BEHOLDING DARKNESS

BEHOLDING DARKNESS

NELLY ALIKYAN

To MMA.
Mariam, Mher, Ando.
My biggest pains in the ass and my best friends.

After all that time, one would assume revenge would be forgotten. Especially since the people the vengeance is toward are gone. But when the species is still alive, retribution is a constant reminder.

And when there are multiple species in the mix, the revenge is never-ending. It takes over a life.

But that's what happens when everything keeping one sane and content is gone. That's what happens when they're taken without mercy. That's what happens when it was all done to hurt one person.

Well, the pain is there.

It's there, and even a millennia later, it's not going anywhere.

It must be remembered that after a millennia of vengeful thoughts, there's no going back. It takes over a person and becomes wholly who they are.

The species responsible, every single one of them, must pay for what they've done.

A millennia has harbored a ruthless person, but it's also harbored a patient one. Waiting a little longer won't matter, if in the end, what's deserving is given.

Not until the species are wiped out, and those remaining cower at one's heels, will it feel like retribution has been cast.

It must be remembered that some people were only made to love and cherish their family. Without them, there is no life. So it must be remembered that when they're taken away, the world will pay for it.

Every.

Single.

Living.

Organism.

They will all pay for what was taken.

ne Month Later

"How much longer do we have to stay?" Vera shouted at Camilla over the loud music. Camilla was only half listening, dazed and content as she was dancing in Warren's arms.

"Go find Maya," she shouted back. "I can leave with Warren."

"I tried. I couldn't find her."

Camilla stopped moving a moment and opened her eyes, taking her sister by the shoulders. "She loves people judging. She's around here somewhere," she said with a smile, which dropped as her gaze moved past Vera's shoulder to the grand staircase beyond, and a grimace lightly took over her features. "What is *he* doing here?"

Vera turned.

Hunter Delvaux was walking down the stairs, his hair lightly askew, enough of a change from his usual perfectness that it was noticeable, and he was tucking his shirt into his trousers with a smirk on his face. He still looked elegant and posh in his expensive clothes, just rumpled, and obviously satisfied.

Gross, Vera thought to herself. "It *is* a party for all magical beings," she responded aloud and somehow heard Camilla snicker behind her over the blaring music.

It had been an entire month since they'd last seen Hunter. Not once had they run across him since leaving the Bridgers coven, where they'd allowed him to take the coven leader, Melusine's, power and kill her. Even though he was Warren's older brother and they'd seen plenty of Warren, Hunter hadn't been around.

And what a glorious month it had been without him.

Even with the other crap they'd had to deal with, not having the extra burden of the demon made their lives all the better. Though, unfortunately, they were both magical creatures, and that hiatus couldn't have lasted forever. Vera knew they would've seen each other at some point, especially with his familial relation to Warren. She'd just hoped it'd be further into the future. But it seemed the Christmas Eve party would be the end of said hiatus.

With a final glance at the demon, Vera turned back to her sister, who had moved her gaze away from one demon and back to the other. Her arms were wrapped around Warren, reminding Vera of going to Christmas parties in years past, before she found out she was a witch and she had two younger sisters.

But that's all she remembered: going. What happened when she got there, how she left, those were mysteries to her. She'd had fun surely, so she knew she should be allowing her college-aged sister to do the same. Problem was, that didn't mean she also had to go through it again.

Vera turned around, time to do another sweep for Maya.

Vera found her middle sister in the kitchen this time, although she was sure Maya hadn't been there before. But now,

Maya lounged lazily on the counter, her back to the cabinets, one leg bent with a drink held over it, and the other splayed out on the countertops. Camilla had been correct, she was people judging. Either that or people watching in Maya's case just meant there'd be disgust in the eyes at all times.

Vera pushed her way through the crowd, stopping in front of her sister. "You look like you're enjoying the party."

Maya gave a sly smile. "Yes, it truly is a joy to behold."

Vera propped herself up on the counter beside her sister and faced the crowd. Just about any creature—besides humans, of course—had been invited.

The ghosts were known for throwing parties and leaving no one out. Since they were the most neutral of creatures. How they kept the civility, Vera didn't know, but she was sure getting everyone so drunk they forgot their own species was part of the ploy.

Vera leaned back against the cabinets and crossed her arms. "Camilla said she'd leave with Warren. We're free to go."

Maya turned her way, seemed to think about it for a second, then called out to Harry. He popped in front of them, swayed lightly with a flirty smirk, and ran a hand in circles in the air before bowing. "Ladies," he said in a seductive tone.

Vera and Maya looked to one another and laughed.

"Yup." Maya pushed off the counter and pulled Harry's arm so he righted himself. "Time to go home."

Harry's flirty smirk grew as he threw an arm over her shoulder. "That was easy."

Maya looked to her sister with a disbelieving laugh that Vera mirrored as she jumped off the counter and took Harry's other arm.

He pulled his arm away and threw it over Vera's shoulders too. "We're going to have a lot of fun." He leaned into Vera's ear, screaming so loud the rest of the kitchen would also hear, "Don't tell, but I like you more."

Maya and Vera looked to one another again, laugher bubbling out of them. Vera turned to look Harry in the eyes and shook a finger out in front of him. "Behave!"

"Yes, ma'am," he seductively drawled. Or as much of a seductive drawl that a pissed Brit could muster. He tucked both of them in closer to him and ported home.

<hr>

The next morning, Vera walked into the kitchen to find Camilla asleep, her hands crossed over the table and her head drooping over them. Across from her sat Harry, elbows on the table, holding his head up by sheer will. He was moaning lightly, eyes closed.

Vera smirked.

"Merry Christmas!" she screamed out, jolting both of their heads up. They both looked at her angrily before closing their eyes again, their groans growing louder. Vera laughed and walked over to the island, getting the blender and ingredients needed for a hangover smoothie.

Bananas to soothe the stomach, coconut water—which Camilla hated—to restore electrolytes, some Greek yogurt to bring back digestive balance, then some avocado, celery, beetroot, ice, chia seeds, frozen berries, and three handfuls of kale.

Vera threw in all of the ingredients she had memorized after her college years and placed the top of the blender to a click. Before pressing the button to turn the machine on, she looked over to the table with a smile. This would be fun.

She watched both her sister and friend freeze, then shoot their hands over their ears as the machine began to mix, both groaning in desperate pleas as they dropped their heads to the table.

Vera stopped the machine, hearing sighs of relief from the other side of the room as she opened the top to sniff. Gross, just as she remembered, but maybe that was just because she wasn't a fan of half the ingredients.

She looked to the vial of relief potion she'd taken from the stash Maya kept in the attic. A drop from this would speed up this process. As much as she would've enjoyed playing with Camilla and Harry that morning, they had other matters to worry about, even on Christmas.

The vial would be the thing that really made this smoothie disgusting. Just opening it had Vera nauseated. She allowed a couple of drops to fall into the blender and closed it once more.

This would be over soon, so might as well enjoy it now, she thought as she looked over to the table again and turned the machine on. They each shot their heads down, covering themselves as if an explosion were taking place.

So dramatic.

Vera laughed and stopped the blender, pulling out two cups and pouring them to the tip. She walked over to the table and placed a cup before them. "Drink up."

They looked at the putrid smelling mulch, then to one another in pleas for help, then back to her desperately, as if she could do anything to get rid of the hangovers without the drinks.

Vera pushed the cups closer to them, then watched as they helplessly brought the glasses to their lips. They looked to her desperately, but Vera remained unmoved. "Pretend it's all the alcohol you two were downing last night."

They grimaced and began to drink.

Vera watched them in amusement, then looked up as she heard the front door open, and a few moments later, Maya walk into the room. "Merry Christmas!" she screamed, watching Harry and Camilla stiffen and cry out their pleas.

Maya took one look at them, then screamed back even louder, "Merry Christmas!"

Harry and Camilla dropped their attention to the cups in hand and continued drinking with renewed speed.

Vera laughed, looking over to her middle sister and taking in her sweaty form as she walked over to the fridge to get breakfast started.

As Maya turned, Vera spotted a bruise on the side of her neck. "What happened?" Vera's tone lost its playfulness as Maya looked over in question and followed Vera's hand as it pointed to her neck. "Your bruise."

She looked down at it, although Vera seriously doubted she could actually see it, and shrugged. "I was the target to a football on my jog this morning."

Vera's brows furrowed. It definitely looked like *something else*, but if Maya didn't want to talk about it, then they wouldn't. And Vera guessed she could give her sister the benefit of the doubt—why would she lie about it anyway? They were all adults.

As Maya readied breakfast, Harry and Camilla began coming to, their hangovers diminishing by the minute. Camilla pushed her glass away and grimaced. "That was disgusting."

"But it worked," Vera said as Maya placed a meal of omelette, toast, and fresh fruit onto the table before them. "And right on time. We can talk and eat."

"About?" Camilla asked, looking at the food, unsure.

"About the call I got this morning," Vera answered, placing some eggs onto her toast and popping a strawberry into her mouth. They all waited for her to continue as they readied their breakfast. "It was another warlock, from Virginia this time. More dead witches. We've got thirty-seven so far, not including Mom." They still weren't sure if their mother's death had anything to do with these witches. Vera took a bite of her breakfast before continuing, "A couple of warlocks are looking them over right now, finding their estimated times of death, just like the others."

After finding that first witch in the woods a month ago, they'd been unlucky in all the others that continued to pile up.

"Nothing new?" Maya asked.

"No, but they know it was at night. They've advised witches to stay home. I've sent out an alert to the other covens, but I'm not exactly sure that'll be doing us too much good."

"And on top of everything else, this isn't adding up to have anything to do with Mom's death," Maya added bitterly.

Camilla nodded. "Which means we have two things to look into. And as much as I hate to say it, we have to focus on this right now. We could possibly save people here."

"I know," Maya sighed. She'd been the most adamant the last month about looking into their mother's murder, but they still hadn't found anything that could be a lead.

They remained silent for the remainder of breakfast, Harry standing as they finished. "I'll clean up and head over, see what I can get, though I doubt any more than they've already told us."

"Well," Camilla began, "this is an exciting start to our first Christmas together." There was no joy in her tone. They knew they would be spending much of their first Christmas together trying to figure out what was happening with this hunt.

Not that they necessarily celebrated Christmas, so it wasn't too big of a problem, but Camilla had wanted a normal human Christmas between them that year. Vera had to admit, she had wanted the same.

But these matters were more important.

They could have a normal Christmas next year, with hopefully no other witches winding up dead, and the mystery of their mother's death put to rest.

2

hey'd tried to enjoy their first Christmas night together, but with each of their minds constantly returning to the dead witches and what it could possibly mean for the deaths of Loretta and Bishop Whittle, it'd been difficult. So they'd gone to bed early and tried to revive for a new day.

It was not a common occurrence—Vera wanting to go out for a run, for any sort of exercise really—but she wanted the excuse to be with her sisters.

Problem was, Maya was already up and back from her morning run when Vera walked down to join the rest of her family. So, no sisters' run, since the middle Whittle was already on her way up to the showers, but she could still get Camilla to go with her.

Camilla was more like Vera in the matters of exercise anyway. Both knew they should do more of it, but neither necessarily enjoyed the thought of doing so. But when Vera mentioned the aspect of quality time between the two of them, Camilla had smiled warmly in her direction and agreed.

With Harry trying to hide the laugh at hearing the two of them would be going on a run, he told them he'd be checking in with the other covens while they were out. His eyes though, they showed the mirth their plans brought him.

Vera started off the jog, taking Camilla in the direction that Maya had shown them countless times before. Realistically, it was the only route she knew. But she did find that, like Maya, she enjoyed the private tranquility it offered.

And unlike Maya, both she and Camilla were complete novice runners, so they didn't need others seeing them huffing and puffing for a single breath.

They'd just stepped into a small clearing with trees littering their every direction when Vera got the tingling from her fingers to her neck that indicated a demon was around. If she had to guess—and she did, considering she'd only had these powers a couple of months and hadn't completely learned them yet—the demon was to their left. Just as she thought that, Camilla shot across the little clearing, hitting a tree. Luckily, her arms looked to take most of the brunt.

The adrenaline spiked through Vera, wanting to make sure her sister was all right, but knowing it would be more important to fight off the demon first. She followed her sense and swung her arm out, using her levitation to throw the animal demon—the demons that looked like monsters rather than regular people—against a tree, though she had to dodge a hit aimed her way.

It was tall and lanky, almost like thin tree barks strapped together, with the most perturb looking moss falling out of its mouth, eyes, and nose. Honestly, out of every hole in it.

Though it was most definitely not dead or vanquished—Vera had been surprised to learn that vanquishing didn't actually kill demons, but just sent them back to Hell—Vera couldn't help her instinct to turn to her baby sister and see her getting up to her feet. As Camilla reached for Vera, the demon ran at them with another blast of power that felt more like a strong gust of wind that knocked them back more than anything else.

Still hurt like hell though.

They were thrown through the air, Vera's back hitting the tree trunk as Camilla, luckily again, landed with her arms cushioning the fall.

Vera shot her hand through the air, trying once more to throw him across the woods as she turned to her sister, making sure to keep an eye on the animal demon picking itself back up. "Find the vanishing spell, Cam!"

There were different lists of spells for different types of animal demons, which simply meant they could not use the same spell for every single demon. Things would be far too simple that way. And creature demons were a whole other level, each requiring their own spell with special ingredients that Vera didn't know about. All she did know was they were lucky to be getting attacked by animal demons rather than creature demons.

Camilla ducked behind a tree and pulled out her phone as the demon sent another gust of wind her way. They'd written out the different types of spells in each of their notes app.

Vera turned and used both hands this time, hoping the thing would go crashing too hard to get up so quickly this time.

Camilla rushed to her side, taking her hand—though it wasn't needed—and holding the phone out in front of them as the demon ran for them once more, unperturbed. "It's one of these two."

Vera nodded quickly as the thing shot out a gust of wind that the sisters ducked down from.

They recited the first spell Camilla pointed to and watched as the lanky demon combusted before it could reach them.

With a breath of relief, Vera slumped against her sister. Partly with ease and partly because she was exhausted from the adrenaline-induced use of power. She was slowly training up her power to be able to use more without getting tired, but she still had a ways to go.

And lucky for them, animal demons hadn't been too big of a problem. They'd only dealt with them a few times the past month, but it was getting annoying.

Harry had explained that it was likely creature demon families sending them. Even if they didn't do the killing themselves, killed by their command still gave the creature demon power and control. And it was all a power game with creature demons.

A slow smile rose on Camilla's lips as she looked at the spot the demon had just been standing. "We did pretty damn well."

Vera looked to her baby sister, the same smile meeting her lips as she felt the warmth fill her heart. "We sure did."

With another look to the spot the demon had just been, Vera nodded down the path they had been on, choosing to walk rather than jog the rest of the route. They'd had the fighting of a demon for exercise.

It may have been a small feat—that animal demon was surely not the most powerful of them all—but they had taken care of it on their own. It was something to be proud of.

***

As they walked down the path in the woods, passing large trees rising high above them, they both wore huge grins. "I think I'm going to tell My that we beat him in minutes, so quickly she truly wasn't needed. She'll narrow her eyes at me and threaten that with her fire, we would've beaten him in seconds."

Vera's smile grew as Camilla spoke.

Camilla was glad she'd had this time alone with just her older sister. Yes, she loved Maya and never wanted to not include her, but it was also important to have her time with Vera.

And now they had this little victory under their belts.

"Yes, I bet Maya will take it all well." Vera laughed, and Camilla joined in.

Until they crashed into an invisible force, and their laughs died immediately. Bouncing back, Camilla quickly turned in her spot to see a body moving toward them.

Then another.

Then they were being surrounded.

"They're not demons," Vera whispered.

That was a small sort of relief.

Camilla remained close to Vera as they got surrounded; masked in plain white, Camilla could not tell who or what they were.

But there were eight in total in an even circle around them.

With nothing to go off of but a strange feeling—almost like when she noticed a witch, but different somehow—Camilla regarded the members around her. It was too odd a feeling for her to place at the moment.

"Who are you?" she asked, figuring it was as easy a question as any to begin with.

"We're friends," one of them spoke in a feminine voice, "here to warn you to back off from your investigations."

"That sounds more like a threat to me," Vera stated, keeping her attention on the quiet ones. It still astonished Camilla that Vera could be so brave to speak back during moments like this, but in their normal lives, she was the quiet and shy one.

"Tomato, tomato." The woman said the same word in different accents.

Camilla rolled her eyes. "Warning and threatening are not the same thing."

"And friends don't threaten," Vera added.

Everyone remained silent after that, Camilla keeping her attention on as many as she could manage, constantly jumping from one member to another. Vera's focus looked to be settled on the quiet ones while Camilla's jumped, landing mostly on the one communicating with them.

After some moments of silence, Camilla said, "Why kill all those witches?"

The same one answered, "We have our reasons."

"Why not kill us?" Vera asked, turning her attention to the communicator. Now Camilla's gaze jumped to the quiet ones.

Although she couldn't see her face through the mask, Camilla was sure the speaking one was smirking as she said, "We have our reasons."

Annoyed, Camilla blurted, "Which are?"

"We're not done using you yet," another answered.

Another female.

Obviously as frustrated with the silence of those around her as Camilla was, Vera's arm stuck out.

Probably not the smartest of ideas, considering she was the only one of the two of them with an active power and they were already outnumbered one to four.

Vera was able to throw two of the standing masks back before defenses were thrown up.

Shockingly, no counterattack was made.

Vera shot out her arm again, but before she could throw anyone else up, both she and Camilla were body slammed to the ground and held down by whatever creatures these were.

Camilla tried to struggle, tried to wiggle out from under the creature above her, but to no avail. The thing was ridiculously strong for its small stature.

Since she couldn't move out from under the female, Camilla took that moment to read her mind. Her thoughts sounded more annoyed than hateful, *Why are pure bred witches such martyrs?*

Pure bred witches?

She'd never heard them be referred to as 'pure bred,' which meant only one thing to Camilla: these were halfies. Half one creature, half another, and if she had to guess, she'd argue one of those halves was witch, and that was the odd familiarity she felt around them.

"Step away," the original speaker, whom Camilla was beginning to guess was their leader, said to the two holding them down. They did as they were told, a little too quickly, so Camilla couldn't get more out of the one holding her down.

Camilla turned to make sure Vera was unhurt before they rose to seated positions and watched as one of the lot threw a potion into the air. Then something Camilla had read about in the Book, but hadn't imagined seeing popped up: a portal.

All eight figures turned and jumped through, the portal closing behind the last one, and it was only in retrospect that Camilla figured they could've tried to fight them at least a little.

Camilla followed Vera in picking herself up off the ground and turned in a circle to assess their surroundings. Everything was once again quiet.

With a final look to one another, they yelled in unison, "Harry!"

3

Harry ported into the forest to find the girls glued to their spots, staring out at nothing with curiosity and astonishment. He'd only been able to pick up from Vera's gaze that it wasn't a pleasant reaction.

He ported them to the foyer of the house, having understood only that they'd been attacked and they believed it was the people killing the witches. That little bit of information was enough for his protective instincts to kick him into gear. He'd grabbed them and left the forest immediately.

Harry watched them take a few calming breaths before Camilla pulled away. "We have to get Maya," she said through a frantic whisper as she came out of her reverie. "We have to talk about this." She lunged without waiting for a response.

"This thing we must discuss," Harry began as he followed, "you say you believe it's eight, possibly more, creatures, maybe even half witches?" He reiterated the entirety of what he'd gotten out of them.

"Yeah," was Vera's only response as they ascended the top step and turned in the direction of Maya's room.

Before they could take more than a single step, the bathroom door opened before them, and out walked the woman in question, wearing her silk white, thigh-length robe. Her hair was dripping down her back and over her shoulders as the dark strands lightly curled into themselves.

Maya paused at the sight of them just beyond the threshold of the bathroom door, looking oddly shocked to see them. Well, Harry could understand that. The entire family wasn't normally standing outside the door whilst one finished a shower.

Her mouth moved to speak, but Camilla cut her off. "There you are. We have to ta…"

Camilla's voice trailed off as *someone else* stepped out of the bathroom, stopping just behind Maya. Clad in only a loose hanging towel, water droplets falling down his chest, stood Hunter Delvaux.

Harry stared at the creature demon that had somehow wiggled his way into their family a month prior, then his gaze shot to the witch standing just before him, both dripping water. Harry had assumed when they'd given him Melusine, Hunter had been satisfied enough to let them be.

Apparently, he'd been wrong.

At least for one member of the family.

And from the look of comfortability between the two, Maya was completely fine with Hunter's presence in her life.

It took only about a second before that disbelief turned to accusation as understanding began to dawn on Harry, because their comfortability together indicated to him that this was not a first time occurrence.

In the seconds since he'd stepped out, Hunter went from unexpected shock at seeing them to gleaming joy, a smirk forming on his lips as his hand reached up to pet Maya's hair. "Well, would you look at that, love, I told you they'd return early." His hand stopped at her shoulder as he threw his arm around her and seemed to delight in their reactions.

Harry hadn't been able to help the recoil his body made at

the way the demon touched the woman he'd begun looking to as a sister. He was sure his lips were downturned as he stared at them, and though he wanted to give Maya the chance to explain first, he couldn't help the judgement he threw her way.

Camilla and Vera threw the same looks, though he doubted Camilla's was as unforgiving.

Maya tossed Hunter's arm off, giving him a reprimanding look before turning back to them, and again, Camilla interrupted before she could speak. "What the hell is going on here?"

Harry didn't want to jump to conclusions or be of any kind of judge—he certainly didn't have a pure past—but he couldn't help the demand for an explanation.

Maya sighed. "Wait for us downstairs. We'll get dressed and come down, and I promise I'll answer your questions."

Harry didn't like it. Didn't like the possibility of them being alone together—ridiculous considering what he'd just walked into—but he knew she was right, as always. They should dress and have a civil conversation.

After a moment, he took a small step back and was followed as he turned and walked numbly down the steps. Neither Vera nor Camilla spoke as they walked into the kitchen, and each chose a spot to lean against the counters, waiting.

A t her family's departure, Maya's composure broke, her hands flying to cover her face. Hunter, for his part, was more amused than before, giving a laugh at her reaction.

Maya rounded on him, smacking his arm. "It's not funny!"

Her reaction only made his laugh grow, black eyes twinkling with delight. Maya growled and walked past him to her room.

Hunter followed her in and shut the door, turning to face her as she disrobed and allowed the silk to fall smoothly down her skin. He watched as she pulled out underwear and began to dress, her periphery telling her his towel was beginning to tighten around his hips.

Good, let the asshole feel some discomfort.

Walking up to her as she pulled the panties up her legs, he stopped the lace with one hand before it could cover her and flicked a finger out, touching her as he held the underwear in place at the tops of her thighs, his other hand skimming up her waist to pause on her breast.

Maya looked up at him with all the annoyance she could muster, a feeling she both felt and had to feign. "Not now."

His eyes darkened, smirk only lightly covering his face as he traced her breast with his thumb, circling her areola before lightly brushing her nipple. Her breath hitched as the finger of his other hand dipped between her folds.

"Not now." She threw anger into her whisper, though Hunter would be able to immediately tell it was a futile demand. He could smell her desire, and it wouldn't take much more to convince her, and he knew it. He'd learned *that* very quickly.

He moved closer so his lips brushed hers. "Afterwards then." His finger flicked at her sensitive nub. "I'll lick up every drop." His tongue darted out, licking her lips, before he retreated entirely.

Maya stood motionless for a moment, hating that she had to calm her racing heart from the short encounter. Then he dropped his towel, exposing his hardened length to her, and her annoyance was back on, now for an entirely different purpose.

She knew her eyes gleamed as she looked into his. "I hate you."

He smirked and eyed her like she were a meal. "Good."

They dressed fairly quickly, both in blacks the way they preferred, before walking into the kitchen, where Maya felt accusatory eyes flicker to them before turning to disgust.

Harry was standing at the end of the island by the table,

Camilla and Vera at the side, sitting on stools, cups of tea in their hands.

Maya walked to Harry's opposite side, Hunter in tow behind her. She stopped near the corner and leaned against the island. She allowed her fingers to tap lightly against the countertop before she spoke. "What do you want to know?"

They all looked at her a moment before Vera answered, "Why?" After another moment. "How? Why?"

Hunter was leaning against the counter behind her, arms folded across his chest, as he no doubt enjoyed every moment of this. "Ask your sister," he nodded to Camilla, "demons sure do know how to give a good time."

Maya sighed in some strength and turned on him as Camilla gasped at his remarks. "*I* will be doing *all* of the talking." Hunter's arms lifted in defense, though the mischief in his eyes suggested he wasn't sorry in the least.

Camilla stuttered before getting her words right. "Warren and I have not done anything. And he's only *half* demon."

"Meaning only half the fun?" Hunter's grin grew.

Maya struck out her fist, punching him on the arm. "Shut. Up."

Hunter mouthed an *okay* before Maya turned back to her sisters. "Why and how?"

"To start," Harry stated.

Maya glanced at her family before looking back to Hunter, the twinkling black orbs transporting her back to Delvaux manor that first time.

"A month ago, after the Bridgers coven, I stopped by Delvaux manor looking for Hunter. I wanted to say thank you… for helping us." And then she'd wound up in Hunter's literally-no-one-but-her-knows-the-location-to manor.

Camilla scoffed, the look she gave Hunter worse than any she'd given before. "Thank you? For what? He stole multiple powers. He should be thanking us!"

Maya took in her family's reactions, knowing if they didn't like that part, they most definitely were not going to like the next part. "And to show my appreciation, I gave him..."

"Sex!" Vera interrupted.

Maya rolled her eyes. "No. I gave him a vial of vanquishing potion I'd made, a way to send him to Hell. He wouldn't have been dead, but it'd take some time for him to make his way back up here."

They looked more astounded than angry.

Vera was the first to speak up. "Where...how did you find out about a vanquishing potion for him?"

"And why haven't we used it!" Camilla, of course, jumped in.

"I found a potion that I figured I could manipulate to work in the Book. The necessary ingredient was difficult to come by, so I only made one batch." She turned to Camilla. "And I didn't use it on him because I had no need to. He hasn't done anything to us to deserve it."

She already knew the tirade Camilla was likely to spew.

"And it *did* work," Hunter pitched in.

"You're still here," Harry stated matter-of-factly.

Hunter's lips quirked up. "To get rid of it, I had to use it. I dropped it on some of my blood. Gone. It definitely would've worked."

That's a fact he likely shouldn't be telling *her* family.

"What is the necessary ingredient?" Vera looked more unsure now.

"Sperm," Maya answered honestly. "And before you get mad, I had a lackey of his get me some. I had no part in picking up that ingredient."

Hunter rolled his eyes, a prideful smirk at her cleverness rising on his lips. "My lackeys are better trained now."

Maya hated the look of betrayal in her family's eyes, especially because even as she'd made the potion, a large part of her knew she would never use it. Knew it would only make for an excuse to see him. Even at the beginning, she'd never wanted to send Hunter to Hell or truly hurt him in any way. But that was a fact no one else had to know.

"So how did that lead to sex?" Harry asked.

Maya wanted to be honest with them, but she couldn't do so while staring at their hurt and accusing gazes, so she turned to Hunter, finding him already watching her. "I knew the real reason I'd gone to the manor that night, the same reason I'd stopped myself from going on many nights before. I'd wanted it from the moment we met, and I knew by the way he was around me that he did too." Purely sexual, fully passionate, entirely animalistic sex.

The how was fairly simple, didn't necessarily need an explanation.

The why, though. Maya paused at what exactly to tell her family. She turned to them and gave a shrug. "As for the why, sexual attraction. We'd felt it from the beginning, and we were finally alone together, finally able to give in to it."

No one spoke for some time before Vera, as suspected, broke the silence. "Okay," she began, though it was obvious she was still trying to process, her tone conveying her desperation to understand. "You gave in to lust. But a second time? Really?"

Before Maya could answer, Hunter snorted beside her. "Second, third, hundredth…"

Again, all eyes shot to Maya in disbelief. She had a feeling they'd known it was more than once, but definitely expected far less than the real number.

Great, she thought to herself and sighed out, "We haven't stopped."

"Why?" Camilla asked, her face lined in a grimace, and a hateful accusation shot to Hunter. It was in that moment that Maya knew Camilla would be the hardest on this relationship, not only because she already hated Hunter the most, but because they'd grown up together. Camilla was more protective of her than the others, and Maya had a feeling this new revelation would be the reason Camilla's animosity toward the demon would grow.

"We didn't want to," Maya answered honestly. All three of them began to argue, so she shot out a hand to stow them. "And I'd really rather not discuss it right now."

Shockingly, they all obliged.

Vera watched her like she was trying to decipher the inner mechanics of Maya's mind, then she nodded toward Maya's neck. "So I'm guessing that wasn't from a football?" The way she said it was lined with the fact that she'd known all along it wasn't from a football.

Maya gave a small smile of apology.

An awkward silence lingered for some time after that, even Vera not breaking it.

Eventually, it was Camilla who asked, "Did you get any vials out of it?"

Harry and Vera looked to Camilla with grimaces as Hunter snorted and Maya looked on with an expression that read 'really?'

Camilla's hands shot out in defense. "You never know!"

"No," Maya answered before her sister said anything else, "and I don't plan on using my body to get any vials for anyone."

With that understood, the silence grew once more.

4

Like he was trying to instigate a fight, before leaving, Hunter grabbed Maya by the back of the neck and brought her face up to his, kissing her a little too passionately. Her body melted into his for only a couple of seconds before pushing him away, but it had been enough. She could feel the anger and disgust coming from her sisters.

He bit his bottom lip as his eyes sparkled down at her. "I'm glad I could do that whenever I want now."

Her eyes screamed 'I hate you,' while he smirked down at her, his features responded with a smug 'Good,' before he shadowed out of the room.

To her surprise, no one spoke of her little revelation after Hunter left. No one berated her for her poor decisions or tried to convince her otherwise. Unfortunately though, their gazes spoke volumes.

Harry cleared his throat, breaking the silence of the room. "We were looking for you to tell you about your sisters' interaction on their run."

Maya's brows furrowed as she stopped at the island opposite Harry. He'd taken out a cutting board and begun with some breakfast, keeping his eyes busy chopping vegetables when he spoke.

She'd completely forgotten how they'd rushed up and been in a hurry to tell her something before Hunter had walked out of the bathroom.

"Interaction?" she asked.

Vera looked up from her helping ministrations getting the eggs for the omelette. "Yeah, we think we met those responsible for killing the witches."

Maya paused, her mouth hovering open to speak, but shut it before anything came out. Her eyes widened in concentration, attempting to understand what her sister had said. The danger both her sisters had been in while she was fucking Hunter in the shower.

Vera interrupted any attempts Maya made of speaking with another shock. "And we think they're half witch."

That little statement pushed Maya out of her shocked state as she huffed and crossed her arms. "Why does *that* not surprise me? It's like witches always want the worst for their own kind."

"Yes, demons are so much better, aren't they?" Camilla's icy tone rang out from behind Maya as Camilla came to stand by the fridge, her arms crossed before her.

Maya looked her sister up and down before answering. "I mean, you are dating one."

Maya knew she shouldn't make snide remarks—Camilla was still shocked—but she couldn't stop herself. Of everyone there, Camilla should be the most accepting. At least Maya was just sleeping with a demon. *She* was in love with one.

Camilla's eyes darkened. "*Half* demon."

Maya quirked a single brow as a slow smirk grew on her face. The same weak defense.

"Anyway," Vera cut in and began to relay the story of their morning run, beginning with the attack from the animal demon, to their acquaintance with the eight members, to their reasonings to believing the half witch theory.

"I just read one of them," Camilla began, "but they all felt the same somehow."

"And still kinda different," Vera added. "I felt a familiarity and complete opposition from them. I don't know how to explain it."

Harry and Maya looked to one another, the same bit of confusion mirrored on their faces.

Camilla ignored their looks and nodded. "Which is why I think they're half witch. The reason we feel something around them. But I think their other halves are all different species, the reason we feel the oddity surrounding us."

"You said they weren't done using you?" Harry asked.

Vera and Camilla nodded in unison as Vera said, "That's what they said. I don't know what that means, though. I tried thinking about it earlier, but I have nothing."

As they set the table and began to sit for their first meal, the silence carried through. Maya sat about thinking about why halfies would want to kill witches. And more importantly, what could have happened to her sisters while she wasn't with them. It was a risk they had to take living in their new supernatural life, but Maya didn't like the possibility of them getting hurt while she was off frolicking.

She was sure her family was thinking about the halfies they'd had a run in with *and* the fact that their sister was sleeping with, essentially, the enemy.

He wasn't an enemy to them.

But his kind were the enemy to her kind.

It was a silent meal of deep thoughts that even Vera didn't break.

They made an attempt to forget the revelation of Maya's relationship and look onto the facts of the eight halfies that were killing off innocent witches, but it just wasn't happening. The entire family needed time before they were able to process the information and look each other in the eye without grimacing.

It was for that reason that they parted ways, finding solace in different parts of the property.

Maya headed to the home office, figuring she could get some work done—they owned the house, but they had other things they needed money for—while her family took their time away from her. She was already coming to terms with the fact that her sisters were fine. That this was the life they signed up for and she couldn't be with them at every moment. Now, she needed them—and Harry—to move past Hunter.

She huffed out as she took her seat and grabbed for her tablet. Opening a half-finished project, she stared at it for some time as she thought about her family and their reactions. Their attitudes from now on would undoubtedly be different.

She gave a loud sigh, hearing the faint note of keys, before attempting to clear her mind and focus on her project.

Harry sat against the wall in the hallway outside of the piano room, listening to Vera's song. He bunched his knees up and lounged his arms over them, trying to make sense of the melody she played. It was a jumble of different scenes, he thought. Their attack, Maya's relationship, and likely more beating down on Vera's shoulders, causing the song to exaggerate a pain of confusion.

He laughed silently to himself as he thought that the song made complete sense for his feelings at that moment. His mind was a state of utter chaos, and it had nothing to do with the day's revelations.

Vera sat at the bench, her thoughts racing at the idea that her sister was sleeping with the enemy—though she knew he hadn't technically done anything to them—the attack by the eight halfies, and most distressingly, a familiar face.

A longing followed the picture of him, and she closed her eyes to erase all thoughts from her mind, and slowly, her fingers played a melody. A story of confusion, a confession of her life now.

Finding this family had given her something to look forward to in life, to have people to come home to and laugh with. It had given her him. And she was grateful for it all. But sometimes, the pain of knowing she wanted him and couldn't have him was too much.

The melody played on and on without a single thought needing to come from Vera; it all just flowed out of her. Her father had always told her she'd gotten such pure talent from her mother, and Vera still wished she could've heard her mother play.

She stared out the full windows that covered the two sides of the room, leading to a small maze garden beyond. It was something she often did when there was a lot happening in her mind whilst she played, but this room offered what none other had before: a beautiful garden to look out to.

Maybe Loretta had been the same as her.

She saw Maya walk out, though it looked almost like she was trying to stay out of view from the windows, obviously knowing Vera was in the room and playing. All Vera could wonder was whether she did it out of respect to Vera or because she just couldn't fathom seeing her after that morning.

She looked to have stopped by a tiny stone bench they had placed by one of the maze bushes, where Vera could barely see, a cup in hand, black coffee no doubt.

Vera thought of her middle sister, of her past thoughts for the darker girl, the one of them who was undeniably attracted to the more unforgiving side.

And because she'd always known, even from the very first day, that Maya was interested in the dark side, Vera couldn't help but think back on every interaction she'd witnessed between her sister and the demon. From the woods, to the fight at the Bridgers coven, to her sister's disappearance at the Christmas party, and her reappearance after Hunter walked down the grand staircase, obviously satisfied, to everything in between. She must have chosen to be blind to their interactions. There was no other explanation.

The melody turned from the pained confusion she'd been feeling before to curiosity at the relationship they'd stumbled upon that day.

Vera gave herself a break, knowing she was never one to pick up on romantic interactions, but still, some of those moments had been obvious now that she thought of them.

Her sister, whom she'd only known a couple of months, was falling deeper into the dark side, and she didn't know if there was anything to do about it.

Vera breathed out, focusing her attention on her breaths instead of the sister outside her window. She didn't need to be thinking of the implications of this relationship Maya had gotten herself into, whether only sexual or not, when all her thoughts were always around a certain relationship she'd like to be in.

Her mind cleared of the darkness as she forced herself to think of nothing.

Then she heard the light screech of a chair behind her and her breath hitched as her body froze.

She forced herself to relax as he placed the chair behind her and took his seat. She made no tells that she knew he was there, continuing the new melody her fingers had chosen—one of anticipation?—as her skin prickled and her heart raced.

She knew from pervious encounters in situations very similar to this one that Harry had taken his seat behind her and dropped his elbows to his knees, watching her fingers dance across the keys. He'd told her once that her songs brought clarity to his mind, and she hoped she was helping erase all thoughts of the troubling world to allow space for only her melodies.

Hoped his heart grew calm in the moment.

<hr>

Camilla walked out to the backyard, taking her shoes off to step bare feet into the cold, wet grass. The light snow they'd gotten the night before had melted before they'd even awoken, leaving a dewiness to the yard.

The faint sounds of Vera's piano reached the yard, but Camilla couldn't focus on her melody. She couldn't even focus on the fact that they'd been attacked just an hour earlier by the same people that had killed the thirty-seven witches.

Her thoughts, no matter how much she tried to change them, continued on one path. Every picture in her mind replayed the sight of Hunter walking out behind Maya. Of their wet, almost naked bodies leaning toward one another before everyone. Of the way he had grabbed for her before shadowing out, the kiss he had given her, the way she'd leaned into it.

All of it.

Camilla took in breaths to empty her mind as she walked circles in the garden, forcing her thoughts to move to the feeling of the grass under her toes. To the touch of the earth beneath her flesh and the healing nature of walking bare footed in grass.

To the feeling of the crisp air around her that was just warm enough to not require a large coat. To the way her body relaxed in the natural elements the planet had to offer.

Alas, she could not fight it forever, and more thoughts of her sister and Hunter, this time their presence together in the kitchen, plagued her thoughts. The way they'd stood beside one another. The way they'd stared at one another as Maya told the story. The little bit of pride in Hunter's eyes when he'd told them the vial had worked.

The worst part of the entire situation was had the entire thing happened a month prior, Camilla knew she would've blindly brushed it aside. Hell, if it had happened yesterday!

It was like seeing Hunter corrupting her sister made the rage in Camilla's blood boil, like she hated him more now than ever before. Because he was doing to them worse than if he'd attacked. He was slowly taking advantage of Maya, Camilla's most beloved person.

She stopped in the middle of the garden, bringing both palms to her eyes and pushing hard, attempting desperately to clear her mind of her precious sister and the monster.

All Camilla knew was she needed time away from her family, from one sister in particular, to calm her mind.

It's funny in a humorless sort of way that she took that time away by calling the brother of the man responsible for this retreat: Warren.

She hoped some well spent time with him would ease her.

Warren's flat was clean, for a college boy's apartment, and Camilla was glad it was winter break and no one else would be home. She went over right after her call, burrowing into his room and taking pleasure in his presence.

She brought some of her favorite poetry classics, and Warren had prepared a picnic of breakfast foods to take on his bed, something she hadn't been expecting. And though she'd already had breakfast that morning, she wasn't opposed to having some more. It was one of the best meals.

They spent a few minutes in delightful silence as they took a few bites of the breakfast—pancakes, a variety of fruits, toast, hard boiled eggs, orange juice, and coffee, sweetened excessively, just to her liking—as they stared at one another.

Camilla took a strawberry to her lips, biting down as she tried to hide behind her smile. "Stop!"

"What?" His eyes widened as his tongue dipped out to clean the syrup from the side of his lip.

Camilla narrowed her eyes at him. "Being so goddamned handsome. It's distracting!"

"You're dramatic," he said with a roll of his eyes, but the smirk that graced his lips told her how much his ego had been stroked.

"Really?" She rose her brows. "Then you won't mind if I have some." She slid a finger onto the plate with the pancakes, picking up some syrup and bringing it to her lips.

And, of course, she added the dramatic moan as her tongue darted out and her lips closed around her fingers, eyes almost closing but for slits to show her his reaction.

He adjusted his spot on the bed and cleared his throat. "Fine, it's distracting."

"Oh?" She feigned ignorance. "What?"

He smirked behind his glass of orange juice, throwing a piece of fruit at her.

She scooted closer to him and picked at her food. "Tell me about your Christmas morning with Matty's family."

He'd spend the morning with the family of one of his flatmates and experienced his first real Christmas morning, an experience he had been looking forward to, and Camilla was excited to hear all about it.

By the time he finished the tale of Matty and his expansive

family, they'd finished breakfast, taken everything to the kitchen, and come back to the room to cuddle up in bed.

Camilla pulled out one of the poetry collections she'd brought with her so they could randomly open to a page and read out the poem, talking about their interpretations and understandings of each one.

It was Camilla's turn again when she noticed the intensity of Warren's gaze on her and turned to look at him. "What?"

"You going to tell me what's wrong yet?"

She drew up to her elbows. "What?"

He quirked a brow with a small smile. "C'mon, Cam, when you called earlier, I could tell you needed to be out of the house. I'm glad I've done so well to distract you, but I'd like to know what happened, if I can help with it."

"Nothing's wrong."

He didn't even try to argue back, just stared at her with a quirked brow until she huffed out and dropped to her back beside him, switching positions so he was up on his elbow staring down at her.

"I really don't like your attentiveness sometimes."

"Liar." He pecked her lips and sat up against his headboard, bringing her into his embrace.

Camilla told him about their interaction with the eight creatures, how those halfies were responsible for the killing of all those innocent witches.

He seemed to freeze at the mention of a group of witch halfies, but recovered quickly. Maybe he was just surprised, Camilla knew she was.

She left out the relationship between her sister and his brother, still unable to voice it. More so unwilling to voice it so as not to speak it into existence. Stupid, since it was already in existence.

Though recovered from the mention of the halfies, the concern was growing on his features, and Camilla couldn't help but feel the slightest tinge of happiness that he was worried for her, like a reminder he loved her even though they were different species.

"We weren't hurt. And, honestly, likely won't be until we're done being useful to them. By then, we should be able to figure out how to stop them." She tried to calm him, but Warren seemed just as down as she'd been when she'd called, except her reaction had been worry for her sister.

It was sweet, the worry he had for her.

He finally feigned the same fake calmness she had before arriving to his place and nodded in thought, promising to look into it from the demon side. He insisted that there was surely something he could learn that could help them.

Realizing now that they both needed to clear their heads, they agreed to forgo thoughts of the magical world for the time being and enjoy their little date.

It was a difficult transition, but Camilla forced herself to relax back and grab another one of the books she'd brought with her. Warren peeled it from her hands and opened it to a random page, reading the poem as dramatically as he could muster.

She laughed so hard, she snorted.

One laugh turned to another, and slowly, they truly forgot about the outside world for a few hours.

Hours consisting of plenty of kissing, laughing, and a promise from Warren to take pristine care of two of the poetry books he asked to borrow, wanting to read them all the way through. It was exactly what Camilla had wanted when she'd gone to Warren's that morning.

5

There was a peace in the large dark luxury that was Hunter's bedroom.

The silk sheets beneath her naked skin, the four poster bed larger than any two people would ever need, and the fireplace at the other end of the room with the chairs to lounge on before it. And rugs that made the entire place feel more regal.

Maya had never been into the gold, gilded luxuries, the modern plainness that mansions carried, but this type, where everything was lined in blacks and silks and a fineness that didn't scream 'Look at me, I'm rich!' to any passerby? This was her type of luxury.

She listened to the shower, knowing Hunter would be out in moments, as she laid back and allowed her fire to dry the remnants of her own wet hair. She stared up at the ceiling, covered in a slight sheen, like he'd taken the barest bit of the night sky and placed it in his bedroom.

Her family wouldn't be happy with her. Not with the knowledge that she'd been with him, and not with the fact that she'd stayed with him all night. When she didn't show up for breakfast that morning, she was likely to get calls or texts.

Or maybe she'd be ignored, all three able to guess where she was.

Camilla most of all.

She knew they didn't like it, but there was a contentment that she didn't feel anywhere else. Not just in his room or his bed, but in the entire manor. She loved just walking about in it, finding a spot to work on her drawings and taking long walks in the large expanse of greens outside.

Hunter walked out of the en suite, dry of all the water from the shower, and moved his naked body toward her. She dropped her gaze to take in the flexing muscles with every step he took, to enjoy the way his form moved as he walked her way.

She turned to her side, facing away from him, when he pulled the covers and got into the bed beside her, causing a chuckle to rise from his throat. He wrapped his arm around her waist, bringing her back flush against his chest as he kissed her shoulder. "Love, are you still angry with me?"

She rolled her eyes.

He bit her shoulder, not so hard to leave a mark, but enough to send a burst of pleasure through her. "You realize rolling your eyes is answer enough?"

She grit her teeth. "I just don't understand why you *have* to infuriate my family."

Another chuckle and a kiss to her shoulder blade. "I don't *have* to. I merely enjoy it."

Of course he'd *merely enjoy* calling Camilla—the one member who most strongly opposed him—in the middle of the night to leave a voicemail about their endeavors while she'd been in the bathroom.

Another reason she didn't expect a call or text that morning.

He'd told her only after they'd finished another round that morning and she wanted to punch him for it.

He kissed her shoulder blade again.

He could kiss her ass—no pun intended—if he thought they'd be doing anything else that morning.

"Well, if you enjoy fucking me on a nightly, then you'd better find another way to cope with being an asshole."

More chuckling. Why did he sound so exquisite when he chuckled?

A kiss just under her shoulder blade, and another only a centimeter to the right, then left, then farther.

She could be mad at him and still enjoy the kisses. No harm in allowing herself that, just didn't have to tell him.

She tried to pull herself out of his grasp, but he tightened his arm around her, holding her as his teeth scraped down her back.

Okay, if she didn't want to make noise, she'd have to distract herself.

And easily done so. With one glance to the nightstand beside her, her gaze flickered to a gold pocket watch.

She leaned over to pick it up, feeling the weight of the highest luxury, as he continued to kiss her back, obviously uncaring if she went through his things.

The watch was engraved with a drawing of the oceans, a beautiful depiction of one of the scariest places on this planet, one that held creatures even the supernatural world would be afraid of.

She opened the watch to see the beauty of the Roman numerals within, a craftsmanship she couldn't imagine must've gone into this design.

"Where'd you get this?" she asked, knowing she should remain angry with him, but unable to push aside her curiosity.

He rested his chin on her shoulder. "I had it made. I have a friend…"

"You have a friend!"

He bit her again, a little harder this time, and she could feel the smile on his lips. "I have a friend in Canada that makes crafts like these. Enchantingly beautiful. I have more of his pieces throughout the house."

If she hadn't frozen at the mention of Canada, he may have continued his speech of which pieces and when he'd gotten them, why. But Hunter had always been keen to her reactions. And freezing against his body was quite the obvious one.

"What is it?" His tone deeper now.

Her brows furrowed, knowing she was being ridiculous to even still be thinking of it, but unable to push it aside.

She turned in his arms, lying on her back so she could face him as he hovered over her and leaned on a forearm. She still held the watch, feeling the coolness of it against her chest now.

"Back when we thought Lila was a part of killing my mom, we had to do a locator spell to find her. That's how we were able to interrupt your tirade." He smirked down at her but didn't interrupt. "The thing with the locator spell is, you need to use something of the person you're looking for. Luckily for us, Lila had made our mother a frame to hold a picture of them when she was a kid. We used that because technically it had been hers before it was my mom's."

"Right." His patient encouragement was nice, to know she could take her time in telling him as much as she wanted to.

"When we performed the spell, Kent came up, of course, but we also got Quebec, Canada."

Understanding dawned in his eyes.

"I know my mom isn't there, but I have to wonder what it was. Had Mom been alive, the locator would've likely given two locations because it had belonged to both of them, I think. But she's not, so what could've called out to the locator spell? We hadn't known about Vera. Is there something else, someone else, we don't know about?"

His fingers skimmed her belly as he watched her. That action alone was reassuring to Maya.

After a minute, he pushed out of bed, and Maya felt his absence immediately. "Where're you going?"

He was slipping on his boxers, moving to his closet for a pair of trousers. "Get dressed, love."

She rose to a seated position and watched him put on his trousers. "Why?"

He stopped and looked her in the eyes. "You said Quebec? Let's check it out."

Her eyes widened, and she felt a skip of her heart that she chose to ignore in the moment. Then she was out, moving to his closet for the clothes she'd left there.

She was dressed in a deep red small sweater, black jeans, and her thigh high boots when she turned to find him putting on his trench coat. Their fire power indicated they never really needed coats, so that was different.

He turned to her with one of his sweaters and dropped it over her head. "It's quite a bit colder in Quebec, better to keep you naturally warm than have to use your power."

His sweater engulfed her fully, and though she knew she could pluck it up and try tucking it into her jeans, the fact that it flowed to her thighs only meant it'd also be keeping her ass warm.

She smiled at him, more annoyed with herself for wanting to smile at him after what he'd pulled with Camilla, but she couldn't help it.

He was wrapped around her and shadowing them out only moments later.

---

6

*M*aya sat isolated in the home office after their failed trip to Canada where she found nothing remotely linking to her family. She finished another client design as she listened to a playlist of 90s and early 2000s music, trying to forget about the entire thing altogether. Her mother was dead, the spell had probably just malfunctioned to Quebec. She didn't have any more family she didn't know about.

She colored in the different aspects of her drawing, 'I'll Make Love To You' by Boyz II Men playing in the background and causing a momentary pause as her thoughts turned distracting.

Salacious smile, shining black eyes, and wicked hands.

She was still angry with him for the voicemail he'd sent Camilla. A voicemail which was immediately thrust into her face when she'd stepped into the house after Hunter had finally dropped her home.

Camilla had been royally pissed, but Maya had to admit, it hadn't been as bad as she'd been expecting.

"Hello, Little Sister." A chuckle. "Look at us now, you're my little sister from Warren and Maya. It seems you're only tightening your

hold on our relationship rather than ending it. Don't worry, I'll be a great big brother."

Maya'd had to force her laugh down when she'd heard that part with Camilla standing in front of her, but she couldn't fight the smile in the comfortability of her office.

"Anyway." He sounded satisfied, and Maya could almost guess the exact way he'd look leaning back on his headboard lazily. "Just wanted to call and let you know that your sister is being well taken care of, nothing to worry about here. She is well satisfied." A moment's pause. "Oh, you want her more than just well? Okay, for you, I'll make sure she's intoxicatingly satisfied. All right, well, to do you this favor, I've got to warm up. Maya and I have quite the night to look forward to. Thank you, Little Sister."

Honestly, the voicemail hadn't necessarily been bad. If Maya were honest, she thought it was sort of funny. The only problem was knowing Hunter had only sent it to piss Camilla off, even though he insisted that wasn't the case.

At least he hadn't lied to her sister—she had been intoxicatingly satisfied. So much so that waking that morning had been a task itself.

Celebrating all through the night indeed, she smiled as she swayed to the song still playing, the scent of the half-thousand sweets Vera was baking taking over the house.

A smile grew at the knowledge that baking was the best job Vera could have ever given herself, the thing that made her happiest, like Maya's graphic design, and she was finally pursuing it.

Finishing the last edges of the character she was drawing, Maya placed her tablet onto the desk, leaned back, and stretched as she looked about the room. The only other dark room in the house outside of her bedroom.

Her mom had let her and Camilla choose the themes for their rooms, but the rest of the house had been up to Loretta

Whittle, and Loretta Whittle wanted the entire house inviting and open.

Maya normally didn't mind it, but there was a comfortability in her bedroom, in this office, in the entirety of Hunter's manor that she couldn't find in the other rooms.

Her gaze dropped to the table, the pocket watch with the engraved ocean sitting on her large desk. She hadn't meant to take it, but when Hunter had gotten out of bed and rushed her to dress, she hadn't thought to put it down. She hadn't even realized she'd put it in her pocket until she'd gotten to her bedroom earlier and changed into sweats.

Maya took it in hand again, her thumb running over the engraving. The meticulous detail was so beautiful she felt a pride in knowing Hunter carried it.

She flipped it open and lightly brushed over the clock inside, the *Delvaux* engraved onto the top half.

It would merely be another excuse to end up at Delvaux Manor, not that she necessarily needed one, but she couldn't come out the thief in this situation.

She lightly bit down on her bottom lip and softly placed it back on the desk, leaning back and closing her eyes as another song started.

Camilla had texted her sisters to gather in the kitchen for a small meeting when Harry ported her in. They found Vera seated at the table, peeling the white bits off of a mandarin and throwing the clean pieces into her mouth, and Maya by the counter, making a sandwich.

Camilla took a seat at the table with Vera as Harry relayed the story of the New York coven's witches that they'd just gone to see. "The coven had been looking for them for a couple of days. They finally sent out some scouts. One of their warlocks found them lying on the roof of a building opposite theirs." He picked at the pieces of cucumber Maya had left on the cutting board. Popping one into his mouth, he chewed before continuing, "They were brought in and assessed. The warlocks believed it to be the same as the last thirty-seven, so they called us. One was a mother of three, mid-thirties. The other was likely only a few years younger."

Harry sat at the head of the table opposite Vera, and Camilla added, "We asked if they knew any half witches or anything that could help in why they were targeted." She looked to her sisters' curious gazes, then added sheepishly, "Nothing."

"So essentially," Maya began, "we're not even back at square one, we're at square negative one. We have more dead witches," she lifted one finger, then another, "and we're no steps closer to figuring out why and for what. Even those halfies that you met, we have no way of knowing who they are."

Maya was frustrated. *Weren't they all.*

Just as Camilla was getting up to comfort her sister, a shadow embalmed before her.

Hunter was there.

Of course he was.

He met her gaze, and one would think it was a genuine smile he gave her, if his eyes didn't flicker with joy at her reaction. "Hello, Little Sister."

And the memory of his voicemail was like an echo in her mind. She grimaced, no longer in a comforting mood, and plopped back into her seat.

Hunter walked over to her, hand outstretched with something in it. Camilla looked down quizzically until she realized it was her book. Her poetry collection.

"My brother asked me to return this," Hunter explained as she ripped it from his hands.

"And you agreed to do your brother's bidding?" Camilla questioned, disbelieving.

He just shrugged. "Brotherly affection. Siblings do things for one another." He spoke entirely with a glint in his eyes. Camilla didn't buy a second of his explanation as he staggered back, moving in the direction of Maya, who stood against the sink.

"Please," Camilla rebuffed. "You only wanted to listen in on our conversation. Let me guess," Camilla's anger moved from Hunter to her sister, "someone told you more witches were found."

Hunter reached Maya, took her jaw in hand and planted a smiling kiss to her lips. Camilla grit her teeth as she watched Maya's eyes twinkle, though her face remained unforgiving at Hunter's antics as he pulled from the kiss.

He was tainting her sister, using her, and there was nothing Camilla could do to convince Maya that the demon had an ulterior motive. She knew he did, and she had to do something to stop him before he hurt her sister.

Hunter turned back to face Camilla, resting against the sink beside Maya. He crossed his arms and answered, "You're right. War didn't ask me to return it. I saw your name and used it as an excuse. Happy?"

"Jump off a cliff and I will be," she bit back.

He laughed in response. "I'd like to know your theories, is that such a bad thing?"

"We're not sure it wasn't you," Camilla answered swiftly, a smirk across her face. Not a single ounce of her trusted the conniving demon.

Hunter's posture didn't change, but his face shifted. His eyes twinkled wickedly, a salacious grin forming. "Oh sweetheart, I was *deep* inside your sister during each of the killings."

Camilla's smirk immediately dropped.

He was deep inside her sister? She was going to throw up.

She turned away from Hunter, noting Maya smacking him on the arm as she faced Vera and Harry. Camilla felt better in seeing that Vera and Harry were also trying to avoid looking in the direction of the demon.

"He's an ass," Maya began, "but he's right. The warlocks have estimated each of the witches' deaths. Hunter's been with me."

Unable to hold back, Camilla's gaze found her sister's, throwing a bit of hate into it.

Knowing she could never, would never, hate Maya, at that very moment, she hated her sister. Hated her for choosing to bed that monster and refusing to give him up. For choosing to spend her time with him. For choosing to defend him.

And at the same time, Camilla knew it was not her fault. Maya had fallen under Hunter's spells—figuratively, of course—and that made her the victim in the situation. Camilla couldn't judge her for that.

Hurt ebbed into Maya's features, but Camilla also knew she would not break—Maya didn't believe she was in the wrong.

Camilla moved her gaze back to the table and noticed Vera's face as she also watched the two by the counter. There was no hatred there, just simple annoyance.

No one moved or spoke for a long while, until the feeling of another presence in the room pulled their attention. Camilla turned in her seat to find Warren standing at the end of the kitchen, his gaze falling immediately to his brother.

Confusion was written all over his face at Hunter's presence, and part of Camilla felt bad for not telling him before about the relationship between their siblings. He turned to Camilla after a moment and smiled. "Hey, I got your text. What's up?"

Camilla heard Maya scoff from her spot by the sink and looked over as she said, "You're allowed to tell and I'm not?"

Camilla didn't grant her sister with a response, instead turning to Warren and replaying their earlier conversation to him, knowing Hunter was hearing the information he'd come for as well.

What the hell was Hunter doing with them without an attack in the process or a threat in the making? Was it another deal? What did they need to have to make a deal about?

As the conversation finished and everyone left the kitchen, Warren grabbed his brother's arm, dragging him to the side of the hall and leaning in to whisper through grit teeth, "What are you doing here?"

Hunter grinned, a twinkle of pure joy erupting from the darkness of his eyes as he placed a hand on Warren's shoulder. "You didn't know?" Before Warren could question him further, he continued, "I'm doing what you've spent months trying to." He leaned in closer. "I'm fucking one."

Warren froze in his spot as his brother gave him a wink and a pat to the back before walking off.

Fucking one?

Impossible.

Not only did he know that the Whittle sisters all respected themselves too much to stoop so low, but Hunter was not one to sleep around. In the past, he'd taken only a lover at a time and been careful never to lead to the possibility of children. He also never made it known who he'd been with so there would never be a way for someone to blackmail him.

But he was openly admitting to sleeping with one of the sisters? With the animosity he felt from Camilla, it could be true. Though Warren knew Camilla hated his brother the most, there was an extra bit of tension that he could imagine would come if Hunter *was* fucking one of them.

Warren looked to his brother's retreating back, disgust ringing through every cell in his body as he thought back to the twinkle in Hunter's eyes as he'd said it. Like there was pride in the matter.

It was that, along with the mere fact that he'd admit to it so openly, that told Warren it was true.

His brother was sleeping with one of Camilla's sisters, and as Warren allowed that reality to hit him, it didn't take much to settle on the sister in question: Maya.

7

———————

Hunter's hand was clasped around Maya's as she pulled him to the attic. She'd told him that a new set of eyes on the Book may give them some new information, and he'd been open to view it. Of course he had been. Any demon would want to view the Book.

Though he'd pointed out her family wouldn't be happy with his presence anywhere near the Book. A fact she was quick to push aside.

If she didn't mind, he wouldn't either.

She dropped her touch when they reached the room and moved to stop at the pedestal the Book sat on, placing both hands on the edges and waiting for him.

He moved to stop behind her, his body pressing against her every curve as his hands landed on hers.

He engulfed her in his warmth and had to push aside any risqué thoughts. They needed this done without distraction.

She moved a hand to open the Book as his face came to rest by her ear, his light stubble chafing her jaw and reminding him of the softness between her thighs.

No. No distractions.

Then they were looking through the Book. And though he was interested in stopping at most of the pages and studying them, he knew that wasn't the purpose at the moment.

The thing about these books that witches had was that every coven's was different, and every family within the coven could have a different spell in theirs. But usually, the same spell could be found in multiple books. It was just the combination that was unique to each family. So no other copy had these exact pages, but in all likelihood, whoever was behind these killings had a spell that they may find in this Book. That may only be in this Book, like the unique one that Maya had used for his vanquishing potion.

And even after an hour of flipping through pages, they found nothing of particular interest to their predicament. Though they were only a small percentage through the tome.

As Maya went to flip the page once more, Hunter's hand shot out, pushing the page back down. "Wait." His eyes flicked over the symbols written all over the page.

Ludacris.

"What is it?" she asked, turning her head to watch him. Separated by only an inch, he could feel her gaze studying him as his eyes ran over the drawings.

Incredible.

Hunter drew his fingers along the symbols. "Do you know what this is?"

Maya shook her head as she looked back down at the page. "I've been translating parts of this Book since we got it, but I wasn't able to get to this. I don't know where to start with it."

"It's an old demonic tongue," he answered, her shocked breath hitting his jaw as she snapped her gaze up to him before turning back to the Book. "Why does your witches Book have an old demonic tongue in it?" he asked as she shook her head.

Hunter didn't know what to think, whether it *was* incredible or completely ludicrous that they had demonic tongue in their *Book*. A Book that was meant to stay far away from demons.

And before he voiced another word, Hunter felt himself fly across the room, hitting the wall hard before he could shadow himself out of the situation.

As he took in a breath and looked up, he found the other residents of the house standing by the door and rolled his eyes as he picked himself up and turned to Maya. "Told you."

The others looked to Maya, anger radiating off of them.

"What the hell is *he* doing looking at the Book?" Camilla asked vehemently.

Hunter took a step forward, but stopped when Vera's hand twitched. Maya folded her arms across her chest, moving to stand before him. "He could help."

"We don't trust him," Vera announced.

"He hasn't done anything to betray us," Maya argued, and Hunter had to bite the inside of his mouth to stop the smile that was bubbling on his lips. She would surely be getting his thanks for her defenses.

"Yet," Vera simply stated.

"Maya," Harry said softly, "I understand that you think you can trust him, but you must remember that you are natural born enemies, and demons are the least forgiving of creatures. The fact that they cannot easily care for others already makes them more dangerous, but adding on that they are born to be your enemy. You cannot be so naive."

It was obvious Maya didn't like being talked down to. "I'm not being naive. My trust in him comes from the simple fact that he hasn't done anything to break it, to betray us. Why is that so hard for you to comprehend?"

"Because he's using you, My!" Camilla was frustrated. "And you're walking right into his traps. He already has full access to this house, now you're giving him full access to the Book. It'll take literally no time before he gets what he's come for."

Maya stared at her sister, squaring her shoulders. "And there's no possible way I'm what he's come for, right?"

"Maya," Vera tried, "he's a demon. They're known for not caring and for using whatever means to get to their goals."

Maya scoffed but didn't respond.

Hunter internally rolled his eyes, but didn't argue with them. Technically all they were saying was true, though he felt a twinge of annoyance that they were all ganging up on Maya like that.

Instead of arguing, he lifted his arm to the page that was still open to the demonic tongue. "That page is written in an old demonic tongue. It says 'midnight of a new era will bring the power for blood renewed.' Midnight of a new era is a New Year, like the one coming up in a couple of days," he explained, looking to the hostile faces watching him, and again, tried not to roll his eyes. "Blood is a powerful ingredient. Not to mention the energy of hundreds of magical beings," he paused before adding, "They could have taken the blood from your witches."

At that revelation, their faces changed to ones of worry, and he knew they were all finally thinking the same thing: there was a magical creatures New Years' Eve party they needed to attend.

8

*I*t was the morning of the eve to a new year, and Camilla was worried about their outfits.

She rolled her eyes at herself, *so* not the problem she should be worried about at the moment.

Alas, she could not let it go. Making sure they all had a beautiful dress with space for vials to hide was an important part of the night. They needed to blend in and be ready for anything, though hopefully, they wouldn't need any of it.

As Camilla took another look at their outfits, she heard Harry and Vera walk in with the tea and snacks they'd prepared and glanced over with a smile.

Maya never slept late, and Camilla didn't know whether to be worried or comforted that her sister was getting some rest.

Pushing the thought from her head, she used the next hour to drive Harry and Vera crazy with questions about their outfits. Did they match? Were the pockets too obvious? Would the pockets be too obvious if they put vials into them? Would the vials fall out? Maybe the men should carry the vials in their pockets and stay by their sides. But wouldn't people think it odd that the sisters were glued to the sides of either Harry or Warren?

It was at Harry's breaking point that Maya walked into the room.

"Up late?" Harry quirked a brotherly smile—and a thankful one—in her direction.

Maya smiled back as she began to pour herself a cup of tea, no sweeteners, causing Camilla to scrunch her nose. How her sister did that, albeit it was the healthier option, Camilla couldn't fathom.

Maya took a seat at the ottoman by the fire. "I was at Hunter's."

The mention of her demon lover wiped the joy from each of their faces.

And although she knew she shouldn't, Camilla couldn't help her next remark, any mention of Hunter sending her blood boiling. "So while we're preparing for this party, you're sleeping in?"

Only an hour ago, she wanted her sister to be sleeping in, but she couldn't help the accusation in her tone at the thought of her sleeping in with Hunter. *Because* of Hunter.

Maya's face darkened, an annoyed tinge growing in her eyes as she met Camilla's gaze. "I wasn't sleeping in. I was having sex."

Maya was picking up her little friend's behavior.

At Camilla's narrowing eyes, Vera stepped in. "We've got other things to worry about. How about we not fight about this right now?"

Vera's gaze moved to Maya as Camilla noticed the annoyance in Maya's eyes at everyone's reactions to her *relationship* with the Delvaux demon.

"Okay," Harry clapped his hands together, "we have no strategy."

That simple remark dispelled the tension between the

sisters, eliciting smiles and poorly fought chuckles.

"No," Vera said, "we don't know what we're walking into. And I have no thoughts on how to strategize."

"Okay." Camilla tried to reason. "So we have no strategy. I figure, we break up at the house and let each other know if we find anything. It's no masterplan, but we have other things to worry about."

"Like?" Vera asked.

"There haven't been any more bodies. It's the eve of the new year. If they were to kill more, then I believe it would have happened. Which means they're stopping at thirty-nine. Why?" Camilla answered, looking into impressed sets of eyes, she rolled her own. "It wouldn't take a genius to come up with this. Move on, please."

Vera bit her lip to keep from laughing, then answered, "I don't know why they'd choose thirty-nine, but if I were to break up the numbers? Nine is a triple perfection. I bet whatever they're up to, they'd like a perfect result."

"Three is half demon," Harry added. "Maybe the other half of the halfie mix is demon." He turned to Vera. "You already know you can't sense half demons. It could be a possibility."

"Half witch, half demon. I can see why they're angry with witches, likely thrown out from their coven for that demon half," Camilla commented matter-of-factly, throwing a sideways glance to the fire witch in the group.

Maya rolled her eyes. "Lest you've forgotten, which you seem to do often, *your* boyfriend is *half* demon." Maya placed her cup down and got up, looking to Camilla. "You should find him, by the way, get yourself loosened. I'm sure Hunter could give him pointers if it's needed."

Camilla gasped, watching her sister leave the room as the doorbell rang. Vera answered it and walked back in with the man in question carrying a suit bag over his shoulder.

Warren handed the suit to Vera to place with the rest of their outfits as Camilla placed both hands on his chest and reached up on the tips of her toes to kiss him.

His hands cradled her face and brought her in closer.

Two kisses. Three. And she was lost in him completely.

Coughs brought them out, and she had to breathe him in a moment before stepping back, a wide smile greeting him. "Hey."

"Hey." He smiled back as he followed her to the couch. "So I looked into those halfies. A couple of them may have been half demon. I wouldn't say all of them though."

"Why not?" After their little conversation, if they were wrong about the demon side too, then they really weren't making any progress.

"Demons may be an uncaring lot, but they're also a smart one. The most demon halfies are mixed with witches, and families always keep track of their halfies, especially the witch ones."

"Because they don't trust them?" Vera guessed.

Warren shook his head. "More because witches and demons are the two most powerful beings. With a mix, the families are more likely to utilize them if they turn out powerful."

"So you're saying you don't have eight missing half demon, half witches? Could they be doing it in secret?" Harry questioned.

Warren shrugged. "It's a possibility, but I don't think so. Plus, a demon halfie would utilize other creatures because they know they would have better control over them. I was able to get a few names, but even from that list, we don't know who is actually involved. I'm trying to look for them now to question them, but it's a lot harder than you'd think."

"They wouldn't have told anyone?" Vera asked.

"Absolutely not. Half demons normally tend to take their demon side in not caring. I was an exception, and there are other exceptions, but generally, they're uncaring. If I had to guess too, within those you encountered, they don't care much for each other either."

Camilla looked to the outfits she had hanging around the room as they all nodded in agreement. This would be all the more difficult if those halfies didn't even care for one another.

Maya walked into the kitchen, having spoken to Harry earlier and learned the news Warren had brought with him. She stopped at the corner of the kitchen counter, preparing the coffee machine for a cup. As she pressed the button to start brewing, she felt a presence behind her.

A hard, definitely male presence.

Musk and bergamot and sandalwood.

His hands gripped her hips, moving so his front pressed to her back as his hand slid up her form, grabbing at her hair and moving it aside to open her neck to him.

His breath tickled her skin as he dipped to the junction where her neck met her shoulder and kissed it. He'd shaved, but there was still a prickliness to his face.

He pressed another kiss before his tongue darted out and licked a trail from the spot to the back of her ear.

Maya tilted her head to rest on his chest as his hands began to wander, one slipping under her shirt as his teeth tugged on her ear. She let out a silent breath as his fingers circled lightly around her navel before wandering up.

His lips kissed their way back to the junction at her shoulder.

Maya gripped the counter as Hunter's other hand reached for the button of her trousers, popping it open and letting his hand skim the edge of her panties. He rubbed himself against her back, his other hand reaching her breast and cupping it as his length pressed into her. His thumb rubbed her nipple as the fingers of his other hand reached her wet slit.

Her head turned to the side and reached to bite Hunter's jaw to keep silent, noticing he'd come dressed in a fine tux.

He bit down on her neck as her fingers tightened on the counter, his fingers expertly moving through her wetness and slipping into her. At her gasp of pleasure, his lips moved to find hers, thrusting his tongue to meet hers.

As their tongues fought for purchase, his hand moved from one breast to the other, giving each their deserved attention, as another finger met the one inside her. Maya felt herself tightening around his fingers as his palm pressed to her clit, deliciously rubbing her.

He kept pace with his fingers. His tongue thrusting into her mouth as his fingers filled her. Again and again and again.

Maya let out a whimper, biting down on his bottom lip. From his attention to her nipples, to his erection pressed against her, to his tongue, to the fingers inside her, Maya was ready to explode.

"Oh! My! Lords!" Two very distinct voices came from behind them.

They froze, eyes widening.

Maya forced her breath to calm as mortification settled in, and she turned to see her sisters turning their heads from them.

Hunter slowly removed his hand from beneath her shirt and his fingers from inside her. Her insides clenched at the feeling, but embarrassment kept her body frozen.

As she buttoned her trousers, she turned to see her sisters looking at them in the worst form of disgust. And to her horror, Hunter decided to play with them by bringing the fingers that had just been inside her up to his lips and suckling.

Maya heard her sisters' exaggerated nausea as she stared Hunter down, not finding any pleasure in this situation, and breathing in to keep herself calm. She grabbed his wrist and pulled his fingers free from his mouth. "I swear I'm going to kill you."

He smirked down at her like the asshole he was. "Yes, ma'am."

Maya growled, but didn't give him any more attention, turning to her sisters as Vera exaggerated, "You had sex this morning! How often do you two do it?"

Maya shrugged sheepishly. "We weren't doing it."

Vera's eyes narrowed. "You know what I mean."

She blew out a breath. "A few times a week."

Before either sister could respond, Hunter unhelpfully piped in, "That could mean a few days out of the week or," his grin grew as he said, "a few times per day. Depends how your sister is feeling that day. And let me tell you, it's normally the latter."

Maya elbowed him in the gut.

The ass was enjoying this far too much. He deserved it.

"Hunter," she barked and pointed to the hall, "shut up and go wait up front."

He raised both hands, the smirk never leaving his face, and left the kitchen, fingers finding their way back to his mouth again.

Maya looked back to her sisters as Vera snickered, "I still can't believe he's coming with us."

"I was kinda planning around the fact that he'd get stabbed through the chest and we wouldn't have to deal with him anymore," Camilla added.

Of course both of them would've been imagining the night without Hunter there; they would much prefer that outcome. But Maya would not.

She wanted him there with her.

And she was in no mood to argue over him again, so she turned to the pot of coffee and poured herself a cup, feeling the glares from her sisters on her back the entire time. Camilla's glare was especially brutal.

She left the kitchen without facing them.

9

This party, like the Christmas one, was hosted by a ghost family.

They'd walked into the mansion as a group but broke into their couples and went in separate directions almost immediately after entering.

The worst part? They were all at a loss as to what exactly they were looking for.

Vera knew Maya felt entirely clueless since she hadn't been with them when the eight creatures, which they had come to refer to as 'The Eight,' had attacked.

She and Camilla may not have seen any faces because of the masks, but they were still able to feel the presence. Hopefully that did them some good.

Vera watched Camilla keep one hand around Warren's arm as they walked the crowds, her free hand shooting out to touch as many passerby as she could manage. Any reading she could get could help them.

Unfortunately, it looked like she was getting nothing of use.

Vera clasped her hands at the crook of Harry's arm as they walked the party. It was an intoxicating kind of reprieve, to be able to use this search as an excuse to hold him, to be this close to him.

She'd been able to force her thoughts aside, but from the moment she'd found out that Harry would be hers alone, to the few moments after he'd taken her hand, she'd been in paradise.

But thoughts of her warlock aside, they were at the party for a purpose. And as they walked the halls, through the hundreds of people, she came to the realization that she did not like parties any more. Rather annoyed by them, if she were honest.

Or maybe that's because she wanted to be alone with Harry?

On their walk around the rooms, Vera kept her eyes open for anything that seemed to call to her, but nothing really stood out, especially not past the sensation of touching her warlock.

Ready to give up hope after about two hours on the search, Vera read the time on the mantel piece: two minutes 'til midnight.

She glanced around at the excited forms of every creature—except humans—getting ready to wish one another a happy new year.

Midnight.

As her gaze moved from the mantel piece that confirmed the exaggerated yells of the partygoers, Vera froze in her spot, recognizing a feeling she had before.

She looked up to find a cloak making its way down the stairs, face hidden behind the hood. No wonder she hadn't felt anything. In the moments they'd been on the upper levels, this halfie must've not been at the party yet.

Or she was just great at avoiding them.

Vera leaned in to whisper in Harry's ear, "Text them. Bottom of the stairs."

Vera hadn't moved her gaze from the cloaked figured, but with the amount of people surrounding her, she was blocked only a moment. That moment's disappearance was all it took. She was gone.

When the others met them at the bottom of the stairs, she was still looking about for the cloaked figure. "Fuck," Vera heard herself curse aloud. "She was just here."

"It's fine," Camilla said and pointed up the stairs. "She came from up there?"

Vera nodded, and they all made their way up the stairs, no need for discretion given they'd walked up and down those stairs multiple times; given anyone at the party may have walked up and down those stairs a million times.

Unknowing which room would've been used, but figuring the attic was the best choice, they began opening doors in search of the room.

Finally, Warren yelled out, "Found it."

The six walked up the mini set of stairs into the attic to find a burn mark on the ground in the shape of the natural circle of salt and candles that many a spell required.

Hunter bent at the knees before the burn mark, touching the residue with the tips of two fingers and bringing them to his nose. "This isn't just salt," he stated.

"No?" Harry asked.

Hunter shook his head. "It's a mix. You need the salt for the spell, but based on the spell you're attempting, the ingredients may not disappear entirely."

Harry stared at the demon with a 'I'm aware' expression, but didn't interrupt.

This spell had plenty of residue left over, which meant plenty of the other ingredients were used. Or what little ingredients they'd used weren't the sort to have vanished like those of the herbs and hearts when they'd been hiding the Hell's Gate key.

He paused to look at the entire burn on the ground before continuing, "If she was using the symbol as merely a form of extra energy, mixing the ingredients wouldn't be needed. She gets the extra energy from all the partygoers. Mixing the ingredients with the salt, rather than separately, though, could give her a more effective result with the blood."

"Blood?" Maya questioned.

"I'm assuming that's what happened here. The demonic tongue in your Book said blood of a new era, and blood was likely taken from those witches. Mixing the ingredients in this residue would give them the right mix of blood they required."

"What would they require the blood mixed in residue for?" Harry asked and Vera had a feeling this was a spell more likely found within demons.

Hunter shrugged. "I don't know their purpose or what spells they're using."

Camilla looked to him suspiciously. "And yet you know so much about this."

He looked up from his crouched position and smiled. "You don't get to where I'm at in life without paying attention, Little Sister."

10

To their horror, in a round of testing the residue they'd found at the New Year's party just days ago, they'd found it to, indeed, be a mix of salt and another ingredient. The ashes of creatures.

Well, to everyone's horror but Hunter's.

He merely found it interesting.

And he'd been the one to figure it out.

Maya hadn't had to argue with her family to allow Hunter to help. This was a matter they didn't mind him helping on.

Before getting called on a business trip and leaving the job to the Whittles, he'd been quick to find it was creatures in the magical world that were mixed within the residue.

Before departing, he'd told them it was unlikely they'd find an actual individual, but knowing which species lay in the mix could help them narrow down what it was being used for.

The four had then taken turns in the attic testing the residue, Harry being the first to come out successful. The ashes of a gargoyle.

Or possibly multiple. They couldn't be sure of quantities.

It took almost no time after that for Maya to find the ashes of both demons and witches within the mix as well, something they had expected, yet still wanted definitive proof of.

The potion used to test the residue was fairly simple. The problem was picking out a piece of the residue that would tell you what you were looking for.

Harry believed there to be at least another two creatures in the mix, if not more, so Vera was taking her round in testing the residue.

For their part, Camilla, Maya, and Harry had started the calls to the different species. If there were any missing, it may help them in narrowing down their own search.

Camilla had already put Warren to the job of learning anything new from the demons. She'd heard nothing back, which they'd taken as a good sign, and their call to Uzark about a dead gargoyle revealed nothing.

"Maybe they took a part of someone that had already died," Maya hypothesized.

"Maybe," Harry agreed, "but that doesn't mean they did that for all of the creatures in that mix."

"Or maybe they haven't taken from a dead creature at all. If they only need a piece, the creatures may still be alive," Vera added as she dropped a small piece into the potion. "We already know that their aggression seems to be pointed at witches in particular."

"So it *could* be just an energy source of sorts?" Camilla added.

"But that wouldn't make sense. With all those creatures about during the party, she would've gotten all the energy she needed without anyone being the wiser," Harry rebutted.

"Maybe something to make the spell she did stronger. Every-one's energy would've made her stronger, but it would've done nothing for the spell," Maya tried.

Harry nodded. "A possibility. But for now, we can look into

the dead or missing. The gargoyle they took from may have remained alive, but that doesn't mean all the victims did."

And so the calls continued until they found a missing mermaid, a dead sphinx, and a dead werewolf couple.

Vera knew her entire focus should've been on testing the residue, but couldn't help her attention as it wavered over to the warlock time and again. It was quite distracting. She needed him to leave.

"Maybe they tried with the two of them." Harry referred to the couple, giving up trying to think of what spell could be used with these specific creatures as ingredients. "And it didn't work, so they tried again with others."

Maya nodded her acknowledgement. "Or maybe they got the one they needed, but it's mate came in to protect, and they were both killed."

Camilla solemnly agreed with Maya's conclusion. "That sounds more accurate. Werewolves are protective, especially towards their mates."

Realizing she was getting nothing done with her attention on a certain member that seemed to insist on being around, Vera stopped her test and walked over to the others, dropping onto the little couch beside Camilla. "Your turn. I couldn't get anything."

As Camilla moved to the makeshift worktable they'd set up at the side of the room, Harry looked up with the clap of his hands. "Right, while you do that, we'll check in with the werewolves."

Oh, now he decides to leave.

Camilla's disdain was written all over her face. "Yippee!"

Vera stifled a smile as she joined hands with the others and ported out to the woods the couple were still lying in, given they'd only been found a few hours ago.

Hayes, a man of two inches past six foot and over two hundred pounds of muscle, looked smaller than most other werewolves, but stood as their leader and escorted them to the bodies.

He was a genuinely nice guy. Cute too, with his light bronzed hair, tousled short and wild, and hazel eyes to match. "We had a scout find them this morning, but our healers have estimated they've been dead about a week. We're guessing they were recently dropped here. There's no way my men would've missed them otherwise."

The three nodded as they stopped before the two bodies lying together. Vera knelt opposite Harry to evaluate the pair, knowing this was no moment for his distractions. But she did notice him paying particular interest to the male, moving his shirt up slightly to reveal a mark twinkling under the sunlight.

"What is it?" Linc, one of Hayes's seconds, asked.

"A demonic mark," Harry breathed out, his brows furrowed as he evaluated it. The type of furrow that caused that dip between his brows that made Vera want to smooth it out with a kiss.

No.

Focus, Vera.

This was not the time!

"So it *was* demons," Linc hissed, his fists clenching at his sides.

"No," Maya said as she looked on from above Harry's shoulder before crouching beside him, "but yes."

Hayes's brow quirked. "Well, which is it? Yes or no?"

Maya didn't answer for some time, taking her time to assess the mark. "There's something blocking it."

"Meaning?" Vera asked, wondering how her sister even knew enough about these marks to know something was 'blocking' it.

"Meaning a demonic mark is blocked when another creature is involved. They can still create the mark, but it comes away different." Maya's gaze moved up to meet hers. "I'd wager a half demon."

Harry's gaze shot up to them as they all thought the same thing: The Eight had plenty of halfies to get the job done. No doubt at least one of those was half demon.

Harry turned to Hayes, Vera moving to stand at his side as Maya's attention remained on the mark like she was trying to make it out. "We don't know much about those marks, but we'll inform you if we learn anything as soon as possible."

Hayes only gave a dip of the head. "Wouldn't want to begin an undeserved war, would we?"

Just a bit of incentive to make sure they *were* informed.

Hayes kept his eyes on Maya as Harry grabbed for them and ported out.

On their return home, they found Camilla with her nose scrunched as she did her job with the residue. She looked up, and before she could ask, Vera piped in, "There was a halfie's demonic mark on one of them."

Camilla stopped what she was doing and placed everything back on the table, giving them her full attention. "Please tell me that doesn't mean what I think it does."

Maya huffed out a breath and dropped onto the couch in an effortless way.

Vera shrugged toward Camilla, then turned to Maya. "How did you know?"

Maya didn't answer. Except in this instance, not answering was like screaming the answer right in their faces.

Vera froze, noticing Camilla stiffening from the other end of the room as Harry immediately stepped up to Maya, placing a comforting hand on her arm. "Has *he* hurt you?"

The emphasis on the 'he' showed a bitterness Vera was not accustomed to hearing from Harry.

Maya breathed in to keep from rolling her eyes. "Hunter hasn't done anything to me I didn't want him to."

And just like that, the concern turned to disgust.

Camilla grimaced through a shiver, something Vera definitely felt. "Ugh, has he marked you?"

Maya looked as if she couldn't help the smile that erupted on her face as she moved to the Book, placing her hands on the blank pages she'd flipped to.

Harry stormed closer, raising his hand to heal her, but Maya shot hers out before he could do anything. "He removed it," She shrugged. "I was only curious. Not that you *could* heal a mark anyway."

Vera normally didn't like to show her distaste for Maya's relationship with Hunter, choosing not to judge, but there was no way to hide the grunt she shared with Camilla and Harry in that moment.

Maya ignored their reactions, likely fully expecting it, and shut the Book in front of her. "Hunter's gone right now, but I'll check in with him when he gets back. Don't want to write any inaccurate information here."

She was right on that matter. Writing about demonic marks would be very helpful. Didn't want to get anything wrong.

Vera tried shoving her distaste aside to show her acknowledgement that Hunter was, in fact, coming out helpful to their cause as Camilla added, "We can't rule out a full demon working with them though."

Maya looked to her and smiled. "I know."

Camilla's hesitations came from her distaste for the creatures, Maya's was merely out of open mindedness, and Vera felt like she could easily fit in the middle of their opposite approaches.

Leaving them with only one thing to discuss—the fact that this may have nothing to do with Loretta, or Bishop's, deaths—they moved to the kitchen for dinner.

On top of the fact they still weren't sure if Bishop's death was like Loretta's—a murder—or if his was a real, human reason. Vera didn't know why, but part of her hoped the former, like she would somehow be able to avenge him if he were murdered.

The discussion wasn't long, just opening the possibility to continue looking into their parents' deaths like they had at the beginning. Maya's expression the entire conversation seemed reserved, but Vera couldn't be sure if that meant she was hiding something, or if it merely meant she was hiding her feelings about the matter.

Vera didn't have the chance to sit in her quietude to think about it because only moments after dinner, Camilla asked for a sister's walk. She threw a sheepish grin in Harry's direction, making sure he understood he wasn't invited, and they all watched him laugh and walk off.

Somehow, going out individually on their walks or jogs always left them untouched.

But the second at least two of them were together, an attack was almost expected. It was rather annoying. And even more annoying given the fact they always seemed to forget that particular detail until they were being attacked.

So, it was as they walked along a park not far from their house in the darkness of the winter evening when Vera's senses rose. She shot out a hand to her sisters and whispered, "Behind us."

All three turned and ducked barely in time to get out of the way of a shot thrown their way. Three slobbering beasts stood before them.

Like, really slobbering.

Like, almost-make-you-vomit slobbering.

Disgusting.

Vera shot her hand out, trying to throw one back, as Maya's fire bolted toward the other two. But these demons were fast.

Way too fast.

And they weren't well enough trained to move against them.

Maya seemed better equipped though. Somehow, she was able to hit them, her fire just getting the tips of their skin before they moved. But still, she was hitting.

And Vera was missing.

How the hell was Maya so good at this?

Camilla's voice rang from behind them, calling for Harry, just as a shadow emerged to their side.

It was the Delvaux guard, Loki.

Vera had only seen him once, from a distance when Warren had mentioned it in the weeks where Hunter was not a problem to their family.

Stopping before them just as Harry ported in, he ignored them completely, rather turning on the slobbering beasts and casting a shield to cover the five of them.

He was protecting…them?

The demons looked to be thinking the same thing, if those things *could* think, as they stared at Loki in confusion. Or what Vera assumed would be confusion on a slobbering monster's features.

It seemed even animal demons understood that demons and witches were known enemies.

"Warren Delvaux has made it clear that the Whittles are to be left alone. It is recognized throughout demons. Any demon to attack them again—including the hiring of animals—will meet with the Delvauxs for their consequences."

The beasts only stared at the guard before turning and disappearing as if into thin air. But animal demons couldn't shadow; they must have a different form of moving.

Loki turned to face them, and before they could get anything out, he stated, "Those animals have gone back to whomever hired them. They'll either ask for more incentive or back out. This doesn't mean you won't be attacked, just a precaution. But it'll certainly be less now. "

And just like that, he shadowed away.

Vera looked to the others in pure astonishment as Harry grabbed for them to port home. Luckily, they hadn't necessarily been in much of an attack, lasting only moments before Loki showed up, but Vera realized in that moment that Warren had literally put his ass on the line to make sure no more creature demons got animal demons out to kill them.

Now that was love.

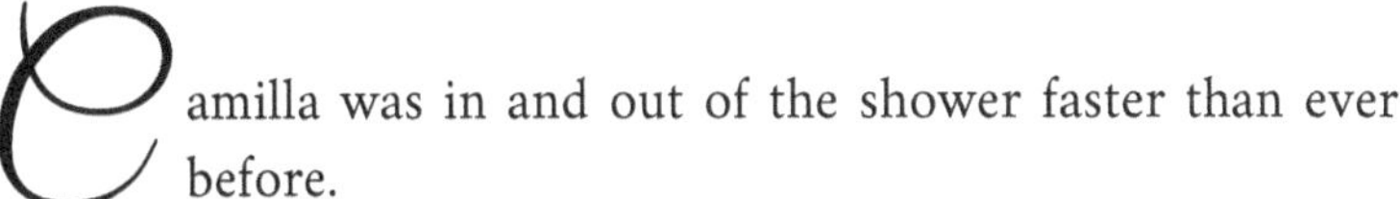

11

Camilla was in and out of the shower faster than ever before.

With a sneak into Maya's room while her family sat downstairs, she borrowed—stole—a set of red lingerie. She knew men didn't actually care, but she wanted to look good. Really good.

And Maya liked wearing lingerie to look good for herself, so it was time to take a lesson from her sister's book.

Camilla rolled her eyes as she thought of any one of the remarks that would come from Maya's lips—*Finally gonna give your bits what they're asking for?*—but she wanted to see Warren.

Her family lounged on the couch when she went down and quickly let them know where she was headed—no need to give Maya the chance to make her comment, especially after seeing the spark in her eyes.

There was a bright smile warming Camilla's face when she knocked on the flat door. And she didn't have to wait long.

Warren was there, and Camilla's heart skipped a beat as his lips broke into a smile and he leaned against the door. "It must be my lucky day."

He was shirtless.

Fuck, was she happy she wore the lingerie because damn, she'd be competing with jaw dropping deliciousness. Every indecent thought that had ever popped into her mind barreled to the front, demanding attention. She pushed them aside—or tried to—and stepped up to give him a chaste kiss before making her way inside.

Calming her nerves, she did the usual and walked to his room to place her things on the desk at the edge of the room and felt him follow. She turned and leaned her hands on the desk, taking him in entirely. Those blue jeans hung low and really didn't help in pushing her dirty thoughts aside. "On the contrary, it must be *my* lucky day."

He was leaning against the door jamb to his room now, arms crossed before him as he looked her up and down. "Oh?"

She made dramatic nods with her head. "Yes. It seems my boyfriend," she shrugged nonchalantly, "do you know him?"

Warren's smile grew a bit wicked as he looked on, taking a breath as he thought about it. "I think I may have heard of him."

"Tall, dark hair, sexy."

He snapped his fingers, pushing off the door jamb to walk a little closer. "Damn, no idea."

"Shame." Camilla sighed. "Anyway, it seems he's placed a protection on my family, something about if anything happens to us, his family would reap consequences?"

Warren moved to her, stopping about a foot away and smiled sheepishly. "You heard about that, huh?"

She pushed herself off the desk and placed her hands to his chest. "Sure did."

His hands slid up her arms until they caged her face between them, his thumbs lightly skimming her cheeks. "That boyfriend of yours must really love you."

Her fingers locked behind his neck as she reached up on the

tips of her toes. "Making me one lucky girl, to love a man who loves me so much."

His eyes twinkled at her words, but he had no time to respond before Camilla pushed closer and kissed him, soft and slow.

Pulling away, she brought her hands back to lay against his chest and pushed. He stumbled back until his legs met his bed, and he toppled over it.

Sitting there, Warren watched as she stepped back a foot and grabbed the bottom of her shirt and began to slowly peel it off.

He grunted, his gaze latching onto the bra she wore—or her breasts spilling over it—Camilla couldn't be sure and honestly didn't care. His tongue darted out to wet his lips as his gaze shot down to where her hands made their way to the button of her trousers. His gaze shot up to meet hers. "We don't have to do anything," he choked out.

Camilla smiled as she unbuttoned her trousers. "I know."

Then she was only standing in the stolen set in the middle of Warren's room, allowing him to drink her in, and boy, did he look thirsty.

Stepping into the space between his legs, she played with his black locks as his hands found their way to the backs of her thighs, skimming her skin.

"It's a nice set, huh?" She played with him.

"Mhm." He looked like he'd say yes to anything in the moment.

"It's actually Maya's. She doesn't know I took it, but honestly, if she knew why, I feel like she would've given it to me in half a second. She's good like that. And horny. She…"

"Camilla…" his voice begged.

She laughed and leaned down to kiss him, knowing she was torturing him and enjoying every moment of it. Her hands skimmed down his body and over to her own. She watched his eyes light up as her fingers ran up her own torso.

She unclasped her bra and let it fall between them, baring her breasts to him and watching the control shift within him as he stretched his neck, veins straining.

"Don't you want a taste?" she asked innocently, watching as his eyes lost the hazel and erupted in black desire.

He flipped them, throwing her to the bed, so he hovered over her, and stared down for only a moment before taking a tip into his mouth. A moan instantly found it's way past her lips as he sucked, hard.

His hands caressed her body. Slowly.

He moved to the other tip as a hand landed between her legs, touching her through her panties. She was wet. Really wet. The walk to his place plus her suppressed desire all erupting at once. She wanted him. Now!

He groaned at feeling how ready she was and suckled her tip harder, his teeth raking it before he moved back to her lips. "I can't wait long."

She felt his length pulsing against her thigh. "Then don't."

He pushed off the bed instantly and stripped naked. What a delicious view.

He stopped at the edge of the bed and grabbed for her panties, slowly pulling them down her legs, his fingers exciting her nerves every inch they traveled.

She arched off the bed, wanting him inside her.

"Warren." Her breaths came out rugged. "Now!"

He let out a purr as he crawled back over her, layering kisses as he moved. When he reacher her lips, he kissed her softly before positioning himself at her center. He looked her in the eyes as he pushed in. A moan escaped her lips as a deep groan escaped his.

Then he pulled out and pushed in a little deeper, a little harder. Again and again and, fuck, again.

"You're so fucking wet, baby," he moaned into her ear.

Her whimpers were her only response. She'd wanted this too long to be able to comprehend anything else.

He kissed his way down her neck, his tongue showing special attention to the junction as his fingers found their way to her center. She pushed into him, her nails lightly marking their way down his back as she looked into his eyes and knew in that moment that she had made the right decision, that he wouldn't hide anything from her, that he loved her.

Just when Camilla thought she couldn't take it anymore, she felt a new sensation. It was like suddenly her pleasure had doubled and she was feeling everything tenfold. Like she was feeling what he was feeling.

Unable to focus, she came, her walls clenching around him as her screams took her to another world. As her body shook, she felt him find release, her name his every prayer as he mumbled into her skin.

He pulled out and slumped down beside her, their heads turning in post-coital bliss to look at one another. As she stared at him, all Camilla could think was that whatever that feeling had been, it had been extraordinary.

Following the almost-attack-and-interference-of-Loki-slash-the-Delvaux-family, Harry and Vera went back to testing the residue, this time trying it against the werewolf couple that had been found in the woods. It was the first time they'd actually have something to test the residue against.

With Maya off doing lords knew what—surely not Hunter, since he was apparently still on business—and Camilla spending her time holed up at Warren's, they had the afternoon to themselves.

Harry watched Vera watch the potion that would let them know whether there was a match or not. If the smoke that came from the cauldron was clear, no match, but if it came back a deep white, they'd add another party to this residue.

It was an important finding.

Even more so since this test would tell them if the individual matched, not just the species.

And yet, Harry could not help when his gaze settled on the eldest Whittle witch rather than the cauldron before them.

Her hair, curls just past her shoulders, was held back with a clip, yet a few pieces demanded to escape. They'd settled just over her face, and Harry had to focus to hold himself back from reaching out and taking those curls in his fingers.

"It's a match," Vera announced, knocking Harry out of his reverie. "It was the boyfriend."

"And they both died for it. It's a shame." Harry looked to the white smoke.

Vera shrugged, her shoulder brushing his and causing every cell in his body to stand at attention. "It's love. Werewolves are protective of their mates. Their love means protect until death. I think it's romantic."

"I think it's idiotic," Harry muttered.

"Have you ever been in love, Harry?"

Shock hit him at the question before he looked to her and shook his head.

"Then you wouldn't understand. And if you don't understand it, you have no right to judge it."

Sweet.

But did she understand?

He turned to face her fully, noticing a shiver run across her skin at his attention, or maybe he was making that up? "Have you ever been in love?"

Hopefully the jealousy that was making his heart beat a million times a minute wasn't obvious in his tone.

She blushed as she looked up at him and whispered, "No."

Relief hit him like a truck.

This was ridiculous. So what if she'd been in love in the past? It was in the past. And he was only her warlock, nothing more.

Vera cleared her throat and turned away from him, her attempt to change the subject adorable. "We're the single ones. We shouldn't be trying to understand this. The others should have more insight, I'm sure."

His lips twitched as he felt a smile coming. "Yes, Camilla has been spending quite a bit of time with Warren hasn't she?"

"Young and in love, baby," Vera joked as she began cleaning the table.

A small chuckle escaped him as he helped her. "Can we say the same for Maya?"

Her nose scrunched. "She says they're just sleeping together."

Harry crossed his arms and leaned against the table until their faces were only a few inches apart. "You're right. It's not love. Just hot, sweaty, dirty, wet, filthy," his eyes twinkled as her cheeks turned crimson, "passionate, carnal, animal…"

"Okay," she screeched, smacking him away and turning from his gaze.

"Sex," he teased, then pushed away from the table laughing and finished the clean, making sure to remain behind the table. Nonchalant as he was on the outside, there was no hiding the erection he'd just caused himself. No need in allowing her to see it.

But the thought of carnal sex and Vera standing before him wasn't something he could ignore.

She turned to him. "You know, sometimes you can be an ass too."

He feigned ignorance. "How so?"

"You say things like," she waved her hand around, "that!"

He laughed. "Surely you do not blush at the thought of sex, Vera. You are shyer than your sisters, but I wouldn't think a prude."

She narrowed her gaze on him. "I am not a prude. I enjoy

sweaty, carnal sex as much as the next guy." Her blush was dark on her deeper skin.

Good to know.

"Then what?"

She stared at him, really stared. Then grabbed the rag she'd cleaned the table with and backed up. "I just don't want to hear about Maya's sweaty, carnal sex life."

She was out of the room before he could respond, but he didn't believe her answer. Surely that was part of it, none of them wanted to think of Maya with *Hunter*, but that definitely wasn't the entire story.

He had to push away the part of him that insisted she rushed out of the room for the same reason he hid behind the table. She wanted him. But that surely couldn't be the case.

12

$\mathcal{W}$hat better way to keep her mind occupied from Hunter's departure than looking for the missing mermaid?

Maya found herself driving to the private beach that the mermaids owned before she'd fully decided that was the task she would be taking on. She'd checked in with Devon and Bianka, the mermaid leaders and parents to the missing girl, and found nothing of use. Understandably so. If they'd had any information, their daughter would've surely already been found.

There was the option of going back home after the short encounter, but so close to the ocean—and on a private beach—sticking around made better sense.

The mermaids mostly stayed in the water, meeting in a cave off the edge of the beach when other species came by for a visit, so Maya had the beach to herself.

She watched the waves crash against the sands in silence. The water moved back and forth onto the beach, too far from Maya to touch her.

She listened to the crashing waves and thought of her family and the stress of this problem they had somehow found themselves in the middle of.

How had they become the detectives on this problems?

All they'd been doing before was trying to find who had killed their mother—and possibly Bishop—and now they had an entirely different situation taking up their time.

She still thought about it daily though—what happened to Loretta Whittle? Why it'd happened? Still thought about what she would do to the person who hurt her family.

Daily.

And yet, they'd been so sidetracked with The Eight and the dead witches and that residue they still hadn't figured out that they hadn't the time to think about their mother's murder. And realistically, they had no leads.

Nothing.

At least before, they'd thought they had a lead with the headstone that had the piece of the Hell's Gate key in it. At least they'd thought they'd had a lead with the Bridgers coven.

And the trip to Canada hadn't brought anything useful up.

So they were back to square one, and all she knew was that no one had a problem with her family. Not that she could find. Not that even Hunter could find, other than the demon's glory for killing a witch like Loretta. But he'd even admitted the Whittles were a coven of ironies for demons. On the one hand, they were powerful, so defeating them would bring respect and control like no other. But on the other, they were the most linked with dark magic, likely the best to be on a demons side.

He'd told her that last part with a wide smirk.

And they'd already covered it wasn't a demon.

She hated thinking about it, the fear that she'd never find out. That she'd never be able to avenge her mother.

She closed her eyes and breathed in the ocean air. No, even if it took some time, they'd find another lead. But for now, breathing in and out was all that mattered.

A ting came from her pocket, and she opened her eyes to look out at the ocean for another moment before pulling her phone out to a message from Hunter.

I think you'll notice a change in my arms when I return. They're ridiculously sore from thoughts of you. Stay out of my mind. I'm on business.

A smile broke immediately on her features, eyes brightening and core tightening as she stared down at the message, shaking her head.

She hated that man.

As she looked back up to the waves, smile still bright on her face, she jumped in her seat. There was a girl, not even ten, standing beside her. She dropped to sit without a word.

Maya put her phone away and watched the child. "Hi."

The girl stared out at the water, then turned to look at her. "You're looking for my sister."

The girl was tanned, dark haired, and beautiful, the resemblance to Bianka shining through her features. "You're Brynn's sister?"

She nodded, staring out at sea, giving Maya a moment to watch her. She was small, but even in that minute of acquaintance, Maya could tell she was fierce.

"You know there are a lot of us. Magical creatures." Maya's brows shot up at the abrupt change in subject, but she remained silent. "But somehow, each species remains within their group and makes babies."

Maya's lips twitched at the corners as she forced herself not to smile. She had no idea where this girl was going with this speech, but she didn't dare interrupt. She nodded in agreement as the girl looked to her.

"Don't you think it's odd to believe that the species never cross?" she asked.

Maya's brows furrowed at the question, but she answered honestly, "They do."

The girl was watching her intently, like she was trying to read her, learn her thoughts. "My parents say it's intolerable. Those couples are a taint to the magical world."

Maya scoffed at the revelation and looked back out to the ocean. She knew that most people within the different creatures took offense to the crossing of species relationships. She found it absolutely ridiculous. How was it that they were allowed to love someone but their peers weren't just because it was a different creature? They were all still human at the base of it.

"You don't believe that?" the girl asked.

Calming her expression, Maya turned back to her. She knew her eyes still poured the anger she felt, giving the girl her answer, but she spoke anyway. "No."

Unexpectedly, the girl smiled. "Good."

Maya's anger switched to shock. And a bit of confusion. "Excuse me?"

"I don't know exactly where Brynn went, but I can help you find her."

"You know something? Why not tell your parents?"

"They'd find her intolerable," the girl simply stated, intently watching Maya to see her reaction.

Maya's heart jumped a beat as realization struck. "Which species has she crossed with?"

"Gargoyle."

Maya took a moment to think it through before asking, "She told you?"

The girl shook her head. "Brynn was too scared to tell anyone because of our parents. I followed her one night and saw them."

"How do you know they're together? Maybe they're only friends," Maya reasoned.

The girl looked to her and smirked, far too knowing for a child. "They were kissing. A lot."

Laughter burst from Maya. That smirk said they were doing

more than kissing. "You're right. Probably more than friends. But if you know she's with him, then I don't need to find her. I was just making sure she wasn't one of the dead we're looking for."

"I know, but I want to know my sister is okay. I don't know anything else, just that she's with a gargoyle, but I have to know she's happy and safe," she whispered, turning back to the ocean.

Maya understood that entirely all too well, and that was the only reason she would agree to find this missing mermaid. Well, and maybe because this fierce child called to something in Maya. "You should go back to your family. I'll look."

The girl nodded, rose to her feet, and looked Maya in the eyes. "Thank you."

Maya watched her walk off before calling out, "Hey!" The girl turned to face her, "What was your name?"

She smiled. "Bella."

Maya smiled back. "Maya."

Bella's eyes shined, and Maya knew that the girl would be formidable when she grew up.

Maya watched her go until she was no longer in sight, then turned to look out to the ocean again. *A gargoyle?*

Running off with a gargoyle could mean Brynn was dead. They did have a dead gargoyle on their hands.

Maya pushed up from her seated position, smacking the sand from her hands and butt, and looked out to the ocean a bit longer. They would have to be near the ocean for Brynn to get her swims in if they had run off.

Maya chose to believe they were alive and well. At least until she found a reason to think otherwise. Until then, they were just making their happily ever after.

Gargoyles liked wooded areas.

Mermaids needed a watery area.

Maya had scrolled multiple areas around the map, assuming they'd stay within the country, and found a little more than she cared to admit. She'd figured she could have Hunter shadow her around when he got back, but she couldn't help but know that this Brynn girl wouldn't have gone far.

She had a little sister.

And from what Maya understood, the sisters loved one another like she and her sisters. So that left only a few places Maya would think to search. They were all private beaches by the woods.

It didn't take long for Maya to drive to the first one and find it completely empty.

The roads were empty because no one went to the beaches in the winter, so getting to the next one was a breeze. These beaches were so remote, Maya almost believed even the mermaids may not know of them. Her mother had always had a knack for finding hidden places. Now, Maya understood, that it was all magic. The same sort she'd used on the map to find this place.

It was when she got there and out of her car to walk the beach that she found a small house where beach met woods at the far end. She watched as a man walked out laughing, a woman following in his stead.

She looked just like her sister.

Maya smiled at the knowledge that they were okay, that she could take back good news to Bella. She stood with her hands in the pockets of her jacket and watched as the man turned to Brynn, cupped her face softly, and kissed her.

As he looked up, Maya knew she'd been caught.

Their gazes met from over Brynn's shoulder, and his entire body froze before pushing Brynn behind him.

Their expressions grew cold as they watched her walk up to them and stop about ten feet away. "Bella sent me to look for you."

Brynn's eyes softened at the sound of her sister's name, but they remained defensive. "Who're you?"

"A friend of Bella's."

"You're a witch," the man stated in a tone that wasn't very friendly.

"And you're a gargoyle," Maya responded matter-of-factly.

"How do you know my sister?" Brynn asked.

"We just met. I was looking into your disappearance, and she so kindly informed me that she'd seen you kissing a gargoyle in the woods, asked me to find you and make sure you were okay. Said she wouldn't tell your parents because of the prejudice. "

Brynn's eyes expanded—surely by the fact that her sister knew of her relationship—then narrowed—likely because such a deep secret had been easily passed on to a stranger. "Why trust you?"

Maya gave her a knowing smile. "My lover is a demon." Both their brows shot up. "I'm not here to judge you. Don't tell them where you are. Don't tell them who you're with. But let them know you're okay," Maya continued solemnly. "With all the species being hunted right now, they should know that much."

Brynn nodded slowly, like she was unsure of the motion. "Thank you…"

"Maya."

"Maya," she said. "I'm Brynn. This is Alloy."

Maya smiled at them with a single nod.

13

———

*O*n the day she'd been home, Camilla played her every *time* with Warren in her head. Every time she lost control of her powers and got to feel what he was feeling.

Every.

Time.

And yet, he never lost control of his powers.

She'd reasoned with herself that it must be a witch thing, but lying to yourself could only go so far when you knew the truth —it most likely wasn't *just* a witch thing.

Especially with how similar witches and creature demons were. Unlikely.

And that marked the best thing about having sisters who were going through the magical world alongside you.

Camilla found Vera in the kitchen baking for another freelance job she'd gotten to make a few hundred cupcakes. And she was glad for it. The last thing she wanted was to learn anything of Maya's current sexual relationship.

Camilla stood awkwardly at the corner of the island, fidgeting her hands, and watching her sister ice the cupcakes in the most effortless technique. How was she supposed to bring up a conversation like this?

Vera glanced up at her and furrowed her brows. "What's up?

A blush grew immediately on Camilla's cheeks. "Have you had sex since unlocking your powers?"

A narrowed gaze shot her way as Vera cautiously responded, "No."

"Oh," Camilla said, looking down at her fingers. Whelp, then no need to bring this up.

She began to back away when Vera called, "Why?"

Blowing out a breath, Camilla stopped and looked at her sister. Might as well. "Every time Warren and I have sex, I lose control of my powers."

Vera's lips cracked in an obviously suppressed laugh. "Excuse me?"

Camilla slumped against the island. "It's not funny."

Vera held up her hands. "Of course not. Please, continue."

Camilla blew out. "I don't read his mind or anything. It's more like I feel what he's feeling. Like instead of reading his mind, my body is reading his body."

She still didn't know how she hadn't read his mind. As uncontrolled as she'd been in those moments, she'd assumed his every thought would be plaguing her.

Vera nodded, biting down on her bottom lip. "Right. And why are you coming to me for this?"

"Because it seems like it only happens to me. His powers haven't been affected at all, and I wanted someone to talk to about it."

"Well," Vera picked her icing back up, joy twinkling in her eyes, "I think we both know who you should be going to with those types of questions."

"I don't want to," she whined just as Maya walked into the kitchen.

Vera looked up to her. "Speak of the devil."

Maya grabbed a glass of water and stopped at the island opposite Camilla. "Why are we speaking of me?"

"Is Hunter the only one you've been with since unlocking your powers?" Vera blatantly opened with.

Camilla gasped and hissed, "Vera!"

"Only one the past couple of years. It was depressingly dry before him. My bits didn't speak for anyone."

"Ugh, gross," Camilla whispered, looking down at her fingers.

"Okay," Vera said slowly, "then I have a question about your escapades with Hunter."

Maya choked a laugh on her water. "Escapades?"

"Yup," Vera said without a care in the world. Placing her icing back down, she began to pack up the cupcakes for pickup. Maya waved a hand for her to continue. "Have you ever lost control of your powers while you two were together?"

Maya's brows furrowed a bit as she drawled out a yes with a question mark at the end.

Camilla really didn't want to hear about her sister's time with that demon, but couldn't help brightening at her answer. "Really? What happened?"

Maya looked to each of them in turn, like she was trying to figure out what was happening, before shrugging. "We're both fire powers, so it doesn't really do anything, although, it wouldn't do anything even if he wasn't a fire power." She demonstrated by allowing some fire to caress each of them. It felt like a liquid caress, and to Camilla's surprise, it felt amazing. Tantalizing, inviting. And to Camilla's dismay, Maya pulled the fire away. "But, because we both have it, I kinda flame up, and he catches on. Eventually, we're both on fire."

"While you're having sex!" Vera exclaimed, stopping her work to look at their middle sister.

Maya nodded. "It's absolutely amazing."

"So it is a witch thing? Losing control of your powers in the moment?" Camilla asked, knowing there was a hopeful tint to her tone but unable to suppress it.

"No," Maya answered, crushing her hopes. "Hunter loses control just as often as I do. Sometimes I lose control first, sometimes he does. It actually happened to him first. He shadowed us through two floors." Camilla could feel herself deflate with that. He'd lost control first? How? "Why are you guys asking? You don't like hearing about my relationship with Hunter."

Camilla ignored her question. "Had it happened to Hunter before you? With other people?"

Maya's eyes darkened at the mention of Hunter and *other people*, a fact Camilla really wanted to ignore and pretend like she hadn't noticed. "Hunter says it doesn't happen often with any creature. It had never happened to him."

"Do you know why it happens?" Camilla felt her heart racing a little faster.

"He says you have to completely let yourself go in order to lose control. He'd never trusted anyone else enough for that."

"So he trusts you?" Vera quirked in. "Enough to completely let go? And you him?"

Maya didn't hesitate. "Yes."

Camilla watched Vera's reaction, something akin to understanding, maybe acceptance, written in her depths. She narrowed her eyes at her sisters and turned on Maya once more. "So, giving him the vial made him trust you?"

Maya watched her again. "No."

Camilla was sure her features showed the confusion she felt in that moment, more so at the thought that Maya would trust *him* enough to lose her own control.

Maya crossed her arms before her chest, surely taking in all of Camilla's reactions. "I'm not saying anything else until you tell me why."

A blush broke across her cheeks immediately, but she folded

and told her everything, about each of the times she'd lost control, and about none of the times Warren had.

Maya's eyes softened as she heard the insecure tone. "It didn't happen our first time. Don't worry too much about it."

Camilla looked back to her in thanks. Maya was right. There was no reason to worry about it.

Except for the fact that Hunter had opened up to Maya first, and Warren was obviously still holding back from her.

Vera smiled at them as she finished her packing of the cupcakes, then turned on them, the smile dropping from her features. "Speaking of love…"

Maya interrupted, "We were speaking of sex."

"Speaking of love and sex," Vera continued, "not so fun news with the residue."

"It wasn't a match to the werewolves?" Maya asked.

"It was. The good part for us is now we know one more creature in the residue," Vera answered. "But that's also the not so fun part of it. The boyfriend was the match. We're assuming that his mate tried to protect him, and they were both killed for it."

Camilla grimaced, noticing Maya doing the same from her periphery. It was hard to imagine her only problem in life at the moment—not including her mother's murder, which they still had no leads on—was her boyfriend not losing control in bed.

"The good news," Vera looked to her, "is the mermaid is okay. She called her family. They still don't know where she is, but she's okay. Apparently, she'd run off with a gargoyle lover. Smart thing too, because her parents sounded angry, even disgusted, when they told me. The parents didn't even sound happy to tell me their daughter was happy and safe and in love. It sounded like just pure disgust that she would choose a life in a cross relationship."

Camilla shuddered at the thought.

How was that possible? Even she wasn't purely disgusted at

Maya and Hunter's relationship, and she was only a sister. She couldn't even imagine a parent's love.

As much trouble as she gave them, and would continue to do so, she could see that Maya was happy in her relationship—whatever type it was—and so she lived with it.

Before anyone else could make a comment, Harry rushed into the room, face grim. He'd gotten another call from a coven.

14

a survivor.

They had a survivor.

Vera couldn't think of anything else from the moment Harry walked into the kitchen and told them that a ten-year-old girl had just been found, a similar mark on her hip to that of the werewolf.

A ten-year-old girl, the youngest they'd seen by far.

Before her, the youngest reported was seventeen, and even that had crushed Vera's soul. They were babies.

How she had gotten away, he hadn't known, but they would find out soon.

Harry ported them to the edge of a farmhouse, acres of clean grass in every direction. They were met with two men at the door.

"Harry," the one in front said. "Thank you for coming."

"Thank you for calling," Harry responded as they followed the men into the house, standing to the back of the living room as one of the men walked up to a little girl, sheltered in the corner of the couch.

She was small, even for her age, her light brown hair short

94

and haphazardly thrown about. She still looked frightened as she clenched the cup of tea between her hands and huddled closer into the corner of the couch.

Vera couldn't take her eyes off of the girl, her heart pounding in pure hatred for what had been done. She'd been affected by the other bodies before, but something about this time, about seeing how frightened she was, tore at Vera's chest.

Harry turned to the man left standing beside them. "Do we know what happened?"

He turned to them slightly, most of his attention remaining on the little girl. He would obviously never want to lose sight of her again. "She's frightened now, but we got her to tell us. They hid her in a cave, but she's our little warrior." He laughed humorlessly, taking a longer glance at the little girl. "She waited, endured what they did to her, and waited. Once she was alone, she ran. Sharpened a rock enough to break free and ran out of the cave." He paused and looked to her, solemn eyes taking in her sheltered appearance. His gaze didn't waver from her, couldn't waver from her as he continued, "Her power is flying, but she had almost no energy. She ran a bit, randomly, in whatever direction to get away. Once she had some energy in her to carry herself, she flew a few miles." His eyes flew back to them, and Vera read how responsible he felt for her. "When her energy drained, she stopped to rest until morning. She said she thought she was far enough away, so gaining energy was her best bet. She awoke in the morning and flew away, landed in some town, and called us." He scoffed at the last bit. "Lords, we ported to her so fast, but we can't take away what happened."

Vera placed a hand to his arm, unable to break her gaze from his forlorn one. "It wasn't your fault."

He looked to her and gave a small nod, but they could all see he didn't believe a word of it. He cleared his throat and pulled out a piece of paper from his pocket, handing it to them. "The town we picked her up. She doesn't remember any directions."

Vera smiled encouragingly at him as she took the slip of paper. "Thank you."

She turned to leave, knowing the family likely didn't want any more people around, but Maya stopped her. "We can't go yet."

"Why not?" Vera asked.

Maya looked to the man—Vera thought she heard someone call him Vaughn. "I need to see the mark. I have to make sure it's the same one."

Right.

They still had to make sure this was even the same person. Vera's stomach grew sour at the thought that it could possibly be anyone else. They didn't need any more trouble. It was obvious Vaughn didn't like the sound of it, but he relented, knowing this was what they'd been called in for.

He walked up to the little girl, crouched beside her, and whispered in her ear. When the little girl fought the fear that crawled across her skin and nodded, Maya cautiously walked over and settled beside her.

The girl's feet curled at Maya's thigh as Maya slowly lifted a hand to place on one of the hands gripping the cup of tea. The girl stiffened, but didn't pull away, and allowed for Maya to rub small circles on her hand. Maya smiled to her, nothing that reached the eyes, but something to encourage the girl. "I'm Maya."

The silence carried as the girl took her in, and in a raspy voice responded, "I'm Vikki."

"Vikki." Maya studied the name. "You know, when I was your age, I was adamant that my daughter would be named Viktoria."

Vikki gave the slightest hint of a smile. "No more?"

Maya smiled, her thumb running light, unconscious circles against Vikki's hand. "You'll find your mind changes a lot when it comes to kids. I'm almost positive my kids won't have the names I have picked out right now."

Vikki's smile grew a little more. "What names are those?"

"I can't tell you! My sisters might steal them!" Maya admonished, catching a laugh from the girl. It was small, but it was still a laugh.

Vera's heart jumped, a small smile forming. Maya was trying to relax the girl, and it was working.

Maya made a show of turning to look at them, undoubtedly seeing the love they felt for her in that moment, and smiled back before turning back to Vikki. She leaned in and whispered, "Okay, I'll tell you, but promise not to tell."

"But if you're positive you won't name them these names, what does it matter?" Vikki whispered back.

Maya's free hand rose and she pointed a finger. "I said almost positive."

Vikki laughed again, nothing large, but she was growing more comfortable with Maya as the minutes passed. "I promise."

Maya whispered, but it was just loud enough that Vera heard her, "Right now, I'm thinking Myles for a boy and Esther for a girl."

Vikki's nose scrunched. "Esther?"

Maya dropped her mouth in feign disbelief then pursed them at Vikki. "Well, good. That means you won't take them either."

"I could still steal Myles." There was a sheen of joy in Vikki's eyes, slight, but there. Everyone let out little laughs at that.

Maya's thumb continued to stroke Vikki's as they spoke. She was good at this, especially for someone who hated comfort. She was exceptional with the child.

Vikki looked to Maya and became serious. "You want to see the mark?"

Maya nodded, her smile dropping, but her thumb never seizing. Vikki hesitated, waited another moment, then moved slightly to give space for her shirt to be raised. Sitting on her hip was the exact demonic mark they had seen on the werewolf.

Maya's fingers moved to touch it, but she caught herself at the last moment and began to pull away, but Vikki's hand shot out to grab hers. "You can touch it."

Maya looked at her with an encouraging smile, then back to the mark. It shimmered on her skin, almost like a raised, glittering tattoo. Vera still wasn't very knowledgeable about demonic marks, but she hoped they could get Hunter or Warren to come by and remove this one. Maya pulled Vikki's shirt back down and looked back at her. "Thank you."

Vikki just whispered, "Thank you."

Maya walked back to them, Vikki's family settling around her, and they left the house. They ported back to the attic to check their map for a spot the cave could be. Vera simply watched Maya.

"You know I hate when you stare like that," Maya said without turning her head from the map on the table.

"It's nothing," Vera said in a whisper, shaking her head. After a moment, she said, "You were great with her."

Maya looked to Vera with a sigh and a small smile. "Thanks."

Centered in the map was the town they had picked Vikki up in.

Harry sighed deeply beside her. "There are a ton of places this could be, and not knowing which direction, or even how many miles, gives us no starting point."

Camilla looked to the map and shrugged, determination strong on her features. "That means we take it little by little. We can start south. Check a few spots. If we find nothing, we move west. If we find nothing in the southwest, we continue clockwise until we get something."

The Whittles spent the entire next day checking southern location after southern location from the town Vikki had called and come up blank.

So when they returned home just past evening and walked tiredly from the foyer into the kitchen, Hunter was busy cooking away.

And he was rewarded for it just as soon as Maya saw him, her entire form shifting. She grew taller, and her face broke into a small smile.

As the others slumped into chairs at the table, Maya walked to him still chopping at the cutting board. He turned only his head for a chaste kiss, but Maya softly grabbed either side of his face and brought him forward, kissing him once, twice, three times before dropping back to her heels and wrapping her arms around his waist. She leaned in, closing her eyes and taking an exaggerated breath of his scent. "Hey."

Hunter resumed his chopping with a smirk. "Hey."

He looked up and noticed the others watch on, too tired it seemed to be disturbed by their shows of affection. Maya had messaged him to let him know what was happening, so he'd figured they'd be tired when they got back, and as much work as his trips tended to be, he normally felt some exhilaration at the end. But they weren't doing this for fun. They were just plain tired.

He stopped chopping again and pulled Maya off his back, turning to face her. "Go shower. And take your family with you. I'll have dinner done when you come down."

She didn't say anything, but smiled thankfully at him, and leaned up for another kiss before leaving and taking her family with her.

When they returned not even an hour later, they were completely renewed. Showers sure could work like magic sometimes.

This time when they walked into the kitchen and saw Hunter, bitter expressions instantly appeared, causing a smile to form on his lips. "Ah, that's more like it."

Maya rolled her eyes as she helped her sisters set the table, telling Hunter what their day had consisted of. "But now that you're back," she paused at the back of one of the table's chairs and looked to Hunter, who was leaning against the island, arms crossed before him, listening intently, "I need to know what cross this mark is. It looks just like a demonic mark, but it's more pink in color. Like, light pink. Closer to the color of a fading scar than the darkness of a true demonic mark."

Hunter thought back to the different types. "Well, you're right on one thing. It's not a full demon. We only give black or dark purple marks. A half gargoyle is blue. Faeries and pixies are the hardest to tell apart, but they're more purple to light purple. Mermaids are coral or peach, so it could be that, depending how light it is. Werewolves are green. Nymphs, light brown. Dwarfs, light red, and elves, yellow. My dear brother's is a deep red. Witches are the closest to white, so it could also be that if it resembles a scar."

"None of those are the color," Camilla simply stated.

Hunter looked to her nonchalantly. "These are just base colors, but most everyone has a different coloring. Mine for instance, is deep purple with black around the edges. If it's a light pink resembling a scar, I'd wager witch, but it could be mermaid too. Might even be dwarf."

And just as he'd thought, they didn't like the sound of their own kind being involved, even though it had been their own kind that had drugged and killed hundreds, even thousands, of demons and witches not a few months earlier. He knew that even though they'd only found about a hundred bodies in the Bridgers coven, it didn't mean the coven hadn't killed more many times before. For generations.

Camilla scoffed. "Please, you're just trying to get us to turn on our own kind."

"Correct me if I'm wrong," Hunter quickly retorted, "but it was your kind that tried to kill you not two months ago."

Camilla's eyes narrowed at him. "A few rotten eggs."

"And there could be a few more, Cam," Maya said softly, obviously trying to stay on her sister's good side.

Camilla's head snapped to her sister, hissing, "Stop defending your boyfriend's kind!"

Hunter noticed the darkness fill Maya's eyes as she casually looked her sister up and down before meeting her gaze. "He's not my boyfriend, but last I remember, it was *your* boyfriend's kind. Especially being that this is a half demon."

Camilla froze momentarily at that remark, then huffed out and began to leave the room. "I'm having dinner with Warren tonight."

Maya rolled her eyes skyward, gripping the back of the chair as Hunter moved behind her, feeling her relax as he gripped her shoulders, massaging the tension away. Maya closed her eyes, head falling back to rest against his chest.

Vera cleared her throat. "She's mad, but I'm sure it's only because she feels helpless. I know I do."

Maya looked to her but didn't move. "You feel helpless? We're trying to find them."

"I know," Vera said as she placed the last plate on the table. "But with my two powers, I still can't seem to be too useful. Even when we were getting attacked by animal demons, by the time I sensed that they were there and turned to throw them back, it would be too late. It feels hopeless, and it makes me feel helpless."

Maya watched her in the silence for a moment before breaking it. "Train with Hunter."

Hunter stiffened behind her, and he noticed the others do the same.

"What?" Vera asked like she'd heard wrong.

"He's a demon. He could train you to sense him and attack quickly so that you're ready next time. We train my powers all the time. If nothing else, it'll make you more confident in your powers."

Vera looked over to him. "Would you…" She didn't finish the question, obviously feeling as awkward with the request as he did.

Hunter looked down to Maya who peeked up at him. He gave a squeeze to her shoulders and a kiss to her crown. "Whatever you'd like, love."

She smiled up at him, and he could see just how thankful she was for it. This would be helping her sister in a fight, keeping her sister safe, and Hunter knew how important her family was to Maya. "Thank you."

He leaned in for a kiss, cherished the feel of her lips softly pressed against his, already thinking about them running across his body.

Harry cleared his throat from beside Vera. "Shall we eat?"

Maya pulled away and smiled at their efforts before nodding and moving to take her seat, Hunter following beside her.

15

Hunter had gone home after dinner to handle family matters he'd missed in his time away. Maya knew it was ridiculous to be angry with him for being responsible enough to take care of his matters, but she'd been looking forward to the release his home coming would bring her.

And now, he was late.

Maya had called Hayes to let him know they would be coming over to see the werewolf with the mark at ten in the morning. It was a quarter past, and Hunter had yet to shadow into her house, something he'd well and truly made himself accustomed to doing.

Sat at the table in the kitchen, empty tea mug before her, her fingers tapped about her irritation.

When, at last, he arrived, he showed no concern for his lateness. "Ready?"

Maya's fingers paused, brows shooting up as she cocked her head to the side. "Do I look ready?"

Hunter's eyes narrowed as he drawled out, "Yes."

"Hm, that's good." She rose and walked to him. "Especially since I did say we were to be there fifteen minutes ago."

Hunter's face broke into a grin she was ready to smack off. "You're mad because I'm late? Seriously?"

Maya crossed her arms before her, which only made him laugh.

He stepped up, circling one hand around her waist and tangling another in her hair, forcing her to look up at him. "You're real sexy when you're mad, love."

Her arms remained crossed before her, trapped in his hold. "I know."

His laugh grew as he shadowed them to the werewolves.

They landed before a cabin Hayes had instructed them to come to, and her irritation grew when she saw him sitting out front waiting for them. Then again, when she tried to step away and couldn't move. "Hunter. Let go of me."

His lips dropped in a plea, and he oozed sarcasm as he whispered against her lips, "Forgive me."

Her anger only grew as she pushed him away. "I hate you."

He let go, but not before shining a winning smirked her way, and followed as she walked to Hayes, smacking her ass in the process. "Good."

Her deep inhalation only resulted in a poorly suppressed laugh.

Hayes didn't say anything about their late arrival, or the matter in which they arrived, which Maya was grateful for. He didn't even seem bothered by the fact that they were of different species and so obviously in some sort of relationship. Though that wasn't too surprising since wolves were the most accepting. He simply rose and began to walk inside, expecting them to follow.

They moved through the cabin, which hosted as their morgue out in the woods, and followed Hayes to the room they kept their dead before burial. It looked like any morgue Maya had seen in shows before, felt as cold as they'd been referred to in the shows too.

The dead wolf, a man named Robbie who seemed to be around Maya's age, lay on the table fully dressed, with only his top pulled up to his navel to show the demonic mark.

Hunter walked right up to him and looked at the mark closely. "Well, I don't even have to think about this one. It's obviously half witch."

"How is it obvious?" Hayes asked, standing to attention at the quick conclusion Hunter was able to make.

Hunter flicked his gaze to Hayes. "Marks only shimmer like that when in contact with a witch." As he said that, his eyes moved to meet Maya's, heating up a moment as they both remembered when he'd marked her, before returning to Hayes. "Since our victim is obviously not a witch, the halfie has to be." Hunter crossed his arms as he evaluated it again.

"Do you have any ideas who it could be?" Hayes asked.

Hunter scoffed in response. "The most common demon halfie is a witch. There're hundreds for sure. Our species may be enemies, but that only leads to hate sex."

Hayes's brow quirked as he looked between Hunter and Maya, causing a flush that Maya wasn't accustomed to to form over her cheeks. "I bet."

Hunter shot a look to him and smiled wickedly, moving his gaze to Maya and checking her out as he licked his lips. Why the flush chose that very moment to burn a slight tinge deeper, Maya wasn't sure. She never got embarrassed about stuff like this. But then again, she was never actually fully accepted for what she had with Hunter. Hayes hadn't necessarily accepted it, but his indifference made it seem like they were just any other couple that he could joke about.

"And do you know why it was left?" Hayes asked, bringing Maya out of her thoughts.

Demonic marks were left for a plethora of reasons, the most

common a form of branding. Like letting the person with the mark know that they were property. It was sadistic if nonconsensual, but Maya could feel her core heating as she remembered the mark Hunter had left on her. She was slowly beginning to regret having him remove it. Maybe she'd ask for it back.

But it was usually nonconsensual.

And it was something only creature demons could do. No other species had a form of branding someone where only that specific person could remove it.

Hunter breathed out. "It could have been a tracking method. Having the mark basically brands you as property, and with property comes a sort of tracking device. It's unlikely, given it doesn't do too well of a job. Might tell you a general location, but won't exactly pinpoint."

"Or?" Hayes listened.

Hunter shrugged. "Could have been a method of inflicting pain. If enough energy is put into it, you could push pain into the person through the mark. Like if I were to do it, I could push fire through the mark, and they would feel it like it was inside their skin, not to mention the stolen powers I have."

Hayes' brows shot up as he looked somberly on the dead man.

"There's the chance it was for control. Depending on who performed the mark—there aren't too many halfie's with the ability—but those that come from more powerful families have the ability to control the person through the mark. Kind of like taking over every function of your body. If they wanted you to push a knife through your own heart, you wouldn't be able to control it."

"So complete control." Hayes looked so lost, and Maya was glad to see how much the leader cared for his people.

"Depending on how sadistic, his mind would've been left alone, so he'd know exactly what he was doing. Some halfies can even control facial expressions, so to everyone else, you look like the killer, but you know it's not actually you." Hunter shrugged. "Torture."

"Only halfies have the ability?" Hayes asked.

Hunter tsked. "Plenty of demons do, just the more powerful though. Part of how they became most powerful."

"Do you?" Hayes asked.

"Of course." Maya wasn't shocked with Hunter's answer. Not from personal experience, but she knew how powerful he was. She wouldn't have doubted him the ability.

"Or could've just been a sadistic game the halfie was playing at. If nonconsensual, those marks could be painful to apply, and even worse so knowing you are forever marked," Hunter finished.

"Nonconsensual?" Hayes looked to Maya, teasing accusation in his gaze.

Her cheeks flushed a deeper red that she was glad would be harder to see in the dimly lit room—albeit werewolves had perfect night vision—and spoke nonchalantly, "Usually they're nonconsensual."

Even with Warren's help, trying to find the location that Vikki had been kept, and in turn any others that could've been captured before or after her departure, could take days, even weeks.

There could be others.

That'd been Camilla's biggest fear, her greatest motivation, to get to the location quickly since hearing of what had happened. Which left her with the one thing she really didn't want to do.

Go back to Vikki.

With Warren left behind, since seeing a demon might cause

unnecessary fear in the little girl, Camilla would go back and try to get a look at her thoughts. She hated having to make Vikki relive the moments all over again, but for the safety of any others, any other children, she had to.

Harry contacted Vaughn ahead of time and didn't even have to put up an argument. Vikki was okay with the visit, and like the little warrior she was, wanted to help.

Even the little girl was braver than she was. There was something Camilla could learn from her.

Vikki was seated crisscross on the couch, knee jumping, when they walked in. She was nervous, Camilla could see that, but she didn't know how to calm her. How Maya had done it before astounded Camilla—especially coming from Maya, the girl never comforted—but maybe her time in Hell's Gate made some things easier.

Camilla was more used to comforting adults, and even then, she did so by letting the person know she was there.

Camilla awkwardly sat beside Vikki. "Unfortunately, I'm not as good with kids as my sister is. But I promise you won't feel anything. I just need you to think about your escape."

She truly hoped her promise would hold up.

Vikki nodded shakily and closed her eyes, taking a deep breath to ready herself.

Camilla took a nervous glance at the girl, then placed a hand to her arm. Most of all, Camilla was nervous this wouldn't work, since she couldn't see people's thoughts, she could only read them. But what people normally didn't realize was that their thoughts were narrated in their heads...majority of the time, at least.

Vikki's thoughts were frantic as she thought about escaping the cave.

Camilla soothed her arm. "Slowly."

The scenes slowed, and Camilla felt a boost of elation hit as she found herself outside, looking up at the sky.

Before hitting the sky, Vikki's eyes took notice of aspects of the area she hadn't deemed important. *The twin rocks across the small clearing were a reddish tint, the size of sumo wrestlers. The sun is hitting my left cheek, my shadow chases me to the right.* Camilla smiled at that quick thought—she was facing north.

Then she ran.

Camilla cringed at her frantic thoughts—*Run, run, run, run, run, RUN!*—and wasn't able to pick up anything useful in the bushes and trees Vikki ran through.

Then she was flying.

Not high, but they were in the air and zooming in the same direction. And again, it was all trees and bushes, nothing distinguishing for Camilla to pick up.

At last, Camilla felt Vikki's thoughts calming as darkness fell overhead and she stopped at a tree, branches hanging so low nothing could be seen. She felt the relief and safety of finding a hiding spot in Vikki's thoughts and paid extra attention to pick up on any details about the location, noticing the little details that Vikki's mind threw out as inconsequential. *The branches were hanging low to my left when I descended from my fly. Falling under them, I looked out in front, to the left, clear woods. To the right, more hanging branches to hide under.*

Then the narrations stopped.

"Are you okay?" Camilla softly said to Vikki and heard the shifting about the room as her family no doubt forced themselves not to run to her.

She hesitated only a moment. "Yes...I went to sleep. I think I slept a long time, but then I woke up."

"Do you want to stop?" Camilla soothed her thumb over Vikki's arm. If she didn't want to continue, couldn't, Camilla would just work with what they had.

"No." Camilla heard the deep swallow of nervousness and hated that she was making the little girl go through this all over again.

When she awoke and came out of the branches, she moved slowly like she was aware not to make noise. She looked around before the fear struck her all at once, like she'd forgotten what had happened, then she was off again.

Again, Camilla paid attention as Vikki pushed herself into the air and began zooming. To Camilla's delight, the inconsequential detail of flying over more low hanging branches, branches that had been to the right of Vikki when she had slept, meant they were flying back toward the cave.

Because of the renewed energy from the night's rest, Vikki was able to fly longer, over and past the cave altogether.

The branches swayed lightly in the breeze. Those trees were much shorter than those. Those are some big rocks. There must be water around, those rocks are bluish. Huh, those are reddish. Nope, those are normal again. Wow, those are some big trees.

Her thoughts sounded like she was trying to keep her mind busy so the fear wouldn't eat her alive. Smart.

But those thoughts had revealed something—the red twin rocks.

She had passed the cave, and from what Camilla could gather as they stopped in the town, facing the convenience store whose phone Vikki had used, it was only a few miles, five at most.

As Vikki began the call to her family, Camilla pulled away and opened her eyes, watching Vikki do the same.

"Good?" Vikki asked.

Camilla's emotions immediately altered, and the fear she had felt while in Vikki's mind was gone, now replaced with empathy. "Perfect."

Vikki's smile was unsure, but she nodded her thanks.

Camilla soothed the girl's arm a few more moments, hating that she'd had to experience any of it, and turned to her family, a small smile on her lips. "Got it."

H arry, Vera, and Camilla wasted no time in porting straight to the location Camilla gave Harry. With the invisibility potion Vera had secured from Maya's stash for emergencies, the three landed just short of the twin rocks.

Harry left them about twenty yards back so he could port closer and check for any protection spells. After a minute, he was back. "Nothing. We'll take the potion to be safe."

Invisible and by the cave, Vera realized there was truly nothing of consequence out there. Perfect spot for a hiding—or dumping—ground. They walked into the cave, the light from the sun shining quite brightly inside.

Where they'd found nothing of consequence outside, the interior of the cave was an entirely different story. There were chains littering the ground and attached to the walls, and blood smeared everywhere, most of it dried up, but some looking fresh.

And no one around.

That was both a positive in Vera's eyes and a negative.

No one was being held captive at the moment.

But also nothing around that could help them figure out what was going on.

She walked deeper into the cave, checking every part of the interior for a clue of what was behind all this, when a mere fifteen or twenty yards from the entrance at the back of the cave, Vera turned into a nook in the rock to find a girl. A woman, really. She was closer to Vera's age.

Vera gasped and couldn't help the little scream that escaped her mouth at the sight of the woman, bloodied and chained to the wall.

Camilla's hand stifled a scream when she stopped beside Vera.

Taking a large inhalation, Vera stepped forward. Slowly, so

as not to frighten the woman, though she was unconscious at the moment, Vera crouched by her and lightly placed a hand to her shoulder. Luckily, the invisibility potion was beginning to wear off, so when the woman's eyes slit open, she saw them.

And her breathing heightened in fear. "No, no please."

Vera's hands shot away, watching the woman crawl back into the rock. "We're not here to hurt you."

The woman looked frantic, the immediate chance of savior obviously spiking her adrenaline. She begged, tears falling down her face. "Please! They took me because I'm half demon. Made me perform marks on people." She was shaking. "Please!"

Vera didn't even think, just helped her out of the chains with Harry crouching beside them to aid in the process. He took most of the woman's weight as they helped her up.

With a hold of his shirt, they ported home.

The woman, who informed them her name was Colette, asked for a bath to wash off what had been done to her, something Vera really didn't want to imagine.

And so they took her from Harry and walked her to the bathroom off the foyer, helping her into it.

"I should be fine in here." Colette gave a weak smile.

"I think I should stay. You're hazy," Vera said, sitting atop the closed toilet.

Camilla's smile was forced as she responded, "Good, I'll grab you a change of clothes."

They remained in comfortable silence as Colette bathed. A quick one too.

"I thought you wanted to soak for a bit?" Vera asked as she began to get up and grabbed for the towel Camilla had brought in.

"Changed my mind." Colette smiled warmly and took the change of clothes Vera handed. Vera turned away to allow some privacy before helping her to the living room.

Harry had a tray of tea and biscuits on the coffee table, a cup ready for Colette, when they walked out. He sat opposite her, his form rigid as he attempted to sit as far from her as possible, likely a caution in case Colette became frightened by his touch. "Do you remember anything?"

Colette shook her head shakily. "Just some parts of being… there." She closed her eyes tight and shook again. "Nothing from before." The agitation was evident on her face as she reopened her eyes, causing Camilla to move to comfort her with a small touch. A touch that was immediately retracted when Colette jumped at the contact.

Camilla was likely also trying to read the girl's thoughts, get a better idea of what had happened. It seemed they would have to wait a bit longer for that.

16

Maya walked into the foyer alone. Again.

She rolled her eyes as she thought about Hunter having to run off again, a family matter he had to help his brother settle. Yes, she was happy he was helping his brother, but damn, she wished he could've waited until after he'd satisfied her body.

She turned toward the living room at the sounds of activity and stopped short at the unexpected guest sitting on the couch to the left, Vera beside her.

At her arrival, everyone in the room stood, Camilla and Harry turning to her from the couch opposite and Vera beginning to speak, "Maya, this is Colette..."

Colette.

Maya knew that name.

She sharpened her gaze to the girl standing beside her sister.

"...she's a half witch," Vera continued, but stopped immediately at Maya's reaction.

Cutting her off, Maya threw out a demon spell Hunter had taught her to entrap someone in a space for a period of time. It only worked for short periods unless it was renewed, but that was all Maya needed at the moment.

Gasps flew as the entrapment settled around their guest.

Colette, the half witch, half demon.

The resemblance was almost remarkable if you paid attention. At first glance, she looked nothing like her brothers, but closer inspection showed their shared features. Features, Maya was sure, Augustine Delvaux would undoubtedly have.

"Maya!" Camilla's sharp cries rang out.

"Maya, what are you doing?" Vera yelled, turning to watch Colette's frantic pushes against the entrapment.

"Maya." Harry's voice grew hard and demanding, something Maya had never heard from him. "What is this?"

They all watched her for an answer, but Maya couldn't remove her gaze from the halfie in their living room. "Hunter has a sister," Maya began calmly. "A halfie. Witch by blood, possibly, but demon through and through." Maya turned to face Camilla. "If you hate Hunter, you're not gonna like the stories about his sister." She turned back to the entrapped halfie. "And her name?"

Everyone turned to the entrapped halfie, then back to Maya, like they knew what she was about to say but couldn't believe it.

"Colette Eloise Delvaux."

Again, everyone turned from Maya to Colette, this time finding the scared little captive turn into the poisonous wicked halfie she was.

"Well, well," she began, the fear completely leaving her appearance as she crossed her arms and looked Maya over, "aren't you the bright child?"

Sputters erupted from the others around her, but Maya never moved her gaze from the Delvaux sister. No one spoke as they took in the complete one-eighty Colette had just performed before them.

Breaking the silence that even Vera couldn't do, Colette

spoke, "I am shocked though. My family never speaks of me. I guess that's changed."

"It hasn't," Camilla whispered, looking between Colette and Maya and back again. "Warren never mentioned anything about a sister."

Colette scoffed as her eyes flew to Maya. "Soft little War didn't mention me, but Hunt did?" Her brow cocked as she assessed Maya again, her gaze registering more this time. "Well, maybe big brother Hunt does have a soft spot, huh. Never thought I'd see the day." Colette took her time evaluating Maya in the silence before moving to evaluate Camilla, then back again.

"What?" Camilla narrowed her eyes at the halfie.

Colette made a shake of her head. "Nothing. Just...my dear sisters-in-law are sisters. It's a bit odd."

Camilla rolled her eyes. "We're not your sisters-in-law, and she's not *with* Hunter."

Colette scoffed and rolled her eyes like she was tired of entertaining Camilla. "You may not be my sister-in-law. War never told you about me. But her," she nodded to Maya, "she sure is."

"Really?" Vera asked sarcastically.

"Of course," Colette answered matter-of-factly. "The only reason Hunt would ever mention me is because he's serious in his relationship, because he trusts the girl. That's why he's never told anyone before. I truly never thought he would."

Maya assessed her a moment longer, then turned to her family. "The entrapment should hold about an hour." She nodded to the kitchen—they needed to talk.

Away from the halfie, but only a step away from setting their sights on her, they stepped into the kitchen. "Well, first things first, call your boyfriend." Maya told Camilla as she, too, pulled out her phone, dialing for Hunter.

Camilla shook her head. "He's with Hunter. You're already

calling."

Right, he'd left her to handle business with Warren, how could she forget?

Picking up on the third ring, Maya could hear the smirk in his tone, "Miss me already, love?" Maya rolled her eyes. She truly did hate him sometimes. "Don't roll your eyes at me. It's turning me on, and I need to be serious right now."

Maya breathed a laugh at both the fact that he knew she rolled her eyes and at Warren's disgruntled reaction in the background. "No, love," she remarked sarcastically, "I haven't missed you. I just wanted to call and let you know I just met your sister."

"What?" The mischievous tease was gone.

"Yup," Maya answered nonchalantly, "in fact, she's in my house right now."

It took less than a second between Maya finishing that sentence and a shadow appearing before them in the kitchen. The brothers had arrived, and Hunter's black eyes were on Maya immediately, demanding.

Maya pulled her phone down, placing it away as Hunter spoke in a deadly soft tone. "Don't fuck with me, Maya."

Maya knew this wasn't the time, but her body reacted instantly to his domineering nature, to the way he said her name. Her mind told her to get back to the problem at hand, but her body screamed to jump him. She could already feel herself soaking at the look Hunter was giving her.

She had to snap out of it.

Maya said nothing in response, but moved to the entrance to the hallway and shot her hand out as if inviting them to step out. The brothers walked over, heading straight for the living room, the others following behind as they all came to settle before the entrapped halfie. It was clear from the brothers' reactions of tightened jaws and stiffening backs that they weren't happy to see their sister, and especially not in the Whittle house.

"Brothers!" Colette remarked in a hearty tone. "So glad you could join us so soon." The brothers said nothing as they stopped a few feet from her, staring at her carefully as Colette's attention settled on Hunter. "Especially you, big brother. Tell me, are you to have a wedding like the witches, or just claim her as yours like the demons?"

Hunter didn't make a sound, didn't move a muscle.

Maya watched from the side, standing beside her family as the Delvauxs reunited. Hunter was angry. Really, truly angry. Something she'd found didn't happen too often with him.

Colette continued, "You don't want to tell me about your romantic endeavors with my sister-in-law?" She spoke in an animated matter, an enthusiastic fluttering about her that dripped condescending. "Nothing?" She pouted. "C'mon, we all know you told her about me because she's to be family."

Hunter stepped up at that remark. He stopped when he reached the edge of the entrapment, as close to his sister as he could get without breaking the barrier, and looked down at her, disgust lining every inch of his face as he spoke to her in an unflinchingly condescending manner. "On the contrary, sister, we were sharing our greatest shames. But what else is to pop immediately to my mind when thinking of shame than you?"

Colette's expression dropped to a grimace, her eyes blazing hatred, a look that was mirrored in her brother before he turned his back entirely on her.

Warren looked just as angry, but where disgust lined Hunter's features, embarrassment lined Warren's.

He hadn't kept this from Camilla because he didn't trust her. It was because he didn't want it to be true. Hunter had told her enough of their past for Maya to understand that much. But the other part of her knew he should've mentioned it, if only for Camilla's safety.

Maybe it was his human side.

Maybe he was just plain scared.

Both entirely understandable.

But he didn't speak to his sister at all, only looked at her like he wished she would disappear as Hunter faced him. "Go home. Grab the power cuffs."

Warren nodded once in his direction, seemingly glad to be away from Colette's presence, and shadowed out.

And maybe Hunter knew that. Knew that his brother didn't want to be in her presence and sent him away, however momentary.

Or maybe that was Maya's humanity.

Hunter moved to stand across from Colette, leaning against the wall. An act that Maya didn't fail to notice was only a step away from her unmoved position by the hallway. He wouldn't show his sister, but he was there to protect her if needed. Maya didn't allow the smile to show on her face, but she allowed her earlier anger at Hunter to vanish.

As they waited for Warren's return, Maya thought to what Hunter had just said. *We were sharing our greatest shames. But what else is to pop immediately to my mind when thinking of shame than you?*

Maya knew it was a lie but said nothing. Witnessing the sibling dynamic between them was a far cry from her relationship with her sisters. Even a far cry from Hunter's relationship with Warren. And she couldn't even fathom what Warren's relationship with his sister was like.

When he returned with the cuffs, Hunter looked to Maya to loosen the entrapment so he could maneuver in and cuff his sister. Realistically, he could've done it, and to all Colette knew, he had done it; but it helped him focus to trust her to do it.

With the cuffs on, he took her down to the basement and chained her to the walls. Funnily enough, Maya had never realized there were chains on the walls down there. Interesting.

The cuffs ensured she could not use magic of any sort. The chains ensured she could not move.

Making sure she was secured, they left the basement.

Vera and Harry walked off to begin dinner as Camilla and Maya stopped at the foyer with the brothers.

"We have to go," Warren said, his gaze hard. "We left in the middle of our…situation, which just means it's going to be a bigger problem when we get back."

Camilla smiled warmly at him. "It's okay, go." She gave him a chaste kiss and backed away as he shadowed off.

Hunter watched Maya, now alone in the foyer. "Am I free to go as well?"

Maya smiled up at him, her hands in her back pockets as she stepped up to him. "If I say no will you stay?"

"Absolutely." He stepped up and placed his hands over her pocket-clad ones, giving her butt a small squeeze. "Tell me, notice a difference in my arms?"

Maya's head fell forward against his chest as she let out a laugh she'd attempted to hold in. She shook her head before looking back up at him and sliding her hands up his arms, stopping at the biceps to give a little squeeze, before encircling around his neck. "Wow," she drawled sarcastically, "from a pebble to a rock."

He scoffed. "Really?"

"Oh yeah." She mocked seriousness as he leaned in to kiss her. It was a kiss that told her he was as affected by her as she was by him, hard and desperate and wanting.

And a kiss that told her he had feared, if only for a second, that his sister had hurt her.

Maya felt him harden against her, his hands grabbing a firm hold of her ass. "I think," she said breathless, "you should go. Your brother is waiting for you."

Hunter shook his head. "Say no."

She laughed and pushed away. "Hunter, you're free to go."

He grunted and shadowed away, his gaze never breaking from hers.

17

Maya had gone another night without Hunter, and she was well and truly horny.

She knew she shouldn't be angry since he was helping his brother, and she could understand that better than anything. She was always in a situation with her family. Well, more like a species problem, but her family always seemed to be involved.

She knew all this, yet her body still screamed—yelled—at her to get out and find him.

Sitting back in her office chair, she placed her work on the table and let her head fall back, closing her eyes and taking in a deep breath. The only reprieve she could find in this situation was that she wasn't alone in her desires. She pulled out her phone to look back at some of the messages Hunter had sent her while away.

I dreamt of your mouth last night. It was doing naughty things. Lords, I miss that mouth.

Loki told me not to play with my food today. Guess he doesn't know the fun I have while I feast on you. I need you, I need to be between those thighs.

Continuing to scroll, her thighs pressed together. This was

definitely counterproductive to getting her mind off Hunter and her needs.

I think you'll notice a change in my arms when I return. They're ridiculously sore from thoughts of you. Stay out of my mind, I'm on business.

Maya smiled reading this one, remembering his beg to stay the night before. Yeah, she definitely wasn't the only horny one.

Dropping the phone, she tried to push him out of her mind as she spun in her chair, and her gaze settled on the photo they had placed back onto the mantle in the office: one of Loretta Whittle and a baby Lila Bridgers.

She thought back to the locating spell they'd performed to find Lila a couple of months ago, when they thought she'd been responsible for killing their mother as a form of revenge, since Loretta had been the reason Lila's own mother had been killed. And the spell had brought up Quebec, Canada along with Kent, England. She'd gone back after they'd finished off the Bridgers coven and tried again with the frame, wondering what it had meant.

And Quebec hadn't come up.

Not then, and not every time she'd tried since then. And nothing special had come up when Hunter had taken her to Quebec. It'd been beautiful, and in any other circumstance, it would've been an amazing date night, but she couldn't help but focus on the part of her that knew there was something about Quebec. There *was* a reason it had come up alongside Kent.

She'd asked Lila and Tamire if they had any significant hold, and they'd denied ever having a connection to the place. So it left her with the final thought: did it have anything to do with how Loretta, and possibly Bishop, were killed?

Her thoughts were interrupted when the doors to the office were thrown open and Vera and Harry stormed in. What now? "What happened?"

Vera dropped a note on the desk before her. "It was left by

some compelled kid, doesn't know anything, hardly knew where he was at."

Maya opened the note.

You have our sister. We have yours. Trade with us, and she'll be fine, but leave her here, and watch her burn. We'll be nice, allow you to think, but know we can't hold out too long. Meet at the skate park on Grand and she'll be fine. But remember, we must get what we want first.

Maya shot out of her seat. "Let's go."

She pulled out her phone as they headed for the basement, shooting a text to Hunter. *Skate park off Grand. Trade Colette for Camilla.*

He definitely wasn't going to like this.

"Ah," Colette smiled as they filled the basement, "I see my friends are here to get me."

Harry unchained her, leaving the cuffs on, and grabbed her arm so tight Maya could imagine the pressure against her muscles. He took Vera's hand softly in the other, and it was both shocking and attractive to watch Harry so domineering.

And yet still so kind with Vera. Interesting.

Maya grabbed Vera's hand, and Harry ported them to the outskirts of the park, somewhere humans wouldn't notice a sudden appearance of four people.

"Over there," Colette instructed, indicating a bench in the middle of the park. A very public place.

They stopped by the bench the same moment two others did. "That didn't take long."

They were two women around Colette's age, maybe a bit closer to Vera's, and if Maya had to guess, they were at the bottom of the barrel in this group her family was calling The Eight.

"Where's our sister?" Vera asked, ignoring their smug tones.

A bob of the head to the side. "Under the bridge."

Under the bridge was basically an urban cave, hollowed out

to a dead end in the back. And there were a bunch of teenage kids skating at the mouth of it.

None of them moved when Vera asked, "How do we know you're not lying?"

A simple shrug.

Harry looked to them, his gaze settling softly onto Vera. "Go. If she's there, then we'll trade."

Maya didn't hesitate, moving to the entrance instantly, though keeping her pace as normal as she could muster so she wouldn't draw attention.

And once she got past the kids and toward the back of the cave, she found her little sister. Lying unconscious.

Maya ran to her, lightly picking her head up and moving it to her lap before trying to wake her. Then she noticed Vera stopping from her periphery and turning back to the edge of the little cave to give Harry a nod to confirm they'd found their sister. Maya didn't pay any more attention to them as she focused on Camilla's now waking form.

She looked dirty, very dirty. But unhurt. Or as unhurt as Maya could make out. That really all depended on how much Maya trusted The Eight when they said they wouldn't hurt them until they were done being used. And from what Maya picked up, they weren't done being used.

Harry and Vera were by their side as Camilla's awareness came to, a groan shaking her as she moved.

After a few moments, Harry helped to softly move her to sit against the cave wall and breathe in. From the story she'd heard of how they'd found Colette, this must be almost like deja vu to Harry and Vera.

Except Colette's had been staged.

Watching Camilla take in her breaths, Maya's body stood to attention at the new member joining their group. Hunter stood across from Camilla, somehow looking both smug and annoyed.

"What's got you looking so smug?" Vera broke the silence that had settled over them.

He shrugged nonchalantly. "I got one. The other got away."

"Got as in killed?" she asked.

He smirked giddily. "As in a nice snap of the neck. No blood, you know, too obvious."

Maya turned her attention back to Camilla. "You okay?"

She nodded slowly, obviously feeling the small movement in every area of her body. "My face hurts. And I can't remember anything." She closed her eyes and flinched as the kids skating only ten yards away yelled.

Hunter turned to them. "Hey! Beat it."

They were far back enough that the guys wouldn't be able to see what was going on, but they gave Hunter a dirty look anyway, though the yelling did stop.

Unfortunately, they remained in the cave, skating back and forth. And every groan Camilla made at the sounds of the boards made Maya flinch with the need to help her, to move her and take her home so she didn't have to endure it any longer.

Maya threw an annoyed look over at the kids, then looked back to Camilla. Her mistake, truly, because Hunter noticed the look. And didn't hesitate to turn around. "What part of beat it didn't you get?"

Maya knew part of the anger was at losing Colette. And Colette made him angry. Really angry.

She had to get him out of there before he did something stu...

"This is a skate park, man, fuck off," one of them yelled back.

Wrong move.

Maya shot to her feet just as Hunter's head tilted slightly and a hand moved, barely noticeable, blasting out a shot of water.

Well, looked like Melusine's stolen power was coming in use.

He blasted each of the six skaters in the face with the water, in what Maya could assume made them feel as if they were drowning. And lucky for Hunter, being in the cave meant they were blocked off from the public, and he could have his fun.

"Hunter!" Maya growled over the protests from her family, stepping toward him. "Stop it!"

Hunter laughed cruelly, turning his gaze to her but pulling the water away. "Angry you can't counter this power? Shame I didn't use fire, huh?"

Okay, so losing Colette made him angrier than she'd thought.

Maya's eyes narrowed on him just as the same kid yelled out, "Hey fucker, what's your problem!"

Seemed they weren't concerned with *how* it had happened.

Vera had Hunter thrown into the wall as he turned away from Maya and tried to hurt the skaters again.

Another wrong move.

Black, angry eyes moved to her older sister, and Maya read the cruel intent there. He shadowed behind the kid that had told him off, grabbed either side of his face and smirked at Vera.

Maya felt her heart drop, knowing what was coming next. "Hunter! No!"

Too late.

Snap.

He ignored Maya as he calmly stared Vera down. "You have five more chances to hurt me. I'm actually having fun." He dropped the body and stepped up, giving Vera a clear strike.

Vera backed off, her face showing the utter horror she felt as Harry yelled, "Enough!"

Vera would likely now blame herself for the kid's death rather than Hunter. Great.

Harry moved to the five remaining guys and wiped their memories entirely before shooing them away.

Maya glared at Hunter as the two men made their way back to the end of the cave. Harry reached out for Vera, who was holding Camilla up, and took her hand, his other reaching for

Maya, as if waiting for her decision: would she go with them or with Hunter?

Maya threw a withering look in Hunter's direction as her hand slipped into Harry's and he ported them out. They would most definitely be talking about this later. She didn't care how angry he was with Colette's situation.

Warren was waiting for them at the house, having gotten a text from Hunter that Camilla may be hurt and no other information. Having no answer when he'd tried calling anyone in the family, he'd shadowed to the house, waiting impatiently for anyone to show up.

He jumped to attention as the members ported into the living room, and ran for her as Camilla settled onto the couch. He dropped to his knees before her, softly touching her to make sure she was okay. "Thank the lords you're okay."

Camilla allowed his inspection. "How did you know?"

"Hunter texted me."

She grumbled, "Oh."

"What happened?" he asked as his hands lightly touched her hips, and he felt her stiffen. "Did that hurt?"

"No." She furrowed her eyes in question, pushing two fingers under her trousers and pulling out a piece of paper.

"What is that?" Maya asked.

Camilla shook her head. "I don't know. It was held under my underwear strap. I must've hid it when they had me. I don't remember anything." She opened the paper and shook her head. "I don't know."

Maya took the paper from her hands. "Whatever happened, you hid it because it would help somehow." She looked the piece over and stiffened. "It's a list of ingredients, a list that includes the blood of thirty-nine witches."

It could be exactly what they had been searching for, what it was the thirty-nine dead witches had been needed for.

Maya flipped the paper to look at the other side. "There's faded ink back here, but it's definitely the ending to a story."

With that said, Warren watched as they all dispersed, likely to rest themselves, if not to begin the search for that story. He rose to sit beside Camilla on the couch and played with her hair as she let her head fall back to rest.

"I'm so sorry, Camilla." He spoke just above a whisper.

She didn't open her eyes. "You didn't know."

"I know Colette. I should've warned you."

Her eyes opened and watched him intently. "Why didn't you?"

His thumb skimmed over her lips as he brought himself to speak. "Human psychologists say that sometimes things are so traumatic we suppress them. She's my thing."

Her hand circled the one that caressed her face, as if he was the one who needed comfort in the moment. "Will you tell me about it?"

He didn't want to, but she deserved to know.

He gave a small nod, but before he could speak, she did. "Help me up to the bath, and you can tell me while I soak."

Of course.

She was the one who'd just been taken and likely beaten. Dirty and bruised as she was, how could he not have offered the bath?

He pushed aside the self-loathing he felt and picked her up into his arms, shadowing them to the bathroom across from her bedroom.

He locked the door behind them and began the bath as she stood and watched him. "Help me with my clothes too?"

And he knew it was widely inappropriate, but his dick jumped at the invitation.

He turned and slowly helped her lift her shirt off, unhook

her bra, and pull off her panties and trousers. She was covered in dirt from only a day with those animals. The urge to kill was strong within him.

He helped her into the bath and sat on the ground beside the tub as she wet her face and hair, getting some of the grime off before emptying the bath and refilling it so she didn't sit in the dirt. When all was settled, she gave him her full attention.

Right, time to give his side. The reason he had never mentioned having a sister when Hunter had told Maya.

He knew it had bothered her to learn that even Hunter had been open enough with Maya to give that information, but he had to make her understand that Hunter was the one Colette feared, and Colette was the one *he* feared.

"Colette's never really been a part of the family. Sometimes she would be around for a couple of months, but it was never more than that. My father had always put his interest in Hunter and me. And it's not because we're boys. I don't even think it was because she was a witch. I think it had more to do with which witch she'd come from. I know, sounds crazy—if he hated her so much, why even have sex and lead to the possibility of children?—but it's the one thing our two species do best: hate sex."

Camilla didn't move as he spoke, kind eyes watching him.

"It's why Hunter doesn't sleep around. His total body count is lower than mine—not that mine is so high, but you get the point—he doesn't sleep around. Maybe…a handful of women, including Maya. It's because of Colette. He's never wanted to fall into a position where he has a vile child like her. And honestly, this is one of those aspects of Hunter that I need to follow, that I began following a year ago because I realized he was right. I mean, I was only sleeping with humans, but still, didn't want the possibility of having a Colette-like child."

Even the talk of other lovers didn't seem to bother Camilla.

She was likely readying herself for the part that actually mattered.

"She wasn't around too often, and about ten years ago, my father stopped allowing her to be around at all. He won't admit it, but I think Hunter had something to do with that decision. And honestly, on top of the fact that they are my family, I think keeping her away from me was a big reason why I've been so loyal; because at the end of the day, they must have done something, scared her somehow, to keep away from me. She's had so many opportunities when my family weren't around, but I'd never heard from her."

Her wet hand reached out to his, a thumb stroking the top of his hand. His gaze dropped to where their skin met, and he didn't look back up.

"She's only a year younger than Hunter, five years older than me. I came at the perfect time for her experimentation. I don't remember any of it since I was a baby, but I'm told that she was specifically kept away those first few years because she thought it funny to scratch me and see if I'd heal on my own, feed me shit from the animals outside, throw me around to see if I'd land on my feet, my ass, or what she hoped for, my head. And that's only from what I've been told. I'm assuming there was more.

"My earliest memory is from when I was six. She was visiting for the month, and we were left alone. I was messing around with some toys, and she was ridiculing me from the side. And that's the day she found out about her power. We were staring each other down—she'd just called me every name her little eleven-year-old head could think of—and the hatred in her eyes was so evident…then I felt it, like I'd stuck my finger into an outlet. She electrocuted me. It was only a moment. She was shocked too. It was the first time she'd seen her power, but then she looked at me with pure joy and did it again. This time, she didn't stop until Hunter ran in to find out what my annoying screams were about and tackled her to the ground. He set her on fire to get her to stop."

Camilla leaned over and kissed the hand that Warren still stared at. He didn't want to look up at her.

"She was sent away after that, but she was still a Delvaux so it wasn't the last I'd see of her. Every time she came back, she found a way to torment me. The next year, she'd learned how to electrocute utensils to shock the person holding them. It works quickly, but she knew what she was doing and I was small and naive, and when she'd get in trouble for it, she'd send animal demons after me to scare me because it was my fault.

"Hunter's an asshole now, but he was a good brother then, at least because he hated Colette more than I annoyed him. Every time she did something to me, he'd do something worse to her. He began stealing his first powers at thirteen, so soon it wasn't just his powers he was using on her. It's why she never tried anything on him."

Camilla gasped. "How many powers does he have?"

"Tons. He doesn't use most of them on a regular basis. A lot of them work best for the situations he put Colette in—torture."

"So that psychopath fucking my sister has a million and one ways of hurting her?"

Warren didn't respond but looked guiltily at her, as if it were his fault they were sleeping together.

"I'm sorry. Please, continue."

He really didn't want to. "The reason I never told you about her was because of everything she's done to me, but mostly because of the last thing she did, the reason she was sent away from us."

Warren knew she wouldn't dare read his mind at the moment, that she'd only hear what he wanted to tell her, so he knew she was fully comforting him when she leaned in close and brought his hand up to her lips. "If you can't do it, you don't need to tell me."

Warren shook his head. He did have to tell her. "I got my power when I was ten years old, younger than she was when she'd gotten hers. She didn't like that. She wasn't with us when I got it, so when she came for the visit a couple of months later, she was astonished to find out that little halfie-human Warren had gotten his power at ten, when *she*, a half witch, had been eleven. It didn't matter to her that Hunter had been nine—he already scared her enough that in her eyes, as the only full demon, he was deserving and I wasn't. So she decided that I didn't need powers. It'd be better for me to 'rot a plain human' than to disgrace her, so."

Camilla stiffened as she held his hand, but she didn't utter a word.

"Stealing powers works if the person is too weak or restrained to do anything about it. Usually, it's that they're too weak, basically dying. Hunter was able to do it at the Bridgers coven because they were all weakened by the fire, being aflame would kinda immobilize you from fighting it. Colette decided that she'd take my power, then she would have a stolen power like Hunter, and even worse, because it would be my melting, she'd be able to control a lot with it. If done correctly, you can get into a person's bloodstream and begin melting everything."

She gasped. "How is *that* a medium-level power?"

Warren couldn't help the small smile that graced his lips. "I said if done correctly. It's not as easy as melting anything else, and it would take far too much energy. You'd be out of it for maybe a week."

She scoffed like that wasn't a good enough answer but didn't say anything more.

"Anyway, she wanted my power so that I wouldn't have one and she'd have two. My father and brother were in the study discussing business. Hunter had just started the trips, so they always had a ton to discuss—how they could do more, who they could hire, who they could scare. Basically, they wouldn't be out for a while. She'd silenced the room so that only she would hear me scream, then electrocuted me from the inside out. She'd gotten me by surprise, so I was barely able to melt a couple of vases onto her. She might still have a scar from where it burned into her leg, before she brought me down. Her power is more painful, but mine can immobilize if I melt onto the right spots."

She shook her head and whispered beneath her breath, "How is that a medium level!"

Warren bit back the smile and continued, "She chained me up with those cuffs we used on her earlier, then electrocuted me again to make sure I was weak enough not to fight the steal. I wasn't though. I fought it. It took another two tries before I couldn't fight it anymore, but by then, Hunter and my father had walked in. I never saw her again after that. They had me taken to my room and taken care of while they took care of her."

"Until yesterday?" she asked softly.

"Until yesterday. Hunter's an ass, and I truly hate him some-times, but he's always taken care of me against her. Even yesterday when he was more concerned with protecting Maya, I know he was still looking out for me."

"You think he was protecting Maya?" she asked, shocked.

"Undoubtedly. Probably not the smartest move, considering I'm positive Colette picked up on it too, but with how open he is in his relationship, he likely didn't care."

She looked confused with the new information, but pushed it aside as her fingers brushed a curl that had fallen to his brow, continuing the caress until he looked her in the eyes. "I still hate him." He couldn't help the grin. "But I'm glad he protects you. And I'm thankful that you could tell me this. I love you, Warren, and I am so sorry that she was so awful."

This time he didn't speak, just leaned in for a kiss. He stayed pressing his forehead to hers until her bath began to run cold.

18

Whatever book this story was ripped from, their mom didn't have a copy.

With Warren staying the night to take care of Camilla, Maya'd had the chance, along with Vera and Harry, to go through all of the books Loretta Whittle had left lying around the house, and more importantly, the attic.

Given this storybook wasn't part of Loretta's collection, it was time to look into contacts, see if anyone recognized it. And since she wasn't talking to Hunter at the moment, her contacts would be the first to use.

And Warren's and Harry's.

Though she wasn't dumb enough to think Warren's contacts would even compare to those of Hunter's in the demon world, it was still something.

They'd each taken a picture of the page, capturing the ending of whatever story this came from, then broken up.

Warren would obviously take the demon side. Harry was to contact Uzark and Hayes for the gargoyles and were-wolves, along with looking into any of his contacts that may know of anything, like his old friend Rupert. Vera would call

Lila, and Maya, Brynn. It wasn't all of the species, but it was a start.

A call with Brynn told Maya that she'd contacted the wrong sister. Bella had always been the one to love stories, usually memorizing them to retell later.

Which meant a visit to Bella was required, a fact that Maya was secretly happy about. She didn't even know her, but Maya missed that girl, missed the fire and determination and fearlessness in those eyes.

And Brynn wanted to see her sister.

The excitement that came from the older mermaid as she sat inside Maya's car for the ride over to the mermaid's private beach was palpable. Maya could only imagine. She'd only met Bella once, and she was—secretly—excited to see the girl again. Brynn must've been over the moon.

"How long has it been since you've seen her?" Maya asked as they drove toward Bella's beach.

"A month, I think," Brynn answered. "I've missed her so much, but I was just never sure. She's young. I didn't know whether she'd understand that cross relationships aren't a bad thing. I didn't at her age."

"How'd you come around?"

She was silent for a minute. "My parents really ingrain it in us that it is all right to be friends with other species; allies are always needed. But that was it. And by friends, they meant acquaintances. They didn't want us truly friends with anybody but other mermaids. I never really cared much. I was a quiet kid, preferred to be on my own."

"Bella seemed to me to be the same," Maya said.

"She is." Brynn looked out toward the waters they passed. "But she's a lot nosier than I was. I was truly content with being of my own mind, truly didn't care about anybody else's business. She would make a far better heir than I anyway."

"What a formidable thing to behold." Maya smiled.

Brynn smiled back before dropping it. "I was content with my life, with being friendly to other species at events in order to build a sort of allyship, but not putting much effort into it. Hell, I didn't even put much effort into friendships with other mermaids."

Maya could understand that much. So far, she wasn't liking much of the witches she'd been meeting.

"I'd swam past our borders one day. I did that a lot. I'd go and go and be gone for days sometimes, but I'd come back with souvenirs, and I was genuinely so wide eyed and uncaring that my parents knew I wasn't going on any rendezvouses. Plus, they'd had me followed before and realized I truly was just a lame explorer. So, when I'd go, they'd let me. They saw it as an exploration, something I could use to my advantage when I began to rule the North American group."

"Let me guess, you swam up toward shore and Alloy was bathing in the waters?" Maya smiled.

No answer.

"Brynn?" Maya's grin rose.

Nothing.

She barked a laugh. "Seriously?"

Brynn's flush was light on her skin. "I actually swam up toward shore, and beneath the water, I saw...*him*."

"You mean you saw his cock," Maya clarified.

The blush deepened. "If you knew what I meant, there was no need to say it."

"On the contrary, there was much the need to say it." Maya smiled and glanced over to the mermaid, trying to stop her laughter.

She shook her head and spoke through her smile, "I saw him, and I looked up and he was so beautifully fit. I'd never been... affected by anyone before. It hit immediately. I rose from the water and kinda scared him, but he relaxed after realizing what

I was and that I'd just happened across the area. I was already blushing, so he knew I'd seen him."

"And?" This was a fun story.

"I apologized. For swimming up on him like that. He," she bit her lip at the memories, "he just shook it off, asked if I wanted to go for a walk. I was so embarrassed, but at the same time, I wanted to be near him. I wanted any form of time I could have with him. It was so confusing. I'd gone two decades never feeling the need to be around another person, and now it was hitting, and it was a gargoyle, and I truly didn't even think of our two different species until I was swimming back home the next day."

"Lust at first sight?"

"Absolutely. But it quickly moved to love. Very quickly." She paused, staring out the window, before continuing her story. "I got out of the water, changed into my human form, and waited for him on shore. I knew I should've looked away, given him his privacy, but I couldn't. And he felt my stare. He told me later that he loved that I couldn't peel my eyes off him, but at the same time, he really wanted me to. He was very affected from seeing me in the water with him, from seeing me on shore. But he said he chose to act nonchalant about it. If I wasn't gonna be shy about staring at his naked form, he wouldn't be shy to show it to me."

"Could you tell he was a gargoyle right away or did he tell you?" Maya didn't know why, but she was curious.

"I knew. It's easier for me than it would be for you. I grew up around the species."

Very true.

"Anyway, he came out, naked. And I nearly glued myself to the tree I was leaning against. It was a spot like where we live now, water and woods, so I just glued myself to the tree and watched him walk toward me. There was a small hut about twenty feet behind me. He thought he'd been alone on the beach, so he hadn't brought anything out. I couldn't take my eyes off of *him,* and for the first time in my life, I was pressing my legs together and my mouth was almost drooling. When I finally met his gaze again…he was enjoying my reaction."

"So what happened?" Maya asked.

"We went into the hut." She shrugged. "People would think I was naive and easy, and he got lucky. I didn't care. I wanted him."

Maya smiled. Good. "So you had him."

"And I kept coming back. He'd been at the hut that day by chance. He'd been out on his own searches and found it, wanted to rest. After that night, he came back every chance he got, and I'd meet him as often as I could. Sometimes we'd meet some-where else, deeper in the woods, but we made our own dates. In only a couple of weeks, I knew I was his completely. I guess he felt the same."

"Guess?" Maya scoffed. "He was damn near ready to rip my head off for coming onto your little beach, for forming any sort of threat to you."

Brynn smiled around her flush.

Maya parked a bit farther away from the mermaids' private beach, knowing Brynn didn't want to be seen, nor would she necessarily be accepted now that her parents knew she was with a gargoyle.

Leaving Brynn by the car, Maya went to ask for Bella alone.

It took no longer than five minutes for the little girl to walk out and see Maya standing in the cave. She looked almost relieved to see her.

"Hey, twerp," Maya called out.

That brought a wider grin to her face. "Hey, witch."

Maya motioned for the beach. "Let's walk."

Bella didn't hesitate to leave, an almost thankful breath leaving her as they stepped out.

"You okay?" Maya asked as they walked in the direction of

the car, a direction that seemed to have little Bella confused but that she didn't question.

She shrugged in response. "Everyone knows about Brynn and Alloy now, and they won't stop with all the comments. I needed to get away."

"Well then, you're welcome."

Bella didn't look too impressed, but laughed anyway. "Thanks." After another minute, she asked, "Where are we going?"

Maya didn't answer, rather pointing to her car and the woman leaning against it. A wide grin broke across Bella's face.

Then she was running.

Brynn caught her as she threw her arms around her sister and they hugged something fierce. Maya felt her heart beat calm in seeing the two together. It was so nice.

Maya allowed the sisters a moment as she looked on, smiling at their enthusiasm before joining them. "Okay, kid." She sat at the trunk of the car, looking out at the ocean beyond the cliff they were parked at. Bella joined her on top, Brynn taking the other end of the trunk as all three looked out at the ocean.

Maya pulled out her phone, opening to the picture. "Brynn tells me you like stories. Happen to know this one?"

Bella took the phone, looked at the fading words, and in seconds answered, "Yeah, that's the ending to 'Grandmama Told Me.'"

***

Finding nothing in his searches, Harry decided to give someone else the chance to find something while he joined Vera in the attic in the search for the last creature in the residue.

Taking the now separated ashes, they added them to the potion with a bit of griffin features. If the potion smoked up white, it would be their creature. At that point, they hoped for it to be a griffin. Not that they wanted any griffin dead, but in the hopes that they'd finally find the missing creature.

They'd just finished with sphinx; not it. So the dead sphinx wasn't killed by The Eight.

Most likely.

It was difficult to hold much belief that a griffin would truly be the other species as they waited for the smoke. Griffins were some of the most difficult to come by. It would've been quite the feat to find a griffin, then attack it enough to get what they needed. Whatever the reason for this residue, The Eight must've really needed it. And both knew they were running out of alternatives.

Vera looked stiff as she watched on.

"Are you all right?" Harry asked, trying to hide the ample amount of concern that came for only the eldest Whittle witch.

Her gaze seemed glazed over before settling on him. "I'm fine, just not looking forward to later today."

Later today?

Ah, Hunter, of course.

"You have your first training today?" Harry asked, equally not enthused to have her alone with Hunter, albeit happy she'd finally be getting proper training, something he could not help her with. Something he never thought any demon would help her with.

Plus, if there was any man he could trust to be around Vera in a non-sexual, non-romantic way, it would be one of the Delvaux brothers. Their attentions were already set on the younger Whittles.

"Yup." She popped the word on her lips, bringing his attention to her mouth. "Not only was I already not looking forward to being alone with him, but now that he and Maya are in the middle of an argument because of what he did at the skate park, he's going to be in a foul mood."

Harry didn't want to laugh because he knew that was true, but he couldn't fight the small chuckle that escaped his lips.

She smacked him on the arm. "It's not funny. I need Maya to make up with him so he won't be as much of a pain in the ass, but you know Maya, she won't do it."

Harry took her hand in his, loving the feeling of holding her, and looked her in the eyes. "Vera, it'll be a fine session. He may be annoyed, but he's not going to do anything else to get her angrier."

"How do you know that?"

He smirked. "I saw the way he watched her when we were porting out of the skate park. He already knew he'd messed up. He'll be crawling back to her in no time, so adding another thing to piss her off with isn't going to help his case."

Her fingers played with his hand, and his heart dropped to his stomach as he held still. It was like every fantasy he'd had of her fingers caressing him had gone out the window because this felt an eternity better. And it was only on his hand. Just imagining this same feeling on his face, his arms, his chest, his...

He cleared his throat as she looked back up at him. "Let's hope you're right."

She didn't release his hand as the white smoke rose from the cauldron, and their attentions snapped over. With a meeting of gazes, the relief of finding the final creature was overruled with worry for the griffin.

Just because it was in the residue, did not mean it was dead. It could very well have been injured and was now doing well.

"Maybe," Vera thought aloud, "the dead sphinx was used to find the griffin. It wasn't used for this spell directly, but as a tracker. If it were offered something good enough, or just didn't care, it could have worked with The Eight."

Harry's eyes studied her before giving a short nod. "Killed when they were done using it."

"Sounds about right," Vera said solemnly.

Harry had no control of his hand as it shot out, his thumb lightly grazing her cheek. She flushed almost immediately as her gaze met his. He would do anything to see that happen over and over and over again. Anything to know the desire he saw in her eyes at that very moment was true.

"I hate to see you so upset," he whispered to her.

He was standing a whole arm's length away, but he could feel her around every inch of his body. Could feel his own need to be closer to her, hold her, arouse her.

Her breath hitched, and she barely managed a response. "We'll figure it out."

His thumb grazed across her cheek, barely brushing over her lips as he said, a serious glint in his eyes, "We will."

<hr>

Vera stood in the empty room across from the living room waiting for Hunter. They'd agreed on four in the afternoon, but ten minutes later and still no Hunter. She was ready to call him when a tingling began to shoot through her fingers and up her neck. She turned to find him leaning against the trimming to the hallway.

"You're late," she seethed.

"And you're slow," he rebuffed.

She scoffed. "Excuse me?"

"It took too long for you to recognize that I had shadowed in. I could have easily killed you."

Her brows shot up. She didn't know what she'd been expecting, but he got right to the point. He was there to train her, and it started immediately. In a real situation, recognizing he'd shadowed in instantly truly could mean life or death.

"Sorry." There was no real apology in the word, but she threw it out anyway.

Shadows, and he was gone again.

Vera turned, expecting him to be behind her now, but found nothing. "Hunter," she grumbled.

"Yes?" he asked from exactly the same spot just as the tingling shot up her fingers to the back of her neck.

"What are you doing?" Annoyance didn't even begin to describe how she felt.

"Your response time is slower than I thought. Those must've been some weak or slow animal demons that came after you because they should've been able to kill you before you processed they were there."

"Well, gee, I did only get the power a couple of months ago."

He narrowed his gaze at her. "How does it work?"

"What?" How Maya ever kept up with him Vera couldn't fathom, the man was all over the place.

"The power. How does it work? How do you know a demon is around?"

"Oh." She looked down to her hand. "I get a tingling feeling in my fingers that shoots up my arm to the back of my neck."

"And does that feel nice?"

"Seriously, what? You're here to train me!"

"Answer me."

Vera narrowed her eyes at the demon. She didn't want to answer him, but something told her things would go a whole lot easier if she did. "Yeah, it does."

"How nice?"

She breathed out heavily. She had no idea what this had to do with anything, but she answered anyway, "Like fingertips caressing you, but from the inside."

He smirked.

"Why?" she bit out.

"That's why your response time is so slow. You're taking your time enjoying the feeling rather than taking the hint and turning to the enemy."

She scoffed. "That's ridiculous."

He shadowed and was gone again. She felt the tingling begin to shoot up just as a breath tickled her ear from behind. "Is it?"

She gasped and jumped out of the way. "Do not touch me."

His smirk only grew. "Sweetheart, I am interested in only one woman, and you most certainly are not her. And it is because of her that I am doing this, so stop being so over sensitive. You won't learn anything if you are defensive all of the time."

Her heart jumped. He was right. She needed to push her personal feelings out of the way. He was here to help her for Maya. "Fine."

And it was nice to know that Harry had been right too. The eldest Delvaux wouldn't do anything else to get on bad terms with Miss Middle Whittle.

"Good." And he was gone again.

Tingling.

"Too slow." A breath from behind her ear.

She turned and found nothing. The tingling was gone again. Then back.

"Vera," he said her name.

She turned with the tingling to find him leaning against the fireplace in the empty room.

"Stop that! How is this training?" Yeah, she was really regretting agreeing to this.

"We will continue doing this until you stop thinking of the tingling as Harry's touch and begin thinking of it as mine."

"What?" This time she was well and truly flabbergasted.

"When you get the tingling currently, it feels nice, like if Harry were to touch you, but…"

"Why Harry?" She could feel her cheeks growing warm.

He scoffed. "Please. I could scent your arousal, both of yours, when you're around each other. Not to mention, you two aren't very discreet about your relationship."

She stuttered, "We don't have a relationship."

"Fine, in the relationship you want, but don't have."

Wait, he could scent it? "What do you mean you could scent it?"

"A stolen power, heightened smell. Though I will admit, the power is much weaker on me than it had been on the host."

Then she was blushing. Deep. He could smell how affected she was around Harry. That was wrong. So wrong.

"Back to our strategy, you need to stop thinking of it as Harry caressing you and start thinking of it as me caressing you."

The grimace was quick to her features.

He smiled. "Perfect."

He shadowed out.

Tingling and from behind her.

"Still too slow." He was leaning against the trimming to the hallway again. "Don't tell me you'd enjoy my touch." He didn't look too pleased by the statement.

And she certainly felt the gag rush up. "Absolutely not! It's just not as easy as you seem to think it is."

And she couldn't get out of her mind that he knew of her feelings for Harry. That it meant Maya likely knew.

He didn't seem to care. "Try again."

He shadowed away.

Tingling.

She was never gonna get this.

19

There was a woman, the Grandmama. She lived at the top of a mountain, about a two days hike from the village. She lived alone in her cabin home, spending her days sleeping and her nights witching. Spending her evenings dancing and her dawns enchanting.

She knew no end to the days, the weeks, the months. Her only saving grace was the knowledge that the sun would awake later one day, remaining high up in the sky until evening had passed. The day the sun chose to stay out late was the first day of the trek to the cabin at the top of the mountain—a trek her seven children had done time and again.

And so, every year, Grandmama waited for the sun's late ascent and began counting the two to three days until she once more saw her family. Her kids would be coming to her, and years later, when they were old enough, her grandchildren would join the trek.

By the time all were old enough, Grandmama would ready her cabin and the surrounding area for the inclusion of her seven children and her thirty-two grandchildren. She had long since not permitted any in-laws to join the voyage, claiming only those with her blood were to see her.

And so, when they were all of age, the thirty-nine family members of Grandmama would begin their trek to the top of the mountain at the start of the long days. It truly was a sight to behold.

This continued on for years, until her youngest grandchild was sixteen years of age. Then the year came when Grandmama prepared for the arrival of her family, and they did not show.

Not a single one of them.

She waited the three days she normally permitted them. Then a fourth in case they were delayed. A fifth day passed, and still, not a single member of her family had made an appearance.

Believing it a sign that it may now be her turn to make the trek, old as she was, on the sixth day, Grandmama set voyage to the village at the bottom of the mountain.

Half way down, about a day's worth of journeying, she came about the reason her family had not shown up. Scattered there, in the middle of the mountain climb, were each and every thirty-nine members of her family, staked through the heart.

Every one of them, from her oldest child to her youngest grand-child, lie scattered within a quarter mile of one another. And every single one of them lay dead, eyes staring wide into the bright sky.

Grandmama's heart broke that day, yet not a single one knows what happened to her. Some believe her to be on a new voyage now, one of revenge. Some believe the sight of such a horrific scene sent her to Death's doorstep as well. But not a single one knows what truly became of her.

Bella closed off the story. "I have the book, if you want. It would probably help you to have the real story."

Maya's brows shot up. "Yeah, that'd be perfect, Bel."

Bella hopped off the trunk. "I'll be back."

Brynn smiled over at Maya. "I miss her so much. It's the worst part of leaving."

Maya looked back out toward the ocean. "I take it your family didn't take the gargoyle news well?"

She knew the answer.

Brynn laughed humorlessly. "Essentially said it was a good thing I left. I couldn't be embarrassing the family with such things. Can't be tainting Bella's mind like that. Though I'm sure everyone's speaking of it now."

Maya shook her head and scoffed as they sat in silence for a while, listening to the ocean crash against the sands, before Brynn said, "You said you were with a demon."

Maya knew her face twisted into irritation while her eyes shined as she glanced over to the mermaid. As annoyed and angry as she was with Hunter at the moment, she knew she'd never feel differently about her choices regarding him.

Brynn laughed at her expression. "I take it he's in trouble right now."

"You take correctly," was Maya's simple response, her lips twitching into a smile.

"How do your family take it?"

Maya shrugged. "They don't like him. They've tried getting me to break it off. Mind you, the one most opposed is dating his brother." Brynn's brows popped at that. "Apparently though, being that the brother is half human, he's moons better."

They'd moved at some point until they were seated together at the middle of the trunk, shoulder to shoulder. "But they accept it?"

Maya looked to her a moment, thinking of her family. "Yeah, they still give me trouble, but they accept it."

"Good." Brynn smiled and knocked her shoulder against Maya's, shoving her a bit. "Now, how much trouble is he in?"

The two laughed, looking back out over the ocean.

Maya returned home to an empty house. Her sisters had texted in their group chat that they wouldn't be home, Camilla going out with Warren and Vera and Harry out picking up some potion ingredients.

Vera had also let her know how her training with Hunter had gone and surprisingly, Maya had gotten no complaints of the demon.

She walked up the stairs and straight for her room, the book Bella had given her in hand, and stopped two steps into her room as her gaze shot to the figure taking up presence in the armchair in the corner.

Hunter's eyes shined, a small smile already growing on his face. "There's my girl."

Maya threw him a dirty look as she walked to her dresser, casually placing the book on top, though her heart raced at his words. She removed her leather jacket, roughly placing it on top of the book.

"Oh, c'mon," he began from his seat as she walked back to the bed, sitting to remove her shoes. "You can't still be angry with me." The look Maya shot him said differently as she removed one boot, moving onto the other. "Love," he moved to sit at the edge of the armchair, "we haven't been together since New Year's Eve. It's killing me!"

As she removed her other boot, socks falling over the shoes in turn, she got up and moved to her dresser, throwing him a look through the mirror. "Keep killing innocents, and we can guarantee it'll be longer than that."

He leaned back into the armchair, moving a hand over his heart. "Oh, my bleeding heart, he wasn't so innocent."

"Being a skater doesn't make him a delinquent!" She turned to face him directly. "Neither does yelling at you."

"I agree," he said calmly. "But we demons recognize a lot of the truly bad people." She dropped her head to the side, expression reading complete disbelief. He moved from the armchair to stand before her. "Love, I don't hurt truly innocent people, even when I'm angry. I may be a demon, but killing off innocents would cause more problems with the humans than it's worth.

All those kids at *that* skate park have histories of abusing. I'm sure you'll see the kid on the news soon. I'm helping the humans."

"The priest?"

His jaw ticked beneath his smirk. "Occupational hazard."

Maya remained leaning onto her dresser, arms crossed before her. She was angry with him, even if what he was saying was true. And she knew it was. He had yet to lie to her, and she didn't see him starting with something as inconsequential as this.

But she was still angry with him.

Apparently though, her body didn't get the message.

The moment she'd walked into the room, she'd been on high alert, skin prickling with desire.

"Maya," he said slowly, knowing the effect saying her name had on her, "it's been ten days." He took a step forward, her body freezing as she tried to control her reactions to him. He smirked. "I'm ready to combust just looking at you." Another step. "And smelling that you want me too doesn't help."

She was angry, he knew that. But he also knew she wanted this as much as he wanted her. It was something she could never hide from him.

Her eyes were drinking him in entirely, and her scent was growing stronger with each passing second. He stepped up closer, only a foot away now, and took in a large whiff of the air. She was desperate. He could smell that much.

His eyes gleamed, a wicked grin erupting across his face as he grabbed her around the throat and threw her against the wall beside the dresser. His other hand slammed beside her head, trying to hold onto his control. "Don't torture me, love. Don't torture yourself."

He rubbed himself against her and breathed in her moans, soft and wanting and effectively over being mad at him. At least for the time being.

He took a bite of her chin before licking up and into her mouth. "You're angry. How about a bit of hate sex?"

"Hate sex?" She bit out. "Apt. Considering how much I despise you."

His cock throbbed against his trousers. "You're teasing, love."

She smirked and he caught a final look in her eyes before their tongues met. The desire was strong, but there was definitely a tint of 'I hate you' there, and Hunter knew, everything was all right with them. Her tongue fought him for control the moment their mouths collided, a control they both knew he'd win.

And she was finally giving in, her breaths growing more heady and wanton.

Her hands were on him, ripping the buttons free from his shirt and exposing his chest to her. He had to fight his body for control as his hand tightened around her throat. As he scratched down her walls.

Ten days surely had had an effect on him. There would be marks left on her wall, and he grew harder knowing every time she looked at this wall, she'd remember this, him.

And surprisingly, he grew harder at the knowledge that he'd never felt this before, the need and all-consuming thoughts of a woman.

Her hands teased his chest, his back, left little marks that disappeared in only a few days, far too soon for Hunter's liking. He wanted to be marked forever by her.

Then those fingers were at his belt, unbuckling. Hunter pushed away, throwing his shirt off and moving to unfasten his trousers as he growled, "Naked. Now!"

They were moving back together, like magnets, in record time. His cock pulsing as their skin touched, desperate to be inside her. He threw her onto the bed, watching her bounce up with the impact before falling to the edge. His cock was desperate to be inside, but so was his tongue.

It'd been that long since he'd tasted his favorite meal.

He took a rough hold of her thighs and pushed them apart, giving himself a grand view as she gripped tightly to the sheets, her head popped up to watch him. "Hunter," she growled out.

Yes, his girl was ready for him.

He licked up one thigh, biting hard at the top. He wanted to mark her.

With his face only an inch from her sex, he breathed her in completely and almost came right then. "Be a good girl and scream a little louder for me, love."

His tongue flew from his mouth, taking in every drop of desperation that slicked her center. He watched her fall back with his name on breathless lips as he slid up her those folds and played with her clit. As he circled her little nub and suckled it. Then he was tasting back down and fucking her with his tongue, tasting her clenching walls.

Hunter hated clichés, but this was like a giving water to a man stuck in the desert for a month. Intoxicating. He couldn't get enough.

It took almost no time to get a rough scream of his name, her thighs closing in around his face as she came.

He took pleasure in the hold her thighs locked him in, tasting only her, breathing only her. He could happily die right then.

When her thighs dropped, her chest rising in large inhalations as she looked over at him, his cock cried out—it was *his* turn to be inside her.

Hunter moved up to his knees, placing himself at her center. He grabbed her jaw, pulling her up to meet his lips. His tongue pushed into her mouth as his cock pushed into her. "You're mine, witch." He pulled out and slammed back in hard. "All." Again. "Fucking." Harder. "Mine."

Her clenching pulses almost broke him as he growled out, dropping her back to the bed and pumping into her. His thrusts grew harder, but he never broke his pace, feeling the way this specific one affected her. He wanted her to have everything she desired, and right then, she desired this. This speed, this pressure, this.

Her name flew out of his mouth along with some grunts as he thought about giving her everything. He looked down at her as her hips moved against his and had to bite his lip to a bleeding point to keep from combusting. She needed to go first. He needed to feel her milk his cock.

Her hands scratched at any bit of skin she could get a hold of, and she screamed for him. It was a good thing they were alone in the house because if any Whittle heard her, he'd be farther down the despicable garbage barrel than before.

And yet, even if they heard, even if this caused more problems, he didn't care. He wanted to hear her, to drown in the sounds of her.

And part of him wanted her family to hear, to know she was his. To *know* it.

She stared up at him, and all his thoughts centered on knowing she was it, on wanting to taste her and feel as much of her as possible, on needing her to know it.

"You're it, love," he grunted through another thrust. "All it for me."

Her lips were on his, her tongue playing with him before leaving him with a chaste kiss. "Good, baby, because there was no way you were getting away."

His tongue was on her skin, licking and sucking his way from her jaw to chest to ear to lips, anywhere. His hands holding her tight enough to leave bruises on those creamy thighs, one slipping between her thighs to send her to her climax.

Because he was ready.

"You're mine, baby. Mine, mine, mine..." Her words were begging him.

And they were working.

But he wanted—no, needed—her to come with him. "Now, baby," he whispered in her ear. "Come with me. Now."

He grunted her name with a fuck or two and felt the sting of her nails digging into his ass as her head fell back, screaming his name. And she did as she was told and came with him.

Then he was losing grip on himself, finishing inside her with a final deep thrust. He made sure to remain as deep as possible, to know his seed filled her completely.

He held himself up for minutes, catching his breath and bringing his thoughts back to Earth.

Yeah, she was it.

He fell off of her, breathing hard, and lay shoulder to shoulder as they caught their breaths.

His cock was already singing for another round when Maya shoved up and moved to straddle him, sitting on his lower abs. Her wet folds touching him as if knowing it wouldn't be long until they had a repeat performance.

Maya lowered herself over him, licking her way up his chest to his mouth. Against his lips, she whispered, "Do you have enough money to pay off that manor?"

Hunter's brows furrowed at the sudden subject change. "My manor is paid off."

"Fine." She bit his chin, then looked up at him through her lashes, hardening his cock instantaneously. "Then do you have enough money to cover your expenses?"

"For probably two lifetimes. Maybe three." He grinned at her. "Why?"

Her eyes gleamed at his response, her teeth biting down her

giddy smile. "Good." She lowered her body until she was rubbing against his cock, her dripping slit drenching his cock from tip to base. "Because you're never going away on a business trip again."

***

They got in another two rounds before her family began showing up.

It was close to midnight and Maya knew it would be time to get back to reality, so reluctantly, they'd taken their showers in turn and readied to meet the others downstairs.

Maya grabbed the book and followed Hunter down the stairs and toward the noise in the kitchen. Unsurprisingly, her sisters stood around the island with Harry and Warren, all laughing about a scene Warren and Camilla had witnessed on their date. It was nice of Warren to take Camilla out on a date, good for her to forget what may have been done to her.

Hunter grabbed the chair at the table, pulling it out and sitting backwards on it so that his arms rested against the back as Maya walked up to the island and placed the book down. "Found the story."

The room grew silent at the sight of the book.

Harry grabbed for it as Maya continued, "The story itself is only about a sixty pages. The rest of the book is recipes and drawings."

Camilla, Vera, and Warren huddled around Harry as he flipped through the book. A tug on the back of her trousers turned Maya's attention to Hunter. His eyes questioned where she got the book.

Bella, she mouthed to him, turning back to the distracted four taking their turns with the book. Maya didn't know the reason, but she'd kept Bella and Brynn a secret from her family. No, not a secret, private. They never asked, so she never told.

Hunter knew, of course, but that was because of the intimate moments they shared, both sexual and otherwise. She couldn't help but tell him everything. And at the current point in their elusive relationship, she knew she trusted him fully.

He pulled her belt loop so that she fell against the chair's back and circled his arms around her waist, holding her there. His forehead rested against her back as she began to speak, her hands falling over his. "It's left with a cliffhanger. No one knows what happened to Grandmama."

Maya retold the story Bella had told her, feeling the condensed version was more apt for the moment than the actual thing. She'd read it after dropping Brynn off and hadn't found anything to help or add to Bella's version.

Her family watched her intently, putting together all the pieces as she finished her explanation. "But, if you flip to the end of the book, there's a page where a theory was written out —that the stakes were made to kill magic doers, which Grandmama definitely was. Magic doers are the demons and witches. Attached to that we have gargoyles and werewolves, who are believed to be the protectors of the village and mountains, yet they did not protect. And griffins, which is what I'm assuming the final creature to be, were meant to warn of trouble, yet Grandmama was given no warning. If you put it all together, you get the Grandmama's revenge of the village, whatever it may be."

Silence followed her, then Vera said, "We tested the residue again today. It was a griffin."

Another round of silence, then Harry said, "Well, this is a perfect start. We'll all take turns reading this." He still held the book, shaking it for effect. "See what we can find."

Everyone nodded in understanding.

"Until then," Harry continued, "I think we should all rest up."

With his final words, the room emptied.

Harry and Vera each off to their respective rooms, Warren

shadowing home, and Hunter pushing his chair in and walking back to her room. Maya wasn't sure if they would be spending the night here or if he'd shadow them to his place, but was happy with either outcome.

Before she could follow him, Camilla placed a hand to her arm, and Maya turned to see something akin to confused curiosity on her sister's face. "What's wrong?"

Camilla met her eyes, shaking her head. "Nothing. Nothing serious. Just…I wanted to ask you something."

"Okay."

Camilla hesitated a moment, then said, "Was he telling the truth? Hunter?" At Maya's questioning look, Camilla clarified, "He told you about Colette because you guys were talking about shame?"

"Oh." Maya relaxed, having expected something far more serious. "No. No, it was just some random thing he mentioned one night." Maya's brows wiggled, her lips forming a suggestive smirk as she joked, "You know, post coital conversations."

"Just…a random thing?"

She shrugged. "Yeah. It was kinda his way of telling me he knows and trusts that I can protect myself but would never want to risk me around her."

"That sounds kinda serious." Camilla sounded almost shocked now.

"Don't worry." Maya smiled. "He's still just my delicious fuck buddy."

Camilla smiled back at her sister, both hints of disgust and playful understanding lining her eyes. "Oh. Okay, I was just curious."

Maya wasn't sure if she believed that, but she allowed the excuse to stand, turning and leaving the kitchen. "Goodnight."

"Night," Camilla called back, though it was obvious she was barely paying attention.

20

$\mathcal{A}$ugustine Delvaux was a proud man, but more so, he was a smart man. If there was one thing he knew, it was that pride could cost you more than it was worth.

And it normally did.

So Augustine Delvaux almost never allowed his pride to direct his decisions.

He knew one thing, if he wanted the Delvaux name to continue holding strong, he was to know what was happening at all times. So that Monday evening, just over a week since the reappearance of his daughter, his sons joined him for dinner.

Sat at the end of the long table, with Hunter to his right and Warren his left, the men readied for dinner. The table may've been long, but he'd no need to scream across it to his boys when they could just as easily sit beside him.

It was time to get some news.

And what better way to get news about his daughter attacking the Whittle witches than the boys currently involved with the Whittle witches?

Augustine shook his head, unbelieving that even Hunter had

fallen for one, albeit unwilling to admit so. "Tell me, boys, how are our Whittles doing?"

Both boys looked to him, then one another. Hunter sat back, quiet. Warren seemed to read the situation, knew someone must speak, and Hunter wasn't going to indulge him with any information regarding his relationship with Maya.

"They haven't been bothered all week. They think Colette was sent to get something from the house. As you know, it's enchanted, so just anyone can't get in."

Augustine smirked at his son. "Yet both my boys have access. That sure does make me a proud father."

Warren ignored his jibes. "They've been looking into the witches that were killed, the missing or dead creatures now, but nothing new, nothing from Colette either."

"Yes, Colette," Augustine said slowly, bringing his drink to his lips and taking a swing. "How is your dear sister?"

"Rotting away, I hope," Warren sneered.

Augustine laughed. "That's my demon." Warren rolled his eyes and continued to eat. He hated his sister, more so than any of the rest of them, and Augustine couldn't blame him. If there was one thing he regretted, it was having that daughter.

Warren took a bite as Augustine continued, "Tell me, Son, how is Miss Camilla doing?"

Warren's stony gaze met his father's. "She's well."

Augustine waited a moment. "Is that it, Son? Merely well?"

"She misses the normalcy of not knowing she was a witch. Misses only having to worry about school and boys, uh, me. But she hides it a lot. Like she knows she wouldn't change anything because now she has Vera and Harry. I think she likes being a witch, but hasn't fully accepted it yet."

"Sounds like a sweet girl." *Sounds like a boring girl.*

"What would you like to hear?" Warren retorted, annoyed.

"I'd like to learn more of the witch that has stolen my son's heart. Tell me, how is *she*?" It was quite obvious the relationship would go nowhere, no demon, no matter halfie or not, would ever speak of his mate to anyone who could use the information. But Augustine could have fun while it lasted.

Warren shot a glare in his direction, eliciting a laugh.

Augustine took another sip of his now refilled drink and turned to his other son. "What about you, Hunt? Tell me about this Maya girl. She must be gloriously dirty to have held you in her grip all this time."

Hunter maintained the bored expression he'd mastered as a child, a single finger tapping his lips as he stared back. That was Hunter, bred to keep his private life so hidden no one could use it against him. "You aren't to think of her. That's all you are to know."

Bingo.

This one was mated.

Amazing.

Augustine's laugh was hearty as he turned to Warren. "Well, boy, I can see which of you is in love, and I have to say, it isn't you."

Warren's eyes shot to his brother's as Augustine looked back to his older son. To anyone looking, Hunter's exterior showed boredom, a man lounging about a chair waiting for dinner to be over. Even to his trained eyes, it was all Augustine saw. After all, Hunter had trained his emotions long ago. What he felt for Maya, whether they were merely fucking or he was falling in love—and Augustine would bet his entire fortune and power it was the latter—was nowhere to be seen.

Hunter didn't make any show that Augustine's comments affected him, but something in him, maybe it was the father feeling, told Augustine he was correct. Miss Maya Whittle would become a true member of this family. Would become Mrs. Maya Delvaux. There was a ring to it.

And what better luck than a witch with such a powerful high-level demon power.

"Well," Augustine called out into the silence, "what problems will Colette cause us now?"

Back to their true problem, he would learn more of his sons' relationships in time.

Takeout was a heaven send when no one wanted to cook. With delivery on its way, Vera busied herself with some piano practice and Maya with her graphics in the office, leaving Harry and Camilla in the living room with the Book. They'd been trying to see if there was anything within it to help them with the storybook Maya had found, but were still coming up blank.

"I'll get us some tea. It seems we may be here a while," Harry said, leaving Camilla alone on the couch.

She nodded distractedly, staring down at the Book in her lap. Her frustration increased as she listened to Vera's melody, a piece that sounded wanting, and tried to figure this out.

She grunted, muttering to the Book, "C'mon, I know you have something! Give me something. Help me!"

And just as Vera's piece turned longing, the pages of the Book began to turn. Camilla had no time to analyze what could have shifted her sister's mood, her attention moving with each quick flip of a page, until finally, it stopped on a set of blank pages. Camilla groaned, ready to slam the Book shut and throw it across the room, when the blank pages began to fill. Words and drawings taking up both sides.

"Woah!"

At its fill, the pages showed a spell Camilla had never seen before, with small drawings around the edges she was sure had been added in generation upon generation. There were pictures of baby animals turning to humans, humans turning to magical beings, magical beings to humans, magical beings to other magical beings. It was almost grotesque.

"Feed each the amount that they have born, and together they will create anew," Camilla read a part aloud. Listening to the longing in Vera's piece reach it's crescendo, Camilla turned to Vera's method—thinking aloud. "Okay, the amount they each bore. That means each person is to have as much of something as the amount of children they've had? Feed means they are consuming whatever it is. Each means there are multiple people partaking. Create anew… but what does this have to do with the storybook?"

Her brows furrowed, staring at the page another moment before turning to the storybook and opening it. "Grandmama had seven children. That's seven people to consume each of whatever. The seven children each had three to seven of their own, making thirty-two grandchildren." Flipping to the drawing of the family tree in the storybook, Camilla looked to Grandmama's children. "That would mean her first child would consume four, her fifth child would consume six, her sixth child eight."

The music stopped, and Camilla was left alone in the echoes as it all clicked together. "That's it! Whatever the halfies are doing, that's why they needed the number thirty-nine!"

She stared at the now filled page, trying to make out what the halfies would need with this spell, and came up with nothing. "But what are they doing?"

There was something she was missing, but hopefully her family would figure it out.

Just as those words left her lips, Harry walked in carrying a tray of tea. The excitement of finding this new spell died on her lips as she glanced up and stopped short at the look in his eyes, a longing likeness to match Vera's piece.

Camilla watched him as he placed the tray on the coffee table, handing Camilla her tea. With a slow grab of the saucer, Camilla allowed her hand to graze his, catching a flash of Vera in his thoughts. She was normally careful to keep from encroaching on other's private thoughts, but couldn't help it this time.

Pulling away, Camilla knew this was not the time to broach the subject, so she changed it entirely. "I found it!"

"What?"

"The thing we didn't know we were looking for," Camilla stated as if it were obvious. "I just spoke to the Book and it flipped to this page." She turned the Book to show Harry, repeating her thoughts for his ears. "What I haven't gotten is what they would be consuming. Or what they're doing with this."

Harry's eyes seemed frozen to the spell within the Book, placing his cup down and taking the tome in hand. His stony expression met hers. "They're creating a new life. Whatever or whomever it is they need."

Camilla's tea scorched her throat as she took in too much in her shock. "Excuse me?"

Harry turned the Book to show her, pointing to the drawings Camilla had found both beautiful and disturbing. "This here indicates they're creating a new life, a new being of some sort." He turned the Book to face him once more, taking a few moments to digest his thoughts before voicing them, "And if I am correct in my theory, they will be consuming the blood of the thirty-nine dead witches. With seven volunteers, or more likely forced victims. If each of them drinks four to eight of the witches' blood, one for the child they represent, then another for each grandchild that they brought into the world, they'd get their new life."

There was something he wasn't saying. "And?"

"I merely fear what it could be for the halfies to put themselves at risk to bring about. If the halfies are included, I fear what it could mean for the species," Harry said, staring down at the page.

Camilla huffed out a breath as she took another sip of her tea. "Great."

<hr>

Harry and Camilla explained their findings not twenty minutes later.

"We need to warn the covens," Vera began. "If they need seven more witches, then covens should know to be on higher alert."

"No," Maya interrupted, receiving shocked looks from each of them, Vera herself feeling the pound in her chest that her sister was beginning to not care. Like demons. "It doesn't specify that a witch must be used. We need to notify them all. And that's on the hopes they don't just use humans."

Vera breathed out in relief. Of course.

Then she felt the nagging hatred in the back of her mind that she would even consider otherwise.

"Well, if they do, there isn't..." Harry began but was cut off by a ring.

They remained silent as Harry answered the house phone, then hung up after only a few seconds.

The faeries had called and their presence was requested.

Porting to the faeries immediately, fearing something to add to their list of dead and missing, Vera was confused at what they landed in the middle of.

They were on faerie property but stood before two witches holding a protective circle around a faerie and... a human?

All looked to be about Maya's age, maybe near Camilla's. Vera wasn't sure what she was witnessing and had no time to speak as Finlan, the faerie leader, stepped up. "Perfect timing. Take your belongings and leave."

Vera looked to the others in hopes that they would know what he was talking about. Nope. Even Harry stood rigid, the crease between his brows inviting her to smooth it out.

"What?" Camilla asked.

Finlan lazily pointed to the two witches. "Your belongings. Take them and leave our lands."

Their belongings?

The witches.

He was referring to the two witches as *their belongings.*

"Excuse you! Who…" Maya began but stopped immediately as Harry jumped in.

Good. They did not need Maya's temper at the moment.

"They are not our belongings. But please do inform us on what is going on, and we'd be pleased to help," Harry stated, stepping before the three of them and acting as head of the Whittle household.

With Finlan's nose rising to meet the sky, Vera turned to the four within the protective circle, waiting on an explanation.

The faerie in the circle stepped up. "My name is Kellan." He pointed to the witches on either side. "These are Cora and Rory, my best friends. And this," he turned slightly, keeping himself on the defensive in case he needed to protect, "is Celine, my mate."

Faeries didn't mate like werewolves, but understanding hit Vera anyway—another cross species relationship.

And this with a human.

And out to his species leader, proud.

And worse yet, cross species friends to aid and protect.

Normally cross species friendships weren't looked down upon, but preferred. It was important to make sure to have supporters in different species, but when those friends were helping you in a romantic relationship with someone other, it was definitely frowned upon.

Vera looked from the circle to Finlan and his six lackeys as Harry turned back to the faerie leader. "What exactly did you need from us?"

"To take your meddling kind away so we can deal with our problem."

Maya stepped up, the fire caressing her arms as she held in her control. "You're not going to hurt the human, or the faerie for that matter."

Finlan's eyes narrowed, definitely taking in Maya's power and the seriousness in her eyes, but he did not hesitate as he responded, "Then take them all." He turned to face Kellan. "You, Kellan Sterling Archibald Leander Finlan Channing, are hereby cast out of the faeries. All of your possessions are hereby confiscated to be held by the crowns."

Finlan gave the rest of them not even a second's glance as he turned and left, his lackeys following behind.

That was it? He just left Kellan behind with nothing.

Even the mermaid leaders had been glad to see their daughter gone when they'd found out about her romance with a gargoyle. It was flabbergasting.

Vera was still processing it when the two witches dropped their protective hold.

The four friends moved to reach for one another as they stared at Vera and her family. Their gazes spoke the question no one voiced: would they be judged as well? Saving them from the faerie leader didn't mean they were supported.

Without the faerie leader to stand up to, Celine's bravado dropped as her gaze found Kellan's. "I'm so sorry. This is my fault. How are you supposed to support yourself without your things, your money!" Her attention then flew to Cora and Rory. "And how are we supposed to help you with nothing to our names?"

Vera stepped up, too upset by what she was hearing to allow it to go on. "By doing just as Finlan said. You'll come home with us."

The four sets of eyes shot to her before Kellan spoke, "You do not have to burden yourselves with this responsibility. We *will* figure it out."

"We have no doubts on that matter," Maya said. "But we can help to get you started."

The four friends stared at them as if trying to figure out what was happening. Then to one another like they were trying to figure out if it were real. Then they were nodding their agreement.

Harry had his hold on them all, and they were ported back home.

The entire thing took all of ten minutes, but Vera felt the impact it would leave on her life.

Landing in the division between the foyer and the living room, they moved to settle around the couches, Harry falling to rest after porting such a large load.

After hearing the third apology for the intrusion and the fifth thanks for allowing them to stay for a few days, Maya finally raised her hand, waving it at them, and asked, "How?"

"Maya!" Camilla hissed her sister's way as Harry and Vera sent her bulging looks.

"What? We're all thinking it," she defended.

Celine laughed. Having been the quiet one of the lot, Vera had not expected for her to answer. "We're kind of a ragtag team of orphans."

Seriousness fell upon the room at the revelation.

Cora continued, "Rory and I are from a coven in the hollows of New York state. Likely only see woods if you were to research it."

"It was an orphan coven," Rory picked up, "where truly

orphaned witches, or those running from their families, could take refuge."

"The coven fell through years ago," Cora picked up, "We were eighteen, nineteen years old, and suddenly, we no longer had a coven to call home."

"So the two of us kinda set off. And in the process, we found Celine making ends meet as an orphan thrown out, younger than us by years," Rory said.

"We became inseparable, the three of us," Celine picked up this time. "I knew they were witches, and I envied them so much for it. We worked and supported, protected each other. We made a family for ourselves."

Everyone's eyes flew to Kellan to understand how he fell in. "I knew Cora and Rory from events when we were younger. As kids, we worked for the same magical creatures to make ends meet. We became really good friends, but we only ever saw each other a couple of times a year. And by the time they met Celine, I had stopped working for those creatures, moved up. Making good money within the faeries. I was orphaned, but I had a good background to fall on."

"And we ruined it all for him," Rory teased.

Kellan smirked, his eyes glinting with mirth. "They sure did."

"We were in the forest, teaching Celine archery. We did it at least once a week, usually more, and we'd never been interrupted," Cora said.

"Until I was sent one day to pick up some berries that were known to only grow in those woods, in that area specifically. Magical creatures sure do know how to hide away from humans, yet they do an awful job of hiding anything from each other." Kellan smiled.

Garnering a laugh from Celine as she tightened her hold around his arm, she continued, "Cora and Rory had left me for a few minutes. They were hungry, so they portalled back to the city to grab us a picnic. Not two minutes after they left, Kellan walked into the clearing we'd been using. He was alone, but I knew what he was. I'd studied each of the creatures and their giving features with Cora and Rory. As a human, it's harder for me to pick up on it, but I had studied them vigorously."

"Like she'd studied archery." Kellan laughed, turning to look Celine in the eyes. "And she pointed her bow and arrow at me and threatened to shoot."

They looked into one another's eyes as smiles split their faces. "I didn't hurt you," Celine said.

"But you shot me," Kellan rebuffed, the smile never leaving his face.

Celine turned back to face them. "But I didn't hurt you."

"Only because he got out of the way," Cora laughed.

"Yeah, Celine's a pretty good shot," Rory said as all four looked to one another and laughed.

Celine's smile grew a bit confident as she continued the story. "Anyway, Cora and Rory showed up. The three of them had their happy little reunion, and Kellan tried to ask me out."

"And she said no," Kellan said with mock indignation.

"And yet here we are," Celine teased.

Cora scoffed. "Yeah because anyone with half a brain could see Celine was moony eyes for you, no matter how much she tried denying it."

Wow, Vera thought as she watched them, they truly were best friends.

"Here you are." Maya smiled at them as she got up from the couch. "And here you may stay until you have your next plans laid out. You two," she turned to Kellan and Celine, "can take my room. I'll stay at Hunter's."

"And the family room has a pull out bed," Vera said to Cora and Rory.

"Perfect." They smiled.

Maya leaned against the fireplace, meeting Celine's eyes and winked. "I'll change the sheets when you leave. And there's a permanent silencing charm around the room. Have as much fun as you'd like in there."

Vera sputtered, but knew she wouldn't be able to hide the laugh. That was such a Maya thing to offer.

Celine burned crimson as Kellan laughed. "Oh, we certainly will."

21

She was still thinking about the connection Quebec had with her mother, if any. And Hunter could see how much it was affecting her, even if she didn't speak of it.

He lay on his side, staring at her. "You're doing it again."

Her gaze didn't meet his as she smiled sheepishly. "I can't help it."

"I know." He kissed her shoulder. "Which is why we're not staying home today."

He was out of bed and getting dressed for a trip to Canada. Again.

She didn't hesitate to follow him. "Where are we going now?"

He winked and finished dressing in almost the exact outfit as their last visit to the cold country, leaning back to watch her. "You still have my pocket watch?"

"The one you refused to take back?" She put on one of his sweaters again, likely understanding they were headed somewhere cold by his coat. "Of course. Why?"

"Would you like to meet the man that made it?"

Her gaze narrowed on him. "Why?"

He winked, taking her face in his hands and shadowing them as his lips dropped down to meet hers. By the time he pulled away from the chaste kiss, they were standing in the snowy lanes of a small Canadian village. If it could be called a village. Really only a few buildings for magical creatures.

And it was close to Quebec. Very close.

So close, the species normally stayed at the inn in this village rather than Quebec itself when visiting.

"Wow." She leaned into him. "This is amazing."

"It *is* beautiful," he agreed, dropping to kiss her crown and breathe in her scent.

She looked up at him, her arms wrapped around his waist. "What're we doing here, Hunt?"

Hunter quirked a brow. "Hunt?"

She rose to the tips of her toes and kissed his chin. "Hunt."

A smirk graced his features, and he hated how much he loved that she'd called him that. Only his family called him that.

"We're seeing Sir Zathrian."

Her brow quirked, a small smirk rising. "You call him sir?"

"I respect him."

She took a step back. "This is not my Hunter. Where has *he* gone?"

Hunter pulled her back into him. "He's reserved for when we're in public."

Their kiss was long, but slow. It was like a fire that warmed icy fingers in the freezing depths of the Canadian mountains. A raging one, given both of their fire powers acted up with each passing moment they remained pressed together.

"How about you show this side to my family?" she said after pulling away and letting the kiss settle, her eyes still closed.

He pulled away, taking her hand and turning to a small hut of a shop. "Absolutely not."

It was layered in brick and looked straight out of a Hallmark Christmas movie. When things were settled, Hunter planned on bringing Maya to one of the small huts that were scattered about in the area for any visitors that didn't want to stay at the inn. They could spend a lovely week shackled up in the bricked hut as a snowstorm blazed outside.

She laughed as he pulled her in, not dropping her hand as he opened the door and heard the ring of the bell informing Zath and Acacia of an arrival.

Sir Zathrian, standing at just under six feet tall with whites beginning to fray into his hairline, was a handsome man. He'd earned the 'sir' title after defending creature demons of multiple families and giving up the power—figuratively, the man was honest and hardly ever stole powers—it afforded him. It was a respect that demons continued to show him, like knowing he could take it all back whenever he pleased.

Hunter included, though most of his respect came from the man's craftsmanship.

And recently, his priorities.

"Hunter!" He stepped out from behind his service table. "Good to see you, old boy."

He moved in for a hug but paused when Maya stepped out from behind Hunter's back as they walked farther into the shop. Still hand in hand.

Zath's gaze shot to her, then to their conjoined hands, and back up to her, before stopping back on Hunter. His questioning eyes turned to delight as the smirk broke across his face. "Well, well, well. A witch?"

"My witch," Hunter clarified.

Maya's hand tightened in his hold like she was nervous. It was probably being in a situation with a demon where she didn't need to stand on defense that was throwing her off.

Zathrian stepped up to her. "You must be one incredible little thing to have control of Hunt so."

Hunter looked down and felt a stab of pride ripple through

him as she smirked at the older—albeit only by about a decade —man and let little flames fly across her skin. "I am."

Zathrian's eyes bulged, and he stepped back. "Incredible."

He stared between the two of them another few moments, taking them in and allowing Hunter to stand tall with her at his side.

Finally, Zathrian stepped back. "So, Hunt. What can I do for you now? Something for the pretty girl?"

Maya spoke before Hunter could. "You don't care? That I'm a witch? A simple high-level dark power okays it?"

Zath smiled and met Hunter's gaze, realizing she hadn't been told. Instead of answering, Zath called to his mate, "Acacia, darling, come here a moment."

In seconds, Acacia was before them, and Maya's hand was squeezing his as her breath caught. "A witch?"

Acacia's smile at seeing Hunter dropped a moment at the newcomer before seeing their conjoined hands and putting it all together. "Impossible! Hunter Delvaux has found a mate? In a witch? Zath, you're playing a game on me."

"Her name is Maya," Hunter growled. He didn't want her referred to as 'witch' by anyone but himself. She was *his* witch.

And the two seemed to enjoy his reaction.

Well, of course Zath would. Hunter had toyed with him time and again for leaving it all behind to be with his witch. Priorities.

Maya pulled for his attention, and Hunter gave it to her. "So you've always been okay with witches?"

"I'm only power hungry, love. I've never had a problem with witches, other than their problem with me. You, of course, annoyingly became the exception."

She dropped his hand and stepped up an inch, taking in the little hut with all the trinkets of creations Zathrian made when he didn't have a special client order. Toys and clocks and mantel pieces and bits and bobs of all sorts.

Then her gaze dropped to Acacia and Zathrian, who had come together, Zath's arm around the witch's waist. She turned to meet Hunter's gaze. "Is this why you brought me here?"

Hunter smiled down at her. This was certainly a bonus, seeing her eyes shine in pure happiness that way. "I'm glad you like it all, but no." He pulled her into his chest and stepped up to the table Zath and Acacia stood behind. "Maya's on a search for something she thinks her mother left in Quebec. I was thinking she may have stayed here on her visit."

Maya gasped, turned in his arms to face him, and for that look alone, Hunter was glad to have brought her. The grateful shine that sat just beneath the pride of having him as hers.

"Thank you," she whispered so low it was inaudible.

He winked and looked back to his friends, who were watching them like a hawk. He saw in Zathrian's eyes that the man knew what Hunter had planned.

When Maya turned back to the others, Zath shrugged nonchalantly. "Can't promise anything, but give me a name, let's try."

"Loretta Whittle," Maya said.

Sometimes, a café was preferred.

Sitting around a circle table, they drank their coffees as Vera thought aloud, her eyes absently staring ahead. "Now humans are involved."

Camilla shook her head. "Tell me about it. Literally every species is beginning to intertwine. And on top of that, we don't know what The Eight want with the spell they're planning on casting, or if that has anything to do with anything else."

Harry clinked his cup to Camilla's. "Jumbled thoughts. Something we can all relate to."

Harry did seem to be extra distracted that morning, like

there was something more than just what had happened the previous night on his mind, but Vera didn't question it. If and when he wanted to tell her, she'd be ready to hear it.

But she couldn't fight off the piece of her that wanted him to tell her, if only to show how much he trusted her.

"We can't assume The Eight don't have anything to do with the mixed couples suddenly coming out, but I don't see how the connection would be there. Maybe the fear of it all has been sending them together?" Vera's stare continued to look absently at the table before them.

The waitress came by, placing their food on the table and walking away with a shy smile toward Harry. There was a pang of jealousy, one easily dismissed when Harry hardly glanced up at her but for the simple nod of thanks. But she also felt for the waitress. Harry was a beautiful man. Dark hair slicked back, hazel eyes, tall and built but still lean.

Perfect. For Vera, at least.

Breakfast was hearty for them all, each getting a full plate of savory foods to keep them full throughout the day.

"It's nothing new," Maya began, looking to each of her family when the waitress walked off. "Look at all the half breeds. This has been happening for a while. We're just new to the world. Mixed relationships aren't a big problem. They just happen to be something in the magical world that's frowned upon."

She was right, of course. Vera had been overthinking and overcomplicating things. The situation that Kellan and his lot were in had nothing to do with the craziness they were dealing with. It was just another part of being in the magical world.

And though Maya's comment was more directed to Vera's statements than anything else, Camilla's interest seemed to be piqued. "I agree. But I also read that halfie's mind. They hate purebreds, but I feel like they would protect each other. I mean, look at Colette. It took almost no time to get her. But they can't afford to go deeper than that, can't care for those of us that aren't judged by our own species for something we can't control. It's understandable."

Vera cracked a small smile, now looking at her sister. She placed a light touch to her hand. "You're always finding the best in people. That's your truest gift. No matter what wrong has been done, you look for people's good."

Camilla smiled back, squeezing her hand in thanks as they began to eat their breakfast. Just as the first bite hit Camilla's lips, Maya muttered under her breath, "Not always."

Camilla's smile faltered, and she looked to the middle Whittle, Vera's heart sank at the knowledge that Maya was right in matters regarding a certain Delvaux brother. Camilla wasn't always fair. But that had more to do with the fact that Hunter was with Maya. Camilla was worried for their sister.

Looking her in the eye, Camilla stated, "No, not always. I won't ever find the best in Hunter because he is an awful person, like his sister. I cannot fathom how you can forgive him everything he's done. Everything he continues to do. He hurts innocent people."

Vera's back stiffened. She wouldn't go so far as to compare him to Colette, not after all she'd seen in his protective instincts for Maya, no matter how jumbled a mess it seemed.

Maya took a bite of her food and chewed slowly as she evaluated her younger sister, eyes narrowed in irritation. A glance at Vera and Harry showed they were trying to stay out of this, and with a swallow, she simply stated, "I won't bring it up again. You three can hate him all you like, but he's mine, and he's staying until *I* don't want him anymore. I'm tired of your little remarks, or the look you two give to agree with Camilla. You hate him, but Hunter satisfies me and my wants and needs. Considering he's with *me*, that *is* the important part." With the swallow of some coffee, she added, "This is why we didn't tell you."

A light dash of pink filled Vera's cheeks at the admonishment, knowing Maya's argument had merit. She still didn't like Hunter, couldn't fathom doing so, but she did feel bad that the attack was always on Maya. Like any other couple, Maya couldn't help choosing him. Vera understand that all too well as her gaze involuntarily shot to Harry before dropping to her food.

"Maya," Camilla breathed out. "I'm telling you, I don't trust him. He's got an ulterior motive, and he's purposely not betraying us so you can get him anything he wants. He's going to betray us, betray you, and you're going to be left hurt."

Maya's gaze was lethal. "What of Warren? Will he betray us too?"

"Of course not. Warren's half human."

"And Colette is half witch."

"My." Camilla looked almost desperate to get Maya to understand. "Hunter has never been shy to admit he's greedy and power hungry. We're new to our magic and from a powerful line. We're easy targets, and you're the easiest. He's found a way to slither into your more wicked thoughts, and you don't see it. The Maya I grew up with wouldn't fall victim!"

All was quiet for moments. Long, insufferable moments as Maya stared at Camilla. Then her gaze softened, and she said only once, with no passion in her tone, "Like I said, I won't bring it up again."

Camilla looked like she wanted to continue, but Vera shot her hand out to grab for her arm and shook her head. Maya was tough, but she would need the time to at least think about everything Camilla had said.

Because there was merit. Hunter was greedy. They were new to the world. Maya may be easily susceptible to the dark side. And one Camilla hadn't mentioned, but Vera was sure was part of it: the sex was good. Better than just good. Maya was blinded to anything else.

It took a few minutes, but eventually, Harry opened a new

topic of conversation—one that had nothing to do with the problems they were facing with the magical creatures, or dead witches, or with Maya's relationship with Hunter. In fact, nothing at all to do with the magical world.

Instead, he spoke of the people coming out of the store across the street, playing the game of 'Who Are You,' where they created a whole life behind some stranger in public.

C amilla needed time alone to just be in her head after her little argument with Maya. And with Harry off to who knows where for who knows what—Vera wondered if it had anything to do with what had been on his mind that morning—she and Maya figured a stay with their new house guests was in order.

They were in the formal dining room across the hall from the kitchen, Cora having taken to the room without enough care from others to object.

With Vera at the head of the table, Cora and Rory at the side backing the kitchen, and Maya facing them, and in turn, the kitchen, Vera asked, "Do you guys know what you want to do? What you can do?"

Rory shrugged in response. "We can't really do much. A lot of what Cora, Celine, and I had is gone. We figured even if Kellan wasn't accepted, we could still get his things, his money. We were probably naive in thinking that. Should've grabbed everything first, should've grabbed *something*, anything. But, I don't know...it's gonna be a complete start over."

As she finished, they heard a squeal coming from the kitchen where Kellan and Celine had insisted on making a small dessert for them. They all watched from their positions through the small opening that led from the formal dining room to the kitchen as Kellan grabbed for Celine, pulling her in to dance to no music. Smiles were on their faces so wide they could split worlds. Now that was love.

That was what Vera dreamt of.

Cora and Rory turned back to them, Cora stating, "It's nothing to worry about. We always make it out. We care for each other. We'll make sure we're okay."

Rory smirked and nodded back as another squeal escaped Celine, followed by a loud laugh. "And if nothing else, Kellan would literally put his life down for that girl, and she's our sister. We've got a guarantee through that."

Vera laughed, noticing how Maya's eyes glued to the couple.

She was in a mixed relationship too, no matter how much she liked to deny that she and Hunter were anything more than lovers. She likely understood more than any of them how Kellan and Celine were feeling, pushed away from their species because of the people they fell for. Not that Maya had been pushed aside, but her declaration during breakfast had made Vera realize that this wasn't easy for Maya, no matter how much she liked to pretend it was.

And she felt worse for ever putting Maya in a situation where she had to pick between them and Hunter. And part of her knew she'd do it again, sometimes acting before she thought, and she wanted to apologize for that already.

"You can't use your powers to work yourself back up?" Vera asked, pulling herself out of the thoughts of her sister and her demon.

Rory tsked, her short black hair flowing as she sat back. "We're not very powerful. Most creatures aren't. Other than the portal we make, which we still don't know why that works for us and not others, there isn't much we could do that others would pay for. My primary is flying, and Cora's is speed. We're basically gargoyles at that point. Most creatures aren't blessed with powers like your lot. It's why some families can remain on top."

Cora nodded. "Especially with demons. Other species, they have powerful families that kinda rule over others—like your family over other witches, but you don't really hold that over them. Demons tend to work more like humans. The more power and control they can get, the more they work it over others."

"Like the Heisenberg's, the Delvaux's, the Okoro's. There're at least like five families in each territory," Rory added.

Surprisingly to Vera, Maya didn't defend. She shrugged. "True."

At least her sister wasn't in denial.

It didn't take too long after that for the dessert to be placed before them and for Celine to shrug at Rory's, "What is it?"

Celine took her seat on Kellan's lap as he sat at the other end of the table. "I have no idea. I just looked up a dessert recipe and made it."

Being the baker she was, that scared Vera a bit. Only a bit.

She couldn't help it. Baking was something she loved so much, she couldn't imagine not paying attention and loving every moment of the process.

It was good though, whatever it was.

A hint of chocolate, but not overpowering. It looked like a brownie, but even with the hints of chocolate, it didn't taste like a brownie. Vera would have to see what recipe the girl had found and try it herself.

After finishing half her piece, Vera looked across the table and asked the question she'd been wondering since they'd brought them home from the faeries. "Why now?"

No clarification was needed. Everyone around the table understood.

Kellan gave a small shrug, holding Celine a little tighter to him. "We had a banshee friend..."

"Wow, you guys are literally friends with every species," Maya interrupted.

They all laughed as she apologized for interrupting and waited for him to continue.

"We had a banshee friend, have one. She went missing. Her mate couldn't do anything about it, couldn't ask the species for help because they didn't know about them, and he couldn't very well tell them without her. They wouldn't believe him. He's still out looking, and we'll be joining him soon, but we didn't want that, to live in secret anymore." He gave Celine's jaw the lightest of kisses.

Vera saw their love, heard it in the way they spoke, and her heart ached a bit more at the knowledge that a piece of their hearts would always be with the people they left behind, the people who refused to accept them.

It looked like Maya'd also noticed this, but like the compartmentalizer she was, she straightened to another part of his statement that definitely demanded more attention. "A banshee is missing?"

Cora nodded solemnly. "We have hope, but no matter, we won't stop looking until we find her. Felix won't stop until he finds her. Even if it's only a body."

That brought the conversation to a dark corner.

But it was yet another thing to consider. Did this missing banshee have anything to do with The Eight, or whatever they had planned with the blood of the thirty-nine witches?

Their guests didn't know about The Eight, and at this point, Vera knew it wasn't something to mention at the moment.

Instead, she watched the four and thought of the two others —this banshee and her mate—that made up their little family.

It was a mix-match, but it was the love and support, the protection and care, that she'd only ever given to her father, and now to Camilla, Maya, and Harry. And Vera knew in that moment that they may always hurt for those they left behind, Kellan especially, but they had a family. They'd be okay.

22

Their four guests had taken a liking to the piano room, and after becoming accustomed to Vera's playing, Camilla could barely stand what she was hearing. It was atrocious, unpleasant at the kindest.

But they were having fun, laughter heard past the horror of the keys.

Looking for an out, she'd found her sisters in the living room, Vera practicing her sketching—horribly—and Maya staring into the fire.

"Anyone care for a walk?" She knew Maya was still annoyed with her, and she truly did feel badly for it.

There was no answer but the silent rise and move to the front door.

They traveled past their neighborhood, through the local park, and into a different pathway of the forest, Camilla breaching conversation about two minutes into the walk that had nothing to do with apologizing to Maya. That was how they worked. They fought, then got over it.

And she had nothing to apologize for. She was right, and eventually, hopefully not too late, Maya would realize it.

They spoke about nothing—the neighbors or local going-ons—and about everything—their house guests and the growing problems within the magical world. Vera and Maya told Camilla about the new missing banshee, adding that to the list of things to worry about.

But knowing she only had so long on this walk, Camilla pushed the conversation back to the nothings of town. A distraction.

They were not long into the woods when Camilla felt the familiar push back from nothing. Another shield.

They were surrounded. Again.

And the feeling of difference and similarity told her it was The Eight.

This time unmasked.

And Colette was not among them. Had she ever been, or were there so many members her presence wasn't needed? Surely there were, but Camilla didn't want to think about how much that could be. Or what it could mean.

There was no point in fighting back immediately. A large part of her, basically all of her, knew The Eight still hadn't gotten what they wanted from them, so they'd be fine.

Plus, the vague memories she had as their captive was more her bumping into a shield and falling than actually getting hurt. Though she was still unclear on other events.

Even so, the moment one witch dropped the shield, another paralyzed them to their spots. Total paralysis could wipe out any calm thoughts. Instantly.

Okay, maybe it wasn't the best idea to not fight back, even if they'd been in a shield and wouldn't have been able to actually do much.

One of the members stepped up, walking straight to Maya and taking a piece of her hair between two fingers. Her eyes moved to meet Maya's as she threw the piece of hair back. "Your boyfriend killed my sex toy."

Not her boyfriend.

Maya smirked, likely more proud of Hunter in that moment than she ever had been. Camilla was, if only for causing that bitch some misery.

He would be getting rewarded tonight for no other purpose than the fact that this bitch wouldn't be. Camilla was sure of that.

Maya's smirk held as she looked the halfie in the eyes. "Good."

The halfie looked bored. She didn't care for her sex toy's life. It seemed she was merely annoyed that she would have to find another.

She stepped back a couple of steps as another stepped toward Camilla, placing her hands on either side of her head. "Hello, friend."

Camilla shuddered at the halfie's sickly sweet tone. As her hands enveloped her face, she felt the rush of memories run through her mind. It was like watching a silent movie about her life through her eyes. At reaching about a week's worth of memories, the halfie stepped back and turned to the next sister.

Vera shuddered at her touch, likely seeing her past week in memories as well. Apparently not finding what she sought for, the halfie stepped back and moved to Maya.

Maya didn't shudder. Instead, she stared the woman down before getting sucked into the passage of a week's worth of memories.

The halfie let her go, but didn't step back. "Nothing," she called back to her peers and met Maya's stare with a smirk. She stage-whispered, loud enough for all to hear, "That boyfriend of yours sure does give you a good time."

Dis. Gus. Ting.

Maya's expression darkened, her possessive nature taking hold of her body—she didn't like that this halfie had just seen everything she did when she was with him. He was hers.

And Camilla hated that she could guess all that just by looking at Maya.

Yup, this was definitely more than just fucking, and Camilla hated that admission.

Maya sneered at the halfie before spitting on her. The halfie merely laughed, stepping back and turning away from them. Behind her, a portal had been opened, and all eight members softly jumped through, like they were in no rush. The one holding them paralyzed moved last, and with her, the portal closed, and Camilla found movement once more.

It took minutes before they were all ready to turn back toward the house and walk home, no need to speak this time. And Camilla was in no mood to. Whatever they wanted the first time she'd been stuck in the shield was still not found, no need to discuss that.

Plus, all she could think about was Maya's reaction to that bitch seeing Hunter—likely, and disturbingly, in every erotic position and angle Maya had seen him in—in her memories.

Maya was well and truly angry. Possessive, Camilla confirmed to herself. Possessive if she'd ever seen possession.

They were home only a quarter hour when a knock at the door caught their attention. Spread throughout the living room, the members of the household and their house guests waited to see who was at the door as Harry moved to answer it.

And walked in only seconds later with a werewolf. A large, masculine type of guy.

"Felix!" Kellan exclaimed, moving straight to him for a brotherly hug.

The girls followed suit, giving Felix affectionate hugs and wide smiles.

Eventually, Rory turned to them. "This is Felix, the mate we told you about."

"A faerie and a human, and a werewolf and a banshee," Vera merely stated. "You guys have quite the group."

Kellan smiled, clasping Felix's shoulders with affection. "We sure do."

Cora's attention moved to the werewolf, growing serious. "How'd you find us? Where's Juliette?"

"Heard word that Kellan and his mate were protected by the Whittle witches," he answered her before his tone grew desperate. "Nothing on Juliette yet. But I know she's alive."

"How?" Camilla asked casually, then gasped, a hand flying to her mouth. "I am so sorry. I didn't mean…"

Everyone took their seats, Felix beside Kellan and Cora as he interrupted Camilla's apology with a brush of the hand. "It's a wolf thing. Any creature can mate. I mean, look at them." He indicated to Kellan and Celine. "But wolves do it to an extreme. It's more literal with us, something in the DNA that makes us up. I can sense my mate, even when she's not around. I know she's okay. I just don't know where she is."

Kellan turned back to the family. "Felix and Juliette are the last of our little family of orphaned creatures."

"Which, I'm assuming, means we need a space for Felix now? There're these couches," Maya suggested.

"No," Camilla piped up. "Maya's staying with Hunter. There's no reason I can't stay with Warren a few days. Cora and Rory can take my room, and Felix can have the family room. At least then he'd have a bed."

Camilla was glad for the excuse to play house with Warren for a couple of days.

Playing house. It sounded both childish and exactly what she needed.

She watched Warren wash the dishes as she sat on the counter beside him, drying each piece he handed her. He'd laughed at her mention of 'playing house,' but he seemed to be enjoying it too.

"It's not funny," she told him in mock anger, taking the glass he handed her.

"No, you're right. Not at all." He laughed at her. A smack on the arm got him to settle his laughs down. "It is nice, though. Having this place. If I were at my dad's right now, there's no way I'd allow you to spend any time 'playing house.'"

She scrunched her nose. "I wouldn't want to. Especially with your brother around. And no offense, but I just make your dad out to be an older version of Hunter, so, no thanks! Maya might be okay with that, but not me, baby."

Warren's brows furrowed as he watched her. "Why would Hunter be around?"

Camilla mirrored his reaction. "Because he's your brother. I mean, unless your dad got him a little place too. Actually, that would make sense, huh. He is older. But he also enjoys that demon stuff you live away from."

"Hunter doesn't live with us at Delvaux Manor. I figured Maya would've told you." He considered his statement, then continued, "Maybe she doesn't know. I don't know. Anyway, he doesn't live at the manor. He bought his own manor years ago. And yes, he also named it Delvaux Manor. Makes it confusing for people looking for him, but good for him because he doesn't let anyone know where the location is."

Camilla considered that a moment before getting distracted by the splash of water that hit Warren's chest, soaking him in water, when he placed a plate under the water at an odd angle.

Turning off the water, he grabbed for the bottoms of his shirt and pulled it off, tossing it on the countertop. Camilla didn't hesitate in reaching out and pulling a now shirtless Warren between her legs and wrapping herself around him. His hands lightly grazed her thighs before settling on her hips as they stared at one another.

"So, he runs his own demon lair?"

"Yup." His eyes caught hers. "I'd assume Maya would've known, though. My father would've definitely mentioned something about having her at the manor if he'd taken her there."

"Maybe he has another place, a flat like this one." Camilla would have to talk to her sister about that. "But either way, I wouldn't want to see Hunter senior either."

Warren laughed, his hands skimming her thighs. "Cute, but Hunter doesn't look like our father. I do."

Camilla's brows shot up. "Excuse me?"

"They share the black eyes, but I share most everything else. I'm more lean like him, same black and curlyish hair, same looks in general."

"Wow. So you're saying your father's hot?"

He grimaced through a grin. "Gross, Cam, gross."

He moved to turn the sink back on, a few dishes left to clean, but didn't get far before Camilla was pulling him back between her legs.

"I think we can finish the dishes in the morning," she whispered.

Leaning in close so their mouths pressed together, Warren whispered back a quick thanks to the lords as he grabbed her thighs, wrapped them around his waist, and walked to his bedroom.

Camilla kissed her way down his neck and over his collarbones the entire journey. The more she could distract his perfect walk, the more delighted she felt.

And he stumbled.

Twice.

But he didn't stop until he dropped her onto his bed, caging her in as he hovered barely over and kissed her deeply. "I love you, Cam."

With the explosion of her heart, Camilla felt the extra feelings begin to cascade over her body that told her she would be losing control of her power in the moment again, and they hadn't even started yet. "I love you too."

The feeling expanded and tingled, causing a long moan to escape as Warren kissed her neck from one ear to the next, unbuttoning both of their trousers.

"I can feel you, Warren."

He glanced up at her through his lashes and smiled a wolfish grin. When Camilla had told him about her loss of control when they were together, he'd been excited to learn the heightened power of their release from her perspective. And he'd been excited to make it happen again and again and again and...

23

With their guests still on the hunt for their Juliette, they'd gone to checking in with each of the species to look for any missing people who could possibly be used for this spell The Eight had planned.

Maya and Harry ported to the edge of what looked to be a deserted town in the middle of nowhere Montana, but one step through the glamour showed them an entirely different scene. The drab and spooky town that pushed them from moving forward changed before their eyes to one of heightened color. Everywhere they looked was like a six year old's unicorn magic show. Sparks and color and happiness unencumbered.

The two stayed at the edge of the town, waiting for the elf leader while watching the exuberance around them. It truly was like a dream; it didn't seem real. Unicycles and cotton candy and colorful clothes, euphoric laughter and arguments that barely seemed real, and happiness. It was surreal.

Eventually, an older plump man walked up to them. He was cheerful and boisterous, and the picture of what Maya imagined a unicorn pretend world's grandfather to look like. Exactly as would be expected in a place like this: Sir Weylin-Tovor.

Sir Weylin-Tovor welcomed them with a boyish excitement, taking their hands with passion when they shook and inviting them to join him at the Main Street Café.

It was the small walk through town to the café that gave Maya a deeper look into the unicorn world, and…she didn't like it. It was too colorful and cheery for her. Something that could be fun for a few hours, like an amusement park, but no longer.

Taking seats at a round table, Maya got right to the point of their visit, her desire to get out of the town as soon as possible growing by the second. It was a bit too much for her. "We're checking in with every species, looking for any missing residents. We think there's a plan to take seven members by a group of halfie's for a spell they'd like to perform, but we're unsure where the seven will come from. We want to take the precaution and check in with the different species."

Sir Weylin-Tovor's grin dwindled a moment before stopping at a small smile and responding, "Look through the menu. We have amazing coffee." He handed her the bright, laminated menu. "As for the missing, I'm proud to say we have none. It would be hard to take an elf. We all live within these deserted, empty landscapes of Montana. We are not a diaspora like any other creature."

Right. The elves didn't have different territories. They were all within North America. And within the emptiness of Montana, it wasn't too difficult for them to fit thousands of residents into one 'tribe.'

"In perfect sense," Harry responded. "We didn't believe you to be in danger for that very reason, but we felt the need to check."

"The menu, my children," Sir Weylin-Tovor said distractedly.

"Black coffee," Maya said without a glance to the menu.

Either Sir Weylin-Tovor didn't notice Maya's behavior or he chose to ignore it as he continued on, "By a group of half-bloods you say? It doesn't surprise me."

He looked down to the menu like he'd only mentioned the weather.

"Meaning?" Maya's tone grew indignant.

"The crossing of species. It should not happen. Proof of that is in these half-bloods. Look at them, on a mission to kill multiple people for the purposes of a spell. Outrageous! And it is all because of cross breeding."

"But what of romance?" Maya rebutted. "Love?"

Sir Weylin-Tovor groaned at the mention as if he were speaking with a petulant child. "Love happens only between those within the same species. Look at the elves. The only species with no cross breeding. Ever. Not a single half-blood holds our blood, and in turn, we have not a single problem. We are pure."

Maya felt her blood begin to boil, the fire that she so normally controlled seeping through every bit of her. A leader of an entire species that welcomed them so easily, that made the best of friends—distant as they may be—with visiting creatures, but that also held such a high prejudice against those same species.

She almost couldn't believe it—a man who welcomed you openly and happily as a friend, but would push you into the depths of Hell's Gate were you to proclaim any feeling for another species.

Harry seemed to have noticed Maya's reaction and cut into the conversation before she could say anything that would cripple the Whittles' standing and relationship with the elves. "A Mocha Locha Choca for me, Sir Weylin-Tovor."

Sir Weylin-Tovor smiled to Harry, apparently oblivious to Maya's rage across the small table, and walked to the counter, ordering their drinks.

Harry turned to Maya and whispered too low for anyone to eavesdrop, "You have to let it go, Maya. We cannot afford to make an enemy of the elves. Their ideologies are ludicrous, but we have bigger problems on our hands right now."

Maya took several deep breaths as she stared out at the ludicrously happy Main Street, then into Harry's eyes. "It's just hard for me to process. How all of these species, not just Sir Weylin-Tovor, but all of them, they're not forgiving. How do they not see the lives people find together, albeit by combining two species?"

Harry smiled to her, pride shining in his eyes. "I do not know because like you, I cannot fathom it. But we are different. Essentially no warlock finds a problem with cross breeding. In fact, I've never heard of one who has ever minded it. And you? You and your sisters are in a position where two of you are in cross species relationships. It becomes easier to understand when your own feelings are involved."

"Please," Maya scoffed, her eyes traveling to Sir Weylin-Tovor picking up the three to-go cups. "I wouldn't have minded even if I didn't have Hunter. To think that anyone could ignore the feelings between them, between Kellan and Celine, Felix and Juliette, even though I haven't seen them together, even Br..." Even Brynn and Alloy, whom her family didn't exactly know of.

Harry smiled and leaned in to tease, "And that is why everyone comes to the Whittles. We truly are one hell of a household."

Sir Weylin-Tovor interrupted as Maya smiled to Harry, handing their cups over and looking Maya in the eyes. "I got you the Vanilli Camilli. A sweet girl like you should have the same."

She smiled through her teeth, though she wanted to chuck the entire cup at the old man.

Harry stood immediately, taking Maya with him, and apologized for their early departure.

Sir Weylin-Tovor only smiled and insisted to have them over again. He walked them to the edge of the glamour that separated the elves from the rest of the world and bid them goodbye in the most loving, grandfatherly way that Maya almost forgot about his pureblood, prejudice ideologies.

***

While Maya was away with Harry to check in with the elves and the others were out of the house, Vera stood waiting for Hunter.

Time for lesson number two.

Not that lesson number one went all that great. All he did was shadow in and out of the room for three hours and frustrate her to no end.

This time, she felt the tingling just as she was stepping into the empty space across from the living room.

"You're on time," she opened.

"And it took you too long to realize it."

She scoffed. "How would you know that?"

"I saw you stiffen when it hit that I was already in the house. Faster than that, Sister."

"Hunter, I need to learn how to defend myself, not how to detect my power," she seethed through bared teeth.

He scoffed. "I beg to differ."

She narrowed her gaze at him, but didn't speak. She really wasn't in the mood to have him shadowing in and out all day.

"Fine," he stood up straight, "you want to do more, try throwing me back."

He shadowed from his spot and landed to her side, and before she could raise her hand to throw him, he was already behind her. By the time she'd turned around, he was in front of her again.

"Hunter," she growled.

He laughed from behind her and shadowed away before she could turn with her arm thrown. "You said you wanted this." He was beside her, then gone. "You said you didn't need to learn how to use your power." In the hallway. "If you're so capable with that power," by the fireplace, "you should know where I have landed and shoot to the spot before I can leave." Right before her with a wide smirk. Then gone.

The tingling shot up her arm again, and she knew he was behind her. She turned in a slump. "I'm telling Maya you're being impossible."

He shrugged. "She knows that."

She grimaced. "And yet she stays with you."

His smirk was knowing. "This isn't about my relationship with your sister. It's about getting you to react to your powers. You have to make them as much a part of you as breathing. It's natural, and it happens without a thought. The reason you're too slow right now is because you're taking the second to process things before acting. Too long."

She relented. "How?"

His gaze narrowed on her. "I've never trained a witch. I'm not particularly sure." Before she could yell at him through her sputter, he continued, "But I would assume a little incentive. You bleeding hearts make that part a little too easy."

"What are you suggesting?"

He stared at her a few minutes without responding. "Let's see how well your imagination works." He walked around her to the end of the room. "I have your sister, kidnapped her. She got away, running from me, just hid herself away in a room that you stepped into. I shadow in, you have less than a half second to realize I'm there and immobilize me to protect her."

Vera breathed out. "Okay."

He shadowed out of the room, and she was left alone to let the imagination sink in. Maya was running from him, something she definitely didn't see happening. Maya was more the type to stick around and knock him a few, but imagination, right?

Maya was running and just found a spot in this room to hide herself. Pretend there was an ottoman she could stuff herself into, and Hunter was about to come in and catch her. Oh, she could imagine Hunter catching her all right.

Tingling and… a breath behind her.

He was gone before she could turn with her power.

"Seriously?" He was leaning against the trim to the hallway. "You're just going to let me kill you and get to your sister like that?"

"I reacted a second later. I hardly think…"

"Trust me, Sister, I could've easily snapped your neck. *Easily*."

Vera grumbled. "Okay, fine. I got distracted. Try again."

And they did.

And again.

And again.

"Wow, Sister, I'm really starting to doubt this sisterly bond that's apparently supposed to be instantaneous."

Vera slumped against the wall. "I'm sorry, I just can't picture it."

"Your imagination not strong enough?"

She rolled her eyes. "You terrorizing Maya. I've seen the way she looks at you. She wouldn't leave. Not to mention, she'd beat the crap out of you rather than run if there *was* a problem."

He merely…grinned? It must've been a smirk because Hunter Delvaux didn't grin. But that was definitely a poorly hidden grin and pride shining in his eyes. "Imagine it's our little sister."

Camilla?

Well, that just made this a whole lot easier.

Camilla was running—though again, Vera couldn't imagine her sister running. She could see Camilla spitting on Hunter if he tried anything, maybe clawing his eyes out—and she found a spot to hide. She was scared, holding a hand over her mouth to keep the breaths from making a sound, and tears were streaking down her beautiful face.

Tingling and shoot. Her arm was out before she turned to her side, where Hunter had just shadowed out of the way.

He returned beside her. "Good job."

"Not good enough." She looked to him.

He laughed. "I've had my magic since I was nine years old. That's two decades. You have a few months on yours. Even I wouldn't be that hard on you."

"Nine? Wow, doesn't that kinda give you a power imbalance with Maya?" Yes, she saw the way Maya looked at him, but she was still on Camilla's side—she didn't like this guy.

"Trust me, your sister has all the power where we stand."

"Figuratively. But literally?"

He looked her right in the eyes. "Literally. That warlock of yours has a hundred years on you, but I'd still say you hold the power over him. Just wait until your relationship begins. He'll be at your beck and call."

Vera's blush was deep. She could feel it across every inch of her skin. She turned away from him and walked the room. "This isn't about me and Harry."

"And it isn't about me and Maya. It's about training your powers, so stop bringing it up."

She looked to him. He was right. She had to focus on her powers, not her sister's deluded relationship. She had to learn how to physically protect her sisters, then she'd worry about the emotional part.

24

---

amilla took to hobby what Vera had taken to as business—baking. In the kitchen, she and Celine switched out a batch of cookies from the oven for a batch of brownies. With the others out in the hopes of finding Juliette, they'd wanted to have something waiting for them when they returned, small as it might be.

It wasn't long until just that happened, and the kitchen filled with Vera, Harry, Maya, Camilla, Celine, Kellan, Cora, Rory, and Felix—still no Juliette.

Just as they all began to settle around the kitchen, half sitting at the table, half standing around the counters, Warren shadowed into the entrance to the kitchen, capturing everyone's attention. Well, all but the Whittles, as they were quite used to it by that point.

The house guests on the other hand, froze, relaxing only when they saw Camilla walk up for a chaste kiss, their expressions turning from fight to shock.

"You're with a demon?" Rory asked, dumbfounded.

Camilla smiled cheekily, leaning into his warmth. "Forbidden romance, right?"

A part of Camilla swore seeing her with Warren sent a sense of ease into their guests that hadn't been there before. Like they'd known this family was accepting of cross species relationships, but they truly believed it now. With a member in a 'forbidden' relationship, there was an ease of knowing the house they were staying in wouldn't turn on them.

Celine piped up, "I thought demons were the one species not to do the romance part of that statement."

Warren's hand went up with a smile. "Half human."

Camilla went back to her seat at the end of the table, Warren taking the one beside her as she turned back to the group. "So, no news on Juliette. Do we have anything on what The Eight are waiting for? Why haven't they taken the seven they need? Which seven? Anything?"

Yeah, she should've waited for some answers before throwing in all the questions, but she couldn't help it.

"Other than a lovely old man that turned out to be a prejudiced prick?" Maya rebutted from her spot atop the counter.

"Nothing," Harry jumped in before conversation derailed to Sir Weylin-Tovor's thoughts. Camilla had learned only that Maya was frustrated with the man, and knew from Maya's expressions that she probably shouldn't bring it up. "We can't find any creature in danger. They've all been warned, but we have no idea what they'd be waiting for. There must be something they're still missing."

Even with the mention of The Eight to their house guests, no new information had been learned. With their own problems of how to start a new life in their hodgepodge of a group, halfies hadn't ever been high on the priorities list.

It seemed Harry's interruptions were for naught, as Vera turned back to Maya. "Why is Sir Weylin-Tovor a prick?"

She hadn't gotten the news. Or learned yet that some of Maya's looks meant you were safer staying out of it.

"His beliefs on cross species relationships. His superiority complex that the elves don't have any half breeds," Maya said bitterly, then continued with her own thoughts. "Cross breeding isn't new, but it's rarer than those halfie's are making it look. He acts like..." Harry cut her off with a touch to the arm, likely knowing she could get passionate and not wanting her to explode in front of guests.

"Agreed," Felix jumped in. "Normally it is lust, not love, driving two together."

"That's true," Vera added. "I mean, look at Warren. His parents just had sex. Or Colette, Warren's sister," she added for the new members at the table, "she's half witch, that was just sex for them as well, although, that ended with a loathsome creature at the end."

"Hmm," Camilla mocked. "A demon and a witch lusting after each other, funny."

She knew she shouldn't have, but sometimes—okay, a lot of the time—her thoughts just spewed out.

Maya ground her teeth so softly, Camilla was sure only the family noticed, responding in a clear, unbothered tone, "Except, dear sister, Colette was abandoned by both parents. I would never abandon my child."

The others looked between them with quirked brows.

Celine turned to Camilla. "Aren't you with the demon?"

"Half demon," Camilla said. She didn't understand why no one ever remembered that.

Camilla saw the look Vera sent to their guests, giving them a small, apologetic smile. She knew the argument everyone would use—half or not, Camilla was also with a demon—but there was a difference.

Vera cleared up the situation. "Maya is sleeping with Warren's half-brother."

Clarity rang in the air as Cora said, "Full demon, I suppose?"

Vera answered with a single nod, and they sat in silent tension. Kellan was the first to break, turning to Camilla. "You know, lust can turn into love. That's what happened between Felix and Juliette."

Camilla grimaced and whispered under her breath, "Lords, I hope not." She turned to her sister on another bound to get her to drop the demon. "How much do you really know him, anyway? You don't know what he's hiding! You know he has his own manor? He could be doing lords-knows-what there."

She felt Warren squeeze her hand, trying to calm her down, but she ignored it. He was so sweet for looking out for Maya's feelings at the moment, but she had to protect her sister. Even if it meant hurting her a little.

Maya's face twisted. "I know. Where did you think we go?"

Warren sat up straight, shock written on every inch of his face. "He's taken you there? He's never allowed anyone access before. We don't even know the location."

"I know," Maya responded, then turned back to Camilla. "He took me there before we were sleeping together. I think I can trust him just fine. The only thing he's doing there is me."

A poorly hidden bout of laughter from their guests.

At least they tried to hide it. They just didn't understand the importance of the situation.

Camilla's face twisted in disgust, but she didn't comment, allowing the conversation to turn to more pleasant topics. This was no time to be arguing with Maya. They had guests.

***

Takeout was key to a large group like this one.

And Vera had been in the mood for Chinese food all week.

And like clockwork, it was just as the food got there and everyone was preparing for dinner that Hunter shadowed in.

Maya was getting plates out of a cabinet when his presence appeared behind her, and hands gripped her ass, giving it a nice squeeze, as he leaned in to whisper in her ear.

Vera bit the inside of her cheek to hide her secondhand embarrassment as Camilla grimaced from her spot by the table. Their house guests didn't seem to agree with Camilla's sentiment, as they, too, watched the interaction between Hunter and Maya. She'd leaned back against his chest, a smile breaking across her face as his hands rounded her hips, holding her close.

"That's what you're angry about?" Felix scoffed to Camilla. "Those two are far past lust." His tone indicated annoyance, and Vera knew Camilla had lost an ally. Felix was definitely on Hunter's side.

The whole group was settling around the table for dinner, pulling chairs from the formal dining room to make space for the eleven of them.

They spoke and joked together as if they had no problems, like a group of human friends getting together for a night. It was something that Vera hadn't known she'd craved until she had it, friends. She'd been so happy to have a family that she'd forgotten that sometimes these larger groups were just as exciting.

"Stay as long as you'd like," Hunter said to the guests of the house when they informed the group they would be leaving that night. He'd just placed his plate on the island at his back, since it was closer than the table with the way he was seated, and placed his hand to the leg Maya had thrown over his.

Vera knew Camilla would attempt to calm her annoyance at his response but wouldn't be able to hold back her response, and she was rewarded with being right when Camilla grumbled, "You don't live here. What part do you find in dictating any arrangements?"

Hunter looked to her with a smirk, mirth in the eyes. "The

part where I've enjoyed having your sister as lady of my house-hold. I'd like to keep her."

That was…sweet.

And it reminded Vera of her earlier training with Hunter. He'd been prideful when Vera had said that Maya wouldn't run. That if anything happened, she would beat the crap out of him herself. In the moment, Vera had assumed the pride was in Maya's ability to protect herself—and she was sure part of it was that—but she could see now that the other part was their relationship. He took pride in what they had, knowing that she felt for him something that was obviously more than lust. And Vera could see, he probably did too.

Just how much was an entirely different question.

"Then do so. She's right beside you," Felix jumped in. "Ask her to move in with you. At least for just the nights if she wants to stay near her family until this mess is over."

The eyes of all but Felix's little family looked to him in shock at the suggestion. Maybe they'd all been thinking the same thing, or maybe they were so used to Felix that hearing this suggestion from his lips wasn't shocking.

But it definitely was shocking. Vera had to fight the little o her mouth made at hearing it.

Hunter recovered first with a smirk, and his eyes shined with pure greed. "I just may do that, friend."

It was scary to think what a friendship with Hunter Delvaux consisted of, but Felix didn't seem to mind.

Vera had just pulled herself out of her frozen state when Felix gave the demon a wolfish grin, and Maya's smile grew as she looked between the two men.

They wore grins that could rival one another, and it was probably new to Maya, to all of them really—Hunter didn't have friends. And he'd never find one in their family, but it seemed almost telling that Felix would undoubtedly be one.

Something told her that if the two spent some time together, they'd be one and the same, and she didn't know how she felt about that. She actually liked Felix. Maybe that was because her first acquaintance with him wasn't him killing a priest. Or maybe it was because he wasn't a demon, so she wasn't instinctually—or stereotypically—programmed to hate and mistrust him.

Not fair, she knew that much. But Hunter was also not making it easy on her.

Maya leaned her head to Hunter's shoulder, cuddling into the arm that was thrown over her leg, as she watched the group go into a new conversation. She closed her eyes as Hunter leaned in and kissed her crown, and Vera saw it then, what he'd said in their first training session. He only had eyes for one woman.

She'd originally thought he meant in the family, so she'd pushed the comment aside. He'd made it clear time and again that the only Whittle he wanted was Maya. But no, he meant overall. She was it.

And Vera didn't know how she felt about that.

After dinner, the Whittles' five new friends huddled into the foyer, ready to leave, Maya giving them a set of vials, each labeled with a potion that they may find come in handy for their new start.

Warren followed their departure, bidding them a goodnight and shadowing out. Camilla would be going up to bed alone tonight. In a way, that was a good thing. She was young, no need to rush the relationship. Some time between them would be good.

On the opposite spectrum, Maya clutched both fists into Hunter's shirt when he, too, tried to bid her goodnight. Vera watched Hunter's poor attempt to pull away and heard Maya whisper, "Let's pretend my room is still occupied for a few more days."

Vera saw the wicked smile erupt on Hunter's face as he shadowed them out. She'd offered exactly what he'd been aiming for. She stared at the spot they'd occupied for a few minutes, knowing she didn't like Hunter, but growing content with him because of the way he made Maya happy. Perhaps Felix had been right, and this was more than lust. Well, she knew it was more than lust, but maybe it was more than more than lust.

Vera walked to the backyard, sitting on the patio steps to look out at the moon as she huddled into herself in the cold and thought of her sisters and how close they'd grown in such a short period of time. Sisters she hadn't known only three and a half months ago.

How she'd come to love them in such a short period of time.

With sisters in mind, Vera couldn't help but think back to Hunter and the problem he was causing in the family.

She agreed with Camilla's thoughts about him, though she made it known far less frequently than her sister, but she couldn't understand Camilla's arguments given her situation.

Her argument of Warren's human side didn't mask the fact that she was also with the species she was so against Maya being with. Camilla thought with her emotions, Vera knew, and saw only a dangerous man sleeping with her sister. It was those stubborn emotions that may just be what was hindering Camilla from seeing the full story when it came to Hunter and Maya's relationship. A story Vera was sure she still didn't fully see, but a relationship she was sure they had, in more than a sexual manner.

Relationship. What a concept.

Harry.

Thoughts of his face, his presence.

Thoughts of their time together in the piano room that afternoon. They hadn't spoken, yet Vera heard his voice whispered in her ear. They hadn't played the piano, yet Vera could envision the notes filling the room. They'd touched only their sides, yet Vera felt him in every part of her being. She felt her skin boil and grow sensitive with desire.

She squeezed her eyes shut hard. Harry was their warlock. She could not think of him as anything but.

Even though she continued to tell herself that, his presence never left her thoughts. They consumed her.

25

$\mathcal{M}$aya licked her way from his navel to the dip between his collarbones. She felt his body twitch, his arms coiling in the need to move, but she held his wrists down beside his form. He was not to move.

And she would be the death of him.

With the light suckle at the base of his neck, he groaned her name, feeling her smile wickedly on his skin.

Her gaze flickered to meet his as she settled herself over him, straddling his lap, his length pressing against her panty-covered sex. Her eyes shined mischief as they looked to his need-filled ones.

"Yes?" she whispered seductively, nibbling his jaw.

"Love, take those panties off." He ground his hips up and tried again to move his arms. "Now."

Maya rocked her hips against his, keeping her hold on his wrists as she kissed her way down his neck. "I don't think I will." It was the last article of clothing between them, and Maya was having fun teasing him. "In fact," she sat up and looked down at him, "I quite like the idea of just talking tonight." She ground her hips into his once more.

His gaze moved from her eyes, to her lips, to her now prominent breasts, to the spot they touched, and back again, unable to retract from her breasts for long. Two beautiful, peaked brown buds calling for his tongue.

He groaned as his desire grew, but he quite liked this game Maya was playing. "At least let me touch you." He moved his wrists once more under her hold.

Realistically, he could pull his arms out easily, but this was her game, and he wanted her to play.

Her tongue shot out to lick her lips, ending in a bite as she relented and released his wrists, settling her hands on his thighs behind her. He moaned at her new position as it displayed her breasts more fully to him, his hands shooting up to grab a hold, fingers circling and flicking her nipples, taking pleasure at the moans he elicited.

Maya's hips moved, and her head rolled back as his hands grazed down, taking her hips and rocking her to his rhythm. Panty clad or not, Hunter could feel her dripping onto his cock, and he needed the friction of her movements.

With one hand holding her hips, and making sure they continued to move, the other moved back to give her breasts some much deserved attention. Then the one on her hip moved to press through her soaked panties, the little nub begging to be touched.

"Weren't we supposed to be talking?" Maya breathed out, her nails digging into his thighs.

Hunter smirked. "Talk."

She looked at him through hooded eyes. "What's your favorite ice cream flavor?"

Hunter's thumb paused a moment while brushing her nipple, not expecting such a mundane topic of conversation. He brushed the shock away and continued his movements, his hips now rocking with hers. "I don't like ice cream."

Maya moaned louder still, then furrowed her brows as she

looked at him, attempting to keep up with the conversation as if they were seated across the room from one another. "An outrage."

"I bet." He groaned as she dripped down her thighs and onto his cock. "And yours?"

He bucked up, feeling the sensation move toward his spine and knowing it wouldn't be too long. It was never too long when they were together. He'd make her come, then follow right behind.

"Vanilla," she answered, her body beginning to spasm in her closeness, but she continued on. "I leave the flavor for more private affairs."

Hunter gave a small laugh at her response, then asked, keeping with her pretense at normality, "Your favorite city?"

She didn't answer, likely couldn't as her body spasmed as she came without warning, still grinding against him. Her fingers left deep, bleeding marks on his thighs as she cried out, and before she could fully come back from her high, Hunter flipped them so that she was laying beneath him, and continued to rock his hips against her panty-clad sex.

"You did not answer me," he teased through clenched teeth.

He was about to spill all over her.

Maya laughed as his movements grew rash, his climax hitting him only a moment after and marking her with his seed. He groaned and grabbed the base of his cock, making sure to spill every bit onto her stomach. She was his, and he took plea-sure in marking her any way he pleased.

Their breaths mixed as he held himself on his elbows and settled his forehead upon hers, finding peace in his release.

"Edinburgh," she breathed into him.

His smile mixed with hers as he slipped off her and moved to grab a towel and clean her up before laying next to her.

They remained in bed and played a round of twenty questions, each of the questions bits of small talk, but each giving them insight into the other in the most mundane of topics.

Favorite books. Most hated season. Ideal vacations.

By question seventeen, they lay on their sides facing one another and laughed as Maya told him that she had a fear of bunnies because she was convinced they were evil.

"I'm serious!" Maya laughed. "Look at their eyes. They don't lie to you. Especially the white bunnies. I would *literally* shit myself!"

Hunter's enjoyment only grew at the truth of the statement in her eyes—she was being serious—and that made things all the better as he fell to his back with thunderous laughter.

He moved quickly as she hit him, pushing her to her back, and settling his body over hers, planting a kiss between her breasts.

He rested his arms over her chest and settled there, smiling up at her with a spark in his eyes. Her hands moved immediately to play with his hair, a smile lightening her features as she looked at him.

"Do you ever get lonely? This huge place with only you," Maya asked, her smile faltering and pupils dilating as she watched him.

Hunter rubbed his stubbled chin lightly against the top of her stomach, tickling both her chest and abs. "I did sometimes. But it had nothing to do with the manor. I didn't have anyone in my life that I cared to be around."

"Because who could ever be so good as to tempt your attentions," she joked.

Hunter smirked and kissed the spot his chin had just been tickling. "Exactly."

She scoffed, and he began to tickle her, eliciting a burst of laughter and a move from playing with his hair to pushing his arms to retreat. And just as she cried for him to stop, her phone rang on the nightstand.

"Ignore it." He stopped the tickling, but leaned up to kiss her lips.

Maya allowed him a chaste taste, but moved out of the kiss and grabbed for her phone. "It could be important." Hunter groaned, but settled back to his spot lying above her as she picked up the call. "Brynn. Hi."

Her phone was so loud, Hunter was sure he could've heard Brynn from across the room.

"Hey, Maya. I just wanted to call and inform you Alloy heard from some gargoyle friends they've been called by the faeries to help with a situation. I don't know if it has anything to do with the people you guys are looking for, but I thought it could help to check it out."

"Umm, yeah." Maya sobered up. "Thank you. We'll check it out."

Brynn hung up, and Maya dropped her phone to the bed, looking to Hunter. Her gaze said she knew he'd heard. "Could be something there we're looking for."

Hunter's face dropped to hide against her stomach as he shook his head, as if throwing a child's tantrum. He didn't care as long as it meant he got to keep her in his bed. "No, let's not leave."

Maya laughed, but insisted anyway. "Hunter, get off. We have to go."

He looked up, eyes glinting and smirk growing. "Fifteen minutes."

Maya would know that glint all too well. "No!"

His hands reached for the panties she still wore and began to slowly pull them off. "Ten minutes."

He'd gotten the panties off and quickly moved back over her so she couldn't move.

"It's never only ten minutes with you!"

He kissed the spot just below her navel and smirked back up

at her, his arms going to rest atop her thighs so she couldn't move. "Ten minutes."

Maya had texted her family when it seemed futile that Hunter would give up his conquests, and so, an hour later when she arrived back home, they already had information ready.

Camilla had checked the storybook and found only a bit of information surrounding the faeries, including a solely faerie power. "Lightness of foot, lightness of feel," Camilla said. "It was what made it possible for Grandmama to leave so easily to look for her family when they didn't show. The only reason she normally had them go to her is because she had a limited supply."

Maya sighed out, "Which makes faeries a reasonable target."

"Unfortunately." Vera sighed beside her sister.

"Well, let's go!" Harry clapped his hands together as he met them in the kitchen. Surprisingly, he hadn't been home when Maya had returned, and neither sister had known of his whereabouts.

When they landed on faerie property, a few gargoyles still lingered about, but all was calm. Maya checked the area and found no Alloy.

Finlan, who was standing at the front of his manor, saw them immediately and was over in moments. "Gee, so glad the lot of you are here."

Maya ignored the sarcasm dripping from his voice. "Heard you called for help."

"We called the gargoyles, not you," Finlan sneered back.

"All the same, we need to know what the problem is. If it relates to our issues, we need to know," Maya said, not the least bit intimidated by his superiority complex.

Finlan looked displeased and ready to argue, when a faerie who looked like she could rule his entire world called for him. The desire was there and gone in seconds, but Maya knew he would be relenting, if only to get to the woman quicker. "We found a whole group attacked, only one dead." He turned and began to walk toward the manor, Maya matching his steps and the others following behind. "There was a banshee that helped them." Maya's step faltered, knowing it could very well be the banshee they were looking for, but she righted herself before Finlan could speak on it. "Got there just in time to save the others. She's completely out now, but the survivors were up in arms that she was their protector." He'd walked them into the manor and off to the right, down the hall to a bedroom with a single sleeping woman in the bed.

Finlan left them in the room and walked away with nothing more to say. Closing the door, they settled around the room, watching the sleeping banshee.

Just as Vera opened her mouth to break the silence and likely voice the question they were all thinking, the woman began to stir, eyes peeling open. She shot straight up and into the headboard as she came to and faced four strangers.

Maya stepped up. "Juliette?"

Her eyes shot to meet Maya's, and she nodded ever so slightly, as if scrying her mind to try and figure out who Maya was. "Who're you?"

"Friends of Felix's. He's been looking for you for almost two weeks," Maya said calmly, taking a seat at the edge of the bed.

The mention of Felix seemed to steal all the fight left in her body, and she fell against the headboard, looking to the group with desperate eyes. "How is he?"

"He's doing well," Camilla answered.

"Good," Vera said.

"He's well," Harry chimed.

Maya waited a moment, looking Juliette over, and answered

honestly, knowing it's what she would've wanted in this situation. "Awful. I can see not being with you, not knowing where you are, is eating him."

She knew she'd been right to be honest when Juliette's gaze went from uneasy at the answers of the others to trusting, like even though the answer hurt her, it was something she could believe.

She closed her eyes, then opened them slowly, looking to Maya, eyes wet, but not a single drop falling down her cheeks. "I felt it coming, death. I couldn't allow something to happen to them, to Felix especially. I left him a note, but I knew that would do no good but to let him know I left on my own."

Maya wanted to grab for one of Juliette's hands, ease the banshee as she spoke, but she wasn't the comforting sort.

Juliette continued, "All I knew was that it had to do with Kellan's lot, so I left and began looking. I finally found them the other day. I don't remember when, depends how long I've been out. A group of five faeries surrounded by halfies. They were talking about faerie dust, but it didn't seem all that important to them. They said the Whittle secret was all they *really* needed." Her eyes shot around the room before settling back to Maya. "You're the Whittles, aren't you?"

Maya smiled, nodding. "Maya."

"Vera," came from behind Maya.

"Camilla."

"Harry."

A small smile graced Juliette's lips. "I killed one of them, a half demon-faerie, and another attacked me. That's how I ended up out of it. But the rest got away."

Maya shrugged. "You still saved four faeries."

Juliette smiled back, though it was obviously non-convincing. "I know."

Not long after, the five began their venture out of the manor, Juliette having asked to leave with them and go back to Felix.

Finlan met them at the front porch to bid them farewell, as spruced up as before, but Maya had no doubt he'd been having *fun* with his little friend.

He looked to Juliette. "We thank you, Miss Juliette."

"Cross breeding isn't such a bad thing after all, huh? Without her, they'd all be gone," Camilla chimed in.

"We're thankful for the help, but it was half breeds that caused the mess in the first place. I don't see how anyone could see that and believe a good thing."

As with Sir Waylon-Tovor, Harry interrupted before anything jeopardized their standing with the faeries, as thin on ice as it was already. They still needed some type of allies.

At home, Juliette settled onto the couch to rest, Maya moving to her office for the privacy to call Felix. The phone only rang once. "Has something happened?"

Maya couldn't help but smile, even though she could still hear the ache in his tone. "How long until you can get back to my place?"

"Probably a good seven hours. Cora and Rory are out of the potion that allows them to port around. Why?"

Maya smiled at his tone. He was in a desperate need to find his mate, but was still willing to drop everything and come help her family. She smiled, too, at the fact that the girls ran out of the potion that helped them port. She'd been envious to learn that they had acquired the ability to port, a solely warlock power, with the help of a potion.

Unfortunately, the potion only seemed to work on the two of them, something even they hadn't been able to figure out. "I think you should start heading back. There's a banshee here waiting on you."

Even over the phone, Maya knew Felix had frozen in spot, breath leaving him completely. "I'll be there as fast as I can."

Maya smiled as the line cut, and she moved to the living room, where her family already had tea ready and talk open about what next. She settled into the end of the couch beside Juliette, closest to the foyer, and waited.

In the time that passed as they sat about talking, the Delvaux brothers shadowed in, one moving to sit beside Camilla, and the other pulling Maya from her seat.

Maya could feel Juliette's eyes on her as Hunter pulled her out of her seat, took it, then brought her to his lap. He leaned his head back and closed his eyes for a nap, Maya's arms wrapping around his neck and snuggling in to take in his scent. She'd missed that perfect scent.

Juliette's gaze never wavered. Maya was used to it by now, the stares she got anytime she was with Hunter. Especially because it was Hunter.

The demon and witch aspect got them attention, as it did Warren and Camilla, but not as much as the mere fact it was Hunter, an uncaring asshole who'd probably wreaked havoc in most species' lives.

Well, and maybe because she and Hunter were far more touchy than Warren and Camilla.

"You guys are with demons?" Juliette glanced between them and Camilla and Warren.

"Brothers too," Vera piped in from the other couch, playing with Harry's hair as he leaned against her legs on the ground.

"Half-brothers," Camilla clarified as Maya expected she would. "This is Warren," her smile dropped as she pointed to Maya, "and that's Hunter."

Warren had taken the seat beside her, but nowhere as touchy as she and Hunter. So yeah, it could just be the demon and witch thing, and they just made it more obvious.

Conversation was quick to pick back up between the others as Juliette looked around the room and leaned into Maya, though she never dropped to a whisper. "You two remind me of Felix and myself."

The smile was immediate. "Yeah?"

Juliette nodded, but didn't elaborate. Instead, she said, "I can see your Hunter is not accepted, but I think you two are quite perfect together."

Maya's smile warmed. "How can you think that? You don't know me, least of all him."

She smirked back. "Banshee instincts."

They laughed and turned to the conversation between the others, Maya planting a light kiss to Hunter's exposed neck and noticing the smirk that had planted itself there—he'd definitely not yet been asleep and heard Juliette's remark.

It took hours, as she expected, but it was only five hours, rather than seven, before they heard a knock on the door. It was nearing three in the morning, but no one had been able to sleep, so they'd stayed up talking.

Everyone froze at the knock, a now awake Hunter tensing under Maya. She probably should've mentioned she'd called a certain someone.

Hunter's hands tried to grip her waist as she shot out of her spot and went to open the door, a tug telling him she knew who it was and she'd be fine. He still wasn't keen on letting her go, but Maya had a door to get to.

Felix was standing there, rigid and hopeful.

Maya stepped out of the way, knowing there was no need for conversation, and walked back to the opening to the living room, Felix only a step behind, and the others a step behind him. And he froze there, seeing Juliette again after nearly two weeks—equivalent to months, maybe a year, to a mated wolf.

Juliette's gaze met his, and she shot off of the couch, crashing into him without a care in the world. Her arms clung around his neck, her legs gripped his hips as she breathed in his scent. And Felix wasted no time in wrapping his arms around her and squeezing tight.

After two weeks with no contact from Hunter, not know

where he was or if he was safe, would she react that way? Maybe she was more similar to these two.

But maybe not. Would she react like that?

All remained silent as they watched. Minutes passed, and the two merely hugged one another, breathing in each other's scents and relaxing in the thought that they were back together. Maya, too, felt her heart settle, knowing that their pain vanished with each passing moment, unable to imagine what they'd been going through.

Eventually, Juliette pulled away and kissed him full on the lips, long and maybe a bit too passionate for being in a room full of people, before pulling away to whisper against his lips, "Hey."

He smiled, wide and shit eating. "Hi, baby."

It was moments still before they untangled themselves, Felix reluctant to do so, and Juliette turned to the others and threw herself into more tight hugs. When their little family finished with their reunion, she walked to the couch, Felix taking the other end from Hunter and pulling Juliette to his lap. Maya laughed. Juliette may have been right after all.

Kellan and Celine found spots on the floor to tangle together, Celine leaning between his legs, and Cora and Rory brought chairs that lingered about in the foyer to take their seats as Maya settled back on Hunter's lap.

She felt at ease in the presence of the mixed lot. She looked to Camilla and Warren on the couch across from her as they snuggled in close to one another. Holding one of her hands between his on his lap, Warren played with her fingers, and Camilla looked content. That was all that was important to Maya, that Camilla was content with her relationship. It's what she had.

Her gaze then moved to Vera, who still played with Harry's hair as he leaned back into her.

Those two.

How long would it be until they admitted their feelings for one another?

She'd seen glimpses of it before, but when Hunter mentioned it, she'd been shocked to find that she wasn't shocked. She just needed them to be okay with their own feelings.

She then looked on to Juliette and Felix beside her, and felt herself grow warm with serenity at her future because she saw it in those two.

Maya snuggled in closer to Hunter as she thought of it, that at the very least, Hunter would have a friend in Felix and she with Juliette. That no matter what, there was one couple—apart from Zathrian and Acacia—that didn't find a problem with them.

And finally, to the four remaining guests in the house, the first set of 'friends' they'd actually made in the magical world. She'd always be thankful for them.

And the joy they brought one another? Unbeatable.

26

School was back from winter break, and Camilla watched students walk the paths to classes, the cacophony of normalcy that washed over her in being back on campus and in the world she'd grown up in all her life felt nice.

She saw Warren leaning against the brick outside the building to their next class and smiled—another semester of literature with him.

Together, they walked into the lecture hall, where all one hundred students of the class would begin taking their seats. Up front stood a professor Camilla didn't know, apparently new to the school entirely.

He stood well dressed, light goatee, glasses in place. He was attractive, likely only a few years older than Harry. Camilla knew he would catch the attention of some female students in class, his bald head somehow making his appearance more appealing. To top it all off, he began class introducing himself and the class topics, and Camilla relaxed into the idea that most of the female population would fall in love with him—he was attractive, obviously smart, *and* a nice guy.

Warren leaned in as the professor, Mr. Jenkins, spoke of the main topic of the literature course. "You've got a bit of drool there, babe."

Camilla hadn't realized she'd fallen into the fascination, jumping at his closeness, and immediately sat up and pretended nothing had happened. She also couldn't look at Warren after getting caught.

He laughed silently at the blush that took over her features.

At the end of class, they walked out together, both finished with their courses for the day, and headed to Warren's flat, only about ten minutes away walking.

Camilla basked in this small bit of time alone with him, surrounded by hundreds of people. Cuddled into his arm, she felt as if it were only the two of them, taking a walk and enjoying one another's presence.

The intimacy was broken when they entered the flat to find a few of Warren's flatmates littering the space.

"Little Whittle!" Matty, one of the more boisterous flatmates, called out to Camilla as he stormed over, picking her up in a bear hug.

"Cami!" Dane called from the couch. They were playing video games.

"Hey, Whittle," Knox said from his spot beside Dane, unable to even pull his eyes from the television. Lynus and Leonard weren't there.

Camilla smiled, taking a seat on one of the bean bags they had under the mounted TV as Warren handed her a drink, then sat on Dane's other side.

Matty dropped beside Camilla on the bean bag, taking over the entirety of it, and threw his arm around her. "So, Little Whittle, how was your break?"

Camilla moved to the edge of the bean bag, giving Matty's mountainous body more space, though they were still cuddled up on the small bag, and smiled up at him. "Eventful."

He rolled his eyes. "Tell me about it. My sister decided she wanted us to go to the mountains, and we got snowed in. For days! Twelve of us stuck in that house. We were just lucky we had enough food. But let me tell you, the fights we got into…"

Camilla smiled—Matty could talk a lot.

He was known for it within his group of friends. But she liked to listen, so she settled in and listened to his crazy family vacation story, watching Warren take the controller from Knox when he lost.

Warren was about half way through his game when Camilla's thoughts turned wicked. She couldn't help her attention from continuously dropping to his exposed forearms, the veins popping out and the muscle on full display. He may be lean, but the man was mighty fit.

Fuck, I'd do anything to have those arms around me.

Warren jumped in place, eyes moving around the room and brows furrowing. At her next thought—*What's wrong?*—he jumped again, his eyes settling on her.

Camilla watched as Warren threw his controller to Knox, "Take over," and walked straight to her, pulling her from the bean bag and into his room.

Warren shut the door on Matty's protests, "Hey man, we were talking! You couldn't calm your dick for another fifteen minutes!"

Warren turned his full attention to Camilla. "Do that again."

Camilla looked around the room, then back to Warren, her thoughts running wild trying to figure out what he meant. *What the hell is he talking about? Do what again?*

"That!" Warren exclaimed, pointing to her. "Cam! I can hear you in my head. You're talking to me!"

"What?" Camilla was dumbfounded. What was he talking about?

"You said you'd do anything to have my arms around you." Camilla's blush erupted. "Then I heard you asking what was wrong, Cam!"

Camilla stared at him wide eyed, a smile beginning to grace her lips. "Okay, okay. Let me try!"

I wasn't kidding when I said I'd do anything to have your arms around me.

Warren's eyes darkened as the thought flew into his mind, his smile turning seductive. "It wouldn't take a lot of convincing."

He stepped up to her, lightly tugging at the bottom of her shirt.

"Respond back to me in your head. Let's see if it works both ways."

After a moment, Warren asked, "Anything?"

Camilla's lips dipped. "No. Maybe I have to start it. Hold on." He'd began pulling her shirt up, and she now stood in her bra.

Take your shirt off, she thought and watched his face darken in a smirk as he followed her demands.

As you wish, he responded eliciting a gasp from her.

"I heard you!" she exclaimed. "This is awesome! I have a new power."

Warren enjoyed her excitement as he dropped them to the bed. "It *is* exciting. We should celebrate now."

Well, what are you waiting for? Those arms aren't around me yet.

Vera sat, prepared this time.

She'd taken to the room before their arranged time and stood in the middle. She'd wanted to sit cross legged and allow her body to relax and keep control, but she wasn't sure how well her reflexes would work sitting down, so standing it was. Fight or flight instincts made that far more useful.

And she tried to relax her body and mind, something that was more difficult than she would've expected, given she'd dreamt again of Harry and not being able to have him.

She'd dreamt that all the couples—Hunter and Maya, Warren and Camilla, Felix and Juliette, even Lila and Tamire, and every other couple they'd met—were together at a dinner, and she was going to step up to Harry and finally admit her feelings, when he walked in with another witch on his arm. A witch from another coven, something no one would look down upon. And everyone had laughed as Vera had grown red.

When she'd woken straight up, she was angry and frustrated.

But she had to forget that. There was some ass-kickery that needed to take place.

So, she stood in the middle of the room and imagined Camilla running through dark and dungy halls, trying to find somewhere to hide from the demon after her. She ran past Vera into a room, and all Vera could think about was she had to make sure this demon didn't get to her sister.

Tingling, this time shooting from her fingertips to her neck at lightening speed rather than taking its time up there, and shoot.

She didn't get him. Again.

"Prepared. I like that." He was leaning against the unused fireplace.

"And still, I can't get you."

"Remember what I said last time? You have to make it as reflexive as breathing. My instincts are always on alert when I shadow into a room. It would be stupid not to. You never know what you may shadow into, no matter how safe of a place you think it is."

"Okay." Vera didn't want to play around. She wanted to get right into it. "Let's get started."

He seemed shocked that she didn't delay with conversation, but he'd been right. If demons were all so trained as to be on alert when shadowing about, she would have to be a lot quicker. And without the need to imagine a horrible scenario.

He shadowed out of the room, and the fails began.

Again.

And again.

And again, she failed.

Coupled with her frustration from her dreams, Vera broke the next time Hunter shadowed into the room and she couldn't get him. "You have got to be fucking with me!"

"Anger and frustration are normal. They come with training. You're doing well, better than our first lesson by leaps." He was being kind.

But Vera didn't see that.

All she saw was the demon that had entered her life by stabbing a priest with a staff, then looking up at her with a cruel smirk and a glint of joy in his eyes. Multiple times he'd done things that pushed her family into hating him more, and Vera knew those had been him being tame. For Maya. Which only made her imagine what he was like before Maya came into his life. What despicable things had he been doing before?

"What kind of monster are you?" she seethed through her teeth.

His brows furrowed as he looked her over. "What are you talking about?"

"Before we met. What kind of horrors did you commit and walk on like you hadn't just ruined people's lives?" She was being unreasonable, but the anger in her was building, and she needed to know, if for nothing else, than for Maya's safety.

He stiffened and stared at her. "I was never hurting innocent people."

"Bullshit," she spit his way.

His fists flexed, and he stepped up. "It's too much work to clean up the mess innocent people would make. I only play with the ones that have it coming."

"You played with the priest!"

"He tried to kill me," he reasoned.

"Because you stole from him!"

"No," his anger was well hidden behind his calmness, "because I'm a demon. He would've done it had any demon stepped into the building."

Fine. "You played with those kids!"

He rolled his eyes. "Only to get your attentions. I had no intentions of doing anything. Like I said, too much mess to clean up."

Her stomach rolled at his nonchalance, but fine. "You threatened to take Lila's baby!"

He smirked. "They stole from me. That's not innocent."

This was ridiculous.

"You're playing with Maya! She's innocent."

His gaze blazed, the blacks of his eyes filling with fire. "I'd kill myself before hurting her, Sister." He spit the last word out, like *he* was disgusted with *her*.

"Please," she scoffed. "You don't deserve her."

"I'm well aware." His fists clenched at his sides, turning whiter with each passing moment, but he didn't step any closer to her. People were right. Calm anger was far scarier than raging anger. He looked ready to kill, and a part of Vera—so far in the back of her mind she barely heard it—recognized that he was being truthful, but she couldn't see it any other way.

"So stop ruining her life!"

"If she doesn't want me any longer, she's at power to leave," he spoke through gritted teeth. "She knows she'd still have me at her beck and call no matter."

"She doesn't need you, period. She's got the three of us!"

He narrowed his gaze at her. "Is this what you're truly angry about, or is it that you're in love with your warlock and are too deluded to do anything about it?"

"Harry has nothing to do with this!" Lie. Huge lie. Harry had everything to do with this, because Hunter was right, and this entire argument was because she couldn't have Harry, and she was angry that *he* got Maya.

"I'd beg to differ. You're angry you can't have him, but I've got Maya. That she wants me and isn't afraid to let everyone know it."

"She doesn't know what she wants! She'd blinded by her desire for you!"

Hunter only watched her through blazing eyes when the door opened and two people walked in. Funnily enough, the two—one in particular—that their conversations always seemed to center around. Harry and Maya were home.

"What the hell is going on here?" Maya asked as she looked between the two of them, her brows furrowing as she, no doubt, felt the tension in the room.

"Love," Hunter's entire demeanor seemed to calm as he walked immediately up to her, taking her softly in his arms, "you know I'd do anything for you, but dealing with your sister is getting taken off the board."

Maya furrowed her brows deeper. "How is that *anything?*"

"She doesn't train. She spends the entire session talking."

"About?" Maya didn't seem very convinced of the problem.

It wasn't common for her, but Vera burst. "About him being a lowlife, worthless piece of shit!"

Both Maya and Harry looked shocked by her outbreak.

Okay, so technically, that wasn't *why* she was arguing with him.

Maya looked to Hunter.

"About us. Every session gets turned around on how you're with me. She's not focusing, and I'm done. I was helping for you, love, but she doesn't want it, so I'm not going to waste my time."

Maya gave an imperceptible nod, her face still wrapped in his hands. He touched her so softly, as if she would break. Maya? As if *Maya* would break. Please.

Her gaze shot to Vera, and she breathed out. She looked disappointed. In her?

Maya took his hand, and they left before Vera could question it, but her sister was definitely disappointed in her over this. That was insane. She was the one with a psychopath for a boyfriend.

Harry didn't say anything to her, and Hunter's remark from their earlier sessions came back—*you hold the power...he'll be at your beck and call.* Harry wouldn't say anything. Hunter was right. He'd be on her side, but the disappointment was there.

Disappointment.

In her.

27

Camilla returned home to find her family exactly where she expected—the kitchen.

She walked in to find Vera at the island flipping through the Book, likely trying to do what they'd been trying all month: find whatever it was The Eight were after.

It didn't look like she was getting any further, and Camilla had a feeling that the Book wasn't going to be of too much help anyway.

While she looked, Maya and Harry stood at the island, baking—or more likely attempting to bake—some of Vera's perfect cookies. The cookies were perfect, but somehow, only when Vera made them.

They all looked to her with smiles, greeting her and asking about her first day back to classes.

My first day was great. I have a hot professor, she threw the message to them.

Then watched as all three jumped and looked around, trying to figure out if she'd said that aloud or if they truly had heard it in their heads. This was definitely a more entertaining power than the reading minds one. At least with this one, she didn't have to be touching.

As all three gazes landed back on her, watching her mouth, Camilla sent another message. *It works both ways. You can respond to me through your thoughts.*

They gasped as the thoughts reached their minds. Maya was the first to recover—which somehow didn't shock Camilla—by responding, *Can I put down money on how you found out?*

Camilla rolled her eyes and responded, *No*, as another thought reached her.

This is incredible, Camilla, Harry said, and Camilla's smile brightened. For some reason, Camilla took pride in Harry's proud looks and loved receiving them.

Wow, Cam. This is so cool, Vera thought to her almost a second later.

Camilla tried to organize her thoughts, sending a *Thank you* to Harry and a *I know, right?* to Vera. Okay, organizing thoughts when speaking to multiple people was difficult. Really difficult. Her head hurt.

Maybe stick to one person at a time for now.

Maya's thought came back to her just as Harry began to speak, "Well, this is amazing. And a power that can help the three of you immensely, especially if no one else knows of it." *Your bits were screaming out for Warren, weren't they?*

Camilla's sharp gaze met Maya's gleaming ones. Her smirk said she knew she was right, and so Camilla didn't respond, instead turning to Harry. "It is amazing, isn't it? And Warren knows too, but he won't tell anyone."

Maya snickered at the mention of Warren's knowledge as she placed their tray of attempted cookies into the oven to bake, and Camilla asked, "Why are the two of you baking and not the baker herself?"

Maya side-eyed Vera. "Because the baker wanted to look through the Book."

Vera was back to flipping through the tome, glancing at Camilla. "You said a spell just appeared?"

Camilla nodded, but said nothing else as Vera's eyes glazed over. If Vera was thinking and not spewing her thoughts aloud, it meant she already had an idea, and she didn't need to think it out. "What is it?"

Vera looked to her with a small smile, knowing her family had caught on rather quickly to her thought process. "I think that's what we're missing. Or what they're missing, a spell. Something that's hidden, so even if we look through this a million times, it won't come out without the proper encouragement."

"You believe they require a spell from the Book?" Harry asked.

Vera nodded and looked to all three before continuing on, "I think that's why they skimmed our minds. I couldn't hear anything, so they weren't trying to hear secrets or hear a spell be used, maybe that halfies power doesn't work like that. I don't know. They were trying to look through the Book and find the spell they needed. And the fact that they are after us, specifically, makes me believe this Book is the only one with that certain spell. Also why Colette was trying to get into the house and wanted to be left alone in the bath, so she could shadow up to the attic and look through it. I have a feeling, knowing about the relationships her brothers had with us, she wouldn't have risked it if it wasn't important to get to this Book specifically."

Camilla was the first to break the silence that followed. "Then we should stop looking for it." She didn't elaborate, knowing her family knew how badly she wanted to enjoy a bit of normalcy, especially with school having started back up again.

Vera sighed. "We don't know how long that'll help."

She was right, but Camilla needed this. Knew it was selfish to want her normal life back, but wanted it all the same. Plus, not helping out The Eight in their crazy endeavors was fine by her.

———

The next day, Harry found himself on a visit to his old friend again.

With all the visits he'd been doing recently to 'old friends,' it was nice to be back to Rupert. Nice to be back to one of his own old friends rather than one of Bishop's.

Rupert was on a walk along the fields when Harry ported in just a few yards away. Though it was a spontaneous visit, Rupert didn't jump at the intrusion, just looked to him and smiled as if he knew Harry would be coming for a visit that day.

"Were you expecting me, old man?" Harry teased, falling into step beside him.

"I haven't the faintest clue what you're on about." Rupert smiled back.

Harry grinned with a hint of the fact that he didn't believe a word that left the man's lips, then turned to the matter at hand. "I will be back to beat you at a game of chess when this mess is over, but until then, I need your help."

Rupert's knowing eyes looked to him, urging him to continue. Harry repeated the same condensed version of the story of the Grandmama that Maya had mentioned when showing them the storybook then asked, "Have you heard anything of it? A spell, perhaps, that would be used in conjunction?"

Rupert stared out at the fields surrounding them as they walked and shook his head. "No." Harry was close to slumping in defeat when Rupert carried on, "It does remind me though of a story my mother used to tell me. And it sounds to me that it is a prequel to your *Grandmama Told Me*."

There was a boy, unbeknownst to most by name, who lived in a world of magic, yet held nothing of his own. He worked alongside the others left powerless—the humans, they were called—and watched daily the power that the magic doers possessed.

And he wanted it, some of it, at least.

He wanted, almost needed, to possess magic. To hold power in his grasp.

So the little boy did what he thought would get him some magic— he apprenticed the magical beings. From the ages of seven to nineteen, he worked tirelessly in smithies and cobblers and bakers, anywhere that would take him. And in each apprenticeship, he stole a little bit of magic for himself.

He would go to the broken shed that he'd called home and practice with the little magic he'd taken. It was a time where faerie dust and mermaid's water and gargoyle's sweat and all the likes gave a bit of magic to anyone who possessed the ability to hold it.

His second apprenticeship, at the age of nine, he'd worked at a bookstore and there, he'd found a spell book that he believed would help solve his problems, so he'd taken it, like he'd take the small bits of magic before. A week later, he'd been let go to find another apprentice- ship. So he moved as such, trying his luck with any and all the magic he could get his hands on, finding faerie dust worked the best.

And so, from the ages of nineteen to twenty-three, he dedicated his life to finding a way around the faerie dust. He'd been working at a smithy since he was sixteen and knew that was the best course for him. Had made sure not to mess up, to be the best help the shop had ever had so he could have unlimited access to their stores. And so, for years, he stole a little extra power, storing most of it away. He was an orphaned human in a world of magic. Finding a wife was more diffi- cult to him than any other, so he decided he would create his wife. One just for him.

And so came wife made of faerie dust, but human all the same. She was perfectly human in all aspects but one. She needed faerie dust for long distances and large bursts of exertion. The little boy, now a grown man, found no problem with this, having secured his job with the faeries at the smithy. And so the years passed, and his wife bore him seven children, all just as human as he, and they lived in a cabin at the edge of the woods at the edge of town.

The two aged together and watched their children grow and the world around them change—there were more humans. No longer burdened by the shame of not holding magic, they were gaining in power, not magic, but force. And so the man's family grew as one child's marriage led to grandchildren, followed by yet another and another. Until finally, all seven children were married and bringing their own children into the world.

On the day the last grandchild, number thirty-two, was born, the man, now old in age, felt the last breaths begin to take him. And so on that day, he spent his time with his family—his wife, seven children, and thirty-two grandchildren—holding the newest addition in his arms as he sat beside his wife, proud at the life they'd created.

The man prepared for bed that night, telling his wife he would no longer be there to care for her, and that night, wrapped in the arms of his most prized possession, the man fell asleep and never woke again.

The woman, now known to all as Grandmama, grew morose at the loss of her husband, and so she moved, leaving their cabin at the edge of the woods to her eldest daughter, and moved to the cabin at the top of the mountain. There, she found happiness in the solitude and the talks she would have with her husband, whose voice was carried through the winds.

She never left that cabin, for lack of replenishment of her faerie dust, but waited every year for her family to go see her.

28

"You think whatever this is is trying to create a wife?" Maya asked in astonishment at Harry's newest hypothesis as they sat at the table in the kitchen, each clutching a mug of tea.

"No," Harry responded. "I believe whatever comes out of this spell The Eight are looking for will come out an old grandmother because that is the story they are taking from. In the second story, she is only a grandmother, nothing more, but I think we're dealing with something greater than just halfies."

"You believe something else is behind them, like something else was behind the creation of the original Grandmama?" Vera asked.

"I believe so," Harry responded.

"So why create her at all?" Camilla asked.

"That is the part I cannot think of. I do not see how the Grandmama will help their cause, whatever it may be," Harry said.

Vera thought aloud, "Maybe it's about taking power back, the same concept as the prequel, but backwards. If the man created his woman, and the world eventually turned to the humans, maybe the halfies are bringing back Grandmama to turn the power on them."

Their little conversation was broken by screams shattering through their walls. They all jumped, Maya spilling her tea on her hands, thankful her fire power didn't allow her to feel much of the burn.

Loud as the sound was, she'd be surprised if the entire neighborhood wasn't running out to find out what had happened. But no, nothing. When they stepped out, it was clear the sound was coming from a house down their small street.

But no one else had stepped out of their house.

Was this something only they could hear? If so, it had to be magical.

Maya grabbed for Harry as her sisters did the same, using their combined magic to establish a strong hold on the house. If this was a tactic for getting them out, the house would not be left vulnerable. No one would be allowed in, not even the Delvaux boys until they returned.

The sound came from the Featherloo family, a perfectly normal human family.

But this perfectly normal human family was being attacked by an animal demon that looked like the manifestation of darkness in blob form hunched over them. And it looked all too pleased to see the Whittles standing before it now.

So that was a ploy to get them out of the house.

With their added protection to the spells on the house, not a single worry passed Maya's thoughts. It was how they kept others out while all four were gone for the day, a spell on the house that was like those of old vampire lore. Without permission, you could not go about your day within.

But that still left room for the normal demon attack, and apparently this demon did not care for the Delvaux rule that they were to be left alone. Or the incentive it was given was far better than the fear of the Delvauxs.

Harry moved immediately for the humans—two parents and three children cowering and huddled together—and got them to focus on him as he began looking for wounds to heal.

Maya turned her attentions on the blob hovering before them. It didn't have legs or limbs in general, just one oval of a monster. She threw out a burst of fire, which, shockingly, this demon flew toward. With another burst of fire, the demon's eyes gleamed—he was not afraid of fire. In fact, he seemed to love it.

Its fire affinity would not be helpful. Nor would the fact that it was excessively bright in the room. How did the Featherloos live like that?

The demon shot out a bolt of black gush, and Maya came out of her thoughts just in time to jump out of the way, unsure what it was, but not taking the risk of allowing it to touch her.

It was fast too, getting out of the way of Vera's attempt to throw it around or hold it down, and rushing toward Maya's fire. Even when Maya attempted to throw a bolt of flames within Vera's reach so Vera could use her levitation to immobilize the demon, Vera wasn't getting it. Maya breathed out her frustration. Vera definitely needed those lessons with Hunter.

She turned her focus back to the room, and the too much light within it, as her sisters distracted the demon, allowing it to throw the black gush in their direction and jumping out of the way before it touched them.

Animal demons hated light, unlike their creature demon counterparts, who were more like witches and were fine with it to different extents.

Yet, this animal demon seemed to prefer it. Seemed to want to seep out any and all darkness from the room. It was an odd hypothesis, but Maya had to be sure. While her sisters jumped out from yet another black gush, Vera still missing her aims,

Maya moved to a lamp holding the most light and knocked it over. She watched the demon react to the dimming room as Vera finally got a good use of her power, throwing the demon across the room while it was busy fighting off Camilla's kicks—she didn't have an active power, but she had a powerful kick.

The demon had a distaste for the dimmer room. It shrunk back, something Maya wouldn't have attributed to the light had she not been paying attention. But she'd been right; this demon preferred light. Which just meant she needed to make it dark in this room.

Before she could move a muscle to shut off the rest of the lights, allowing only the moonlight to seep through the windows, the entire room plunged into darkness.

Like the thought of wanting darkness had brought it on.

She felt everyone's presence in the room but could not see a single one of them. Like the darkness had completely wiped out any sort of light. But she knew they'd all stopped moving, even the demon. Could feel it.

And though this put the demon at a disadvantage, considering Maya had a feeling it would be shrinking away from this much darkness, it also put them at a disadvantage—they needed light to see and fight the monster.

She needed a bit of light.

And with that thought, the room opened to some light, only enough for her to see around the room, like the squint that your eyes take when walking down a corridor at three in the morning.

The demon seemed just as perplexed at the sudden change. And luckily distracted by it, so Vera could take the opportunity to hold it against the wall. Good thing Vera hadn't been too distracted by the sudden darkness to drop her power.

Maya let out the breath she hadn't realized she'd been holding. Finally.

They walked over to it together, casting the vanquishing

spell used for this particular group of animal demons—blobs in the air. It was amazing how many varieties of animal demons there were, not to mention the variety within those subgroups as well. She couldn't fathom a life without the notes app on her phone.

And just like that, the demon was gone.

And the light was back.

They gathered together and waited as Harry wiped the memories of the family and ported them out before the Featherloos could begin to focus on what was before them. The poor lot would remember nothing, but see their place in shambles and themselves lying on the ground, perfectly unhurt.

Back in their house, Maya felt the extra hold on the house drop as they each slumped into opposite ends of the couches. Maya's mind was running at the new discovery she believed she'd found as Camilla spoke up, "What. Was. That?"

Somehow, Maya knew she was asking about the sudden plunge into darkness rather than the animal demon they had been dealing with.

"I think it was me," Maya said, coming out of her thoughts. "I thought about the need for darkness, and it came. Then I thought about the need for a little light, and it came."

"Another dark power. Low-level, this one," Harry breathed out as he stared at her.

And to her surprise, the others reacted calmly to the mention of yet another dark power on her part, low-level as this may be. Maybe they were now accustomed to the fact that she just happened to be a bearer of dark powers.

"Well, I guess that makes two powers for each of us," Vera claimed.

"Technically," Camilla rebuffed, "Maya has three."

"Technically," Maya countered, "Maya has two, since the portal one seems to have vanished." Maya was annoyed with the reminder of the power that came to her at the Bridgers coven last November and refused to come again.

She'd tried for weeks to open the portal again but couldn't get it. Hunter had helped, giving her vile demons to send down. His theory held that she needed to be angry enough with the person to do it, so he would place the prisoner he held in his father's dungeons before her and tell her all the horrid things they'd done, but to no avail. Her power did not return. Instead, she held the vile things those creatures had done in her head.

"Try it again," Harry insisted, bringing Maya's thoughts back to the conversation at hand.

Maya took a breath and thought about needing the room to darken, and just like that, it was entirely black before them. It was a very sudden change, too sudden of a change. She needed to work on that.

She thought of lightening the room, and again, way too sudden of a change. This one was worse, the light bleeding into her eyes.

Rubbing out their eyes, they focused back on the light in the room, Vera analyzing her. "In theory, this power should be helpful, but how helpful will it be if we're all plunged into darkness in an attack?"

Maya mimicked her sister, then said with a smile, "I'll learn it. With control, I'm sure I'd be able to dictate how dark I want it and where I want the darkness."

They all smiled at her insistence, and Harry spoke, "This is to stay between us. No need in anyone else learning of your new powers. Even better if they are unprepared. Your primary powers are known, as can be expected, but no others need to be known."

Plus, they didn't know how strong this power would be. The thing with primary powers was once you trained, you'd have total control. Non-primary powers didn't work that way. You may or may not have total control. Like Vera's demon control.

She had no control over it and could only sense it to the extent of a full demon being around, whereas Camilla's telepathy seemed to fully be based on her control.

No one knew of Vera's demon-sensing ability—except the Delvaux brothers—and now they would add Camilla's telepathy and Maya's darkness control to the list.

29

The youngest sister began her night with a quick shower before finding herself seated at her vanity, drying her hair. She listened to the loud ring of the hair dryer as it stole the moisture from her locks, trying to clear her mind of all thoughts.

It was a source of relaxation, to have her mind cleared and not constantly overthinking about possibilities. Like the possibility that Maya remained with Hunter.

Fuck. No, Camilla, clear thoughts.

Too late.

She knew it wasn't Maya's fault, knew she couldn't control the powers she got, but the clear preference her sister had for the dark side was too evident. Patched onto that, her desire to keep Hunter.

Camilla shook her head and listened again to the sound of the hair dryer.

Twelve. She managed to keep her thoughts at bay twelve seconds. Still something.

She sighed as the eldest Delvaux came into mind, moving the dryer to the opposite hand.

Hunter Delvaux, the half-brother to the man she loved and fuck buddy to her most beloved sister. She didn't like that. His relationship with Warren was uncontrollable, but she wanted to fight for Maya. Eventually, her sister would see the horridness that Hunter brought to this world. The amount of pain he brought to people. She had to remember that the man had burned a child alive and snapped some random kid's neck. No matter that the child came out unharmed, and the dead kid wasn't exactly a saint. Hunter was a monster.

Camilla breathed again, calming her thoughts back to nothing so she didn't work herself up.

Nine. Nine seconds this time.

But this time, it was another Delvaux who popped into her mind.

Warren brought the devil on her shoulder, calling her a hypocrite for her constant jibes at demons. She knew it was unfair to constantly use the 'he's a demon' attack against Hunter when Warren was also part demon, but she couldn't help the way it always rushed out of her. She had to change that.

She wasn't opposed to Maya being in a relationship with a demon, just this particular demon.

She wasn't.

Demons weren't all bad.

Remember that, Cam.

And to be fair, Camilla knew she was in love with her demon, while Maya claimed to just be fucking hers.

Claimed, main problem. Camilla wasn't too convinced by the claim.

But her demon was kind and loving and cared for others and was all around worthy. Maya's was domineering and greedy and used people for his own gain and was overall worthless. Warren cared for the world to remain in peace. Hunter evoked havoc just to gain more control and power. Her accusations were valid!

She shut off the hair dryer, placing it on the vanity as she brushed out her hair. Ridding her mangled thoughts on demons, she turned to safer ones: Vera and the blush that seemed to never escape when Harry was around. Even now, when it seemed there was a problem between them. Was Harry angry with her? No one had mentioned anything to Camilla, but she swore she saw some disappointed looks aimed Vera's way. But that was unfathomable, especially coming from Harry.

Camilla smiled to herself in the mirror. She was definitely imaging the looks. But she wasn't imaging one major fact: her big sister definitely had a crush, and if Camilla wasn't mistaken, it wasn't unrequited.

The middle sister began her night with a bath. She was the sister who spent the most time in the bathroom, usually for her love of long, steaming baths. With her speaker on the counter playing music to lull her to relaxation—some alternative—she leaned back.

In her state of relaxation, she allowed her head to fall back and her eyes to shut and think of her sisters. Vera had seemed to be coming around to Hunter, small as it may have been, but she'd lost that advantage again. Whatever had caused her outburst against the demon, Maya didn't know how to fix it. Vera needed Hunter's help to get better with her powers, but her hostilities were keeping her back. Not to mention, Camilla was obviously on Vera's side. Luckily, Maya had Harry on her side.

Camilla though. She was too stubborn to let her hatred of Hunter go, and it was causing a problem between them. Small as it may be, it was a problem Maya wanted to fix. But she was not willing to give Hunter up for it.

Thinking of the devil.

Maya's eyes shot open, her head snapping up to attention as his voice broke the monotony of music in the small room. "Like a feast laid out for me to ravish."

Funnily enough, given she was just thinking about bringing her sisters around to Hunter, she was not pleased to see him—though her body never seemed to be aware of that decision.

He sat perched atop the toilet, elbows relaxed on his knees as he watched her. He wore a black set of t-shirt and jeans, but nothing else, not even shoes. She narrowed her eyes at him. "Go away."

He smirked but didn't move. "Still mad, love?"

Maya turned her attention away, trying to get back to the relaxed state she'd just been in.

Hunter laughed. "Love, it was only two days. Well, it was only supposed to be, before you cut it short."

Maya snapped her neck toward him, annoyance and anger running her eyes black. "We had an agreement."

"No," the asshole laughed. "You told me I wasn't to do any more business trips. I never agreed."

Her eyes narrowed, refusing to respond, before turning again to face the wall before her.

Hunter dropped his head to his hands and laughed before looking back to her. She hadn't moved. Her annoyance growing as she saw him from her periphery.

He stood and walked toward her. "I'll make you the promise now. I won't do any more business trips unless you give me permission first." He crouched beside her by the tub and watched her with a shit-eating grin plastered on his face. "How about that?"

She didn't want to give him any attention, but her gaze was losing the battle. She remained stoic, but her eyes moved to the side to meet his. He laughed at her determination to ignore him.

He stood and did exactly what she hadn't been expecting and got into the tub fully clothed. Placing his arms on either side of her shoulders and kneeling between her legs, he seemed to enjoy the gasp that escaped her lips, and leaned in close, so their faces were only a couple of inches apart. "Do we have a deal?"

Maya's tongue jumped out to lick her lips in anticipation, her gaze moving from his lips to his eyes. She bit her lip, her arms rising from the water to grip his shirt and pull him even closer. He kept his hold on the edges of the tub so he didn't crush her, but allowed her to pull, knowing he'd won this time. Asshole.

"Deal," she whispered against his lips, then crushed them with hers.

The eldest sister began her night with a shower. She'd gotten in after Camilla and intended to stay a while, loving the pounding of the water on her skin.

Her thoughts drifted to their most recent events and the discovery of these new powers, the combination of the powers of the three of them. It was incredible.

And she tried to keep her thoughts there. Safe. But it took almost no time for her mind to push her sisters out of the way and bring Harry into the spotlight, her thoughts revolving around him more and more as the days passed. And even though she knew he was still disappointed—rightfully so, she hated to admit—in her for the fight with Hunter, her mind chose a recent dream she'd had about Harry to focus on, and there she stood under the pounding water, re-experiencing that dream all over again.

It had started innocently enough—Harry coming to listen to her play in the piano room—but it had ended with her ass playing the melodies as he pounded into her. Way too inappropriate for her relationship with Harry. He was their warlock. That was it!

She forced herself out of the shower and into baggy sweats and an oversized shirt. It was one of her father's favorite ones from when she was a teenager and had been hers for years. And with him gone now, it made her feel safe to wear it, to have him around in even the smallest way.

She walked into her room, the room that had been her mother's—technically both of her parents' before they separated—and wrapped herself into the duvet. The framed photo of her parents holding her in front of this house sat on her nightstand and stared at her as she lay there.

Yup, any dirty thoughts about Harry were gone.

And on the framed photo was the necklace that her father had always worn, a dog tag with words written on it, a foreign language that Vera hadn't been able to translate. But he had always worn it. Always.

She reached out to grab it and brought it close, running her thumb over the tag. She missed him, more than she dared imagine. And she wanted him back as much as Camilla and Maya wanted Loretta back.

She wished to have met her mother, but knowing her father was the best gift she'd ever known. She wouldn't have traded it for the world. And she wanted him back. Especially with his unexpected passing, the pain of losing him stabbed as deep as it had the day she'd found out.

"Hey, Dad," she whispered as her eyes began to water. She stared at the dog tag and the inscription of the four words on it. "I miss you, every day. I wish you were here. I wish you could know Harry." She scoffed. "You probably know him already, don't you?"

She fell to her back and looked up to the ceiling as she brought the necklace to her heart. "You were a warlock and Mom was a witch, so I'm guessing you wouldn't mind, but then again, you weren't Mom's warlock. Your relationship wasn't looked down upon, not like Lila and Tamire's is, not like mine would be."

She closed her eyes for minutes before opening them again. "Does it matter that Tamire only knew Lila the first few years of her life, then again as an adult? Does it matter that Harry would have only known me for a couple of years, if that, before meeting again as an adult? Does any of that matter?"

A single tear slid down her cheek and nothing more. Just the single tear for what she could never have with Harry.

"I want him. I…I think I love him," she whispered, so lightly she barely heard it.

She turned to look at the picture of her family. He would have been around her age in the picture—by looks. Realistically, he was older than Harry—and he looked so happy and in love with her mother, with his little family.

"What do I do, Dad? I have these new sisters, and I *really* hope they're yours too. I kinda think they are. Sometimes, I look at Maya and see a bit of you. Not Camilla, though. She's all Mom." A small smile inched up her face. "But I always hope they're yours. You would've loved them. They would've adored you."

Vera held the dog tags tighter in her hands as she thought about her two little sisters. "I think you would've liked Warren too. He's a really sweet kid and so good to Camilla. The poor kid is still under his family's hold though, but he's trying, and he loves her. Loves Camilla more than I could imagine. He's a real good kid, Dad. You'd like him."

Warren was a good guy, a really good guy, and part of Vera worried Camilla's constant jibes against demons would ruin what she had going with him. He always acted as if it didn't bother him, but she couldn't fathom how often he'd have to continue hearing from the woman he loved that she didn't like half of what he was before it was too much.

"And Maya, she's a fiery one, and not just because of her

power. And of course, she fell for Hunter. Not that she'll admit it, at least not verbally. I don't know about him. My instinct is to say you wouldn't like him, but that's because we don't like him. I don't know. You might turn it around because you could see how much he cares for her, and that's all that matters. And maybe you're right. Maybe we are being too hard, because if nothing else, he proves time and again that Maya is the only person he cares about." She stared at Bishop Whittle in the picture. "Would you have liked him, Dad?"

She closed her eyes and released a breath before opening them once more. "I know, I know, Maya and Harry are right to be disappointed in me. I'll apologize to her, but I just can't help it. When Hunter's around, all I can think about is how did Maya fall for him? Maya! Miss Logical, Non-Emotional!" She scoffed again, knowing what her father would say to her. "But he cares for her. He's soft for her in a way he would never be for anyone else. And he was right. Maya has the control in their relationship, and she wants him. Maybe she needs him in her life as much as I need Harry? I don't know, and I know what you would say. Camilla is already being hard enough on them, so I'll try to give it a break."

She stared at his picture a long time.

Then brought the dog tag to her lips and kissed it lightly. "I love you, Pops."

She lightly hung the necklace on the framed photo and hugged herself into the duvet, closing her eyes for sleep.

30

Maya was up before her family the next morning —nothing unusual—and off to the cemetery for a talk with her Mom. It was much needed.

She used to come every other week and just lie back on the grass and talk to the headstone. Maya wasn't into the whole spiritual thing, but it felt nice talking to her, even if she couldn't say anything back.

Ever since they'd found out about becoming witches, and the supernatural world that came with that, Maya hadn't had the opportunity to come by alone again. Her sisters had always wanted to tag along, and as much as she loved them, Maya needed this time alone.

Especially considering she had some complaining to do regarding them.

She smiled at the thought as she lay tulips by the grave, then sat on the dewy grass beside it, leaning her back into the head-stone. Another reason she liked coming alone, Camilla would've reprimanded her for leaning against the headstone.

She tilted her head back and stared out at the clouds.

It was a while before she said anything, taking solace in

watching the birds fly overhead in the early morning air. "You think it's kinda messed up that we come to your grave all the time, but Camilla and I have never been to Bishop's?" She closed her eyes and let the crisp air flow around her. "I mean, technically he's buried a few towns away, and we don't know if he's actually our father, but still, we should visit his grave too. If he was as great as Vera says, he deserves that much."

She hadn't come to talk about Bishop, but now that the thought had entered her mind, she'd make it a priority for them to go to his grave. Maybe then Vera would be the one doing most of the talking.

"We're all good. Camilla's a brat, like always, but I already know what you're gonna say. She's young and making her way through life. I know." She opened her eyes to look out to the clouds again. "And Vera's fitting right into our little family. She may have Bishop's looks, but she's a lot like you, plays better though. It's beautiful, when she goes to the piano room. It reminds me of when you used to spend hours in there. The longing melodies are similar too."

Maya breathed out. "You were longing for Bishop, weren't you? The way Vera longs for Harry right now. I always wondered what that was about, but wow, look at history repeating itself. Hopefully, one of them will finally break and put them out of their misery. Vera and Harry would be great together, and we already know you guys liked him." She smiled. "Unless he's lying about that.

"But we're all good, Vera's become as much a part of the family in these short months, as if she'd grown up with us. I honestly see more between her and Camilla, sometimes more than me and Cam."

A bird landed on a headstone a few paces from where she sat, and Maya looked at it. It was beautiful and all black. A crow, most likely, though Maya wasn't too sure. Could be a raven. She didn't really know the difference.

She scoffed but didn't take her eyes off the bird, the black of its feather captivating. "I thought she was coming around to Hunter, but maybe she's more like Cam in that department than I had originally thought. I don't know. Hunter tells me it's her sexual frustration that has her pissed at him—that he can have me, and she can't have Harry. Said he refuses to be her punching bag just because she's too much of a wimp to do anything about it."

She pulled at a couple pieces of grass. "Demon mentality. He doesn't understand why they back away from what they want, but I get where they're coming from. They're scared about what others would think. I was too when I first saw Hunter, and boy, was I right." Her laugh wasn't real. "I get it, the frustration, but what I don't get is why it's thrown at us. He's a demon, I get that, but he's been nothing but good to us."

She looked back up at the bird. "What do I do, Mom? I think Harry's on my side. I think he sees that Hunter's with me, and he's coming around to the idea, but Cam and Vera don't like it, and fuck, they're not shy about letting me know. But I can't leave him. I can't. If I leave him, I'll be the one playing those longing melodies, except we all know I can't play."

Her head rested back on the stone again, eyes closing in the chill of the air. "What do I do? I love him." She felt the breath leave her at the admission. "I've never said that before. I don't think I'd ever let myself think too much about my feelings for him, and when I started getting this, this desire to protect him, to have him by my side at all times, I was so confused because I'd never felt that before. But I'd also never been in love before. And especially not with a demon. And he loves me too, I can tell, but if I didn't even consciously know it until now, he's definitely clueless to the feeling. But I don't care about hearing it. I just want to be able to have him and the family and not play referee every time."

The bird cawed. The sound against the morning breeze and

light chirps from far off brought tranquility to Maya's jumbled thoughts.

Her voice was low, almost inaudible as she spoke to her mother. "You know, I always try to imagine how you would react to him. I always think you'll react favorably. You think I'm being naive?"

And part of her swore she heard a *no* in the air.

"I just remember how you never judged, how you sat back and listened to all sides and gave your best, unbiased decision, and I think you would do the same here. Even without hearing my feelings, I think you'd be able to see it. I think Vera and Cam and Harry all see it. I don't know how they wouldn't. Everything he does is to make me happy, to protect me."

The bird cawed again, and she laughed. "Okay, maybe not everything, but he's a demon. Some things he just does because he genuinely doesn't see a problem with it. But if I told him to stop, he would. If I told him to put his life on the line, he would. I know he would. And I know you'd see how I react to being around him. I just...I think you would like him, if only because of what he means to me." She shrugged, her hair lightly flowing in the breeze. "Or maybe I just want you to like him because you're my mom, and I want your approval. But I don't have it, can't have it, and the only family I can get it from refuses to consider what is so plainly before them."

The bird cawed a final time, and Maya heard the wings as it flew away.

She opened her eyes and let her head tilt so she could see the stone she leaned up against. "What do I do, Mom?"

31

They'd frozen after hearing her mother's name.

"Ah, yes, I see the Whittle resemblance, dear Maya," Zathrian eyed her with a different curiosity now. And a sort of recognition that Maya couldn't place.

This time, when he glanced between her and Hunter, there was more intrigue in it. Maya had been curious what exactly that look had meant, but this was an opportunity to learn what Canada had to do with her mother, so she had let it slide.

"You know her?" she asked.

"Yes, of course. I know both your parents." Zathrian leaned into his counter, reading her every reaction.

Both her parents? He assumed Bishop was her father? Or was he speaking of someone else?

"So you saw her? Talked to her? Would know what she was here for?" Maya's heart skipped with the possibility.

Zathrian shrugged. "I always know when they come around."

Acacia smiled warmly. "Yes, they are the best of guests."

"They?" Maya asked.

"Bishop and Lore, of course." Acacia furrowed her brows at the question.

A light flush touched Maya's cheeks, Hunter's hand pressing into her lower back to remind her he was there. "We never got to check he was my father."

"He is." Zathrian winked at her.

Maya watched them and waited. And waited. And finally gave in. "So, why were they here?"

"They came here every time they needed a break from you kids, needed to be together while you lived apart." Acacia smiled suggestively. "But lately, it's seems they're more cautious about not being found, like they're running from something."

"What do you mean?" Maya asked.

She shrugged. "You know, they spell their cabin, don't mention as much 'for our safety.' They've had the cabin paid in full for some time, so they come in and out as they please."

"It's quite annoying, you know," Zathrian jumped in. "Are you like that too, little Maya? Keep things hidden for others' safety?"

Technically no. She kept things hidden for her own sanity.

"Rest assured," Zathrian continued, "we've offered our help time and again, and they take it, too, when they can afford to, not that they like it."

Hunter stood frozen, too straight backed, and watched his friends. "Zathrian, why do you keep speaking in the present tense?"

There was a twinkle in Zathrian's eyes like he was waiting for them to catch onto something. "Whatever could you mean?"

What was he talking about?

"Bishop and Loretta have been dead for years. Why keep referring to them in the present tense?"

Just then, the door opened and a black bird flew in, landing on a shelf to the side of the counter Zathrian was leaning toward. This probably had to do with Zathrian's power. She'd have to ask Hunter later what gifts the well-respected demon had.

It was beautiful and looked to her like it knew her.

Maya had to pull her attention from it—difficult as it was, since she had the sudden desire to continue watching it, almost like it was hypnotizing her to remember it—and looked back to Zathrian and Acacia, the demon and witch couple.

The demon and witch couple that were apparently friends with her mom—and dad?—and her man.

Zathrian's smirk was knowing, his eyes glittering. "Whoever said they were dead?"

***

Vera and Maya made up.

And Hunter was still refusing to continue training Vera, not that she was complaining. Maya continued to exasperate at the lot of the people in her life. She couldn't seem to do anything to keep everyone happy.

Though her family drama could be entertaining, Camilla put her full attention to school and her relationship with Warren, going out on dates and hanging out with his flatmates any chance she got. Anything to force some humanity back into her life. Funny, she was running to human life, and Celine—the human—was running away from it.

Maya had been able to get some drawings done while Vera got some more freelance baking work for little parties and get togethers. That was about as much of the normal human life they'd clung to; everything else in their lives had remained in the supernatural.

Well, Camilla couldn't do that, wouldn't do it. She wanted to hold on to the life she'd had before.

Though their lives still revolved around what was happening with The Eight, and Maya had brought their mother's death back to attention, it had been a relatively calm week. So much so that Harry had taken the opportunity to visit an old friend he hadn't seen in a long while. He'd known it would be a risk to leave them, since they wouldn't be able to reach him while he was away, but their insistence that they'd be fine had finally worn him down.

He deserved some of his old life back too. Camilla couldn't be the only one allowed to take it.

He'd been gone a few days, and Camilla could tell that Vera missed him every single moment of it. Even if seeing him brought on the disappointed looks, which Camilla assumed would be gone now that Maya had 'forgiven' her. When she wasn't baking or going through the Book and theories about The Eight, she spent most of her time in the piano room. Maya and Camilla had come to referring to the room as *their* room.

Though they each kept individually busy, Maya had made it a point to train their powers often, like a mother reminding her children to do their homework every night. So, they stood in the room opposite the living room, a space that had been mostly empty, save for some rugs and decorations along the sides, and the beautiful fireplace that mirrored the one exactly like it across the house in the living room. The room that Vera and Hunter had used when he was training her.

They'd played a game of powers, each throwing about and practicing their power and ways to block it. It was quite entertaining.

As they laughed at Vera's poor attempt at running from the fire Maya threw her way, their door clashed open, and Colette walked in like she owned the place.

Welp, they'd have to figure out how she just strolled in. The house should've protected against it.

Or maybe it was because she'd been in the house before. Damn, they should've thought to fix the spell around the house before that had happened.

Colette sent bolts of electricity flying their way in record time. This had been what Hunter had warned them about. A demon wouldn't just stand around and wait for you to be ready. They'd simply attack.

But electricity.

Warren had mentioned that was her power. She'd have to talk to him about their powers and what constituted the level of each of their powers. His was a medium-level power, but melting seemed a long way from fire or electricity.

They had just enough time to duck and bounce back up as Colette commented, "We're tired of waiting, witches."

The electricity that jumped around on her arms looked all too ready to come for them. It was mesmerizing in a way it shouldn't be. Camilla wanted to react, but the bolts that shot around Colette's arms held her attention.

Then another bolt came their way, and Camilla snapped right out of it.

And they were in total darkness.

It was a great tactic to stun the enemy into pausing, if only a moment, but it would do nothing to someone with the power of electricity.

And the bolt still made its impact, hitting the wall behind them, just beside the beautiful fireplace, throwing pieces of plaster to the ground.

Vera threw the halfie against the banister of the stairs as Colette's hand shot out a burst of electricity in Camilla's direction. She had just enough time to jump out of the way and fall to the ground, no active powers to lean on. Instead, she pulled out her phone and dialed for Warren.

No answer.

With the darkness reaped back—no use in wasting the energy for it if it didn't help—Maya shot Colette with a bolt of fire, singeing the end of her shirt. But the halfie moved fast. Apparently, with halfie demons, it was a guessing game on whether or not they would be able to shadow, and Colette had taken the short straw.

Probably another reason she hated Warren. He was also a halfie, but he could shadow.

Camilla tried again as Vera threw her arm out, redirecting the bolt of electricity back to its holder. Now that was a cool trick.

Though the electricity wouldn't do anything to Colette, it would still be away from them.

When Warren didn't answer the next call, Camilla tried again.

Fuck, perfect timing for Harry to be uncontactable and for Warren to not be picking up.

Not getting through to Warren! she sent to her sisters.

Just as the second ring went on her call, Maya threw her phone to Camilla, and a voice intruded her thoughts. *Speed dial 1.*

Camilla grimaced. He was on her speed dial. He was *first* on her speed dial.

Her displeasure did not have time to take root as Maya thought out to her, *Now is not the time, Cam.*

She hadn't sent her thoughts to Maya, but her sister seemed to know where they would've gone. Camilla picked up the phone as a burst of electricity just passed Vera's shoulder, barely affecting her, but causing her to stiffen long enough to not fight back.

Maya's fire saved her from another hit, taking Colette's attention. Though the halfie was fast and dedicated, she seemed to freeze at every sight of fire, and Camilla had a feeling it was the memories it brought back of an older brother with the exact power.

One ring, and Hunter picked up.

Camilla didn't give him time to say whatever innuendo she was sure he used at the start of all of his calls with Maya. "Your sister is here."

It took almost no time between Camilla hanging up the phone and Hunter shadowing in behind his sister. He moved quickly, knocking her legs out from under her and moving to grab for her throat as she fell. His strength lifted her off her feet, then slammed her onto her back. Camilla swore she felt the ground rumble a bit with the impact of the halfie's body.

The electricity was ringing around Colette's arms, and Camilla was sure she was sending it toward her brother. But he had no impact.

He took on her electricity and added his flames to it. She was guessing, but maybe Colette's fear of her older brother also came from his acceptance of her power. Maybe it was the fire control in him—technically electricity fell under fire, heat. Maybe Maya would be able to handle it too, maybe be immune to it?

His teeth grit, eyes deep with control and dominance, and Camilla had a feeling none of it had to do with the effect of the electricity, and all of it had to do with the control to not incinerate her in two seconds.

He had her lifted by the throat and hanging in the air again, then his arms were blazing with fire, and she was set aflame, screaming.

Then the fire disappeared, and not a single trace of evidence showed that she'd been touched by the element.

And she was aflame again. Screaming. Thrashing.

He was fearsome like this. Camilla had always hated him for the frightening things he could do, but other than the gymnasium with the kids, she hadn't witnessed any of it.

A new fear edged into her as she watched the flames disappear, and Hunter slam his sister into the ground again, hovering over her. She wasn't fighting any longer, just staring up at him with equal parts fear and hatred.

He seemed almost disappointed that she gave up so soon, but moved, placing a cuff that looked almost like a dog collar around her neck. It was the cuff that took away any power.

He pulled her to her feet by the collared cuff and recited a spell that locked her in place.

Camilla hated him, but she liked the sound of that spell.

She didn't know when she'd gotten off the ground, but she couldn't stop staring at him. Though it helped them in the moment, she didn't like this, didn't like that *he* was a part of *their* team.

Peeling her gaze away, she checked on her sisters, finding they were fine. At least they'd been able to hold their own, if only for a few minutes. She was over a decade into training to their few months.

Or maybe she was purposefully not hurting them because they still needed the spell.

Behind Hunter's anger, Camilla realized, was concern as his gaze met with Maya, checking her over for injury.

"That was fast," Colette baited. The fear was still in her eyes, but she was doing a good job at hiding it, fighting it.

Hunter smirked, but no humor graced his features as he looked over to her. He looked like he enjoyed the way she tried to fight her cower around him. "I began keeping a collar on me when you decided to show yourself again."

Colette grimaced at his answer and watched them all head out of the room and to the kitchen.

Camilla was sure of one thing. Hunter was angry. Very scary angry.

In the kitchen, he turned on them. "Where the hell is your warlock?"

Vera answered before any of them had the chance, anger matching his, "On a much needed vacation. Don't speak of him in that tone."

Hunter was about to respond when Maya placed a hand to his arm, catching his attention. "I'm okay," she whispered. "She didn't touch me."

Hunter's features, his entire body, relaxed at her whisper. His eyes melting as he drank Maya in. Camilla was shocked to see the affection he so freely showed for her sister, but had no time to analyze it.

"They're not going to give up until they have that spell. If not this, they'll start attacking innocent magical creatures, if not innocent humans." Camilla knew she was the biggest advocate for a normal human life, but their lives had no space for that at the moment. "We need to find that spell. At least to find out what we're up against."

Everyone left the kitchen for the attic, Camilla staying behind a moment to call Warren one more time. Part of her worried about what could've happened to him, and the other part annoyed that he still wasn't picking up.

She came out to find Hunter throwing an incantation on the door to make sure no one but those who already had access, being Harry and Warren, would be allowed in. She walked up to the attic and felt his presence behind her as she moved to stand by Vera before the Book. She really wasn't sure what good this would do. They'd checked a million times already.

Maya stood on the other side of the pedestal, her arms crossed before her chest, and Hunter moved to press against her back. His hands settled on her hips, and his face dipped to the junction between her neck and shoulder, as if making sure she was safe and with him.

Maya seemed to enjoy the possessive presence of his form behind her as she looked to the two of them. "Allow Hunter to go through it. We've looked a hundred times. We didn't find anything before and it's not going to change now. He may find something we missed!"

Another argument to allow Hunter a look at the Book. This really wasn't the time.

"Yeah, like all the spells he could use against us?" Surprisingly, this comment came from Vera. Maybe she was still angry with the demon about their argument over a week prior.

Or maybe it was because of the demon's comments on Harry.

Maya sighed. "Fighting me about this is supposed to be Camilla's job."

Well, she wasn't wrong.

Vera's annoyed gaze looked up to the couple standing before them. "I've decided I stand with Camilla."

Camilla smiled as Hunter rolled his eyes and moved backward to lean against the wall, pulling Maya in with him so she settled against his chest. He held her close, his arms wrapping fully around her waist, her hands holding onto his arms.

After about half an hour, Hunter moved them to the chaise at the other end of the attic and sprawled in the middle, Maya on his lap as they continued to watch. His hands stroked her back and thighs, hers playing with the edge of his hair, grazing his neck as they whispered and teased and laughed together.

It was distracting in a way that Camilla could not afford right then. That none of them could afford. Maya should be more focused on helping them than fraternizing with the enemy.

And her anger grew in the knowledge that Warren wasn't there.

She knew he would have a good reason, but she couldn't help the jealousy that raged in her at seeing the way Hunter held and teased her sister.

With hours passed and nothing found, the two finally went back downstairs, giving Camilla the break she needed. As much as she tried to focus, she'd constantly found herself staring at them, even getting caught once when her eyes grazed up and Hunter was looking in her direction.

But he needed to re-amplify the spell that held Colette stuck to her spot, and Maya wanted to grab everyone some leftovers, basically the best way to eat food.

Camilla had long since moved the Book from the pedestal to

the ground, both she and Vera sitting around it, and was glad to have done so when the two resurfaced with the food.

At least when they reclaimed the chaise this time, Maya took her own seat, albeit pressed right up against him, so they could eat.

They were just about done with their meal when Harry ported into the attic. "Why is Colette Delvaux downstairs?"

"Because Hunter is our savior," Maya teased, squishing Hunter's chin in a 'good-boy' gesture. Hunter's eyes turned wicked as they looked to Maya, his smirk growing seductive.

Those two definitely needed to focus on the moment!

"Ugh, gross," Camilla commented, then turned to Harry. "Colette attacked this morning. Apparently, they're tired of waiting. We called Hunter, and he drained her power and stuck her in that spot with that nifty little spell. Now, we're looking for the spell they need so they don't go off hunting for innocents. Not that it matters. We've searched this Book a million times. If it were here, we would've seen it."

"We've been looking for hours." Vera's gaze was gentle on him, but there was a tiredness to her voice. "Nothing."

"I said we should let Hunter look, but they don't agree," Maya threw in. Of course she would try that argument again.

Harry looked between the four of them, as if analyzing every person in the room, then astonished everyone, most of all Camilla herself. "I agree with Maya."

Vera sputtered, "You can't be serious."

"I think it would help. He hasn't betrayed us in any way. Rather, he's been on Maya's side in every possible step these past few months, even before they were sleeping together. I think we can trust him."

Camilla looked between their warlock and the two on the chaise, and saw Maya's eyes warm toward Harry's praise as a small smile graced her features. "Thanks, Harry."

Harry shrugged, but returned the small smile. "It's only the objective truth."

Camilla looked to Vera and felt defeat settle before relenting. Vera would want to agree with him, was already agreeing with him. "Fine."

Hunter's smirk told her he knew she didn't like this outcome, and that fact made him enjoy it more. Asshole.

He took the Book to the pedestal and started back at the first page. And there went his excuse for staying loyal to Maya. The second he got what he was looking for, Camilla feared what it would mean for her older—now middle—sister.

With Hunter's slow progression through the pages, Camilla found herself analyzing *him*.

He looked like his brother in the way you can tell two people are related when they don't share the obvious features. His hair was golden brown to Warren's black; his eyes were black to Warren's hazel—funnily the exact opposites; he was a bit more built to Warren's leanness; he was a million times crueler to Warren's kindness.

But he was also always there for Maya. And even though Camilla knew it had to be because he was after something, he was still there. He still found comfort in her, still teased her, still made that smile brighten Maya's lips that Camilla hadn't seen since before their mother had passed. And even then, the smile hadn't been that wide.

Vera had told her that Hunter had said he was at Maya's beck and call during one of their training sessions, and as much as she hated it, it was true. She'd called Warren multiple times with no response, but a second into calling Hunter, and he was by Maya's side.

There was nothing worse than turning the faults from one brother to the other, but she couldn't fight the evidence. *Warren* wasn't there for her when she needed him; *Warren* had kept secrets from her; *Warren* knew what was happening in her life, that The Eight were after her family, and still didn't pick up.

Then her phone rang.

Speak of the devil.

She felt almost annoyed looking down at the caller ID, but picked up anyway, again not giving time to speak and only saying, "Your sister is here."

Like his brother, it took almost no time between Camilla hanging up the phone and him materializing before them.

"Good for you to finally join us, brother," Hunter called out in a sardonic tease.

Warren paid him no mind, his gaze immediately finding hers.

She didn't speak, just left the attic for her room, knowing he'd follow her. She stood rigid, arms crossed before her chest, and stared at him.

"You're angry with me?" He sounded almost hopeful that she would answer in the negative.

She ground her teeth and tried to calm herself. "I called you. Multiple times, and you didn't pick up. We called Hunter, and he picked up on the first ring."

"Camilla," he said slowly and tried to step closer, but she stepped back, leaving space between them. His eyes stung with the rejection, but he stopped and stared. "Camilla, my father had me in trainings all day. We're not allowed phones. I called as soon as I got my phone back."

She was almost annoyed with herself at feeling her resolve breaking so soon.

But it truly wasn't his fault. And she knew she was more angry that he hadn't picked up her first ring, that Hunter could be at Maya's beck and call, and he couldn't be at hers. It was dumb and selfish, and she couldn't help it.

She was jealous again.

Of Maya's relationship with Hunter.

And she had to stop comparing their relationships if she wanted hers to last. He was doing the best he could with his family situation, and she was being selfish. Maybe being the baby of the family was finally catching up to bite her in the ass.

She felt the tears prick her eyes and allowed Warren to step up and take her in his arms.

Most of all, she was angry with herself for what she was doing to this relationship. Warren didn't deserve the comparisons she made with his brother, and he also didn't deserve when the comparison was in the negative, like the fact that he was a demon too, no matter that he was only half.

32

"What is she playing at?" Hunter growled as he fell into his armchair by the fire.

Warren stood by the bookshelves across from him in the dark room of their father's study. Given how much he'd hated being a demon and working for his father when it came to the Whittles, this room still made him feel protected.

Augustine would never claim to love them, but maybe in his own demonic way, he did. Warren wasn't sure, but he did know one thing. His father had always protected him, sent him to this office to know he would be okay.

And surprisingly, almost always included him on family matters—the almost coming into play when he and Hunter were planning something they obviously knew Warren wouldn't stand for.

But this was not one of those moments.

Any talk of Colette always involved Warren, and for some reason—maybe because she was always torturing him growing up—he was always given final say on decisions regarding his sister.

"Your sister has always been sick, but this doesn't seem like one of her ploys for fun. There must be a motive behind it. And if I had to guess, where your sister is involved, she's looking for someone to care for. Or someone to care for her," their father spoke.

Warren scoffed. Colette deserved to remain unloved until the day her worthless body shriveled up.

Augustine smiled behind his cup of bourbon. "Everyone feels the need, even someone as deplorable as she. Whatever it is they're looking for, it's going to be someone or something that can give her what no one else on the planet will: love."

"If everyone needs it, where do we stand? Demons don't, and she's a demon," Warren fought. He couldn't stand the thought of anyone loving that woman.

"I care for you boys, in my own way. Just because it is different from the way you love, does not mean it is not there." Augustine took the armchair across from Hunter. "And your brother has it in his Maya."

Hunter's gaze shot to their father, raging. He never liked when Augustine spoke Maya's name.

It was odd.

He claimed he wasn't in love with her, but that look spoke volumes. He was ready to kill their father for speaking her name, even knowing Augustine would never lay a hand on the middle Whittle. If he had more human instincts like any non-full demon, Warren would just call it denial, but powerful full-blooded demons like his father and brother didn't suffer from denial. They were never ashamed to admit their shortcomings, and most definitely never ashamed of the things they treasured.

And Hunter definitely treasured Maya.

Warren had always wondered what that feeling must be like. Demons didn't fall in love often—it was very possible, but it just didn't happen—but it was said that when it did happen, it was almost like a werewolf mating. Is that what Hunter was feeling for Maya?

Warren had wondered for some time now whether he would get that way for Camilla. Did it happen to halfies? Did it take time? It hadn't with Hunter. They'd only been together a couple of months. Maybe it worked different with him and Camilla.

"I'm telling you boys, that must be it. She's looking for love in any way she knows how. If what your brother tells me is correct, and there is a master, the real question is, what is he trying to get?" his father finished.

"It's correct. Colette's being more careful than usual. She's following orders. If that's because at the end she will get this thing to love, I don't know. All I know is she's calmer," Hunter spit and went back to staring at the fire.

Augustine was looking Warren's way, and he saw the same thing written in his black eyes that Warren was thinking—Hunter was angry. But more than anything, he was relieved that Colette was put on a tight leash, otherwise something could have happened to Maya. The Colette they knew wouldn't have played safe, especially knowing it would hurt Hunter to go after her. But only after her. Hunter couldn't care less about the rest of the Whittles, but he'd burn the planet down if something happened to her.

Warren just wondered when he would admit it.

Maybe he didn't even know yet. Falling in love wasn't something demons had experience with, especially full-blooded ones, most going their entire lives without it. Maybe he just didn't know what it was that he was feeling. All he knew was that he had to keep his witch safe.

And Warren could understand that much because he wanted to keep Camilla safe. It was harder for him though. He was still under Augustine's line, and until he cut off from his father, he had to continue training—which he honestly couldn't complain about—and continue to possibly miss Camilla's calls for help.

He hated that he couldn't be around to keep her safe at all times, but at least Hunter would be around. He may not care for the youngest Whittle, but he would protect her for Maya's sake, and Warren even thought for his sake too.

But that also brought on the nagging feeling that Warren tried to push aside, but somehow kept making its way to the forefront of his thoughts: was he in love with Camilla?

He loved her, there was no question there, but was he in love with her the way Hunter was in love with her sister?

He pushed the thought aside, definitely not a bottle he wanted to open at the moment. He was. He loved her, no other thought about it.

"So what do we do with her?" Warren asked.

Augustine downed his bourbon. "There's nothing we can do. Colette is only a piece in the mastermind's game. She's worthless to his final outcomes. What we need is to find out what this mastermind is after."

***

Harry had taken her side.

She'd thought so before, but now Maya was more sure he was coming around to the idea of her and Hunter because he'd now visibly been disappointed in Vera for the argument and stated that he trusted Hunter to help them in any case.

Epic milestone in her book.

Maya hadn't realized how much it would affect her, having someone accept her relationship. And although Harry hadn't technically accepted it, he never attacked her for it.

With everything going on, it was nice to finally be alone with Harry again. The training with potions and spells they'd started before she'd gotten her powers was still something she wanted to continue. And she liked that it gave her the time with him. She'd never had a brother, but she imagined him one.

He was cutting up the roots of two barks for the potion he

would be helping her with, and it gave her the chance to watch him.

He was handsome. There was no doubt about that. With the dark slicked hair and shining hazel eyes, clean shaven, and inviting smile. No doubt.

And the British accent instantly harbored favorable results.

But he was more than that. He wasn't perfect. He admitted to not being a mentor because he never wanted to be, because he caused more problems than not when training, because he overall had never chosen this life.

Maya really liked that about him, that he was ready to admit his misgivings.

And he'd quickly become family, protecting them like what Maya expected having a brother was like. Though, to be fair, he didn't exactly fight their lovers, so maybe not entirely like a brother.

But the way he looked to her sister would make him a brother to her the way Hunter called Camilla—and from what she'd heard of their training sessions, Vera—sister.

"Okay, Mr. Mentor Man, what're we learning today?"

She saw his jaw grit and smiled wider at the effect as his gaze flicked up to meet hers. "You're indescribably annoying, Maya."

She feigned a flush. "Harry, you flirt, you're supposed to be going for the oldest sister, and I'm not it anymore."

He shook his head, a wide smile forming on his lips as he looked back to the roots he was cutting. No eye contact. He was shy about this line of conversation.

And that made Maya all the more wanting to follow it.

She leaned over the table and rested her chin on her hand. "Tell me, Mr. Mentor Man, you ever going to tell her how you feel? It's quite obvious."

"Like your *not*-just-sleeping-together relationship with Hunter?"

"Yes." She wasn't too proud to admit that she'd claimed this a fuck buddy relationship when it wasn't. Never truly had been, if she were honest.

His gaze flicked back up to her. "Is it obvious or did that power stealing boyfriend of yours just figure it out?"

She smiled unashamed. "Both."

He shook his head as he finished cutting. "What power does he have, anyway?"

She smiled with a twinkle in her eyes. "Scent. He can smell a lot better than us, and he's told me how you two act around each other, at just the mention of a name."

The flush on his light skin was adorable. "Maybe Vera has a reason behind not liking him."

She rolled her eyes. "Oh, please, we both know it's only because Hunt fucks me whenever he wants, and she's still waiting on you."

His breath caught, skin burning brighter as he turned away from her and grabbed for a few other ingredients—crisp leaves, chewy bark, and tiny berries—to add to the mix already on the table—salt, wax, garlic, three different types of herbs, apples, milk, and the cut up roots.

Her smile grew. "I understand not doing anything because you're unsure—though that sounds ridiculous given how obvious you two are—but now you can be sure. She wants you." He wouldn't look at her. "Inside her! She wants you inside her, Harry."

"Enough!" It was a demand, but it was said weakly, like he was trying to keep the image of what she was saying out of his mind. He looked up at her after a moment, his skin bright with heat. "Do you want to learn how to make this or not?"

Changing the subject. Cute.

She strolled up beside him and began looking into the Book, then the cauldron, as Harry instructed her about timing and amounts of each ingredient needed. He was patient with her. It was another reason Maya enjoyed practicing with him. He had all the patience in the world.

Time passed without her knowledge when she was with him like this. They'd gone through two potions and a spell when her phone vibrated from the table, and she realized they'd been in the attic for hours.

I think it's time you come home.

She didn't realize the warm smile that rose on her lips until Harry spoke. "Hunter?"

Come here. It's almost time for dinner.

"Yeah." She put her phone down. "He'll be here soon."

No sooner did those words leave her lips than a shadow appeared in the room.

"I've got your dinner right here, love. Let's go home."

Harry's eyes twinkled as he looked at her, and she knew there was a light tinge of a blush on her cheeks. She didn't know why. She was open about her sex life with Hunter, but it still came.

"Go wait downstairs, Hunter. We'll be down soon."

His gaze narrowed on her. She could see he was trying to fight an argument as he turned and walked out of the room.

Maya turned to Harry. "Shut up."

"Mhm," he said through a close-lipped smile.

33

Shockingly, Vera and Camilla were already in the kitchen when Maya walked in the next morning. They were never up before her. Ever.

Although, Vera had to admit, Maya's ministrations with Hunter had probably put her to sleep late last night and kept her in bed that morning.

She wondered if he was still up there.

Didn't matter, because at the very least, she was grateful that the silencing charms they'd placed in Maya's room were working wonders. She hadn't heard a thing, and she had a feeling that wasn't the two of them being respectfully quiet.

Vera already had eggs, bacon, toast, and fruits ready at the table, Camilla bringing the coffee and filling each of their cups to the brim, when Maya took her usual seat at the table. "You two are up early?"

"Couldn't sleep," Camilla said.

"Couldn't go back to sleep," Vera added.

The following silence as they ate was comfortable, the kind that even Vera didn't feel the need to break.

Harry walked in as they were finishing, bidding them a good

morning and walking over to the coffee pot to fill himself a cup. He settled at the table beside Camilla and began piling a plate with the still warm food. Vera had a feeling Maya had something to do with the fact that it was all still warm.

Vera couldn't look at him, her gaze having snapped down to the cup between her hands the moment he'd settled down, a fact he seemed too distracted to notice, but that didn't miss her sisters.

She felt the prickle of Camilla's thoughts invade hers. *What happened?*

Vera blushed and sent back, *Nothing.*

Maya watched her blush as Camilla threw back, *Don't lie to me, Big Sister.*

Vera had no energy to fight back. *I had a dream last night. That's it.*

Camilla broke out in a smile at the same moment Vera broke out into a deep flush. Maya's eyes darted between the two of them, Harry still oblivious to the entire scene. He'd come home late last night. From where, Vera wasn't sure, but she'd heard him.

Maya was no doubt asking Camilla what was going on. Great, she definitely did not need to be adding her bits jokes into Vera's very jumbled thoughts.

Camilla looked to Maya with a wicked smile, and Vera felt the thought come to her as well. Camilla had been saying she wanted to try to loop thoughts. It seemed to be working. Vera covered her face as the thought entered her mind, and even the way Camilla thought it sounded suggestive. *She had a dream last night. That's it.*

Maya's gaze snapped immediately over, lips breaking out into a Cheshire grin. "Vera, are you okay?" she said aloud, her tone suggestive, of course.

Harry didn't pick up on the tone, his head snapping to look at her. "What's wrong?"

Vera tried to meet his gaze, then flushed deeper and looked back down.

Maya laughed. "Oh, I'm sure it's nothing, Harry. I think Vera's bits are just acting up this morning."

Yup, there she went with the bits jokes.

Harry's face scrunched in confusion as Camilla burst into laughter, and Vera dropped her head to hit the table. Harry didn't say anything, but Vera felt his stare on her.

It wasn't long after that little scenario that Hunter came down, lazily dressed in trousers and a t-shirt, and hair just slightly askew. Warren shadowed in almost at the same time, dividing the household to begin their days.

They'd chained Colette in the basement the night before, settling on the decision that they'd access the situation again when they were fresh eyed.

Now, Vera still didn't want to access the situation.

So she didn't.

While Warren and Camilla went to the formal dining room in order to get some homework done, and Maya went off to the office to get a final client piece done, Hunter having picked up the Book and followed her inside, she'd be taking their cue and not working on anything supernatural.

She wanted to trust that Hunter *was* fully on their side and that letting him look through the Book would be helpful to them, but it was difficult. Especially after he'd openly told them at breakfast that he found the entire reading immensely interesting. Maya had smacked him with the confession, as if she'd told him not to say that in front of the family and he'd done it anyway. The death glare she'd given him when he'd smirked in response had left no doubt in Vera's mind.

So now, she went to the piano room, Harry close on her heels.

There wasn't much for either one of them to do, as they

were relying on Hunter to find something for them in the Book, so she didn't feel too bad playing rather than working.

She'd try to calm her mind of any thoughts surrounding Harry, which became all the more difficult when he closed the door and took a seat beside her at the piano bench. Her body stood alert, mind racing image after image of her dream from last night.

Harry seemed oblivious, waiting for her to begin playing, but Vera could hear her own blood rushing. Her heart was beating loud enough for the world to hear.

It was almost painful, but eventually, she began to play. But she couldn't get herself to relax—her body was too strung with his presence sitting so close. Her heart was too loud for her to hear the melodies her fingers created.

Harry broke their silence, his gaze following her fingers on the keys. "Are you all right?"

Vera cleared her throat and responded weakly, "Yup."

His hand found purchase on her thigh, just above her knee, and her entire being reacted, each cell her body possessed moving to find a spot in that area. Her fingers faltered, and she stopped playing, letting her hands rest on the keys. Unable to move, she kept her gaze staring straight ahead.

"Why won't you look at me?" Harry asked softly.

Apparently, not so oblivious after all.

She tried to look at him, but her mind blew up in memories from her dream when her eyes caught sight of him, and she immediately dropped her gaze and rested it on the hand he still had on her thigh.

He wasn't moving it, not even a finger, but she felt her thigh boiling beneath the pressure. She wanted to be honest, so still staring down at his hand, she said, "I had a dream about you last night."

She felt him stiffen beside her, then his other hand reached out to tug at her chin so she would look at him. Their faces were only a few inches apart, gazes meeting. Vera felt the need to look away again, but Harry kept a tight hold. She'd do anything to have him lean down in that moment and kiss her.

"I would never hurt you, Vera."

She stared at him and knew he'd misunderstood her. And she didn't correct him. She'd been vulnerable enough for the time being.

With a minuscule nod, he released his grip on her chin. Turning back to look at the keys, he moved his hand from her thigh. "Please. Play for me."

Vera felt the loss of his touch immensely, felt her entire body ache to have it back on her, but she swallowed the feeling down, and turned back to the piano, and did as she was asked. She played him one of her favorites.

***

It was hours before they escaped their confines and met again in the kitchen for another meal. Camilla stood in the kitchen making a quick meal with Vera, Harry, and Warren, before Vera texted Maya to join them.

Before long, they were all in the kitchen, Hunter still clutching the Book in his hands and reading intently as he placed it on the island, but never interrupted his concentration. Camilla had to control her urge to rip it out of his hands.

"Found something, or just trying to memorize as much as possible?" she asked sardonically.

Hunter ignored her jibe and leaned into the Book. "There's a demonic tongue here. Surprisingly, plenty of it." He pointed to the page and the symbols climbing the sides. "A spell to unlock what is needed most."

"Why would *that* be in a demonic tongue?" Camilla asked.

It was Hunter's turn to act smug as he looked up at her and smiled cruelly. "The ingredients wouldn't make you happy,

Little Sister. That's why there's a difference between demon and witch magic, and why it is easier to do demonic magic."

"What ingredients?" Vera asked, placing a sandwich in front of him.

"The normal ones, really. Salt, herbs, blood."

"So why wouldn't I be happy?" Camilla remarked.

"And the eye of a live human child," Hunter smoothly added.

She froze. Her heart literally stopped beating. It had to. Nothing else could've been done to erase that picture from her mind.

"You're lying," Camilla seethed.

Hunter quirked his brow and motioned for the Book. "Your boyfriend can read the tongue just as well as I can."

Camilla looked to Warren desperately, hoping he'd tell her his brother was joking. Warren looked at the page, then back at her. His expression gave her the answer—Hunter had not been joking—but he also softly caressed her arm. "I'm sorry, Cam. It's grotesque, I know. That's why I don't love the demon side."

That's why, not the fact that demons are uncaring. Camilla could feel a scoff wiggle inside her, but pushed it down. She'd promised herself she wouldn't throw the demon thing in Warren's face anymore, and she was going to keep her promise.

"Keep looking," Harry chimed in just as a ringing came. "In case there's something else."

Great, had The Eight done something to require their attentions again?

Except, it wasn't the house phone. It was Warren's.

His apologetic expression when he picked it up told Camilla everything. He was needed at home. He handed the phone to Hunter after letting his father know he'd be there in a moment.

Hunter looked bored with the call. "I'm busy. You can bother me with your needs when I'm finished with Maya's."

Huh, he wasn't running to his father's every call.

He also wasn't living with their father, needing to please him for shelter and money.

Warren stepped up to Camilla and gave her a huge, sloppy kiss goodbye just as Harry made an excuse to leave. He said he would check in with the other creatures to make sure nothing was amiss, but there was something in the way he didn't meet any of their gazes that made Camilla think it was a lie.

Hunter didn't seem to notice he was the only man left in the room.

With their departure, Camilla knew it was time to have a chat with their little friend downstairs, no matter how much she didn't want to.

It would be better this way, anyhow. If Hunter were to go down, she'd be too proud to say anything, the fear and hatred she felt for her older brother clearly evident in her gaze. And if Warren went down, he'd get pulled back into his nightmares, and Camilla would never make him suffer that. The longer she could keep him away from his sister, the better.

She caught Vera and Maya's eyes and thrust her head toward the basement. They looked just as unhappy with their next course, but stepped up anyway, leaving Hunter sitting in the kitchen.

As they descended the stairs to the basement, Colette looked to them. Even tied up and powerless, she was smug. "My dear sisters, you've been keeping me waiting."

None of them spoke as they took different positions around the room: Vera leaning against the wall to the left of Colette, Camilla standing before the halfie, and Maya taking a stand a few feet behind her, though Camilla could see her through her periphery.

Colette's smug tone never wavered. "My brothers kept you busy, I suppose." Her eyes moved from Maya to Camilla. "Well, maybe not you. But those two," she looked back to Maya, "I'm sure they had quite the night. Just waking up?"

Maya smiled sweetly at her. It was a look Camilla did not like on her sister. "I did have quite the night. That brother of yours has come on just about every inch of me."

Colette's face turned down in disgust, and Camilla was not too far behind. "How about you refrain from telling me such intimate details about my brother?"

Maya's smile didn't falter. "How about you refrain from thinking about my intimate moments with your brother? You asked, so I answered."

"Pleased with your little question time?" Vera broke the spat and thankfully moved the conversation from Hunter's intimate times. "Good. Now it's our turn."

Colette rolled her eyes to look at the eldest Whittle sister, her brow quirking for Vera to continue.

"Why? Why do any of this?" Vera asked.

Colette rolled her eyes. "Why do you lot always ask the most boring of questions? Why not ask me something more entertaining?"

Vera didn't take the bait. "That is what I wish to know."

Colette gave a heavy sigh. "Isn't it obvious? We are respected in this group we have created. Half bloods find respect nowhere else because neither side will accept them, and other creatures look down at them."

There was silence following her response.

Not all halfies. Warren was respected. At least, Camilla assumed he was.

"Good. At least we know you'll be answering honestly," Maya said.

Colette gave her a mock-cheerful expression. "You gave me the honor. I shall return the favor."

Maya laughed cruelly at her, but it was Camilla who spoke next. "But they don't actually care for you, don't you know that?"

Colette looked to her. "Of course I know that."

"Then what about it is appealing? The respect is only shown because you guys are working together for something. When it's all done, they wouldn't respect you either," Camilla asked.

"For Grandmama," Colette said sincerely. "She will care for us the way we deserve to be cared for."

Grandmama? Like the one from the book who had her entire family taken from her? These halfies were aware that was only a storybook, right?

"And if she doesn't?" Vera asked, pity beginning to ebb into her voice.

Colette wasn't worried. "She will."

Wow, whoever was playing the wheels really had these halfies fooled. Even knowing Colette was a piece of trash, at the very least for what she did to her brother, Camilla, too, felt a bit of pity.

"Okay," Maya cut in, unsurprising to find no pity on her behalf. "Backtrack. What happens if you don't get what you're looking for? You know, especially considering we don't know *what* you're looking for."

Colette looked at each of them and allowed a small, cruel smile to grace her lips. "The humans are such a simple lot, do you not think? What may their reactions be to our kinds?"

"You'd resort to outing the magical world to the humans?" Camilla asked. "If you think the species hate you now, they'd be all after you."

"Not outright," Colette answered. "A few humans here and there. It'll cause a riot after some time, the believers and non-believers. What havoc humans can have on their own kind."

Camilla had to wonder if all the halfies were this deluded and selfish.

After some silence, Colette continued, "Or maybe we won't do that. Maybe we'd just attack and call it terrorism and still allow the humans to ruin their own kind. They're very good at that, you know." Her smile had turned knowing as she looked at each of them. The pity was falling away. She didn't deserve it. "Yes, maybe that's it. I wonder, are there many people at malls on Saturday afternoons?"

Camilla froze. She couldn't mean *now*.

Maya scoffed through a humorless laugh. "You just arrived to warn us yesterday. Why do anything yet?"

Maya's bravado was something Camilla could not get herself to fake.

Colette gave a small shrug. "We weren't stupid enough to think I wouldn't get caught. I saw the way my brother acted with you. There was no way Hunt wouldn't be here to protect you, and there was no way I would be able to fight off Hunt alone. Precautions state a time limit." Her smile was cold on her face. "And now you have one."

"We're looking for your spell," Camilla seethed, even knowing she didn't want to give them whatever spell they were after. "Tell your lackeys to break it off."

"Can't do that," was all Colette responded.

Camilla looked to her sisters and felt the terror slowly rise within her. What atrocity could they possibly have planned?

"Tick tock." Colette smiled, eyes black with cruel humor.

34

They left the basement calmly, not giving Colette the pleasure of watching them run in a frantic need to stop her friends. Only when they hit the ground floor did they break and begin to rush up to the attic, where Hunter was lounged on the chaise, and called for Harry.

He ported in immediately.

"Colette said they may do something today. Hit a shopping center. Make it look like an attack, cause a riot within the humans." Vera quickly condensed for them.

Hunter shrugged it off and turned back to the Book, and Vera had to calm her nerves and remind herself that demons didn't naturally care for others. His reaction was not his fault.

Harry, on the other hand, turned to them. "How much do you believe it?"

"I don't," Vera said. "But in case it's true, we can't risk it."

"It likely is true," Hunter spoke, glancing up at them stoically. The amount of unconcern showing on his features was astounding. "My sister is many things, but a liar is not one of them."

"We have to do something!" Camilla exclaimed.

"Why?" Hunter asked. "Allow the humans to deal with it. We can't fight everyone's fights for them."

The shock and horror of his comments filled her mind, and she had to remind herself, again, that it wasn't his fault.

Camilla, though, didn't seem to care about that little fact and turned on Maya. "Now are you ready to dump his sorry ass?"

Maya rolled her eyes, taking out a map of the town. "You guys know demons don't naturally care for others the way every other creature does. Why would his reaction now shock you?"

"Because he's been so…different with you," Vera argued.

Maya smiled at them sadly. "Do not imagine something that isn't there. Hunter doesn't care for the lives of people not in his life. He doesn't even care for majority of the lives of the people *in* his life."

"And yet you keep him in *your* life?" Camilla asked, flabbergasted.

Maya looked to her sister, eyes resolute with certainty. "I accept him for what he is, Cam. It honestly doesn't bother me because at the end of the day, he'll do whatever it is that makes me happy. Even if he doesn't care for the people he's helping."

"Maya! That…" Camilla started but was cut off.

"Now is not the time, Camilla," Harry said, looking down at the map of town, Mr. Mentor Man in action. He was really attractive as Mr. Mentor Man. "There are two major shopping centers they could hit, one with an outdoor Americana of stores."

"It's the middle of winter. It has to be the fully indoor one. There'll be more people there," Vera said.

"But the Americana is holding winter events. There's an outdoor skating rink by the edge of that one, little contests. There'll be hundreds out," Maya countered.

Camilla looked skeptically at her. "How do you know that?"

Surprisingly, Maya's eye roll was light. "We do go on dates, you know."

"Fuck buddies don't go on dates," Camilla smugly remarked.

"You continue to call him my boyfriend, so he's doing boyfriend things. You know, to make *you* happy, Little Sister." Maya's eyes shimmered like there was something more to that comment than what Vera could understand.

And the way Hunter barked a poorly hidden laugh and Camilla steamed at the comment, there was definitely something more to it.

"We'll try the indoor one first," Harry interrupted, not even seeming to give the argument any of his attention. He held out his hands for them to take and looked to Hunter. "Are you coming?"

Vera grimaced but didn't say anything as Hunter got up and joined them, wrapping his arm around Maya's waist. Vera turned for Harry's hand, Camilla at the other, and they ported as Hunter shadowed Maya out of the attic.

They landed at the back of the mall, the spot where only shipment trucks passed. "Separating only works if you have some way to escape if something were to happen, which means we can do two groups," Harry stated.

"Right, so you two check the roof, we'll check the lower levels," Vera said, taking the same assumption they all did of the pairings.

"No." Camilla stopped them. "I'm going with them." She nodded her head in Maya and Hunter's direction, catching everyone off guard.

As the seconds passed and Camilla didn't recount her comment, they realized she wasn't joking.

"Okay," Vera said slowly, then turned to Harry. "Let's go."

The two turned to the door leading into the building, leaving the three alone outside. Once inside, Vera turned to look at Harry as they walked, catching his gaze, and breaking into laughs they'd tried to contain.

Harry spoke through his, "What I wouldn't give to see how that goes."

"Tell me about it." Her laugh edged off as they neared the steps down to the basement, and her hormones woke up, her bits processing that she was alone with *him*.

They reached the bottom and Harry's hand moved, landing on the small of her back and remaining there. And just like earlier that morning, every cell and nerve ending in her body found the area his hand occupied and fought for the chance to be there.

She'd been nervous to be around Harry again, but she hadn't worried about it, sure that Camilla would be with them. Never had she expected Camilla to volunteer to go with *Hunter*.

But now she was alone with their warlock as they walked the mall's basement which, to her astonishment, was quite clean. She kept her gaze forward but caught his darting to her through her periphery, like he was trying to fight off staring at her as well.

Maybe it was just wishful thinking.

She felt his hand expand at the base of her back before relaxing back in its spot, but that one movement was enough. Her thoughts raced again to her dream the night before, to her gasping breaths as she awoke in the middle of the night, drenched in sweat and dripping wet between her legs. She hadn't just been wet, that dream had made her come all by itself. That was how desperately she wanted to be with him.

Vera stumbled a step as her thighs clenched together at the memory of it.

His free hand swung out to catch her. "Are you all right?"

Again, she couldn't look at him, but felt her face flush deep. "Perfectly fine." Her voice broke in her attempt to seem unaffected by his presence.

She needed something to happen, needed to not be alone with him any longer.

The Lords must've been listening to her prayers because it was not even a moment later when Camilla texted her.

"We need to go."

They'd been left alone for two seconds, and already Camilla knew she'd regret this, but she wanted to keep an eye out for Maya.

No matter what everyone else said, she didn't trust Hunter.

The three of them went for the outdoor staircase that led to every floor, including the roof. On the climb up, Hunter threw his arm around Camilla's shoulders. "I'm honored you wanted to spend some quality time with me, Little Sister."

Camilla grimaced, throwing his arm off. "I'm here for Maya's protection."

Hunter laughed and threw his arm instead over Maya's shoulders, bringing her close into his side and kissing the crown of her head.

The roof was expansive given the size of the shopping center, and they were unable to break up for the simple fact Hunter's shadowing ability would be required in case of an emergency. They began their hunt of the unknown at the stairs and expanded outward.

Would they find halfies or something the halfies had left behind?

Not a sound was made as they walked the rooftop, and Camilla watched as Hunter remained between her and Maya, knowing it was so he would have easy access to both of them if they needed to leave quickly. She had a feeling he would prefer to stick around and play with the halfies, but hopefully, he also wasn't done using them yet and would choose their protection over his fun.

He was between them, but Camilla could see his natural

gravitation toward Maya, and knew that if it weren't for Maya's love for her, Hunter would have just as easily left Camilla in the moment of an emergency exit. She wondered if her relationship with his brother would have prompted help in that scenario.

Turning the corner behind one of the mall's large electrical sources, they found two halfies standing by a skylight window, devices in hand.

Camilla froze, feeling rather than seeing Hunter and Maya do the same.

Maya was the first to move, sending her darkness toward the halfies, surrounding them in blackness and blinding them long enough for Hunter to shadow behind one and snap its neck without the other seeing. In a matter of thirty seconds, one halfie was dead, and the other was in Hunter's clutches.

Camilla hated to admit it, but they worked really well together. Always had, even before their little relationship began. The memory of them setting those witches on fire at the Bridgers coven was still engraved in Camilla's soul.

These halfies were men. Though she obviously knew there were halfie men, her boyfriend being a prime example, she hadn't thought there were any within The Eight. Maybe she was being dumb in assuming only women because she'd seen only women thus far.

"Hey there, little friend." Hunter taunted the man in his clutches.

The halfie struggled and tried to pull away, but Hunter was strong. Really strong. Camilla seemed to always forget that.

And the halfie wasn't half demon. Or half witch, since Camilla wasn't getting any sort of familiarity.

"Tell me, my little friend, what are we doing up on the roof?"

Camilla couldn't help but wonder if he always played with his victims like that when trying to get information. Or was he being kinder because of their presence?

"Fuck off, demon." The halfie had balls. She'd give him that.

Hunter's chuckle was menacing as he flipped the halfie around and landed him on his knees so that he was looking at Maya now. With a tight hold on the man's neck, Hunter tsked. "Want to try again?"

Camilla could see the light, almost invisible, flames dancing on Hunter's fingers. That was most definitely going to leave burns.

Maya walked up to them and traced a finger down the halfie's face before blackness settled before him. Camilla didn't doubt that Hunter hadn't released the fire.

"My little lady here is quite impatient, friend." Hunter sounded like he was enjoying the moment, enjoying sharing it with Maya.

Camilla didn't know if anything else was being done. Were they burning him somewhere she couldn't see? Was Hunter's hold on his neck getting tighter? Could Maya do something more with the darkness than just take away his sight?

But the man gave in.

"I don't know," he whispered.

Hunter chuckled and tilted the man's head back. Camilla shivered. It looked ready to snap as Hunter sang to the man, "I don't believe you."

There was almost a sizzling sound, which Camilla had to assume was the combination of the man's salty tears with Hunter's small flames.

"I don't." He grew a bit louder. "We were told to come here, and when we noticed an attack through the devices, to throw in a few small bombs."

"And where are these small bombs, friend?" Maya almost sounded like Hunter.

Spend enough time with someone and you turn into them. Camilla had to get Maya away from that demon before she was completely corrupted.

The darkness instantly evaporated, and you would've

thought they were burning the man's eyes with the way he squealed and squeezed them shut. Hunter pressed into his forehead to keep the man's eyes open. Camilla remembered the shock of the light after Maya's darkness. That had to be painful. Almost like setting eyes on fire.

The man pointed a shaky hand to the other side of the skylight window. "There, there. Please, please, plea..." he begged, and Hunter let his eyes fall shut.

The man didn't open them again.

Camilla moved to the bag and picked it up, inside three small bombs. She picked one up to show the others. "How much damage would these do?"

She wasn't part of the questioning, but she needed to know.

"Not a lot." Hunter pulled his neck back, and the man's voice grew more desperate. " I swear, only hurt a few people each. Just enough to cause panic, nothing more!"

"Why?" Maya asked.

"So if you stopped the bomb at the other spot, you would still have to worry about some damages."

"Is the bomb at the other place for little damages too?" Maya asked.

"No." His tears were streaming down his face as he begged for his life. "No, the other one is huge. Everyone is out for winter activities. It could get them all."

"Then let me know this, friend." Hunter leaned in. "Who sent you?"

"Master J. He said we would be valued in helping."

"Who is this Master J?" Hunter's voiced was soft.

"I, I don't know." The tears streaked down the man's face, but his eyes never opened. "We can't meet him until we finish our missions. This was mine."

Hunter laughed. "He was sending you on a suicide mission. No surprise, either. If you were on my team, I would've sent you to get killed too."

Camilla gasped. "Hunter!"

"He squealed at the first sign of danger. He's a liability. This master was just trying to get rid of you." He leaned into the man just before snapping his neck all the way back.

Camilla swore she'd be sick with the sound of the snap. Somehow, she hadn't heard the first one's—maybe she hadn't paid attention—but this one? This would be joining the sounds of the Bridgers witches screaming as they burned to death.

The man lay next to his accomplice as Hunter and Maya moved toward her, taking the bag from her hands.

Coming out of her reverie, she looked to Hunter. "Maybe I can get her to use that new power on you."

Maya was picking up the dropped screens when Hunter looked to her with a smirk turned smug. "Oh, we've had plenty of fun with that power."

Camilla's smile dropped, gaze hardening. She felt her entire face darken. Of course Maya had told him about her new power after they had all agreed to keep it a secret. Camilla was ready to start yet another argument with her sister regarding the eldest Delvaux when Maya interrupted, "Behave, Delvaux."

"Yes, ma'am." He grinned and walked over to Maya's shoulder.

Camilla reached the other shoulder and looked over at the screens. One showed four different angles of the outdoor shopping center, and the other showed a room filled with five halfies.

Camilla pulled her phone and messaged Vera, and within a few seconds, she and Harry stood before them. Maya handed the screens over. "It looks like we chose the wrong shopping center."

"Yes, well, lucky for us," Harry said, glancing back at the others, "each of these four angles are directed right toward the shopping center's managers area. We know where to go this time."

They moved again, Camilla taking Harry's hand alongside Vera as Hunter grabbed for Maya. They landed just outside of the area the cameras caught and right across from a room that looked to have a glow over the door.

It was magical—something only the magic eye could see—which was why they hadn't noticed it on the screens.

"We need to be careful," Harry said, looking to the door. "They may be expecting us. Actually, I'm sure they are."

Camilla turned to Hunter. "Hunter can check for us."

Camilla knew she may be taking her feelings for the man a bit far when all eyes shot to her—Maya's burning with rage—but she couldn't help not caring. "What?" Camilla began. "It's not like we care what happens to him."

Hunter didn't seem to mind her jibes, instead quirking his brow. "You're never gonna believe I'm on your side, huh?"

She looked him directly in the eyes. "I'm always going to know you're ready to let the humans die."

Hunter matched her stare. "I've never lied about that."

Camilla ground her teeth but didn't respond as Maya brought the conversation back to the situation at hand. "Seriously, you guys," Maya said, "we need to figure out what to do."

Camilla's gaze snapped to Maya's. "I wasn't joking."

Maya went to argue, but Hunter stopped her with a gentle tug on her hand. "It's fine, love." He turned to meet Camilla's gaze. "As a show of good faith, Little Sister, I'll go."

Camilla grinned, smug.

Hunter met her grin with one to rival it as he grabbed Maya's hair in a fistful and pulled her to him. He kissed her, there in front of all of them, with vigor, his tongue jutting out immediately to take refuge in Maya's mouth. More like to take hostage of Maya's tongue as they clashed passionately in excited competition.

Camilla grimaced and looked away, finding both Vera and Harry doing the same. Public displays of affection were one thing, but public displays of tongue-clashings was something else entirely.

And between Maya and Hunter too.

It almost looked like they would begin fucking right there in front of them before Hunter pulled away, his eyes finding Maya's. "We'll continue later, love."

She clung to his shirt, shaking her head. "Let's forget about this and continue now."

Camilla strained to control herself before retorting on her sister's blindness to the man she was so ready to take to bed.

Hunter laughed and took her bottom lip between his teeth, giving it a tug before releasing. "I wish that were truly what you wanted." He stepped away from her, releasing her hold on his shirt. "But I know you want this cleared away."

He winked to her, then shadowed out.

M aya stared at the spot Hunter had just stood, then closed her eyes, breathing slowly in an attempt to control her urges to run after him. And her anger at her sister for suggesting he put himself in that type of danger.

She looked to her family, who all held horrified looks plastered on their faces, and tried to hide her giggle at their reactions as she focused on the screen that Harry held showing the inside of the room.

Hunter had shadowed into the back of the room without a notice. He stood there a few moments, allowing for time to pass to see if he would be caught.

When nothing happened, he took a single, small step forward. Faster than even he could react, than she could even blink, two halfies turned in his direction, stunning him to the spot. A mix of electricity and just pure pain hit him, dropping him to his knees almost immediately.

How had The Eight found all such powerful halfies? From what Maya understood, they usually weren't this powerful, rather a mix of normal witch powers, like Rory and Cora.

Maya clutched at the screen, having pulled it out of Harry's hands, and watched intently. The others within the room stopped their ministrations and turned to look at the man on his knees.

The two halfies stunning him stopped, and another stepped up, not giving him a moment to catch his breath as she threw her arms out. And it looked like another rare, very powerful woman, because if Maya was processing this correctly, he was having his life drained out of him. That was a scary, powerful magic.

Another super rare high-level.

The woman's gaze narrowed on him as he tried to resist, and it was all Maya could force herself to watch. She pushed the device into someone's hands, ready to run into the room, when arms wrapped around her.

"No! He wouldn't want you in there."

With Harry holding her back, the four of them watched the screen as Hunter began to sputter on his knees, falling to catch himself on his hands. The position gave her a sense of déjà vu, to Hell's Gate and his first mindfuck. He'd dropped to all fours then too, trying to keep himself strong against the mental torture.

But that had been fake.

This? This was very real. They could literally see the life drain from him as his skin turned ashen and the air before him darkened.

Maya couldn't watch anymore. She elbowed Harry in the gut, hard enough that his grip loosened, and ran past her family's screams to stop.

35

Maya burst through the door, ignoring the sting of the magical barrier as it rippled away. Her arms already engulfed in flames, one hand moving of its own accord to shoot at the one draining the life from Hunter.

She saw from her periphery that he was still writhing on his hands and knees, one of the halfies stunning him immediately after the life taker's retreat.

Maya knew he'd been through a lot of shit in his life and could've shadowed out of this. Knew he stayed so no one would turn on her. Knew it the same way she knew he loved her. But she couldn't stand around and watch it happen.

She was already ducking out of the way as another halfie turned to her.

But it was one against four, five if the one stunning Hunter was included.

She had them enflamed, but that amount of concentration was difficult when attempting to avoid getting stunned. The stunning had to be a control of the cells of the body because Hunter could withstand electrocutions. His stolen power allowed that much.

Two of them looked to be focused on the chants they were whispering beneath their breaths, ignoring the flames Maya had running up their lengths, the way the Bridgers coven had months ago.

This was dedication to the cause. The men up on the mall's rooftop had none of this.

Maya played with the flames as her anger rose at Hunter's position. She knew how powerful he was, and even if he couldn't before, now he could easily get out of it. Shadow away.

And she knew he was staying. For her.

If he stayed, the attention would be kept on keeping him down rather than fighting her. No matter her powerful magic, he had that and decades of training. And a carelessness that was dangerous. *He* was the one they had to keep at bay.

And if he got out, she'd be left vulnerable.

So he took it; the pain, the stuns, the life draining, all of it. He took it so she could take care of them.

The attention of the life-drainer turned to Hunter alongside the stunner, and Maya couldn't control her rage any longer. She enveloped the room in flames, filling the edges and slowly moving in.

In her concentration, the other stunner got the upper hand. Just as Maya felt her form drop, Vera ran into the room, throwing one, then the other, stun-powered halfies across the room and catching the life-drainer's attention.

Hunter immediately released from her hold and fell to his stomach, barely able to hold himself up on his forearms as he breathed in and out slowly.

Maya was back on her feet, watching her family stand off to the edge of the room as the life-drainer moved back to position to resume her earlier work.

Maya tsked. The drainer could play all she wanted, but she would *not* be playing with *Maya's* things.

The room dipped into darkness.

Maya could sense everyone stand still. Another great part of Hunter being around, and now not under their control, the halfies would most likely assume this power came from him.

She took that moment of uncertainty and felt the same rage fill her as those short moments at the Bridgers coven when she'd thought something had happened to Hunter. Felt her form burn, filled with flames so searing, volcanos would feel like winter storms.

Then she let her anger rage.

Bolts of excruciatingly hot fire burst through the edges of the room, purposefully avoiding the front door where her family stood, and moved inward. There went the first scream.

She brought back enough light to see she hadn't gotten all of them, and the life-drainer had thrown a marble to the ground to open her escape portal. She'd have to learn how the halfies made these portals.

More screams were filling the room. And with the heat of the flames, Maya knew they wouldn't last long. The halfies would be burned to crisps in moments.

The life-drainer and another got away before Maya could pull the flames from the edges of the room and direct it toward them.

But the others lay crisped.

Maya pulled the flames back toward her and silence followed.

She released the darkness so the light slowly edged back and listened to the slow breaths from Hunter's form—from her own form as the adrenaline wore off. The spot the portal had been called to her, the nagging feeling of almost having the life-drainer, of almost having the ability to hurt the halfie for even attempting to take Hunter from her.

Hunter slowly picked himself up onto all fours, then again until he was standing upright once more. Maya knew he was staring at her, but she couldn't unglue her gaze from the spot the two had vanished from. The bodies of the crisped lay around the room, and she didn't feel an ounce of regret. No, instead, she felt annoyance at not getting the others too.

Hunter moved until he reached her. He came up behind and wrapped his arms around her shoulders, bringing her in tight.

It was only then that she allowed herself to break her stare and breathe in his scent as he molded behind her.

T he shock of the screams washed over Vera, the sweat dry on her skin as the room began to cool. Those flames had been incinerating. So bad, Vera had started sweating almost immediately.

Which also meant they'd burned. Those halfies who'd been caught wouldn't have had a chance.

She stood frozen and watched as Harry broke and rushed into the room to make sure nothing was left to hurt the humans. And in the middle of the room, in the center of the circle the halfies had been in, shockingly out of the way of the flames, Harry softly pulled out the bomb.

It seemed Hunter was right. His sister was not a liar. They'd truly planned to begin terrorist scares within the humans.

"It's set to detonate in one minute." Harry cleared his throat and slowly moved calm fingers to deactivate it.

He looked like he'd done it a hundred times before. It was another thing that Vera was sure would plague her thoughts later, how adeptly those fingers moved.

Her gaze moved to Maya, whose eyes still burned with hatred as she looked down at the crisped corpses. Hunter hugged her from behind, and Vera could see that his presence helped Maya a bit, that knowing he was okay was helping her.

And he was okay.

Other than the bit of help from Maya to stand, which likely

came from the energy drain from resisting two stunners and a life-drainer, he was fine.

He'd done it. He'd taken it all as a show of good faith. All for Maya.

Vera looked around the room and caught Camilla staring at the two of them as well, and from the looks of it, Camilla was realizing in that moment that this wasn't just sex for them anymore.

It was something they were all aware of, but that Camilla had been the most adamant to ignore—she'd known their relationship had advanced; you'd have to be blind or stupid not to see it—but it was clear that Camilla hadn't wanted it to be true so badly she'd convinced herself otherwise.

But Vera knew it wasn't just sex. There was no other explanation for Hunter trusting Maya enough to take her to his manor, lose control in bed with her, tell her about his sister. For his need to protect her, to pick up on the first ring, and to want her to stay with him in his manor.

There was no other explanation for Maya's constant defenses of Hunter, for her constant desire to be near him, touching him. They had fallen for each other. It was as simple as that.

Harry walked back to them, leaving the scene as it was—he would likely come back to clean up so the humans never found out later—but for now, they would all go.

Camilla took Vera's hand so that she was linked to Harry. Vera hooked her hand into his elbow and waited as Harry slowly moved his other hand to Maya. He would port the five of them out—Hunter being far too drained to shadow himself, let alone both himself and Maya.

The moment they landed in the attic, Hunter dropped onto the chaise, throwing his head back to rest. Maya didn't hesitate in taking the seat right beside him, leaving no space between them, and dropping a hand onto his thigh as if she were laying her claim. Hunter gave a small, silent laugh as his hand slipped into the back of her shirt, resting at the small of her naked back.

He closed his eyes, his body obviously needing to rest after that little attack he'd just suffered. Vera was sure Maya's hand gliding up and down his thigh would settle his thoughts enough to drift off.

Vera turned just as Camilla reached for the Book.

"What's the point of looking through the Book again! There's nothing there." The frustration of not being able to find the spell The Eight were looking for was beginning to get to Vera.

"Look, Vera." Camilla was calm, but there was a desperation in her eyes that was pleading. "I don't know. I don't know what to do, and I just can't live with myself knowing we could've prevented them hurting humans but didn't because of some stupid spell this *fucking* Book is hiding. I just…they need a spell, so it must be in here. It has to be."

Vera slowly walked up to her baby sister and held the Book in one hand as she caressed Camilla with the other. "Okay. I'll go first. You calm down, and you can try after."

Camilla seemed almost thankful with the offer and released the Book.

Vera took it down to the empty room she and Hunter had been training in and tried talking to it. Somehow, it had worked for Camilla when she'd spoken to it, but it wasn't happening again.

When nothing happened, she resorted to flipping through it again—maybe something would jump out at her.

Scoff, yeah right.

Just as she expected, nothing.

Maybe it was something in Camilla's power, the fact that it had to do with thoughts, that had the Book listening to her and not anyone else. Because Vera tried speaking to the Book again and again with no change.

What spell could possibly be in this Book that The Eight couldn't find in someone else's? Why was it only in their Book? What connection did their family have to the spell? None of it made sense.

No matter, her time was up.

She took the Book back up to the attic, where no one had moved from their positions, and gave it to Camilla, who took the next hour.

From where Vera sat across from her sister, Camilla did exactly as she'd just been doing and was finding the exact same results.

Vera had hoped that since it had worked for Camilla before, speaking to the Book would work for her again.

"Maybe it was the Book's way of telling us not to give the spell to The Eight. Like it knows we have no other options, so instead, it's just holding the spell back," Vera joked.

"You know," Harry muttered. "You may be right."

"I was joking, Harry."

"No, but it just may be the case. This is a magical coven Book. It has a life of it's own, built from the generations of witches that took care of it and added to it. Maybe it knows the spell shouldn't be found, so it's refusing to find it," Harry explained.

Vera tried to relax against the wall, given there was nothing more she could do, as Camilla's time ticked away to an end and Warren showed up, taking a seat on the ground beside her.

His gaze seemed to be glued to his brother, who was currently cuddled up on the chaise, looking almost helpless.

Almost.

He still looked like he could, and happily would, crack some-one's neck. He took over most of the chaise with his legs spread wide, but still showed his vulnerability as he held Maya by his side.

It had been shocking to Vera to encounter every time

Hunter showed off his relationship. She'd assumed that he'd try to keep it a secret so that his vulnerabilities wouldn't be known, so that it wouldn't be known at all that he had vulnerabilities.

Apparently, Hunter Delvaux did not care.

He didn't shy away from his feelings for the middle Whittle. And from the look on Warren's face as he watched them, he was still getting used to this new side of his brother.

Harry took the Book after Camilla for his turn, sitting by Vera, yet not close enough to touch. The silence as he flipped through it allowed for Camilla to fill Warren in on the situation. Vera found herself jumping in at times to fill in whatever Camilla's frantic thoughts may have skipped over.

He looked shocked to hear the events of the day, especially his brother's part in it. It did, however, explain Hunter's current position—just woken from his nap, but still resting on the chaise beside Maya—as Warren looked back to the couple.

"The demons were having problems too," he told them. "I was sent out to help a group that were attacked. The attackers left when they found out we were there, and the group is in and out of it right now. We don't know if it was the halfies but I wouldn't doubt it."

"So essentially, this is a fight against every creature, not just us," Camilla said. "At least it's nice to know we're not the specific targets."

Angled toward the chaise, Vera watched as Maya rested deeper against Hunter's side, his had snaking from the small of her back to her midriff, as she spoke. "Well, that would make sense. It's a fight with the halfies. They're a mix of two species. I'm sure there's a mix of every single species."

"Except elves," Hunter commented.

Maya pushed into his gut softly, but smiled against him.

"So, what do we do?" Warren asked.

"We give them what they want," Vera responded. "The spell."

It was clear Warren didn't like the idea, as he went to argue, but Camilla cut him off, "We stopped them this time, but we won't be able to stop them every time. We need to do something."

"And fast," Vera muttered.

Harry slammed the Book shut, grunting in annoyance. "There's nothing. I think it's time we use that spell Hunter found."

Camilla's eyes darkened. "Where are we supposed to find the *ingredients* for the spell that Hunter found?"

"I'll get it," Hunter broke into the conversation. "We have a supply in the Theology building at your school. I'll go pick it up tomorrow."

36

Tomorrow came quickly, and Hunter found himself in an argument with Maya bright and early in the morning. "Love, I'm only going to the Theology building. I can go alone."

"I know that, but I want to come with you."

He quirked his brow at her. "Don't you think you're being a little protective? I've been through far worse than yesterday, my bleeding heart. I can handle it. I'll be fine."

Her eyes warmed. "I know. I just want to come. To be with you." His eyes softened, but he didn't budge. "I know at the end of the day you can protect yourself, but I *want* to be with you."

Hunter watched her, her sincerity and hope. And the formidable creature behind her eyes that told him she was coming. Relenting seemed inevitable as he walked over and sighed heavily, wrapping his arms around her waist and bringing her in close. "You know I always give you what you want."

She smiled and kissed him lightly on the chin as her arms wrapped around his neck. "I know."

He rolled his eyes and smiled back, whispering a quick, "I

hate you" before shadowing them to the hallway that lead to the potions room in the Theology building.

They were alone, no one guarding it this morning, so they headed straight for the room with no problems. Not that anyone would give him problems, but dealing with demons as they stared Maya down wasn't a part of his agenda for the day.

"No guards?" Maya asked, walking around the room and allowing Hunter to pick up any ingredients they needed as she observed.

Hunter looked to her through his lashes, smirking. "Those guards were only placed there because of the pieces to Hell's Gate. Otherwise, no one knows about this place, and even if they did, it's only ingredients. Not important enough for guards."

He walked over to Maya, opening her small crossbody bag and dropping a couple of vials in. She looked away as she swallowed deeply, causing the grin to grow on his features. So, she'd seen the eye in a glass jar that they needed for this spell get thrown into her bag.

His little bleeding heart.

The entire thing took less than five minutes, and as they closed the door behind them—shadowing in and out of the room made impossible by special spells—Maya was thrown far into the other side of the hallway, her body slamming hard.

Hunter's entire form freeze, then turned on the opposite end of the room where a creature demon stood. He stared the demon down, feeling the control on his fury barely holding on as the man spoke.

"Hello, old friend."

"Dashiell," Hunter seethed through his teeth.

Dashiell smiled. "Are you okay, brother? You seem angry."

Hunter growled and began to move, no longer able to keep still as Dashiell's gaze ravished Maya before meeting his again.

Standing between the two, he knew it would give away his intentions for her, his vulnerability for her, but Hunter cared more about keeping Maya safe than the repercussions of his actions.

Though his back was to her, Hunter could feel Maya stir behind him, slowly picking herself up off the ground.

"Ah." Dashiell's smile was full but humorless. "So the rumors are true. You are fucking the witch." Hunter didn't answer, but felt himself grow to cover more of Maya, a move that no doubt didn't go unnoticed by the other demon, as he made a disgusted laugh. "No, I apologize, *brother*," he spit the term out as if it burned him. "You're not just fucking the witch, you've fallen for the whore."

That final word broke Hunter's resolve as his arms came up on their own accord, ready to kill the demon. It was amazing, his usage of both water and fire at the same time, as he threw Dashiell back with the blast of the water and burned him at the same time.

Too bad for Hunter, this demon had control of an element too. It was why they'd gone on trips together in the past. Using both of their elements had made things so much more entertaining.

Dashiell lifted himself off the wall with his air control, moving out of Hunter's reach.

In the air, he shadowed himself behind Hunter, placing himself by Maya's side. Before Hunter could attack, Dashiell held her in front of his body. "Go ahead and attack, brother. I wonder which of us you'll get."

Hunter's looked to Maya for only a moment before his gaze settled on Dashiell, and a wicked smile erupted on his face. "Your problem, brother," more acid dripped from his usage of the word than anything Dashiell had muttered, "is you didn't do your research before attacking."

Before Dashiell could process what Hunter meant by that,

Maya burst herself into flames. Dashiell flew back, trying to break free of the fire, but bits followed him.

Hunter stood back and watched as Maya turned to the demon and threw another bolt of flames at him, enveloping his neck. Dashiell looked to Maya with pure fear and astonishment, and that made the grin on Hunter's features expand.

When his battle began to fade and he dropped to his knees, Maya released her power, choosing to watch him die slowly rather than giving him the satisfaction of a quick, albeit painful, death.

Hunter watched Maya a moment, delight rushing through his form at the sight he was beholding. He would never get tired of watching her dominate.

Now that was his girl.

T he demon lay dying on the ground, Maya standing above it just watching. Hunter stepped up behind her, placing his hands on either one of her biceps. He bent low to her ear and whispered, "He has the shadowing ability. It can be yours."

She stiffened a moment, then tilted her head to the side to look him in the eyes. His eyes bore encouragement but no pressure. If she didn't want to, he wouldn't make her.

She took another moment to answer. "How?"

His eyes grew impossibly blacker, ever the more pleased. And she really liked being the reason behind it.

Both of his hands slid down her arms, landing on her hands and pulling them up to face the dying demon, palms pointing forward. Maya looked to her hands and listened to his voice in her ear. "Allow your body to detect his power."

"I thought you could only steal primary powers?" she whispered low.

He pressed his body more firmly against hers. "That's true.

Primary powers only. Shadowing is so much a part of demons, it is almost like a primary power, so it counts as one of the things you can steal."

She breathed out and allowed her body to relax into his as she listened to him.

"Detect the power you want. It'll be easier for you right now because you know exactly what power you're looking for." He seemed to know better than to ask her to steal Dashiell's true primary power. She was too good for that, too much of a witch for that, and he had always respected her for it.

Maya tried to do as he instructed, looking for the ability to shadow in the gurgling demon. She felt a prickle move into her hands and gasped.

She could feel Hunter smile by her ear. "You felt that? Like a set of pinpricks in your hands?"

She nodded once.

"Good. Now allow that to continue. Allow the pricks to find their way into your body. Allow your body to drop its defenses and make space for the pricks to settle."

The demon was only moments away from dying, but Maya was too focused on what she was currently doing to care. She felt the pricks needle their way into her hands and into her bloodstream. She felt the prickling inside of her, and yet, it didn't hurt. It was odd, but it didn't hurt.

When the prickling hit her chest, her body jerked, then the feeling was gone. Hunter dropped their arms, bringing them down so he could hold her, and smiled into her ear. "Good job, love."

Dashiell took a final helpless breath, his gaze finding Maya's for mercy.

But Maya couldn't find any within her; he'd tried to hurt Hunter. He'd tried to hurt *her*.

He was dead only moments later.

She turned in Hunter's arms to face him.

"Let's test it." Hunter smiled at her and shadowed out of her embrace and across the hall. His lips grew into a seductive smirk. "Shadow to me, love."

Maya's core tightened at the demand, and she felt more of a need to shadow to him just to get him naked than to test her new ability.

She'd learned early on that you did not force your powers into doing anything. You simply desired for it to happen, and it would. So she tried to settle her body to desire to shadow before Hunter, and just like that, she was there.

Given she'd shadowed with Hunter a million times before, the experience didn't make her feel odd at all. Rather, it felt second nature at this point.

Hunter's expression embodied the proud lover, but before Maya could reach out to him, he smirked and whispered, "Try again," then shadowed out of the room entirely.

Her jaw ground as she looked around and dropped her crossbody to the ground, but found no indication to where he'd gone. This was the part of shadowing, and porting for that instance, that always got her—how did they know exactly where the person they were going to was?

Settling into her thoughts, she tried what seemed to always work with powers, simply desiring to be near Hunter. Considering she knew he was within this floor, the ability came easily to her. Maybe this was why a location was always required, but exact coordinates weren't. As long as Hunter knew she was at home, he always found her.

Without any effort, her body shadowed itself, landing directly in front of Hunter, in what looked like an old empty classroom, probably one of the unused rooms at the underground levels of this building.

Maya shadowed closer to him before he could get away, leaving less than an inch of space between their bodies.

He looked down at her, wickedness written on every inch of

his being. "You know, love, with both of us losing control on the same powers, we'll be balls of light fucking through space."

Maya's control broke at just that moment, her arms lighting aflame and eyes darkening to a black that rivaled his, as she pushed him against the wall, the fire off her arms lighting him up.

It seemed this was exactly the reaction he desired.

He allowed her to rip open his shirt, buttons flying haphazardly throughout the room, and nails raking down his chest to the closings of his trousers as flames broke out at every point of contact.

She leaned in and licked him from pecs to collarbone as her fingers unbuttoned his trousers and dipped in, taking his length in hand.

He growled as she bit down at the base of his neck. Then he was finally giving in, moving them so that she was pressed against the wall.

She continued playing with him, pumping her hand up and down his length and feeling it grow as his arousal increased.

His hands found their way beneath her shirt.

She pumped again and again until his growls were vibrations on her throat.

He ripped her shirt open, the pieces falling down her sides as her torso showcased to him. No bra, of course.

He was aggressive as he got to his knees, mouth finding a breast and suckling as he pulled on her trousers, just low enough to get a taste.

With her trousers at her thighs, Maya couldn't spread her legs, instead feeling his tongue on all of her exposed skin and his fingers finding their way inside her. All she could do was pull on his golden hair, hard enough to tell him to stop so she could take the trousers off and spread for him, and to never stop because wow.

It still astounded her how a tongue on her nipple could

cause so much pleasure by itself, how the bites he left on her skin brought her close with no other help.

When she bucked against his hand, thumb playing with her clit as his fingers pumped inside her, another growl, deep and possessive, left him.

He was up on his feet and kissing her again, their tongues fighting for dominance as he peeled at her clothes.

In record time, they were naked and Hunter picked her up by the thighs and wrapped her legs around his waist. He placed his cock at her opening and played with her folds, her scent dripping over him.

There was no need to wait, to take it slow. She was soaking and ready to be filled.

The fire their bodies elicited lit the room in a romantic ambiance as they stared at one another, the flames devouring their every inch, yet not taking from their human forms. It was something only two primary fire holders could enjoy.

Hunter took no mercy in plunging himself to the very hilt.

She cried out with the press of his bare chest to hers as she arched off of the wall, scratching at his shoulders as his hands dug into the backs of her thighs.

"This is it," he growled into her as he pulled out and pushed back in, reaching deeper and harder with each achingly slow thrust.

"What?" she breathed against his lips as she tried to keep her eyes open and on him.

His stare found hers and didn't break. "If I could choose a place to be for the rest of my life, it would be here, plunged deep inside you, Maya Whittle."

He pulled himself to the very edge, then back inside, harder still.

Their flames mixed together, causing a pleasure so deep, Maya was sure he almost dropped to his knees as he wobbled to hold them up. It was like a featherlight graze of fire along every inch of your body, and Maya knew it fed the monster inside him that cared only to ravage his witch, because she felt the same way.

Her screams of pleasure were no doubt adding to his breaking point.

He pounded uncontrollably into her. So blissful, Maya let herself go and only felt each pound her body took. And before she realized it, Maya's control on her newest power broke, and they were falling through the wall.

He'd been right. Balls of light literally fucking through air.

Hunter had the foresight, somehow, to turn their bodies so that he landed on his back when they fell through the wall and onto the ground on the other side.

He landed on a plush rug, which broke his fall ever so slightly, and looked up to Maya, ravaged by flames, landing on top of him.

She pressed against his chest and moved her hips in tantalizing circles as she rode him, feeling her insides tighten with every move. Her breasts bouncing in time to her movements and catching his attention.

She smiled as his gaze latched onto her chest, and his mouth opened like he wanted to take a peak between his lips.

She loved the thrill of knowing that he didn't know what to focus on—her breasts bouncing deliciously before him or her open mouth moaning out his name.

Her eyes remained open to slits so she could watch him watch her. Ecstasy.

Her final scream ricochetted through the room as she came, her walls clutching him so tightly he burst inside her, filling her entirely with his seed.

It was never-ending, and Maya wanted to remain in that moment for the rest of her life.

As their breaths came back down and the flames receded, Maya lifted herself off of him and toppled onto the rug beside him. His loose fist fell onto her stomach—he always had to be touching her, even moments after coming inside her—and a light chuckle left his lips.

She assumed this was what it was like to be a werewolf, hyperaware and hyper-protective of your partner at all times.

"Me too," she breathed out, still trying to catch her breath.

He turned to her and quirked a brow.

"If I could choose a place for the rest of my life, it would be having you inside me, always."

He growled. "Don't make promises you don't intend to keep, love."

"Never."

She intended to keep this, no matter how much her family wouldn't approve.

His features darkened, and she could tell his body was already getting ready for round two, not that they had any time for that at the moment.

As her mind came back to reality, she looked around the room to find it impeccable. It was designed in a plush, romantic array with rugs and soft looking lounge couches and a coffee table. Curtains rung around the walls, even though they were underground and there were no windows.

This must've been a room some of the demons lounged in when they came down to the Theology undergrounds.

Maya turned her head to face Hunter, finding he was still staring at her. She smiled at him in a dark, seductive manner. "When this is all over, we're not leaving your manor for a month."

A grin erupted on his face, all the wicked things he already had planned for that month clear on every inch of him.

37

*B*eing that they were early risers, Hunter and Maya had gone to the Theology building when the rest of the house had still been sleeping.

Back at the house, they found everyone sitting at the table in the kitchen.

Vera watched Hunter place the ingredients, including the eye onto the island.

Like Camilla, she tried looking to the glass jar that held the eye but couldn't keep her gaze on it for more than half a second.

Camilla backed up to the edge of the kitchen. "You know, I think I'm the worst when it comes to making potions. We don't want to mess this up. You guys should do it."

Vera followed suit, edging to the other end of the kitchen. "Harry, you've been alive the longest. Your skill is most honed."

Harry looked about ready to run. "Warren, you're a demon, this should be a piece of cake to you."

Okay, so Harry was just as equally grossed out with the need to use a *live* human eye. Live. Like it was still blinking when Vera glanced at it. How had they even done that?

Warren grimaced. "Maya, I hear you're the master at potion

making in the family. It always was something I never mastered."

Huh, must be the human side.

Maya blanched.

Before she could say anything, Hunter landed a hand to her head, letting in slowly fall until it loosely wrapped the back of her neck, and he laughed. "Don't worry, love. I'll do it."

There was a heavy sigh of relief as she turned and gave him a grateful kiss on the lips. "It seems I'm ever more thankful for your existence."

Maya left the kitchen with the rest of them, giving Hunter the space to make the potion alone, and for once, Vera was thankful for his existence as well. Had he not been around, not only would they not have found out about the potion or had the means for the necessary ingredient, but Harry would've been forced to do it. Vera knew Maya would've turned it on the boys, and Harry's life experience would've put him front of the board. She also knew he would step up to the plate if it were required.

The kitchen cleared in seconds, no one wanting to be there when Hunter took the eye out. Or, like the demonic tongue instructions mentioned, when he cut it up into four pieces and dropped each one into the potion at different intervals.

The instructions actually said the eyes should still be moving when cut up. That meant each of the four pieces should still be alive. Vera could get sick just thinking about it.

Back in the empty room mirroring the living room, Camilla gripped her chest and turned to Maya, seemingly breathing out a sigh now that she was on the other side of the house. "You'll never hear this from me again, but right now, I am so thankful you two are together."

Maya rolled her eyes with a laugh and turned to the others.

They spent their time in the empty room trying to clear their minds of what Hunter was up to in the kitchen by practicing their powers: Camilla's being the most infuriating because she needed another person to practice with.

Harry, given his powers came naturally to warlocks and he had over a century on them, didn't need any practice, so target he became. It could've easily have been Warren too, but his shadowing ability helped both Maya and Vera with their target practice.

Camilla laughed as she teased Harry through her telepathy and tried to get to his mind when he attempted to think of nothing. It was unfounded, but it made Vera jealous.

So jealous, her thoughts moved from Hunter's work in the kitchen to throwing her sister around the room. And almost felt the magic move toward Camilla. Want something and it'll happen, right?

Definitely not the best use of her powers.

Focused on Warren shadowing in and out of the room, Vera still couldn't react quickly enough. He made sure to only pop up in her view since her demon detection didn't work on halfies, but her reflexes weren't honed to that ability.

Eventually, Hunter walked out to find them.

Maya walked tentatively over to him like she was afraid to touch the remnants of the potion.

"My hands are clean, love. I washed up. The kitchen is clean too," he reassured her.

It seemed he didn't need telepathy to know what Maya was thinking.

She relaxed at his reassurances and leaned into him as they walked back to the kitchen to find it immaculate. You would never believe he'd just been in there cutting the eyeball of a live human child.

A potion sat in a vial at the center of the island.

Vera took the spell sheet, having made Warren translate it while Hunter had been out getting the ingredients with Maya. The spell itself was simple; they were to place the Book on the table, then drip the potion along the cover until they formed an *x* along the surface. Then they would whisper the spell. It was something a single witch could do all on her own.

The three sisters huddled and whispered the spell together anyway.

And nothing happened. Odd.

With another try, Vera furrowed her brows. "What the hell?"

"It's likely based off tongue," Harry explained. "You may need to do it in the tongue it was written in. Probably a precaution by demons to make sure just anyone can't use it."

Okay, so a single witch *couldn't* perform it.

Vera dropped the paper Warren had translated on as Camilla waved her hands from the brothers to the vial.

Hunter stepped up. "Anything for you, Little Sister."

Vera stifled a breathy laugh at Camilla's eye roll and watched the brothers recite the spell in their tongue. It's a good thing they hadn't tried it too. There were sounds in there that Vera was sure her mouth couldn't form.

It took a second before the Book began to lightly smoke before fading away. Then it flipped, the pages moving at a speed so fast, Vera barely kept her focus. Then it paused on a blank page and like literal magic, it was no longer blank. Twelve lines made up the majority of the page. The spell The Eight wanted so badly they'd killed and traumatized for it.

The demonic tongue spell worked by creating the potion and dropping it onto an object, then performing the spell above it. While performing the spell, the thing most desired was said aloud, and it should appear on the page.

Voila, it worked.

Closer inspection showed them that this new spell was mismatched lines from 'Grandmama Told Me' and it's prequel. The jumble of sentences made no sense in the order they were placed, but maybe that was the point. For the spell to work, this dumping of lines that simply looked jumbled together would need to be read.

Having the spell put them into a silence Vera didn't want to break. Now that they had it, they really had to think about what to do with it.

Vera didn't realize the passing of time until Warren shadowed back into the house—when had he left?—with three boxes of pizzas.

When they noticed his return, he smiled. "I figured you wouldn't have felt up to cooking tonight."

"I don't like it," Maya began as she pulled a supreme combo into her hands, "but I think we'll need to take Colette to know where to finish this…or start it."

Camilla sighed when no one fought the statement. "I was thinking the same thing."

Warren reached for Camilla's hand and gave it a light squeeze as Vera looked over to how closely Maya and Hunter were sitting.

The distance between her and Harry felt wider now as they sat at opposite ends of the table.

She felt the ache in her build and knew she couldn't keep going like this. She'd need to at least try with him.

The plan was simple: find The Eight, try to keep them out of their minds until they found out what this was all about, then see if there was a way to stop them. Vera had a bad feeling about not being able to stop them.

But they had to. Probably would have to kill them, not that Hunter or Maya would have a problem with that. But the rest of them?

How they would kill them, they hadn't decided.

They needed to see what they were dealing with first. Hopefully, having two demons on their side would help even their numbers a bit more.

It was a weak plan, but with nothing to go off of, it was all they had.

And given the time constraint on the lunatic halfies, a night's rest for an early morning was the best option overall. They needed to be well rested for this.

Hopefully, in another twelve hours, this would all be over.

Or like Maya stated, and Vera feared, the real problem would begin.

<hr>

I t didn't take long for the house to quiet down.

Vera cracked her bedroom door open and looked out to the hallway. Empty.

She silently closed her door and walked to Harry's room, standing outside of it apprehensively for what felt like months, but was likely only a few seconds.

Before she could back down, Vera knocked on the door once, then opened it, not giving him the chance to respond. She needed to get inside before she chickened out.

Harry was sitting at the edge of his bed, bent over his knees. He looked like he was thinking about something important. Vera wasn't sure if she was glad to have interrupted or if she should apologize and leave.

His head snapped up, and his gaze locked onto hers.

Her heart beat so quickly, she was scared it'd throw itself out of her body entirely.

She swallowed the lump in her throat and closed the door behind her, hands gripping the handle as her back pressed against the door.

Neither one spoke for some time as they took one another in. Finally, Vera said, "Are you okay?"

He took a moment to respond. "I was trying to talk myself out of coming to you. It wasn't working very well."

Her heart stopped for a fraction of a second before speeding up, unbelievably faster. She didn't know how it hadn't given up yet.

Her eyes remained trained on him as she slowly released the iron grip she had on the door handle and pushed herself to move. She walked until she was almost standing between his legs, forcing him to sit upright, his eyes grazing her form slowly before staring back at her.

That slow graze shot goosebumps up every inch of her flesh.

Vera didn't know where her confidence came from, but she heard herself blurting, "Can I stay with you tonight?"

She saw the shock fill Harry's eyes before it was replaced with need. His Adam's apple bobbed, and Vera realized he was trying to control himself.

Maybe that's where the confidence was coming from.

Apparently that control didn't expand to his vocal cords because he didn't say anything in response. Just nodded. A multitude of small, eager nods.

Vera smiled, her blood boiling at the look in his eyes, and watched him crawl backwards onto his bed until he was perched on a pillow. His eyes never left hers as she followed suit, crawling over to him. From his perspective, she likely looked like a panther after her prey, and she loved the sound of that.

She lay next to him and he turned to face her.

They didn't touch, just stared.

Harry eventually moved his hand so it gripped one of hers, and they remained like that until they fell asleep.

<hr>

Hunter was staying in her room that night. They'd become accustomed to staying at his manor, but Maya found solace in being under the Whittle house. If something were to happen, she wanted to be near her family; wanted to know she could protect them—Hunter could protect them.

The silencing spell on her room was made permanent about a week after they'd begun sleeping together weeks ago, and there was nothing she was more grateful for at the moment than silencing charms that didn't need to be activated every single time.

They'd just caught their breaths as they came down from their highs, turning to face one another, their bodies pressed together and left not an inch of space between them.

Their foreheads pressed together, noses brushing and eyes closed, as they breathed one another in. Maya basked in the glory of having him beside her and feeling his arm thrown over her waist, bringing her in even closer still.

"I'm never gonna get tired of this," he whispered in amazement.

Her lips twitched into a smile as she glanced up through her lashes to find his closed.

Relaxed, with limbs tangled, they fell asleep.

Camilla and Warren went to bed facing one another. Feet sandwiched under the sheets while they lay a foot apart so they could stare at one another. They laughed and Camilla felt like a schoolgirl at the giddiness that expanded with every passing second.

Eventually, Warren brushed her face and whispered, "I love you."

Camilla's eyes never left his as she thought back on all her arguments about demons. She'd always used that as an excuse for why Maya should leave Hunter, but it had started to settle in her thoughts with the question: could she ever fully trust a demon? Could a demon ever fully trust her?

Warren still hadn't lost control with her when they slept together. Maya had noticed her apprehension about it and had reassured her it doesn't happen all the time. It actually happened less than it didn't.

Though that should've calmed Camilla, her doubts had crept in and stayed a prominent part of her daily thoughts.

They'd been together enough by then for it to have at least happened once. Was it because deep down, he knew this relationship wasn't his final?

And recently, she hadn't been losing control either.

Camilla searched Warren's gaze as she whispered back, "I love you too."

38

Her giggles beneath him caused a wolfish grin as he held her down on the bed. Maya's body racked with laughter as she tried to squirm out from under him, but he was having too much fun to let go. His bites lined the side of her neck as he pushed aside the chuckle that was trying to ebb out of him.

"Hunter!" she squeaked, causing his heart to thunder louder than he'd ever experienced before. All he wanted was to keep her in bed, take her to his manor, and keep her safe and all his.

He paused, hovering over her, his hands just beneath her arms, ready to attack again in a moment's notice. She calmed and stared up at him with a glow of a smile, her hands settling around his biceps. She was so beautiful.

"Tell me again, what're you threatening?" he growled through the wolfish smile.

"Hunter," she said in mock reprimand. She was trying to be serious, but it wasn't working very well. "Either continue training Vera or no more sex!"

His brows rose at her audacity, his fingers slowly strolling up. "Really?"

She squirmed under him, her hands falling to stop another attack. "Really!"

He tsked as he leaned down and kissed the area between her breasts. "I don't think so."

Her hands were in his hair, pulling so that he looked up at her. "Baby! She needs the training, and Harry will talk to her about being an ass to you. Please. For me!"

He tsked. "I think I do enough for you as it is."

His grip on her loosened as he hovered over her, taking her in as his fingers skimmed her sides, not to tease, just a simple touch. Her eyes narrowed on him, and before he knew what was happening, she had them rolled over.

Straddling his hips, she held his arms out by his head and leaned into him. "No threats, baby. You're going to continue training Vera."

His lips quirked. He liked this position just as much as the last. They may have to leave soon to deal with The Eight, but he'd be happy to stay there all day. "Will I?"

She didn't move, just smirked down at him. The glint in her eyes as telling as ever. She was his little dark witch, and he'd do anything for her.

This was a losing battle from the beginning. The moment she asked him to train Vera again, he knew he would do it, but when that threat came out of her mouth, he couldn't help but attack.

She was threatening *him*. With sex. She was almost more insatiable than he, and *she* was threatening *him*.

In fact, to really get at her, he could take the sex away.

But he wouldn't do that. Not only because it would be torture for him as well, but because he always did as she asked. So if she wanted sex, she'd get sex. And if she wanted him to train her sister, he would train her sister.

He knew she saw the resolution in his eyes with the wicked

smile that turned her features. She leaned down, still holding his arms by his head, and kissed him.

She pulled away and just stared at him. "Thank you, baby."

He winked back at her. "You're welcome, love."

<hr>

H unter shadowed home for all of two minutes before he was back with seemingly no change, Maya's gaze narrowing on him. "Why leave?"

He shrugged, ever the nonchalant. "I needed something."

Maya tilted her head like she was ready to question him, but was interrupted when Vera and Harry walked into the kitchen, and Camilla groaned, "I cannot wait to get this over with."

Her family smiled at her. Warren kissed her crown, and older Delvaux rolled his eyes so dramatically it was a wonder they didn't fall out.

She was also more than ready to be done with him.

She looked him over as her family settled into the room, and her gaze caught on his left hand. There was a black ring on his ring finger she'd never seen before. Hunter didn't do jewelry. Or at least, she'd never seen him wear jewelry, and he was at her house *all* of the time.

She turned her attention back to people she actually trusted and knew there was no more stalling. Time to get this over with.

As ready as they could be, they walked down to the basement to grab Colette.

Hunter crouched before his sister, leaning in so he was only a few inches from her face, his tone oozing disgust. "Hello, sister."

Colette ground her teeth but didn't respond. When Hunter backed away and inconspicuously placed himself in front of

Maya, Colette found her voice. "Good job, witches. You really have turned my brothers into your desperate bitches."

Camilla felt Warren stiffen by her side, Hunter unmoving before Maya. She was trying to rile them up, and the longer this went on, the more it would work.

Luckily, Harry interrupted and unchained the halfie, pulling on her arm so she stood.

Colette beamed smugly. "Ah, so you've found the spell?"

Again, no one moved. Instead, they watched her. Was there anything telling in the way she acted now?

No. She looked like she did before, like The Eight knew they'd be getting the spell. From what Camilla knew of sister Delvaux, there likely was no doubt. As witches, they wouldn't allow The Eight to terrorize the masses.

"You guys are no fun," Colette grumbled, then turned to Harry, eyeing him like he were a feast. To be fair, he was quite attractive.

This time, Camilla saw Vera stiffen by her side.

Harry pushed her away and tightened his hold on her arm, giving her a shake so she'd finally cough up the location The Eight were waiting. Good thing too because it looked like Vera was ready to throw Colette's ass through the basement walls.

"You know," Colette made an annoyed turn of her lips, "you could just give me the spell."

"Fat chance," Camilla muttered under her breath.

If shit went down, they needed to at least bare witness to it.

Each of the men took their partner's hands, Harry carrying Colette's extra weight, and disappeared from the basement.

Together, they landed in the middle of a warehouse.

The guys kept hold of each of them in case of an emergency exit. They'd learned their lesson at the Bridgers coven.

The warehouse was mostly empty, only a few large pieces of equipment littered the area that Camilla had to assume weren't in use. Or at least not now. They must've been in use during the day because wow, they were clean.

"Downstairs. We do our work in the basement," Colette muttered, the glint in her eyes telling them that locking her in the basement hadn't been any sort of punishment.

Camilla was too distracted as she looked around the room, swearing she'd seen someone standing by one of the corners but not seeing them any longer.

You see anything suspicious? As much as she wished she had the energy to send it to everyone, Camilla only managed to send the message to her sisters.

Nada, Maya thought distractedly.

I swear I saw a couple people by that machine, but not there anymore. Vera's attention was on Colette again.

I thought I saw someone in the corner too.

Probably left when we showed up, Maya explained.

Probably trying for a surprise attack later, Vera added.

Colette seemed unamused by their lack of attention, like she wanted to rile them up but was coming up blank, and turned toward the stairs, surprisingly in the middle of the warehouse. An odd location, but okay.

Standing alone in the hallway when they reached the bottom of the stairs was a girl who didn't look any older than seventeen, watching them.

Unsurprisingly, they were expected.

The girl said nothing but turned her back to them and walked down the hall. Camilla's hand was growing slightly sweaty even in the chill of the warehouse, her heart beginning to pick up its pace ever so slightly.

When they reached a wide, empty room, the girl walked to the corner and stopped. She turned to look at them as they filled the middle of the room.

Colette moved quickly, pulling out of Harry's grasp and trying to flee to the other side of the room. They were lucky in the moment to have the brothers along, each grabbing her by an arm and pulling her back. Warren's grip looked painfully tighter than his brother's.

It wasn't much, given Camilla knew The Eight didn't care for one another, but Colette was their only piece of leverage.

It was in that sudden moment that the room filled.

Given the fact the Delvauxs trained for moments like this, it felt off putting that they allowed themselves to get surrounded.

More than two dozen women filled the room. Either the men weren't part of the grand scheme of things or they had other plans with the men.

A light shield wavered into place around their small group just as a blast came from one of the halfies. It ricocheted off the shield and almost hit her like her own personal boomerang.

Hunter had put up the shield. It was the slightest of moves, but his jaw tightened as the blast hit the shield, giving him away. It was him, and Camilla didn't know how to feel about that.

Colette shrugged from her brothers, the collar around her neck refraining her from using her magic, but couldn't get away from their grasps.

"So we meet again, ladies," a woman that looked almost like she could be their parents' age spoke up, "and gentlemen."

The one standing behind her, someone probably around Maya's age, was almost giddy in her excitement, while the others held themselves neutral.

"Do we?" Maya answered. "I don't recall ever seeing you."

The woman smirked. "So I've met your sisters only. I believe you were off shagging our demon."

Maya growled, and Camilla hated that she tsked in her head too. He was Maya's demon, not anyone else's. Maya wasn't one for sharing, especially her demon.

But as usual, Harry interrupted before the fight broke out about the wrong matter. "What is it you want with the spell?

What good could Grandmama truly do for you? If you need someone to care for you, you have one another."

Scoffed laughter came from all corners of the room, the woman they were speaking to looking at them like they were crazy. "I do not care about being cared for. I need the respect of the loathsome species that have always ignored us. We *will* have our revenge."

The shield around them wavered once, twice, then held still. Camilla had been so focused on the woman that she hadn't realized that attacks were still being thrown from all ends to get Hunter to break the shield.

How long will Hunter be able to hold it? She sent to her sisters, though only really speaking to Maya.

He's strong. A long time if it's petty attacks like this. She sounded apprehensive.

Then why do you sound worried?

One of them has a primary shield power. They're going to be able to easily break it when they want to.

So they were being played with. And Hunter knew it. But he still wasted his energy. Why waste energy on something so futile?

"How exactly do you plan on getting this revenge? What can an old woman really do for you?" Vera's fists were tightening into balls of white.

The woman smirked and looked to Colette, evaluating, before turning back to them. "Has our representative not spoken to you?"

"She's just as much a liar as the rest of you," Camilla spewed.

She laughed. "We do not lie. I am being honest with you now."

"So how will she help you?" Maya's jaw was tightening, her form rising to take up room like she was ready to go on the defensive.

Camilla just noticed Hunter's form move toward Maya,

making sure she was protected, when the woman laughed. "You'll just have to wait and see."

The shield was a blast of lights and glass that wasn't glass. It was almost beautiful, in a gothic sort of way.

So, Maya had been right. They were waiting to blast through the shield. And what better moment than when Hunter was distracted with her?

Fire was already lining the arms of both Hunter and Maya, but the shield holder had worked immediately, and the Delvauxs were thrown back into the fair corner of the room. Again, they'd been trained their entire lives. How had a halfie beat them? Was being there with Maya and Camilla a distraction they weren't accustomed to?

A shield stronger than any Camilla had ever seen held them to that little corner of the room like an audience to the show.

At the same moment the Delvauxs hit the wall, Camilla felt a hand grab for her but didn't realize what was happening in her distraction to make sure Warren was all right. Harry had tried to grab her and her sisters and port out of the room. Given he only had porting and healing to rely on, he didn't have magic else to protect them. His spell casting wouldn't exactly do them much at the moment.

But his rush to get to all of them had hindered his success. He was thrown to the other end of the room, falling flat to the ground. He was definitely unconscious. They'd thrown him much harder than they'd thrown the Delvauxs.

With Colette trapped behind the shield with her brothers, Camilla and her sisters turned their attention to the many more halfies they still had to worry about.

Okay, so they'd been a bit conceited to think their men wouldn't get distracted in keeping them safe and they would be trained enough to take this on.

The woman they'd been speaking to winked at them, then

just as suddenly as they'd appeared, the dozens of halfies were gone, though the shield holding the Delvauxs stayed in place.

Colette did not seem happy to be stuck behind it with her brothers.

Maya and Vera's backs hit hers as they looked about the room, circling around a few times as they readied for whatever would happen.

Honestly, how was it that all these halfies were so powerful, but the average witch barely had any magic to deem them a true threat? It was then that Camilla realized. "They're the most powerful witch or demon halfies. They want to be respected like the powerful witch and demon families are, that's why they're doing this."

They kept their backs to one another, but Maya whispered back—not because she had to. It was likely just the apprehension of waiting for something to jump out that kept her quiet. "I can't argue with that reasoning."

The first mistake came when Vera's desperation to get to Harry won out, and she stepped out of the little circle they'd created.

The moment she took that single step in Harry's direction, an electrical shock flew their way, hitting all three of them and dropping them to their knees. Camilla had no idea where it came from. She hadn't noticed anyone else in the room, and this wasn't Colette.

Another electrically based halfie! Vera bitterly thought.

Maybe Hunter could steal it from their annoying asses. Coming from Camilla, this caused a laugh from both her sisters.

Wow, sister, coming around? Maya's tone was light in the impending dread.

Camilla was just picking herself up—the shock of the electricity still running through her veins—when another blast hit her, and she felt herself get cuffed in what seemed like the same instruments that held Colette's power every time she attacked them.

The cuffs around their wrists were clipped to chains against the wall opposite the Delvauxs—a feat they had to drag the girls for—before the shock vanished altogether, and all three fell to their knees.

Again, they were left alone.

And Camilla still had no idea where any of it had come from.

In the quietude of the room, Camilla watched Vera look on desperately to Harry. The brothers were safe behind their shield, but Harry had nothing covering him. She could only imagine the pain going through Vera at that very moment.

Possibly even a wish that she had admitted her feelings for him earlier.

She turned to the Delvauxs, finding both brothers' attention intently on them. Warren pressed desperately against the shield as if trying to get out. He looked to be in the same position that Vera was with Harry. She was the one in danger, and he could do nothing to help her. No doubt whatever shield was around them didn't allow for their shadowing ability—or maybe any ability—to be used.

Hunter looked calm, unbothered. His gaze was trained on Maya, his eyes encompassing a storm of rage. When Camilla looked to her sister, she found her gaze glued back to her lover's before flashing to other areas of the room like she was making sure nothing else was around. Then they were back on Hunter.

Camilla's gaze shot back to the siblings behind the shield. Why was it that Harry got knocked unconscious and the Delvauxs were fine?

Colette, like her older brother, seemed unbothered, but where a storm raged in Hunter's eyes, Colette's still held a small glint of joy as she leaned against the wall behind her brothers. "This has been fun."

Camilla could feel the promise of death in her eyes as she

looked at the halfie. Vera turned beside her to face Colette and spit out, "I vow on my life, Colette, I will kill you."

When Colette laughed, Vera's body jerked, and she pushed against the chains holding her in place, her anger making her more reckless.

And that was Vera's second mistake.

From the door they'd entered, directly across from where they were chained now, came a halfie they recognized.

Vera calmed down, settling beside her sisters as the life-drainer that had almost killed Hunter two days earlier strolled in, her attention focused on the three girls.

Camilla noticed the catch of Hunter's attention at her arrival, his entire body going rigid and his face draining of color as his gaze now solely focused on her movements.

The change in manner of the eldest Delvaux brother was uncontrolled. Warren, for his part, showed the same level of concern he had before; he didn't know his halfie, didn't get the danger of having her there.

Camilla also felt her sisters grow cold on either side of her. Maya, especially, felt like the anger was rolling off of her in waves. And when Camilla glanced her way? She was ready to kill, murder written over her features as her gaze locked to the life-drainer. After what she'd done to Hunter, Camilla was sure Maya *would* kill her.

"Hello, girls," the life-drainer began. "I'm Lyric. I believe we've met before." She wore a vicious smile.

Maya stiffened even more, a whisper of a growl escaping her throat.

Her reaction seemed to entice the halfie as she walked right toward her.

Camilla tried to pay full attention to the scene happening right before her, but half her focus was caught by the demon behind the powerful halfie. Lyric's attention to Maya had now garnered Hunter's full focus. He stepped up to the shield, his hands against it, as if beside himself with the need to get out.

Lyric didn't do a thing to Maya but pet the top of her head as she walked around her and over the chains that held them in place. Her fingers passed over Camilla's and Vera's heads too before she circled back to her original spot.

Her gaze moved between the three of them and settled on Maya. Again, as important as it was to pay attention, half of Camilla's attention snapped to the background. Lyric's observation of Maya had broken Hunter's resolve, and he now pounded against the shield with light snarls. His fists slammed into the shield, far more desperate than any attempt Warren had made. But then again, Warren didn't understand the trouble behind Lyric's power.

Hunter's eyes were dry, but the blackness of his orbs somehow turned darker, even more present. He looked lost and like he needed Maya. Needed. Camilla looked to Lyric and noticed her attention now moving to Vera. It had been on Maya for only a few seconds, but that was all it had taken for the eldest Delvaux.

He calmed when Lyric's attention moved, but his body still fought as he held himself against the shield, his gaze unmoving from Maya's form. Camilla couldn't believe the raw emotion in his eyes as he looked at her.

Maybe she had been too quick to judge his uncaring nature. Maybe, somehow, he'd truly grown to care for Maya and only Maya.

Her focus snapped out of her thoughts and back to the entrance as they were joined by yet another halfie. The one who had watched their thoughts before. She looked between the three of them, then landed her hands on either side of Vera's head and easily plucked the spell from her memories. It truly took all of a few seconds.

They had their spell. Now it was time to see what they did

with it. They truly had been naive in believing that they would be able to stop The Eight from any of this.

"Now, that wasn't so hard, was it?" Lyric smiled at them sarcastically.

"Actually was, you piece of…" Vera started.

She tsked. "Language, sweetheart. No one likes a foul-mouthed lady."

Others began to swarm the room, and in no time at all, another dozen halfies made the room just slightly crowded.

Three of them began to prepare the circle they would be using in order to cast their spell, while the others discussed the spell that had been plucked from Vera's memories. Above all else, Camilla was nervous who they would be using for the sacrificial bodies. When the salt, herbs, bone, and candles were laid out in a circle, the halfies began to take their positions.

Colette stepped up against the shield now alongside her brothers in awe and excitement.

As each of the halfies began to take their spots next to the newly drawn circle, one stepped forward and raised her hands in a chant. It was a shield wielder, likely the one who had trapped the Delvauxs.

With the final words of her chant, a shield began to form around the halfies. With her last words, she raised a knife to her throat and slit it—a darker ritual in which the shield may remain until all that was needed was accomplished. One sacrifice for another. She gave up her life.

How they convinced her to do that, Camilla couldn't fathom. What power or respect would she get dead?

With the fall of her body came the erection of the shield that protected the halfies and the evaporation of the shield holding the Delvauxs.

Somehow, the brothers were better prepared, and caught Colette before she could make a move, not that she'd be able to join the halfies now that the new shield was up. Maybe it was a dark magic they recognized when the shield wielder killed herself.

But the brothers also didn't move toward them, and Camilla could understand why. None of them knew what was about to happen, and at least for the time being, they were all safe.

So, they watched in silence.

From within the shield, seven gathered in a half circle around their drawn circle on the ground. The halfies were faced in their direction, though Camilla was sure that had more to do with the spell than for giving them a better view.

Each of the seven pulled out a vial of dark liquid, each with varying amounts inside. The blood of each descendent. They were using their own kind.

Camilla smiled inwardly. At least that was one thing they didn't have to worry about. Albeit none of the seven halfies were witch or demon.

Again, how had they convinced these seven to voluntarily do this?

The rest of the halfies remaining within the shield, including Lyric, stepped to the edges and watched in anticipation. The seven participating in the spell began to chant, raising their hands up and casting out their final lines before chugging their vials down to the last drop.

With the fall of the vials and the shattering of glass, the girls chanted once more. With the end of the final word of the spell, in unison, the girls jerked. As one, they all lurched backward, their backs cracking back so far they looked to be in a ninety degree angle.

Camilla was sure they'd broken every bone in their backs with that. And she was sure she was going to be sick with the sounds of the cracks.

Then as one, they all flew ramrod straight, and smoke began to escape their mouths, their eyes rolling back in their heads. With the last bits of smoke, they dropped to the ground, and

Camilla's eyes drifted to the smoke meeting in the center, the candles encompassing the circle burning brighter and larger.

As the smoke from each of the seven came together, a form began to take shape. An old woman.

Camilla gasped. They'd read about this woman. They'd seen the illustrations of this woman. But it was something entirely other to see her take form.

The Eight had summoned Grandmama.

Grandmama faced them for only a moment with a spark shining in her eyes before turning to look at the remaining halfies within the shield, tilting her head down. The halfies dropped their heads in a bow of respect, even Colette trapped with her brothers, as they faced the woman they'd all been waiting for.

Grandmama didn't say a thing, but as one, they all looked up to her and smiled.

Then one threw down a marble, opening a portal within the shield, and each made their departure, leaving Grandmama behind.

What was the point of this entire debacle if they were just going to leave her behind?

The portal closed, and she turned to the Delvauxs.

Grandmama looked at them for a couple of minutes but said nothing. Camilla couldn't be sure what had transpired between them as Grandmama's back faced them, but given the Delvauxs gave no response, she had to guess nothing. Then, she was gone too with an evaporation of smoke.

And with her departure, the eruption of the shield in the middle of the room and the release of the chains that held them back.

What the hell just happened?

They wobbled up to their feet, rubbing at their knees to brush out the stiffness that had settled in with all the pressure. Maya slowly walked around the circle and the broken halfies within in, taking in the scene from a different angle. Then she looked to Colette.

Something had happened when Grandmama left. The collar around her neck had broken, but she stood weak between her brothers. Like she was using their holds on her to remain standing.

Maya moved for them, and noticed Camilla moving for Warren, when a shield erected between the two families. She saw from the way his head tilted a little higher that it was Hunter who put the shield. Why?

It was nowhere as strong as the one the halfie earlier had thrown, but it would do the trick in telling them to stop, probably in entirely trapping them, considering their few months of training had nothing on his two decades. But that wouldn't be necessary. The message had been clear.

Maya frowned, knowing something had to be amiss. Hunter

knew she could shadow now. This shield wouldn't hold her back if she wanted to get to them.

And yet, he hadn't used anything stronger.

She wasn't sure what was going on, but remained still and watched, noticing Hunter's stony expression on her sisters rather than on her. It was that fact especially that told her something was going on. If he looked at her, she'd be able to read a softness in his eyes that he couldn't afford at the moment.

Like she'd told her mom, he didn't need to say he loved her. She knew it.

It seemed Warren was the opposite, and his stony gaze remained trained on Camilla like he expected her to read there was something else going on in the deceitful way he looked at her.

"What the hell is this?" Camilla said, hitting the wall.

Vera joined her, but they got nowhere. She was no doubt dying to get to Harry's side, to make sure he was all right, to hold him.

The brothers were meant to be on their side.

So they wouldn't answer. If they answered, they would have to lie, and that was one thing Hunter never did. Most definitely not to her.

Maya watched the betrayal hit her sisters at the same moment the brothers silently shadowed away, a smug—albeit weak—Colette between them.

The shield broke with their departure, not that it necessarily mattered. If the brothers had wanted to, they could've hurt them easily.

Camilla turned to Maya at the same moment Vera ran to Harry's side. "I told you your boyfriend would betray us. Because of you, we let those demons *help* us."

Maya didn't argue.

Partly because she still trusted Hunter, and partly because a pang of fear told her he truly had betrayed her. It definitely wasn't uncommon knowledge that demons didn't care for others.

And Hunter *could* have played her.

But he hadn't. He'd taken her to his manner, made her mistress of the household. She was his.

It was Vera who yelled back to Camilla from Harry's side. "Your boyfriend betrayed us too, Camilla!"

Again, Maya didn't say a word. They hadn't betrayed them, but she had no idea what had just happened. Something they hadn't accounted for that meant the brothers had to change course. And Maya believed she knew what it was—Grandmama had told them something. Somehow, she'd found a way to use the brothers to hurt them, to get them fighting with one another.

Maya watched from her standing position as Vera took a breath in, then slapped Harry. He startled awake but remained groggy as Vera gave a quick recap of the events that had taken place only moments prior, Camilla seemingly too angry and hurt to jump in.

They let him rest against the wall, needing his energy in order to port all four of them home.

Her badass brother. Because that's what he was, her brother.

It didn't take long before anger filled the house when they arrived in the living room. Maya could feel it from all directions, not necessarily directed at her, but the situation itself.

She wanted to call him while her family took time for themselves, bathing and attempting to get their bodies to relax, but knew she shouldn't. Whatever the reasoning behind his 'betrayal,' he may still need to be acting his role.

So she took her bath and tried to relax. Camilla was angry with her for her attachment with Hunter, Vera was angry with Camilla for her denial of her boyfriend's responsibility in the matter, and Harry was angry overall for being knocked unconscious and not being able to help them, not that there was anything he could've done.

Overall, they had needed some time away from one another.

Maya laid into the bath, her fire control boiling the water until her skin burned. Just the way she liked it.

She kept her thoughts peaceful. No need in overwhelming herself with the prospects of what Grandmama's return could mean. So she kept calm.

And thought of her Delvaux.

era had stepped out to the backyard, figuring the fresh air could help her in a way she didn't think a shower would. She couldn't believe it, but she had been there, seen it with her own eyes. The brothers had betrayed them.

And for what?

That was the kicker, not seeing any positive for them in the matter. Maybe Camilla had been right, and they'd just been inching their way closer to the Book, and once they had what they needed, they wouldn't need to pretend any longer.

But then why continue the charade? Hunter had looked through the entire thing. If he had what he'd needed, there would've been no point in joining them to the warehouse.

Maybe he'd needed this spell as much as the halfies?

She stood just past the porch, getting the perfect view of the moon shining at the late hour, when she heard footfalls behind her, and her racing heart told her it was Harry. She'd gone outside alone, but had hoped he'd follow.

"You're predictable in the most fascinating of ways," Harry whispered into her ear from behind.

She gasped, not having expected him to be standing so close. Vera swallowed back her nerves and responded, not taking her eyes off of the moon. "How so?"

"When your emotions are shot, whether in a good way or bad, you either go to the piano or you come out here and stare at the moon."

Vera smiled to herself. "And that's fascinating?"

"Absolutely." Vera scoffed, then heard him whisper, "At least to me."

She stared at the moon, heart still thundering with the fear she'd felt when he'd been knocked unconscious. "Are you all right?"

"Perfectly so now."

She closed her eyes to the meaning behind those words.

"Vera." The way his accent formed around her name had her breath catching. "I've been looking into your family."

She froze. That was definitely not what she'd been expecting. "Okay," she slowly let out, not yet turning to look at him.

"You've been worried about being the odd sister out," she froze because wow did he read her like an open book, "especially since you didn't know whether you lot shared a father as well."

She nodded, unable to speak up.

She felt the tickle of his breath on her shoulder. "You do, Vera. Bishop is Maya and Camilla's father as well."

She froze again, too desperate for it to be true to allow her hope to take over. "How do you know?"

"The reason I've been porting out so much recently. I found a lead. Found out where your parents used to meet when your mother couldn't see you, a little town called Les Pouvoirs in Canada. Found out that Bishop was there for the birth of both of your sisters." He paused, stepping up ever so closer, so his body pressed into her back. "Found out why your mother left you."

Her head snapped back to meet his gaze. "What?"

"I owe a couple of favors, but I'd do it all again to get you your answer."

She was too afraid to ask, but she had to know. "Why?"

"You were sick, Vera. I hadn't been around. Your mother had Bishop and wanted me with the European coven, so I hadn't known, but you were sick. Really sick. Too much for a healing power to do anything about it, and your parents loved you too much."

"What did they do?" The question was barely audible.

"Call it a deal with the devil, except the devil in this case is kind of like a genie. You were made healthy, but it came at a price." She really didn't want to hear it, but she had to. "Your mother was not to see you for a quarter of a century or else your sickness would come back, and you'd be gone within days. She stayed away to keep you safe."

Her lids fell closed as their breaths mixed. "When?"

"The clock ran out on it last year."

Last year. Loretta had died two years ago.

She looked back up to the moon and opened her eyes, staring out at it. At least now she knew.

Harry's arms reached for her arms, and he held her firmly against his chest, and all at once, her mind was back to Harry's presence. She could think about her parents later. Right now, she had Harry.

She held her breath and tried to calm her racing heart. After a few moments, her head tilted so her gaze slowly met his. "I wrote a piece for you."

Being that she had begun to see the piano room as their room, it was almost instinctual to write him a piece. That and her constant thoughts. It had led to a piece of heart wrench and passion. She wanted him to hear it.

She didn't want him to ever hear it.

With the intrigue lighting his eyes, Vera turned back to look at the moon, embarrassment tinging her cheeks as she felt his gaze on her.

"May I hear it?"

She swallowed and met his gaze again, whispering, "Do you want to?"

"More than anything."

Her lips twitched at the edges, catching his attention. She didn't say anything but turned to go back inside; to the piano room; to their room.

She'd only taken a step toward the door when Harry's hand reached out and caught her arm, forcing her around to face him. They came chest to chest, breaths catching. "I lied."

Vera found it hard to swallow. To breathe. She couldn't respond, so she allowed the question to bleed through her eyes.

"It's the second thing I want more than anything."

Heart racing at the proximity of their lips, the pressure her body felt pressed up against his, the feeling of his arms wrapped around her, Vera could hardly think. "What's the first?" she barely got out.

Harry's eyes searched hers for a moment, then his lips crashed onto hers. Vera froze for all of half a second, not believing what was happening.

Then her body woke up, and her arms flew around his neck, bringing him in closer. Their lips moved together in a final plea for the feelings that had been growing for some time.

Their kiss deepened as she pulled on the tips of his hair, begging for his lips to part and for his tongue to devour hers. And when he finally did, their bodies melted together, hardly able to remain standing.

Breaking apart for the need of air, they pressed their foreheads together. "That," Harry said breathlessly. "That was the first."

There was something going on. Hunter wouldn't have just left her. As much as her family liked to diss him, Maya's trust wasn't broken.

She just had to figure out what had happened.

And what better way than to speak to the man who raised him.

It'd been two months since she'd stood at the gates of the original Delvaux Manor, waiting for Mr. Black Eyes Uncaring Asshole to take her.

And technically, she was standing before the gates for the same reason.

Except this time, she knew he wouldn't come out. Something in her told her that he wasn't there, that he wasn't anywhere she would be able to find him. So she was left with her next resort: finding out what the hell had happened.

Not that Augustine would necessarily know where his son was. But he knew all of his kids, knew his daughter. He'd know what his kids would be up to.

The gates were just as domineering as they were those months past, but like before, Maya wasn't intimidated. She stood straight backed and waited. She'd stand all night if that's what it'd take to get some attention out there.

Arms crossed, she quirked a brow toward the gate. She didn't know where their surveillance was, but they'd be able to see her annoyance. That was all that mattered.

And finally, he stepped out. Augustine Delvaux.

He stood just passed six feet, the light coloring of his skin shining under the moonlight, short black curls, and sharp black eyes.

His eyes.

Really the only thing about him that looked like Hunter were the black orbs. And it was enough.

The piercing ache that needed to know where he was and if he was all right was strong.

She stood taller as the gates pulled back, and Augustine stopped just before the pass off his land. He stared at her with a wide smirk, black gaze shining like he was really going to enjoy this.

"My son isn't going to be happy with your presence here without him," he opened.

Maya eyed him from bottom to top. "Whyever not?"

"I'm a dangerous man."

"So is he."

"But he would protect you with his life. I don't have the same inclinations toward you. No offense, of course." His eyes glinted with enjoyment.

Maya smirked. "You raised him, you help him. You care for him, in your own deluded ways. You won't hurt me."

His smirk was larger now. "You're right, I do care for him." He took the lightest of steps forward. "But that doesn't mean I wouldn't hurt you."

"I'll trust you to behave."

His smirk turned into a grin, and he nodded his head back, inviting her in. As Maya moved past him to enter the property, he spoke, "I can see Hunt's intrigue."

Maya smirked toward him but didn't say anything as she continued to walk up.

He could've easily taken her hand and shadowed them inside, undoubtedly the way he'd traveled out to meet her, but instead, they walked. All the way up to the manor. And up to the front door and through the foyer.

Where two demons were passing into the back hallway and over to a room at the end of the manor. They paused when she stepped in, eyes narrowed, but didn't say a thing as Augustine stopped behind her.

Then he was leading. All the way to his office.

Hunter had told her about this room. The dark mahoganies and books littering the walls. The leathers and fireplace. All of it.

And she had to admit, it was a nice feeling.

But she still preferred his office, his manor, him.

Her heart ached again with the need to touch him, and at the back of her mind, she heard every sin and emotion cussing him out for not being by her side.

"Sit, daughter." He pointed toward the seats before the fireplace as he moved to pour himself a drink.

She laughed through a scoff as she chose the one to the left, a dark green leather by the fire. "A family trait I see, the calling everyone family."

He shrugged as he turned to face her. "I call it as I see it," a smirk, "daughter."

She rolled her eyes and leaned into the chair, falling into the dents of decades of use.

He was staring at her.

"What?"

"That is Hunt's chair. Has been since he began going on business trips." He looked almost sentimental as he spoke of it.

And she felt almost at home in it.

"Good. Anything that's his is mine."

His brow quirked. "Is that so?"

She gave a small wink, but didn't respond.

He took the seat opposite her and let the drink dangle from his fingertips as he watched her. "Are you going to tell me why you're here alone, daughter?"

"Why do you keep calling me daughter? Hunter and I can break up at any moment. He does it to my sisters to annoy them, but why do it to me?"

This time his stare was almost analyzing. "Hunt will never

leave you. The man has chosen his mate. It is not something that happens with our kind, but when it does, believe me when I say, you don't leave." He took a sip. "Now, if you mean you intend on leaving…"

Her back straightened. "Absolutely not."

The smirk was back. "As I thought. He will give you his mated ring, daughter. And soon. Trust *me*."

Mated ring? What was that?

She rolled her eyes, not the time.

"So you're okay with having me as a daughter?"

"Far better than my own, I can assure you that. And so far, I like you. Possibly more than my kids." He finished his cup and tossed it to the table like it were a light ball. And it landed perfectly and softly. "Now, tell me why you are here."

She stared at him for some time, those black eyes hardening her resolve. "I'm sure Hunter has mentioned The Eight to you, and yes, I know you do not care. The point is, Colette is a part of them. And tonight, they got their Grandmama back. They're planning on retribution on all of the species."

He quirked a brow, waiting for her to get to a point he would care about. Or that was new to him.

She breathed out. "Warren and Hunter shadowed out with Colette. Hunter threw up a shield to stop us from getting any closer and left with her, defended her."

Now he looked intrigued, sitting forward. "Hunt stopped *you*? From getting any closer to *him*?"

When she nodded, he shook his head. "You don't truly believe he's betrayed you, do you?"

"No." She brought her feet beneath herself as she settled deeper into the chair. "But my family thinks they both did. And it makes sense, especially since Hunt has now seen the entire Book. If he *were* looking for something, he would've had full access."

"You're here in hopes he'd be here?" He watched her intently.

"No." She sat up straight. "I'm here in hopes of learning why they would help her, help them."

He shrugged and leaned back, gaze capturing hers in instant resolution. "In order to protect you."

DON'T FORGET TO REVIEW!

Thank you so much for finishing your read! Don't forget to leave a review or rating on all platforms as it helps me as an author more than you can ever imagine!

Amazon and Goodreads ratings help the most but feel free to talk about it everywhere else too—including social medias, blogs, Youtube reviews, and most importantly—word of mouth, and more.

JOIN MY AUTHOR NEWSLETTER

Sign up for Nelly Alikyan's newsletter to be the first to know about new releases and cover reveals, receive exclusive content —like a special scene or two—and be up to date about any other exciting news, i.e. events, signed copies, etc.

www.nellyalikyan.com

ABOUT THE AUTHOR

Nelly Alikyan is a girl from the Los Angeles Valley who moved to Boston for school and found she prefers the East Coast. But really, London is where she'd like to be since it's her favorite city ever. She's the only reader in her family—not her only cause as the black sheep—and has dreamt of being a writer for as long as she can remember.

When she's not working on her books or in the real world, she's on Youtube at Nelly Alikyan!

For more books and updates:
www.nellyalikyan.com

instagram.com/authornellyalikyan
tiktok.com/@authornalikyan
youtube.com/NellyAlikyan
amazon.com/author/nellyalikyan
goodreads.com/nellyalikyan
facebook.com/authornellyalikyan
pinterest.com/insinpublishing

ACKNOWLEDGMENTS

Wow, it's already time for book two!

Honestly, like in the dedication, you can see where this book lies a bit of its focus—siblings. It's about how siblings are a pain and the easiest of people to fight with, but at the end of the day, they're the most important.

My siblings hold that spot for me too.

So, I'll thank them and my mom for continuing to support the start of my career. I thank them for being proud of me even when others may think this a futile dream. I mean, art is the hardest and best of dreams.

But they support it, even if they may think it crazy sometimes too.

I'd also like to thank myself. To be kind to myself and know that I am at the very beginning of my journey and have a long way to go. But I am so proud with how I am starting.

And lastly, and possibly most importantly, I'd like to thank you, the readers. Without you, books wouldn't have a place in this world so I thank you for not only enjoying the escape into magical worlds as I always have, but for giving my books a chance. I thank you for continuing on to the second installment and really getting to know these characters that have routed into my mind.